THE RIPPER'S SHADOW

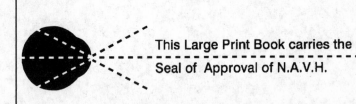

This Large Print Book carries the
Seal of Approval of N.A.V.H.

A VICTORIAN MYSTERY

The Ripper's Shadow

Laura Joh Rowland

THORNDIKE PRESS
A part of Gale, Cengage Learning

GALE
CENGAGE Learning·

Farmington Hills, Mich • San Francisco • New York • Waterville, Maine
Meriden, Conn • Mason, Ohio • Chicago

GALE
CENGAGE Learning®

LIBRARY OF CONGRESS CATALOGING-IN-PUBLICATION DATA

Names: Rowland, Laura Joh, author.
Title: The Ripper's shadow : a Victorian mystery / Laura Joh Rowland.
Description: Waterville, Maine : Thorndike Press, 2017. | Series: A Victorian mystery | Series: Thorndike Press large print historical fiction
Identifiers: LCCN 2016055498| ISBN 9781410496935 (hardback) | ISBN 1410496937 (hardcover)
Subjects: LCSH: Jack, the Ripper—Fiction. | Whitechapel (London, England)—History—19th century—Fiction. | Large type books. | BISAC: FICTION / Mystery & Detective / Historical. | GSAFD: Mystery fiction. | Historical fiction.
Classification: LCC PS3568.O934 R57 2017 | DDC 813/.54—dc23
LC record available at https://lccn.loc.gov/2016055498

Published in 2017 by arrangement with The Quick Brown Fox & Company LLC

Printed in the United States of America
1 2 3 4 5 6 7 21 20 19 18 17

In memory of Simon and
Phoebe Rowland

■ ■ ■ ■

LONDON
1888

■ ■ ■ ■

PROLOGUE

"I never done this before," she says. "What do you want me to do?"

The flickering gas lamps illuminate her, a short, dark woman with brown curls, dressed in a threadbare brown frock and a black straw bonnet, standing by an iron bedstead. The light is cruel to her. It shows the scar on her forehead and the ugly absence of a front tooth. She fidgets with her hands, as awkward as a novice actress auditioning for her first play.

I adjust the camera on the tripod. "You can begin by undressing."

Trepidation clouds her face. "I'm not used to undressing for a woman."

"Pretend I'm a man, if it will help."

"You, miss?" She laughs, incredulous, then tosses her bonnet on the hat stand and smiles coyly in an attempt at playacting. "A gentleman offers a lady a drink."

We both know she is no lady, and gentlemen seldom waste formalities on her. I motion to the wine bottle and glass on the bureau and say, "Please help yourself."

She drinks and licks her lips. Her face flushes, and her eyes acquire a bolder gleam. She strips down to her chemise and petticoats and bends over to unlace her shoe. "How's this?"

I aim the camera, duck under the black cloth that hangs from the back of it, and crank the bellows to focus her image in the viewfinder. "Excellent. Hold still, please." I throw off the cloth, raise the flash lamp, and open the camera's shutter.

Flash powder ignites in an explosion of white light. Shooting sparks burn my hands. I take photograph after photograph while she poses and flirts with the camera.

She leans on the iron bedstead, her bosom spilling from her corset, her round buttocks lifted, the pale, lumpy flesh of her thighs bulging out of garters and black stockings.

The room fills with acrid white smoke from the flash powder, soporific fumes from the gas lamps, and the ripe fish-market odor of her body.

Seated on the edge of the bed, she cups her bare breasts in her hands, eyes twinkling mischievously as she tongues a coarse brown nipple.

We exchange conspiratorial smiles. The thrill of breaking the law — and pride in our daring — add spice to our clandestine business. She begins to relax and enjoy herself. I enjoy her company on what would otherwise be a long, lonely night.

Lying nude on the lace counterpane, sprawled with her knees raised and open, her fingers spreading her womanhood, she feigns an expression of rapture.

After we're finished, she dresses, and I hand her coins, an advance on her share of what the sale of the pictures will fetch.

"If you want me for more pictures, just let me know," she says. " 'Tis pleasanter and safer than my usual work, if you take my meaning."

I nod. Women in her profession experience terrible degradation — and danger — on the streets of Whitechapel. Better she should pass the time with me.

"There's them that would say we're sinners and God should strike us down for what we done tonight," she says. "The coppers would throw us in prison if they found us out. But I say, what's the harm in it?"

1

The East End of London is dangerous even by daylight, and I am a solitary woman abroad at four o'clock in the morning. It is Friday, 31 August 1888, and I have come out to photograph the sunrise over the river Thames. I position my tripod at the top of the stone staircase. I hear waves lapping, but the fog obscures the oily black water beyond a few feet from where I'm standing on the embankment. The sky glows red from a fire burning at the Shadwell Dry Dock. Smoke, ash, airborne cinders, and fog produce an atmosphere like the steam from a witch's cauldron.

As I wait for daybreak, machinery in distant factories grinds and clangs; a train whistle shrills. The city is never silent. I reach for the leather satchel beside me, which contains my miniature camera, lenses, and negative plates. Made by a brilliant, reclusive inventor, the camera cost a small fortune and is my most precious possession.

A small figure darts out of the fog, grabs the satchel, and runs. I cry out in alarm. "Stop!" I pick up my tripod and give chase.

The thief is a boy. As the distance between us widens, the fog blurs his shape. Hampered by the tripod and my long skirts, I pant after him. Grimy brick buildings materialize in the flame-tinted, smoky fog. Gas lamps along the streets glow like miniature yellow moons.

"Help!" I shout. "Thief!"

In these small hours before dawn, a few drunken men stumble along; harlots straggle toward their doss houses; vagrants slumber in the doorways of the tenements. No one comes to my aid. The uneven cobblestone pavements are moist, slick. I trip and fall.

The boy and my satchel have vanished into the fog. I rub my bruised knee, pick myself up, and lament my carelessness. The miniature camera was one of a kind, and I can't afford to buy anything remotely similar. I trudge homeward, alone by habit and choice. A dark place inside me casts a shadow into which other people venture at their own peril. I keep my distance from them, lest their association with me should compromise them in some way — or lest my association with them should injure me.

14

The factory machinery pounds out a funereal rhythm as I enter Buck's Row. This narrow, cobbled lane extends like a gloomy tunnel between a line of dilapidated tenements on my right and Essex Wharf on my left. Yellow light emanates from lanterns in the midst of a crowd. People stand, their backs to me, staring down at something. At the crowd's edge, the boy with my satchel loiters.

My heart leaps. I hurry to him and grab the handle of my satchel. "That's mine! Give it back!"

The boy whirls. All knobby knees and elbows, dressed in a ragged jacket and knickers too big for him, he has an elfin face beneath spiky red hair. Freckles dash his upturned nose. I put his age at twelve years. He is one of countless street urchins who roam London. His blue eyes shine with feral intelligence.

"Hey! Let go!" He recognizes me; he's alarmed that I've caught him red-handed.

As we wage a tug-of-war, a police constable in a blue uniform and tall helmet approaches us. The boy and I freeze.

"What's the trouble, mum?" the constable asks.

If I say the boy stole my property, the constable will make him give it back. But an ingrained fear of police holds my tongue. My only, disastrous brush with them occurred twenty-two years ago — when I was a little younger than this boy. Now I see in the boy's eyes a reflection of my fear: the law is no more a street urchin's friend than it was mine. Our gazes meet. It's rare for me to feel such a mutual sense of kinship with anyone. It's rarer still that I put myself out for someone else's sake, but my instinct is to protect a child whose welfare is in my hands.

"No trouble, sir," I murmur, then let go of the satchel.

The constable looks askance at me — a thirty-two-year-old spinster. My figure is thin like a whip under the damp, threadbare gray coat that covers my modest gray frock. He can see that I am low on the scale of prosperity although better off than many in Whitechapel. My face is too sharply carved for beauty, my hazel eyes too deep, and my jaw too square. My best feature — my thick, straight ash-blond hair — is pinned up in a coronet of braids under my bonnet. Long tendrils escape the hairpins and wisp around my face no matter how much bandoline I use.

"That's good," the constable says, "because I got enough trouble already. There's been a murder, and this here's a crime scene."

As the boy flees with my satchel, I already regret that my fear of the police and a moment's compassion for the thief have cost me so dearly.

The constable marches back to the crowd, which contains many other policemen. I'm free to go home, but I linger even though I'm not interested in the murder. Murder is common in Whitechapel. Rather, my fear of the police contains an element of curiosity, of attraction. When I'm afraid — when my heart is pounding, my every nerve alert, and my body tense with the instinct to run — that is when I feel the most alive. I don't know why; I only know that I've always been this way. Life without fear is like a photograph without dark shadows to contrast with the bright objects. Danger adds a pleasurable thrill to my usually quiet, staid existence. When I see the police, it's as if I've come upon a sleeping wolf, and I feel an impulse to poke it and wake it up. Inhibited by caution yet excited by my own daring, I move toward the police.

People in the crowd shift, and I spy a woman lying on her back upon the cobblestones outside the gate of a stable. Her brown frock is raised above her knees,

17

exposing her scuffed boots, her petticoats, and her thick legs in black stockings. I don't immediately see her face. I see only the terrible red gash across her throat. My breath catches, and bile rises in my own throat. My heart thuds; I hear a roaring in my ears. I have seen death before — victims of brawls, accidents, or other murders — but never a death like this. Horrified, I want to turn away but cannot move. I stare at the grisly red flesh around the wound, the exposed blood vessels. Blood has pooled between the cobblestones, drenched the woman's clothes.

It is her clothes that I recognize first.

I saw them in my studio not a month ago, when she took them off to pose for my camera. The black straw bonnet lies near her motionless left hand. My stricken gaze travels to her face. I see the gap between the front teeth, the scar on her forehead, and I can put a name to her: Polly Nichols.

My hand flies to my mouth. I hold my breath, praying not to be sick. Through my vertigo, nausea, and faintness swims the thought, *Not again.*

The constable says, "Can anybody here tell me who this woman is?"

My lips part to answer, then close, sealed by my realization that I don't want him to wonder what connection I have with Polly. She was my newest model for what I call my boudoir pictures and the police call a crime.

My first model was Kate Eddowes, another woman of the streets. Some eighteen months ago, Kate walked into my studio and asked me if I would photograph her. I quoted my price, and her frank description of the kind of pictures she meant shocked me. Her next words enticed: "I know a man who'll pay ten times your usual price. We'll split it. What do you say?"

I refused the first time she asked, and the second. I did not want to risk running afoul of the law, and I shied from the intimacy that this project would necessitate. The third time, I changed my mind. Customers had been few of late, my landlord had just raised my rent, and if my studio should fail, what would I do? I've no family to take me in. Looking at Kate's haggard face, I saw a future for myself as a streetwalker. And so I agreed to her scheme.

The man did buy her pictures for the sum she'd named, and he wanted more. There is a thriving black market for erotic photographs of models of all varieties. Kate brought other women to pose for me. Although our relations were strictly business, years of solitude had lately become a crushing weight on my spirits, and I appreciated the semblance of camaraderie. I found unexpected pleasure in fancying myself the women's protector, sparing them many nights in fornication with strangers on the dangerous streets of Whitechapel.

A constable is asking spectators whether they knew the dead woman. Each says no, whether it's true or not. Whitechapel folks are loathe to cooperate with the police. *What shall I say when my turn comes?* Would that I hadn't so much to hide!

Polly isn't my first model to be murdered.

The first was Martha Tabram. She was stabbed to death some three weeks ago. At the time, I thought it a random crime, a fate not rare among streetwalkers. But now that Polly has met her end in similar fashion, a chill creeps through me. Polly and Martha both stepped into my shadow and came to harm. Out of thousands of prostitutes in Whitechapel, why two of my models?

"What about you, mum?" the constable asks me. "Do you know this woman?"

I gather the presence of mind to say no. He turns to two men who wear aprons filthy with old bloodstains. He asks, "Who are you? What are you doing about at this hour?" He must suspect that the killer is among us, pretending to be an innocent observer.

The men identify themselves as horse slaughterers from Barber's Slaughterhouse, on their way to work. There are many slaughterhouses in these environs, whose reek of decayed meat taints the air. There are many bloodstained men about at any hour. My gorge rises at the rank, metallic, salty-sweet smell that issues from Polly's body. I sidle away.

"Hey! Not so fast!" the constable says, then demands to know who I am and where I live.

"Sarah Bain, 223 Commercial Street." My fear now overwhelms curiosity and attraction. Excitement and daring desert me. I stare at the ground.

"Why are you hereabouts?" he asks.

The barrier between the present and the past dissolves. I travel twenty-two years backward in time, hear other police barking questions, and for a moment I cannot find my voice. Then I remind myself that this constable can't read my mind and know anything I've done. My visage is as opaque as the fog that allowed the killer to commit his crime unnoticed. I manage to explain that I am a photographer, on my way to take pictures of the city.

"You look a bit upset, mum." I can feel the constable's stare boring into me. "Why's that, if you didn't know the woman?"

I might have said that this gruesome spectacle of death would upset anyone, but of course that's not the whole truth, and what if he guesses I'm lying by omission? The constable draws his breath, and I brace myself to hear him shout threats like those that echo in my memory.

A horse-drawn ambulance wagon rattles up to us. A doctor, wearing a long coat and derby, carrying a black medical bag, climbs out. The constable turns to greet him. I back away, blending with the crowd. I could make my escape, but I can't resist my urge to know more about what happened to Polly.

The doctor winces as he eyes her. "Let's get her to the morgue. I'll do my examination there."

The constables lift Polly; her head dangles from her severed neck. The crowd gasps. The constables load Polly into the ambulance, the crowd disperses, and two men bring mops and buckets and wash Polly's blood off the street. I retreat to the end of Buck's Row and mull over disturbing questions.

Is it a coincidence that Polly Nichols's

murder followed so closely after Martha Tabram's?

What if it is not?

2

Fear comes in a multitude of flavors, and the one I taste now is the raw, animal fear that the killer is still lurking somewhere, his appetite for violence not yet slaked. But I must attempt to determine whether Polly's and Martha's murders are connected, no matter that I'm afraid the killer may notice me poking into his business and come after me.

The clouds and smoke in the sky have lightened to a murky umber color. The daytime noise of hoof beats and rattling carriage wheels has begun. I hear rapping noises from a knocker-upper — a man with a long cane and a lantern, who knocks on the windows of people who can't afford to buy a clock; they pay him a pittance to wake them up for work in the morning. More folks appear in Buck's Row, chatting in clusters, spreading news of the crime. The killer, like the urchin who stole my camera, has dissolved into the fog. I look down Buck's Row at a terrace of brick houses. In the nearest doorway stands a woman — a broad figure in a shapeless dress.

I'm shy with acquaintances and strangers alike, and I have to clear my throat before I say, "Good morning."

The woman has lumpy features and a raw, red complexion, as if scrubbed with a wire brush. Braids of gray hair blend into the knitted shawl around her shoulders. Her shrewd, pale blue eyes regard me warily. Folks in Whitechapel are suspicious of strangers.

"I'm Sarah Bain. I own the photography studio on Commercial Street."

"Oh. You did me niece's wedding picture." Her suspicion thaws, but not much.

Although I'm respected by my neighbors, we're not friends, despite the fact that I've resided and worked in Whitechapel for a decade. At the outset, I rebuffed their invitations to tea, which hasn't endeared me to them. Neither has my courteous but adamant refusal to answer questions about my past, but the murder in our midst encourages conversation.

"I'm Mrs. Emma Green," the woman says. "Terrible ain't it, what happened to that woman?"

"Yes." The next logical thing to say comes to mind. "And it was right near your house. Did you hear it?"

"Not a sound." Mrs. Green shakes her head in surprise and bewilderment. "I were fast asleep."

Across the street, a group of men loiters outside the stable. One waves to Mrs. Green. She says, "That's Walter Purkis, night manager of Essex Wharf. He never heard a sound, neither."

My hope for a hint at the killer's identity fades.

Mrs. Green's eyes glitter with fear and excitement. "This murder were just like the one in George Yard Buildings."

My uneasiness quickens because I am not the only person to connect Martha Tabram's murder with Polly's. Surely the police will, too; and then they will search for links between the women. One link is myself.

"They say she were stabbed thirty times." Mrs. Green's voice drops to a whisper. "And it looked like she'd been interfered with."

I heard that Martha, like Polly, had been found with her skirts up and her legs open. I remember Martha posing for me. A coarse, blowsy woman of thirty-nine, she came to my studio drunk. While I photographed her,

26

she told me that she and her beau worked as hawkers, selling needles, pins, and trinkets by day. By night, she sold herself. She couldn't sit still, even though I told her the pictures would come out blurry, but she wanted to be paid the full price. When I objected, she flew into a cursing rage, wrested the money from me, and stormed out. I'd been glad to see the last of her but was horrified by her death.

"George Yard Buildings is full of people," Mrs. Green said. "They come and go at all hours. You'd think she must have screamed while she was being attacked, but nobody seen nor heard nothing. Just like this time."

"Have you heard any ideas about who killed Martha?" I ask.

"They say he's a fiend." Mrs. Green darts furtive glances around us, as if afraid he's listening. "He's invisible. He's not flesh and blood."

A disembodied evil seems to permeate the fog, and my shoulders hunch; my hand grips my coat collar around my throat. I head down the street in search of more information, but although the other women in Buck's Row are eager to talk about the crime, none can offer anything except speculations. With neither my suspicions nor my fears relieved, I turn homeward.

A gruff, childish voice speaks beside me: "Pardon, Miss."

It's the street urchin. In the clearer light of dawn, I see shame on his dirty face. He holds out my satchel. "Here. You can have it back."

Amazement stuns me. He's no ordinary hardened criminal; he has a sense of right and wrong, and he's repaid my favor of not reporting him to the police.

It's rare that anyone moves me to the brink of tears. I accept the satchel. "Thank you." An even rarer impulse compels me to ask, "What is your name?"

"Mick O'Reilly."

"Thank you, Mick." I realize, too late, that I now must introduce myself and thus turn an encounter into an acquaintance. "My name is Sarah Bain."

"Pleased to meet you, Miss Bain." He tips his ragged cap; he's learned manners somewhere. He regards me curiously as we again experience that feeling of kinship. "I'll walk you home. It's not safe for a lady by herself."

His gallantry is endearing — and alarming. I say, "No, you needn't," and walk away.

Mick grins and matches my brisk pace. " 'S'all right. I got time."

I've unintentionally drawn him into my shadow.

"Did you see the deader in Buck's Row?" he asks.

"Yes." I feel bad because he's seen something no child should see. "It was frightful." I try to think of a polite way to get rid of him.

"I can't wait to tell the other lads. They'll want to 'ear all about it, and I'll be first with the news." Mick sounds more eager and excited than disturbed. "By the by, what's that thingamajig in your bag?"

I tell him it's a camera, and he says, "Did you take a picture of the deader?" When I say no, he's disappointed. "You could've sold it for a whole quid, I bet."

It occurs to me that I should be more careful about what I take pictures of.

On Whitechapel High Street, the morning is scarcely brighter than dusk. Smoke from chimneys blackens the sky; a thin rain dissolves the yellowish-brown fumes belched by factories into acid tears. Soot stains the brick walls and slate roofs of the buildings that rise high along the road, which bustles with carriages, wagons, and omnibuses. I step nimbly to avoid horses' hooves and clattering wheels that splash mud. Hoping to lose Mick in the traffic, I glance sideways to see if he's still with me.

He is.

When was the last time that someone, other than a neighbor who happened to be going in the same direction, walked beside me? When my mother, who died fourteen years ago, was still alive, we walked together by ourselves. She told me I didn't need friends; friends would only turn on me. *Stab you in the back before you know it,* her harsh voice says in my mind.

That happened when I was ten. Overnight, it seemed, for no apparent reason, my mother and I suddenly lost all our friends — the neighbors wouldn't speak to her, let their children play with me, or sit by us in church. I never understood why, but it was a painful experience that neither my mother nor I ever wanted to repeat.

"I'm almost home," I tell Mick. He shrugs off my attempt to push him out of my shadow for his good and mine. He's so badly off that I doubt I could make things worse for him — but that's what I told myself about Martha and Polly.

Saturday is market day, and we navigate through the usual crowd. Farmers drive wagons loaded with fruit and vegetables past women flocking to the shops. Bearded Jews, turbaned Indians, black Africans, and native East Enders jostle. A din composed of voices speaking foreign languages engulfs me, as do the smells of cesspools, exotic foods cooking, manure, and garbage. Amid the decay and squalor, there is a raw vitality that invigorates. There is also an undercurrent of violence. At any instant, tempers may flare into an argument that sparks a fight. Blood spills often. Here, the line between life and death is as narrow as the edge of a knife blade. Now I sense a menace darker than usual. The murderer who stabbed Martha Tabram and Polly Nichols — if indeed it is one and the same man in both instances — could still be among us. Is he that cheerful, rotund hackney driver? Or the thin, nervous clerk at the stationery store? The scene is like an overexposed photograph, its secret, shadowy details lost in the bleaching glare of the flash lamp.

Commercial Street, on the edge of a marginally respectable neighborhood that borders on London's worst slums, has the air of a slattern waking after a bad night. The public house on one corner is closed, the tearoom on the other not yet open. Cockle shells and old newspapers litter the street. Puddles between the cobblestones outside the brick tenements smell of urine. My shop — a storefront wedged between a druggist's and a milliner's — looks drab and forlorn; yet to me, it is the dearest place in

31

the world. As I unlock the door, Mick studies the gold lettering painted on the window, lined with a maroon velvet curtain, which displays portraits of solemn brides and grooms, family groups stiffly posed.

"Bain & Sons, Photography," he says.

I pause, surprised that he can read. Mick says, "I learned my letters from the nuns at St. Vincent's orphanage."

Maybe he isn't a homeless street urchin after all and has someplace to go after I peel him off me. "Do you live there?"

"Not anymore. I ran away. Didn't like bein' told what to do and how to do it all day long and bein' paddled if I did something wrong. Rather be on my own."

"Where do you live now?"

His gaze slides away from mine. "Oh, here and there."

He must sleep in alleys and under bridges. I can't help liking his plucky spirit. When I open the door, he stands on the sidewalk. He's waiting to be invited in, like a dog begging, and I would be cruel to shut the door in his face. If I feed him, maybe then he'll go away.

"Would you like a cup of tea?"

Mick grins. "Sure."

The bell that hangs inside the door tinkles as we enter the studio. Mick pauses at the threshold. His curious gaze scrutinizes the room, darting from my large camera on its wooden tripod to the flash lamp mounted on a metal pole and legs. "Who're Bain and Sons? Your pa and brothers?" He looks afraid that men will appear, object to his presence, and throw him out.

"I haven't any brothers. Benjamin Bain was my father. He's . . . gone." I swallow the lump that rises in my throat whenever I speak of him, despite the fact that new customers often expect the services of a Mr. Bain, and I have to explain that there is none.

"You mean, dead?" Mick asks with a child's bluntness.

"Yes." My father's death is an unhealed wound, even though he died twenty-two years ago.

"How'd it happen?" Mick doesn't realize he's probing a wound.

To shut him up, I explain, "He was killed during a riot."

"Oh." Mick casually accepts the short story; riots are common in London.

The long story is that when I was ten years old, my father disappeared. After weeks passed, my mother learned that he'd been fatally beaten in the riot. I've never told anyone that on the day he disappeared —

before we knew anything was wrong — she sent me to fetch him home from the tavern he frequented. He wasn't there. After his death, I thought that if I'd looked harder — if I'd searched everywhere else, if I hadn't been lazy — I'd have found him and rescued him, and he would still be alive. Nobody needs to know I believe I'm somehow responsible for my father's fate and I live under an unlucky star that will bring harm to anyone else who steps into the shadow I cast. I avoid friendships; I hide my guilt behind a barrier of secrecy.

"My father was a photographer in Clerkenwell," I say, giving Mick my standard speech. "He named his business when he expected to have sons who would work in it, but he had only me — his daughter. He began teaching me photography when I was very young. When I grew up and opened my own studio, I gave it the same name as his."

That's all I tell my customers when they ask about my father. I don't mention my suspicion that my mother's explanation for my father's disappearance isn't true.

"Is your ma gone, too?" Mick asks.

"Yes." After my father died, she and I went to work in a button factory, and she eventually sent me to a charity boarding school.

When she died of cancer, she left me a small legacy that she'd scrimped and saved from her wages, and I used it learn the latest photographic techniques and equip my studio.

"So you're an orphan, too."

"Yes."

Mick smiles. I can't help smiling back. It's another thing we have in common besides our fear of police.

Mick explores the studio while I don my apron and put on the kettle at the rear of the building, in the kitchen that doubles as my darkroom. He ducks under the black drape that hangs over the back of my camera and cranks the handle that opens and closes the bellows. I'm worried that he'll break something. He examines the T-shaped flash lamp, sits on the divan, then jumps up to inspect the photographs that decorate one wall, and opens the cupboards to finger vases, silk flowers, other props, and costumes. He doesn't seem to notice the shabbiness of the furnishings. I invested my limited capital in equipment, and although I earn a decent living, I can never get ahead. I can't afford a better location that would attract a richer clientele.

"I might like to be a photographer someday." Mick pulls down painted backdrops

35

that hang from rollers — a formal garden; the Grand Canal in Venice — then perches on one of the ornately carved chairs in which my customers pose. "I run me own business, too."

I slice bread and measure tea leaves into the pot. "What sort of business?"

"This 'n that. I do jobs for folks. I find things to sell."

Or steals them. He runs upstairs to snoop in my flat, and when he comes back, I'm afraid to ask if he's hidden anything in his pockets. People are unpredictable, dangerous. *Stab you in the back before you know it.*

We sit at the table where I confer with clients, write out bills, and keep my account books. Mick wolfs down his bread and butter and tea. After he finishes, he's restless, like a wild animal confined indoors. He thanks me politely, then says, "Got to go. Be seein' you."

As the door closes on him, I'm glad to be rid of him, yet I feel unexpectedly bereft. Tired because I rose so early this morning, I wonder if it's worth opening the studio today. I have no photographic sessions scheduled, and few customers will walk in.

The door opens with a noisy jangle of the bell.

A man steps into the room. Daylight from

the street silhouettes his dark figure. All I can discern of him is the distinctive shape of his helmet.

My heart jumps into my throat.

He is a police constable.

3

"Good morning, ma'am," the constable says.

His loud, brisk voice pins me to the spot despite my instinct to bolt. He takes off his hat with formal courtesy. His hair is dark brown, almost black. He closes the door, and as he advances on me, I feel like a rabbit cornered by a fox. The police — the enemy — has invaded.

"What do you want?" I say, attempting the stern tone with which I repel folks who barge into my studio to harass or rob me. But my voice is shrill with fear. My studio — my sanctuary, my livelihood — has become a trap.

"Just a word with you, please." He's not above average height, but he stands tall, the better to intimidate, an alien presence in my small, private world.

My senses preternaturally acute, I see that he is perhaps a year or so younger than

I. His skin has an olive tinge, as if from Spanish or Italian blood in his distant ancestry. His face, although molded according to conventional English standards, has rough-cut bones and a dark shadow on the cheeks and jaws from a beard that he must need to shave often. Those features, and his keen eyes, give him an intense, unruly aspect.

"Pardon me if I startled you." Beneath his carefully proper speech, I can hear his East End origins in his voice. I can tell that he imitates his betters and aspires to a higher lot in life. "I'm Police Constable Thomas Barrett. I saw you at the murder scene in Buck's Row."

He followed me home. I didn't notice! The other police at the scene of Polly's death were willing to forget me, but this PC Barrett must think I'm hiding something germane to the murder. How can I throw him off before he can find out what it is?

When I photograph people, they are often nervous, their expressions unattractively tense. To distract them into relaxing, I talk about unrelated subjects. Now, to distract him and calm my own nerves, I grasp at this trick of my trade. "I didn't see you. Were you with the other police?"

"No. Buck's Row isn't my beat," PC

Barrett says. "I'm from Mitre Street Station."

Here arises my contrary impulse to poke the wolf. "Then what were you doing there?"

"I've an interest in the murder." A smile twists the corner of his mouth: he knows I'm trying to direct the conversation away from myself as well as nettle him. "I was the first officer on the scene of another murder, on the seventh of August. It bore striking similarities to the one in Buck's Row. The victim was a woman named Martha Tabram."

What I feared has happened: the police have made the connection between Martha and Polly. How long before PC Barrett draws the line from them to me?

"Are you investigating Martha Tabram's murder?" I ask, even though I mustn't seem too curious. Barrett represents an opportunity to learn more about the murders, and my poking him makes me feel bolder, eases my usual shyness. "What progress has been made toward finding out who killed her?"

"I'm not at liberty to say." A shadow of emotion crosses his features. Years of watching people while photographing them has sharpened my perception, and I can tell that

40

PC Barrett isn't as confident as he would like people to think. His authoritative manner is partly standard police behavior, partly a cover for insecurity. I also perceive that I'm not the only one of us with secrets related to the murders, and his may not be any higher above board than mine. The balance of power between us tilts to a more even keel.

"I'll ask the questions," he says. "What brought you to Buck's Row?"

My impulse is to protect Mick, so I don't mention him. "I was on my way home. I saw a crowd of people around — the body." I almost said *Polly's* body. "I stopped to look."

"What were you doing outside at five o'clock in the morning?"

"Taking photographs by the river. Or, rather, attempting to. It was an experiment. It didn't work." I am uncomfortably aware of talking too much.

His eyes narrow further; he senses lies. "You went from house to house, asking people what they'd seen and heard, whether they had any idea who killed that woman. Why?"

As I try to frame a reply that he'll accept, that won't reveal too much, he looks me up and down. I'm further discomfited because

41

I notice that he's a handsome man. His eyes are a clear, bright gray, like agates under sunlit water. They glint with satisfaction because he's managed to intimidate me. I think he's realized that he betrayed his personal feelings a moment ago, it was unbecoming to a police officer, and he's relieved to regain control of the situation. For my part I thoroughly loathe PC Barrett.

My loathing emboldens me enough to say, "The murder happened not far from my studio. Naturally, I wanted to know about it. I'm concerned."

"Naturally," Barrett agrees, unconvinced by my fib. "What did you find out?"

"Nothing," I say truthfully.

He steps closer, and I step behind the table where Mick and I breakfasted together. "You wouldn't be withholding information from the police, would you? That's a crime."

One heave from him could upend the table. "I'm not."

"You Whitechapel folks are all the same. You always know more than you'll tell the police," he says. "Maybe you even know who killed those two women, but you hold your tongues because you're afraid to speak or because you don't like the police, being on the wrong side of the law yourselves. You keep secrets even when there's a killer in your midst." He apparently understands that Whitechapel has a dark side, like a globe lighted from one direction, and I'm in the middle of it while the police can only peer from the edge. "We're only trying to protect you, and you won't let us!"

I'm surprised to detect passion behind his annoyance. Barrett cares about protecting citizens and is only upset because people like me are making his job hard.

"Do you know what, Miss Sarah Bain? I think you're more than a busybody looking for gossip to spread. You're conducting your own little private inquiry. Tell me if I'm wrong."

Flustered because he's hit the mark, I stammer, "Yes. I mean, no — I'm not."

"Pardon me if I think you're lying," he says with frustration. "Suppose you find out who killed those women. What are you going to do about it?"

I haven't thought that far ahead. "I would tell the police." I hasten to add, "That is, if I were conducting an inquiry. Which I'm not." Defensiveness sharpens my tongue. "I'm a photographer, not a detective."

"You're the one who should keep that in mind. If the killer sees you nosing around, you could be in danger." Barrett waits a moment, letting his words sink in, observing the fear I can't hide. Then he asks, "Did you know Martha Tabram?"

He's caught me off guard. I almost blurt the truth. "No."

"What about the woman who was killed last night? Do you know who she is?"

When I answer no again, it's obvious he doesn't believe me. "Then why put yourself to the trouble of trying to find out about the murders?"

"As I told you, I'm just a concerned citizen."

Baffled, PC Barrett shakes his head, then begins prowling around, surveying the equipment, backdrops, furniture, and props. Mick's curiosity was worrisome enough, but this feels doubly intrusive because I know what Barrett is doing. I do it myself, on occasions when I photograph clients in their homes. I look at their possessions, the better to understand them and know how to pose them in a way that reflects their characters. PC Barrett is looking for clues to mine, the better to crack me open like a safe.

"Nice place you've got here." His tone says he hasn't missed the fact that my studio isn't prosperous. "Who owns it? Your husband?"

"No. I'm not married." I glance at his left

44

hand, noting the absence of a wedding ring. "I'm the proprietor."

I watch him categorize me as one of the breed of spinsters operating businesses on a shoestring. As I force myself to hold his gaze, my internal barrier against the world strengthens as if fortified with cast-iron thorns. *Stay away from men,* my mother often told me. *They'll just leave you in the lurch.* That my father died was, in her eyes, a poor excuse for his leaving us. My lack of charms has made it easy for the opposite sex to overlook me, a circumstance that serves me well. A single woman operating a business cannot be too careful about her good reputation. My avoidance of men doesn't mean I never have feelings toward the opposite sex, but I keep those feelings firmly in check.

PC Barrett moves to the wall where I've hung samples of my work. Studying the portraits, the wedding pictures, and the family groups, he says, "Not bad," then strolls up to my scenes of London: factory girls with begrimed faces, a legless peddler in Covent Garden, the wreckage from a collision between an omnibus and a train. They're exercises in balancing light and dark tones, attempts to clarify the fine details in both the bright and the shadowy areas and reveal hidden meaning under the surface of their subjects. I manage to sell some, not often.

Barrett leans in for a closer look and says, as if he's surprised, "These are really good."

I can't help feeling pleased. Barrett realizes he's paid me a sincere compliment in spite of himself and undermined his authority. He straightens up, clears his throat, and turns to the other photographs. These soft-focus, lyrical views of the English countryside are not for sale. My favorite one shows a graveyard where daffodils bloom through spring snow that covers the grass between the tombstones. In the woods is a blurry figure — my father. He took the photograph by using a timer on his camera. It is the only picture of him that I have.

"Were these taken by someone else?" Barrett asks.

"Yes." The landscapes are among the few examples I have of my father's work. I display them because they're not only beautiful; they make me feel that he is still with me.

"Who's the photographer?"

I cross my arms against my chest. I don't want to talk about my father with Barrett, but I have to answer or he'll wonder why I'm reluctant. "My father."

"Does he work here?"

"No."

"Why not?" As I hesitate to reply, Barrett says, "He should. He'd bring in customers, and it looks like you could use them."

Barrett isn't interested in my father; he's just trying to hold onto the upper hand and get at me. But if I refuse to discuss my father, he'll switch back to the subject of the murders. "My father is dead."

"How'd he die?" Barrett speaks callously, as if to make up for complimenting my photographs.

"He was killed during a riot." The lump in my throat is harder to swallow this time.

Now Barrett looks stricken by my distress, aware that he's needlessly hurt me. He blurts, "I'm sorry."

His sympathy and apology are genuine. They move me toward the verge of tears. I feel compelled to explain, to defend my father in case Barrett should think the riot was his fault. "My father was a social reformer. He organized workers to go on strike and march through London to protest the dangerous conditions in the factories and demand help from the government."

My mother resented him for it, for putting the workers ahead of his own family, for dying for their sake and leaving her to raise me alone. She repeatedly warned me, *A man will always put something ahead of you. It's better to be independent than left in the lurch.*

"The police used force to break up the marches," I tell PC Barrett. "They also barged into our house, yelled at my father for being a rabble-rouser, and threatened him. Once they put him in jail overnight, they beat him up, and he came home with blood and bruises all over his face." From those days came my fear of the law. Suddenly I'm not just afraid of PC Barrett; I'm angry. What happened to my father isn't Barrett's fault, but he's a handy scapegoat. "My father was only trying to help poor people." I loved him and admired him despite what my mother said. "The police are the ones who started the riot."

Barrett looks ashamed of his fellow police yet offended because I've maligned them. He opens his mouth to argue, but I must close the door to more questions about the murders — and about my father. I can't let Barrett induce me to reveal my most private secret — my notion that my father is still alive.

When my mother told me he'd been killed in the riot, I begged to see him, to say good-bye. She said he'd already been buried and refused to tell me where his grave was. My notion was based partly on this meager evidence, but mostly on the childish, wishful hope that he would come back. When I was older, I realized he must have been buried in an unmarked pauper's grave because my mother couldn't afford a proper burial with a headstone and she was ashamed. But childhood dreams die hard.

"Sir, I've had enough of your invading my privacy," I say to PC Barrett. "I must ask you to leave."

"What if I don't?" His chuckle doesn't hide his anger at my defiance. He strides over to me and stops too near. "You'll call the police?"

As we glare at each other, I am aware that even though he is the police and therefore the enemy, he's not as mean as he pretends to be. I am also too aware that there's a body under his uniform — strong, supple, and intensely male. He has desires in addition to his need to solve a murder case. The thought brings a scarlet blush to my face, for it's as much exciting as threatening. I will myself to look away from Barrett, but I cannot. Strands of my hair are hanging loose, crackling with electricity.

"All right," Barrett says, "I'm going." He points at my hot face. "If I find out you lied

49

to me, your troubles will have only just begun."

He gives me a last glance, smiles with strange satisfaction, and walks out the door. I look down at myself and see what he saw. My hands have wound my apron strings around my wrists in a simulation of handcuffs — a silent admission of guilt.

4

I hurry to lock the door behind PC Barrett. Still quaking with fright, anger, and excitement, I stumble into the kitchen at the rear of the shop. On one side are a black iron stove and oven below cupboards filled with pots, pans, crockery, and food; on the other, the worktop where my equipment for developing, enlarging, and printing photographs sits. Prints hang from clothespins attached to a string tied above the sink. The walls and window are painted black, and rags fill the cracks around the door that leads to the alley. Chemical fumes irritate my eyes, but this is my refuge when life gets difficult.

I light the gas lamp with the red glass shade, close the door to the studio, and sit on the stool by the worktop. The safelight bathes me in a crimson glow that reminds me of Polly's spilled blood. I hastily remove the red shade. In the brighter light, I remember what PC Barrett said: *Suppose you*

find out who killed those women. What are
you going to do about it?

I think more clearly when my hands and
eyes are occupied. I climb off the stool, pry
up a loose floorboard, and remove from the
space below it a box of exposed photographic plates. I have prints from them, but
the negatives are a degree removed from reality, more palatable. I lift out six negatives,
spread them on the worktop, set one aside,
and study the others. The first shows Kate
Eddowes. Unselfconscious about her stringy
figure, she poses on hands and knees, her
bare bottom pointed at the camera. The
dark and light tones are reversed; her body
and the counterpane on the bed are black,
the shadows white. She grins over her
shoulder. On her left forearm is a crude tat-
too — the initials T. C.

Annie Chapman is the model in the second plate. She sits, stout and awkward in
her petticoat and chemise, on the edge of
the bed. Although she lets men have their
way with her body, she'd been shy about
undressing. "It's always dark when we do
it," she explained. "Nobody ever sees me
bare naked."

Next is Mary Jane Kelly. Her long hair
covers her nudity in the manner of Lady
Godiva. She poses with knees raised, flirt-

ing with the camera while she pleasures herself. Her hand between her legs is blurred in the photograph. After we finished, she said, "That was more fun than I usually have with a man."

I turn to the plate that shows Liz Stride. Dark curls frame a face spoiled by drink. Drink is the downfall that puts many of these women on the streets. Naked except for garters and black stockings, Liz coils herself around the bedpost. She leers, revealing the loss of her upper front teeth.

While photographing the women, I didn't think about who bought the pictures. Now I imagine a seated man, his face obscured by shadows, the enlarged prints of my photographs in his lap. His breath quickens as his finger traces mouths, breasts, and loins. His hand clenches as if gripping a knife. I wonder again why the killer chose Martha and Polly as his victims. Has he a taste for prostitutes in general, or unbeautiful, downtrodden ones in particular? Other streetwalkers would have been equally convenient targets. The idea that he may have chosen his two victims from among my photographs is disturbing indeed. What surprises me, then horrifies me, is my ability to put myself in the killer's place. As I study the erotic images of Annie, Mary Jane, Liz, and Kate,

I feel an inner stirring, a flush of arousal. They are the physical sensations that a woman experiences with a lover.

I only experience them in the privacy of my bed at night, by my own hand. I have never had a lover.

The imaginary man turns to a photograph of Polly Nichols. It's the one in which she cups her bare breasts in her hands and licks her nipple. He shudders as the thought of her body violated and mutilated thrills him. Remembering the terrible sight of Polly dead in Buck's Row, I hastily put the negatives in their box. I cannot bear to look at the sixth one that I set aside. As I hide the box in the secret compartment, I am also disturbed by what I've just noticed in these photographs. When I first met the women, I thought them coarse and tough, but here I see their vulnerability. Maybe my photographs haven't brought my models to a killer's attention; I fervently hope not. But if they have — if I am responsible for Martha's and Polly's deaths — then I must do something.

As I reluctantly emerge from my darkroom, a knock at the door jangles the bell. I freeze. Is it PC Barrett again? Then I see, through the windowpanes set in the door, that the man who knocked isn't wearing a uniform. He must be a customer. Relieved, I hurry to let him in. He is a great, black-whiskered bear of a man, dressed all in black, his arms, chest, and shoulders heavy with muscle, his eyes fierce beneath thick, slanted eyebrows. His scowl is so threatening that I step backward.

"You take picture?" His gruff voice is heavily accented; he's a foreigner.

"No!" I've been robbed twice by burglars who pretended to be customers, and this man could be the criminal who murdered Martha and Polly, coming after me. I pick up the iron crowbar that I keep for self-protection and brandish it at him. "Go away!"

He cringes. Tears fill his eyes, which are already red and swollen from apparent weeping. His scowl is a mere configuration of facial features, a mask that doesn't reflect his true nature. I am startled to realize that he is a timid, grief-stricken bear. His big hands sketch a gesture of apology, and he turns to go.

"Wait!" I put down the crowbar and open the door. He pauses, and I notice he's wearing a skullcap — he is a Jew. I've had other Jewish customers who were honest, decent people. "I'm sorry. I'll take your picture. Please come in, Mr. . . . ?"

A shy, grateful smile transforms his face. He touches his broad chest. "Abraham Lipsky." He makes a hasty, awkward bow, fumbles for words, and shakes his head at his inability to communicate in English. "You come." He starts down the street, beckoning.

I shouldn't follow a stranger to a place unknown, but I'm sorry for hurting his feelings, and I can't afford to turn down business. I also think he looks familiar. "Let me fetch my equipment."

As we walk together along Commercial Street, Abraham Lipsky carries my tripod, flash lamp and stand, and heavy camera as if they weigh nothing. I carry the satchel of lenses and negative plates. We head north into Spitalfields, a neighborhood of Jews who inhabit the tenements and labor in the sewing workshops. Signs written in Hebrew label stores that sell furs, dresses, and boots. Men with long beards, dressed in black, cluster outside synagogues. Women in head scarves and shawls haggle at the street markets. I hear Russian, Polish, and German languages spoken. The exotic flavor of these streets fascinates me, and I've often wished I could capture the sights with my camera, but the suspicious glances of the residents warn me that this is a world to which I don't belong, in which I shouldn't take liberties. I can see its surface but not the secrets within, just as PC Barrett saw me but not the things I'm hiding.

We enter the stretch of Aldgate High Street that is called Butcher's Row. Outside many butcher shops, canopies shelter meat that hangs from hooks — chickens, headless lambs, sides of beef. Inside the shops, men wearing bloodstained aprons work at chopping blocks amid suspended carcasses. The sharp steel cleavers in their hands flash; the blades thump as they dismember animals. Thinking of Polly Nichols, I hastily look away, but I can't escape the fetid odors from the shops and the slaughterhouses behind them. I breathe deeply to quell nausea.

The butchers call solemn greetings to Mr. Lipsky in Russian. He nods in reply. Now I know where I saw him before — he works here. He is a butcher.

He leads me through a maze of alleys. Grimy brick buildings shut out the daylight. I begin to regret coming. The alleys resound with a cacophony of sinister foreign voices, rats skitter over garbage heaps, and a family evicted from their home sits miserably atop their belongings beside the dark doorway that Mr. Lipsky enters. I hesitate, then follow him up a staircase that smells of urine, to the third floor.

Wailing issues from an open door. I find myself in a small room crowded with Jewish women, all in black garments and head scarves, weeping around a coffin. Mr. Lipsky speaks briefly in Russian. All but one of the women slip out the door.

"My wife Rachel," he says.

She's small and round; her rosy face would be pleasant if her eyes were not red, drenched with tears, and filled with the same grief as her husband's. She welcomes me politely, thanks me for coming, then indicates the coffin. "Our daughter Yulia."

Now I know the cause of the Lipskys' grief, but its magnitude is beyond my comprehension, for I have never had a child, let alone lost one. My troubles concerning the murders of Polly and Martha and the visit from PC Barrett shrink as if viewed through the wrong end of a telescope.

"We want picture," Mrs. Lipsky says. "For remember."

For folks of limited means, photographs are a luxury not conferred upon them until their funerals. It is not uncommon to take pictures of the dead, and I have done it before; postmortem photography is bread-and-butter business for any studio. I've propped up their bodies to look as though they were alive and posed them with their families, but it's harrowing for me when the deceased is a child. Still, I want to help this bereaved mother and father.

"It would be my privilege to photograph your daughter," I say.

Mr. Lipsky opens the coffin. The girl lying inside is perhaps sixteen years old. Her fine-drawn, lovely face is as white as the simple shroud she wears. Black lashes fringe her closed eyes. Her black hair curls upon the white linen pillow. Her emaciation suggests she died of tuberculosis, an all-too-common disease. Mrs. Lipsky sobs. Her husband wipes his cheeks. As I set up my camera, my eyes fill.

Their grief touches the rugged shore of my own for my father.

Centering the girl's still face in the view-finder, I think about how different this is from photographing Polly, Annie, and the other prostitutes. Yulia Lipsky is as pure as they were vulgar. While I compose the shot, I remember, as I often do, my father's instructions.

"Look for the truth under the surface of what's before your eyes," he said often while teaching me photography, when I was a child. "It's what makes a good picture."

"How do I know the truth when I see it?"

I would ask.

"Your heart will beat faster."

I'm seldom absolutely sure I've captured the truth in a photograph, but I've learned to trust my heartbeat. Now, as I focus the camera on Yulia Lipsky, her truth is obvious: she was a good soul who died too young, and she will be mourned by her parents. I take three photographs of Yulia at different exposures. My tired eyes blur as I focus the camera for the fourth, last shot.

Instead of Yulia in her coffin, I see Polly lying on cobblestones red with blood.

The world spins and goes dark.

I'm lying in bed while a woman dressed in black rubs my wrists. For a moment, I'm frightened because don't know who she is or where I am. Then I recognize Mrs. Lipsky. Her husband looms over me, his scowl dark with worry.

"What happened?" I ask.

"You fainted," Mrs. Lipsky says.

Not only have I disgraced myself on the job, but these people are in the midst of a terrible tragedy, and I'm lying on their bed while they tend to me! "I'm sorry to cause you so much trouble. Please excuse me."

I'm frantic to leave, and not only because my behavior was so unprofessional. Today's events have pushed me into too close contact with too many people, and I crave solitude. But when I try to sit up, black dots swim in my vision.

"You must rest," Mrs. Lipsky says. "Abraham, bring her tea."

He goes to the other room, fills a cup from a shining copper urn, and drops sugar lumps into the cup. His wife takes the cup and gently supports my head so that I can drink, and I'm too weak to resist. The hot, strong, bittersweet black tea revives me.

"Thank you," I say. "You're very kind."

Mrs. Lipsky smiles. Her husband's scowl relaxes. I'm humbled because despite their grief, they have consideration for a stranger.

"You are sick?" Mrs. Lipsky asks. "We should call doctor?"

How long has it been since anyone took care of me? My mother did when she was alive. "No, I'm not sick." I mustn't burden the Lipskys with my problems, but I owe them an explanation. "I've just had a disturbing experience. There was a murder in Whitechapel last night. I saw the body."

"Ah, yes. So I hear from neighbors. They say it was a woman." Mrs. Lipsky lowers her voice, as one does when speaking of horrific things. "They say she was stabbed many times."

My mind swirls nauseatingly with the memory of Polly dead in Buck's Row and posing in photographs I took of her. "I'm afraid that my . . ." I can't say *models*. "That my *friends* are in danger." My models and I aren't friends; I could more accurately call them business partners, but I don't want the Lipskys to ask what sort of business.

"But it is only streetwalkers killed," Mrs. Lipsky says, puzzled. "Why you afraid?"

She must think I look too respectable to have friends who are streetwalkers, and if she lacks sympathy for streetwalkers, I can't blame her. I've seen them throw garbage at Jewish women and yell vulgarities. Like many of the less fortunate English folk, they hate the Jews, convenient scapegoats for their own ills.

"Whoever killed them may attack other women, too," I say.

"But even if it is so, why you think he will kill your friends?"

I am too close to spilling my secrets, and I have taken too much advantage of the Lipskys' hospitality. "I just have a feeling." When I sit up, my head is steady; I ease myself off the bed. I mention the logical yet intimidating solution to the problem of safeguarding my models. "Maybe I should tell the police."

Mrs. Lipsky steps back from me and folds her arms as if I've let a cold wind blow into the room. Mr. Lipsky begins shouting in Russian, gesturing violently. The sudden change in him is so alarming that I cry out. His eyes blaze with fury; his stomping feet shake the floor. His waving hands are big enough to strangle the cattle he butchers.

"Abraham! Stop!" Mrs. Lipsky grabs his arms and scolds him in Russian. He is twice her size, but he submits to her restraint. She says apologetically, "He has bad temper."

"Please excuse," Mr. Lipsky mutters.

My heart is still pounding. I can only nod. Such a strong man with such a temper could do vast harm.

"Not angry at you," he says. "We don't like police."

The Lipskys and I have unexpectedly found common ground. I think of Mick and wonder if I will ever meet anyone who likes the police.

"In Moscow, have pogroms," Mrs. Lipsky says. "You understand, pogroms?"

"Yes." To further my education, I study the newspapers. I recall that during the early years of this decade, the Jews were blamed for the assassination of the czar. The government called for retribution, and the rabble among the peasants in towns and the workers in the cities answered the call. The result was the pogroms — waves of violent beatings, looting, and destruction of property inflicted on the Jews. And the pogroms have continued long since then.

"Police burn our house." Fresh tears spill down Mrs. Lipsky's cheeks. "We come to England."

Her husband's anger is understandable now. They suffered much before losing their child, and they still have kind hearts. Although even more humbled by and grateful to the Lipskys, I shy from their kindness. *Don't let people put you in their debt,* my mother said. *They'll expect tit for tat.*

"London, same as Moscow. Police!" Mr. Lipsky curses in Russian.

"English police, they beat Jews." Mrs. Lipsky gives me a skeptical look. "What would police do for your friends?"

My models are even lower in the social hierarchy than myself or the Jews. The police won't lift a finger to protect streetwalkers. If I reported that my models are in special danger and explained about the photographs, it would be me, not the killer, who would be likelier to wind up in jail. The Lipskys have helped me justify the decision that I have been moving toward all day.

"The police can't be trusted." My anger at PC Barrett resurges. "I shall just have to warn my friends that they may be in danger and tell them to be careful."

5

Mary Jane Kelly, Liz Stride, Annie Chapman, and Kate Eddowes ply their trade by night and sleep by day. Warning these four of my five models is complicated by the fact that I'm not sure where they live. Prostitutes move frequently. I go to the hotel on Union Street where I last saw Kate. It's a three-story brick house amid a row of others that have businesses on the ground floors and lodgings above. A sign announces, "Rooms for Rent by the Hour." Men in ragged, dirty clothes loiter outside a cookshop from which rancid steam issues. When I slip in through the hotel's door, the proprietor is snoring behind his desk. I tiptoe up the dirty stairs. On the first landing, I step around a puddle of urine. A man and woman shout angrily above me. On the second floor, the last door on the right is Kate's. I knock. Nobody answers.

"Kate?" I call.

Above, the man curses and the woman screams; they bump the walls, wrestling their way toward the stairs. I try the door; it's unlocked. Rather than be caught in a fight, I dart inside the room. It has a musky, sweaty, masculine scent. On the bed, a naked man lies on his side, facing away from me, pressing himself against the bed's other unseen occupant. His slim back and legs are firmly muscled. His fair, sleek skin and tousled blond hair gleam. He's not Kate's usual companion — John Kelly, a laborer, is thickset and red-haired — he must be a customer. *How beautiful he is!* I shouldn't watch, but when amazed by such a rare physical perfection, I can never immediately turn away. I would photograph him if I dared.

The lovers roll over, the blond man on top. The person under him isn't Kate — it's a dark-haired young man with the physique of a boxer. As the two make love, their legs tangle; their hands grope; their bodies heave. They kiss, tongue entwining with tongue, and they groan with pleasure.

I stand frozen with shock.

Sodomy is considered a sin, a crime against nature and the law. These paramours probably come from some distant, better part of town. In Whitechapel, they won't be recognized, and the folks here are less likely to report anyone to the police. But instead of disgust, I feel astonished by how natural their passion seems. I am moved by it, and envious. Nobody has ever touched me with such desire. I've never experienced such pleasures with another person, and I surely never will.

The dark man rises up on his hands and knees. The blond man kneels behind him. Their members are huge, erect, not like the miniature genitalia on statues. I gasp because I have never seen a naked, aroused male. The lovers turn their heads toward me. The blond man has a face to match his physique — masculine yet fine-featured and sensitive, breathtakingly handsome. He and his partner blench with fear.

Stammering an apology, I back out of the room. The handsome man jumps off the bed, dragging the sheet, covering his loins with it, and slams the door. I flee.

Outside the hotel, I go from door to door at cheap lodgings. By late afternoon, I'm desperate to find Kate, Mary Jane, Liz, and Annie before another night falls and they take to streets haunted by a murderer. On Commercial Street, the bright Saturday bustle is gone; the crowds thin as market vendors close up their stalls. The moist gray air congeals into a foggy, premature dusk while harlots bloom like tattered flowers under the sulfurous glow of the gas lamps. I hear scuffling in an alley, glance in, and see a woman with her back against a wall, her skirts up, and a man thrusting himself between her spread legs.

It's known as a three-penny stand-up. It's how the streetwalkers and their customers often transact business. One simply ignores them while hurrying past.

I look inside the public houses. The women are not in the Britannia or the Horn of Plenty. My luck changes at the Ten Bells. When I open the door, raucous laughter greets me. The room is dim, filled with the yeasty smell of beer and the acrid smoke from pipes. In the flickering lamplight, the people crowded around the tables appear as brief flashes — a grinning profile here, a hand on a breast there — like scenes from a painting by Bruegel. I hear a woman's familiar voice speaking with a Swedish accent and see a gaunt figure crowned by a black bonnet, a red silk rose on her lapel. It's Liz Stride.

She is relating a story, with dramatic gestures, to three people seated with her. As I head toward her, a hand grabs my bottom; I swat it away. I am trembling when I arrive at Liz's table.

"My children fall overboard. My husband jump in water, try to save them. They all drown. I climb up rope." Liz pantomimes climbing hand over hand. "The man above me, kick me in mouth." She grins. Her upper front teeth are missing.

It's the story of the Princess Alice, a pleasure steamboat that sank in the Thames nine years ago. More than six hundred people drowned. Liz claims that her husband and children were among them. It is her favorite story; God only knows if it's true. All the prostitutes who model for me have bad-luck stories. I feel sorry for them even if their stories are made up. Sometimes the lies one tells, outright or by omission, aren't as sad as the truth. My mother told people that my father had died of cholera. She said that if they knew about his protest marches and the riot, they would think we were troublemakers, too.

Liz tells her story to anyone who will listen. Her audiences often take pity on her and buy her a drink or give her money. Her companions tonight are two men and a woman. The men are factory workers, judging from their grease-stained appearance. The woman is Mary Jane Kelly. I expel a breath of relief; I need look no further for her. She's young, in her twenties, and comely. A green velvet bodice flatters her buxom figure and rosy face; the brown hair topped by her straw bonnet flows over her shoulders in thick waves. She sees me and cries in her Irish brogue, "Look who's here! It's Miss Bain!"

She and Liz have never seen me anywhere except my studio. We enjoyed a semblance of friendship while I photographed them, but there is a barrier between us. I am on one side, with my camera and my respectability, and they are on the other. They don't look pleased to see me now. I've crossed an unmarked line.

"Good evening," I say, uncomfortably prim in the pub's rowdy, freewheeling atmosphere. "May I speak to you a moment?"

"Aye. Sit if you can find a chair." Mary Jane's cold tone says that tonight I am an interloper.

One of the men says, "The more the merrier."

I cannot clearly see his face or the other man's, but the light shines on their hands holding their mugs. Black crescents line their fingernails. Is it dirt, or dried blood? Did one of them kill Polly Nichols last night?

71

"In private," I tell the women, then address the men, "If you would please leave us?"

Either my frosty manner repels them or they think they can find better flesh elsewhere. They rise and depart. I take one of the vacated seats.

"Hey!" Liz calls after them. "Come back!"

"You chased away our fellows! We were all set for the night." Mary Jane's blue eyes flash with anger. Liz scowls.

I'd better beware, for I know, from their own admissions, that they can be mean. Liz has been arrested for drunken disorderliness. Mary Jane's beaux always jilt her because liquor makes her quarrelsome and violent.

"You mustn't go with any men," I say, pitching my voice low so that the other patrons can't eavesdrop. "You must stay off the streets at night."

They regard me as if I'd said, *The queen eats cannibals in Africa.* "Why?" Liz asks.

"There was a murder last night. Haven't you heard?"

"Oh, aye." Mary Jane sounds bored; she tosses her hair. "It's the man they're calling the Ripper. He's done it again."

"So what?" Liz shrugs her bony shoulders under her worn, soiled black clothes. The women are callous because they know murder is not an uncommon fate for their kind.

"It was Polly Nichols."

"We'll send flowers to her funeral," Mary Jane says.

"If you'll lend us three pence," Liz says. She and Mary Jane laugh.

My models are not really one another's friends. They flock together when it suits them, but they view other prostitutes as competition, and they seem to prefer not to develop affection for anyone. Losing a friend would add pain to lives already filled with loss.

I am not one to disagree.

After my father's death, my mother and I moved away from Clerkenwell and lived in a series of lodgings. We kept to ourselves, never stayed anywhere for long, and never made new friends. My loneliness worsened my grief for my father.

Liz claims to have lost seven children, or five, or nine. She claims she's been hospitalized for bronchitis, tuberculosis, and the French disease. I think there actually are serious illnesses and children's deaths in her past and that exaggerating their number somehow makes their memory less real — and less painful — for Liz.

"Martha Tabram was murdered only three weeks ago," I say. "She was stabbed, too."

"What's it to do with us?" Liz looks honestly puzzled.

"You may be next."

Their eyes harden. I suppose they don't like anyone pointing out the danger they court every time they take a customer, forcing them to acknowledge their vulnerability. "Martha and Polly modeled for me. So did you. I think the murderer is selecting his victims from the photographs."

"He won't get me." Liz preens with boastful confidence. "I would never go with a murderer."

"When you pick up a man, how can you tell if he's a murderer?" I ask.

"By his eyes," Mary Jane says, and Liz nods. "If he's evil, they've a certain dirty look."

"Martha and Polly probably thought they knew how to tell," I say.

Liz's snort calls them stupid.

"I'll kick him in the nuts before he can lay a hand on me," Mary Jane declares.

"If he tries to kill me, I'll cut him." Liz hauls up her black skirt and shows me a knife tucked in the garter that circles her thin leg.

Increasingly desperate, I say, "I saw Polly.

There were stab wounds all over her body. Her head was almost cut off. She was no match for him. Nor would either of you be."

"You think so?" Liz says, belligerent now. "Maybe I change your mind." She yanks out the knife and thrusts it at my face.

I recoil and jump up. My chair crashes onto the floor. Conversation in the room fades; people turn to stare at me. The women laugh as they rise. "We'll be off now," Mary Jane says.

I race out the door after them, calling, "Wait! Please!" Their attitude doesn't lessen my responsibility toward them. No one else must come to harm because of me.

Along Commercial Street, people are scarce now. The fog, thicker and colder, engulfs the women. "Where can I find Kate Eddowes?" I call desperately.

"Beats me," Liz says.

I wonder if Kate is lying dead somewhere, slain by the man who killed Martha and Polly. "What about Annie Chapman?"

Mary Jane's voice drifts through the fog. "Try Crossingham's on Dorset Street."

Cheap lodging houses line Dorset Street. Most of their windows are dark, most of the prostitutes who live in them already out on the streets. I approach Crossingham's via a

75

stone-flagged passage. It is one of six brick tenements that face a small, paved yard. Shrill, angry voices emanate from Crossingham's. I follow them through the open door, into a kitchen that smells of the tripe boiled with milk and onions in a pot on the stove. Two women face each other, hands on hips. One is, I'm relieved to see, Annie Chapman.

"You said I could have the soap!" Barely five feet tall, plump as a pigeon, she wears a black jacket over a black skirt, both faded and stained. She has abundant, curly chestnut hair to which she owes her nickname, "Dark Annie."

Her opponent is fair, with a bony, pallid face, no better dressed. "I only lent it to you. Now give it back!" Glaring at Annie, she flings out her open hand.

"Well, I can't, Eliza. It were such a small piece, I used it up."

Eliza responds with a spate of cursing. Annie slaps Eliza's face. Eliza shrieks, falls against the sink, and clasps her hand over her reddened cheek. "You bloody bitch!"

"Bitch, yourself!" Annie reaches down the front of her bodice, pulls out a coin, and flings it on the table. "There! Buy a new piece of soap and sod off!"

Eliza snatches the coin, then punches Annie in the eye and the breast. Annie screams,

"Ow, ow!" Eliza cackles as she runs out the door. Annie sinks into a chair and sobs.

"Are you hurt?" I ask.

"Who . . . ? Oh. Miss Bain." Her eyes are a deep blue, the whites veined with red, a bruise turning purple around the left one. Tears run alongside her thick nose, onto her puffy lips. When she came to pose for me, she told me she was forty-seven, but she looks older.

I find a rag, wet it at the sink, and give it to Annie. She holds it over her eye while rubbing the breast that Eliza hit. Three crudely carved brass rings circle the third finger of her left hand. She once told me she bought them from a black man and wears them for good luck.

"Oh God," she moans, "how did I end up like this?" Annie had told me that her little boy is a cripple, her elder daughter died of meningitis, and her younger daughter ran off to France with a traveling circus. I believe it because she seems, unlike my other models, too simple to lie. She's admitted that her drinking, her temper, and her incessant pleas for money drove her husband and relatives away. "Why're you here?" she asks, suddenly suspicious.

I tell her that Polly Nichols was murdered last night, I think it was the same person

77

who murdered Martha Tabram, and I believe he is choosing his victims from among my models. "I'm afraid you'll be next."

"Oh God." Annie lowers the rag and stares at me in horror.

Hopeful that she, unlike the others, will heed my warning, I say, "You must not go out at night until the killer is caught."

"But I have to. I need to pay for my bed here, and I just gave my last halfpenny to that bitch Eliza." Annie says hopefully, "You wouldn't be wantin' any more pictures, would you?"

"No. I wish I'd never taken them. I shan't be doing it again."

Annie's battered face sags with disappointment. She tosses the rag in the sink, and we gaze out the door at the dark, cold, dripping fog. Somewhere out there is the Ripper. We shiver, as though we can feel his black shadow creeping toward us. Annie twists the three brass rings on her finger.

"Walk me to Commercial Street, would you please?"

6

After leaving Annie, I head back to Whitechapel Road. I glance constantly around me, fearful that the killer is abroad and watching me. Police officers are patrolling the alleys, stopping and questioning people. The killer won't dare strike while they're here, but I fear them even more than usual after this morning's brush with the law.

"Hey! What do you think you're doing?" a man's voice calls, close behind me.

I start as I look over my shoulder. Three constables stand under the yellow halo of a gas lamp. The one who spoke wasn't addressing me, thank heaven. He and his comrade face the third man, whom I recognize as PC Barrett.

"I'm looking for witnesses," Barrett says.

"Not on our patch, you don't," says Barrett's interrogator; he has a long mustache.

All appear oblivious of me. I could go on my way, but I'm curious and, I must acknowledge, not exactly displeased to see Barrett. Fear and attraction are disturbingly intertwined with my anger toward him. Concealed by the fog, I pause to listen.

"You lot at H Division had your chance with the last case," says the other constable, a big, brutish fellow. "Leave this one to us professionals at J."

They're referring to the murder of Martha Tabram, I deduce. There seems to be rivalry between different police jurisdictions.

"It's the same killer," Barrett says hotly. "We should work together."

"We don't need the chap who bollixed things up last time."

I wonder what Barrett did wrong. Perhaps that's why he is so eager to catch the killer, to make up for it. Despite my dislike of him, sympathy stirs in me. He's not the only one living with a mistake.

"Get lost." The big fellow shoves Barrett.

"Or we'll tell your guv we caught you, and he'll pull your badge."

They stride off. Muttering under his breath, Barrett stalks in my direction. My heart lurches. I duck into an alley. The sound of his boots on the cobblestones fades. Oddly, I feel almost as much disappointed as relieved to avoid another encounter.

An omnibus stops at the corner; I board, pay my fare, and sit on a hard wooden bench. The horse-drawn coach is jammed with other passengers. As we ride, the tenements give way to the elegant townhouses of the West End. People in evening dress flock to the theaters and music halls. Cultured accents inflect their chatter and laughter. Women who are expensive versions of Annie, Liz, and Mary Jane congregate outside the Oxford Music Hall. Every man who arrives alone goes in with a girl clinging to his arm. He may take his pleasure with her in a luxurious bedroom instead of against a cold brick wall, but the business is the same.

After buying my ticket, I enter the Hall as the dim, cavernous room bursts into applause. People cheer from the balconies. All the benches on the floor are filled. I crane my neck to see over the standing audience at the back of the theater. Barmaids carry trays laden with glasses through the crowd. I breathe the smells of beer and perfume, the vapors from the gaslights that blaze around the stage. A glamorous brunette occupies center stage, flanked by chorus girls.

Her yellow frock is cut so low that her ample breasts spill out the neckline. She sings, with broad winks and saucy smiles, in a gay, lilting voice:

"I always hold in having it if you fancy it,
If you fancy it that's understood,
And suppose it makes you fat?"

She gestures with her hands, suggesting a pregnant belly. The audience roars.

"I don't worry over that
'Cause a little of what you fancy does you
    good!"

The chorus harmonizes the next lewd verse. My attention focuses on the girl at the singer's left. Even amid this confection of painted faces, pastel ruffles, and youthful prettiness, Catherine Price stands out. Eighteen years old, she has the roses-and-cream beauty of angels painted by William Bouguereau. Her luxuriant hair is pale gold, done up in a pile of cascading ringlets. Her face is delicate and perfect, her figure slim but rounded. I think of the negative I set aside in my darkroom this morning. It was a photograph of Catherine — young, sweet, and innocent, unlike my other models. It is she for whom I fear the most. As I watch her sing, I remember how we first met.

Two years ago, I was at Euston Station, taking photographs. I snapped a picture of the train roaring into the station, then turned my camera on the passengers as they stepped onto the platform. Catherine appeared in the viewfinder. She wore a white dress and a straw bonnet trimmed with a blue ribbon. Her beauty was so bright and startling that I lifted my gaze for a better look. She stood alone on the platform amid the gray, rushing crowds, a wicker hamper gripped in her hands. Her expression alternated between rapture and terror. She personified all the country girls new to London. As I composed a photograph, a man in a striped coat joined her in the frame, tipped his hat, and said, "I bet you've come to London to be an actress."

Her eyes widened. "How did you know?"

"Oh, I recognize talent. I'm a scout for the best theaters in town. Come with me. I'll take you to a nice boardinghouse. Then I'll set up some auditions for you."

"Oh, thank you, sir! That would be wonderful!" Catherine was breathless with joy.

I don't usually interfere in anyone's life, let alone a stranger's, but I couldn't allow her to fall for a trick that has been the downfall of so many girls. I hurried to her and told the man, "Go away!" I grabbed Catherine's arm and marched her into the station.

"I don't even know you," Catherine said, bewildered and resentful. "Why did you do that? The nice man was going to get me a part in a play."

"He isn't nice, and he's not a talent scout. Men like him prey on girls getting off the train. If you went with him, he'd have you working at a house of ill repute before sundown."

She stared at me in horror as she understood what I meant. "Oh. Thank you for saving me," she said, polite even as her face crumpled.

"Do you know anyone in town?" I asked. "Have you someplace to stay?"

She shook her head. Tears spilled from her eyes, which were cerulean blue. I couldn't leave her on her own, so I took her home with me and let her live in my flat for three months. I fed her, showed her around London, and helped her find work in a tea shop. She auditioned at the theaters, where her beauty and her sweet, true voice earned her bit parts. She was soon able to afford her own room in a boardinghouse in Holborn with other actresses. I wouldn't have done it if I hadn't thought she would go

84

away as soon as she was financially independent. But Catherine frequently came back to visit me; she wanted a confidante, adviser, and friend. I grew alarmed. The same protective impulse that made me decide not to tell the police that Mick stole my satchel made me bring Catherine under my wing — into my shadow. Also, I experienced in my relationship with Catherine a disturbing echo of my relationship with my mother. My mother had been distant, critical, and harsh. She often said she was preparing me for adult life in the cruel world. Whenever I said I wanted to be a photographer, she would say, *You'll never make a living at it. Don't be silly.* After my father was gone, she sold his equipment to a junk dealer for pennies, and when I tried to stop her, she scolded me and spanked me while I wept. I had a strange feeling that it wasn't photography she objected to; she didn't want reminders of my father.

I found myself behaving in the same harsh manner toward Catherine. I finally told her that it was time for her to grow up and be on her own. She stopped coming. Now I wonder if she would be safer if she'd never met me. I certainly wish I'd brushed her off before the day she walked in on my photographic session with Liz Stride.

Catherine's brows flew up. She'd seen many shocking things since her arrival in London, but never a naked harlot in my studio. "Sarah, what is this?"

Liz chortled. "Now there's a pretty model for you, Miss Bain."

After I explained about the boudoir photographs of the streetwalkers, Catherine said, "Why don't I model for you? It'll be fun, and my pictures should earn far more than theirs."

She acted on the same rash, naïve impulse that put her on the train to London. I, who should have exercised wiser judgment, agreed. Catherine was between roles and hard up, and I was afraid she would fall to the fate from which I'd tried to save her. One of the resulting photographs was a reenactment of Botticelli's *Birth of Venus.* Catherine stood nude on a large papier-mâché scallop shell. One hand rested against her bare breasts; the other modestly covered her pubis. It was my best boudoir photograph, and it did indeed fetch a high price.

Now I fear that it has brought Catherine to the attention of a murderer.

Amid cheers, applause, and foot-stamping, the curtain comes down. The audience streams out of the hall, and I walk against the tide to the dressing room. The chorus

86

girls chatter as they remove their costumes. I spy Catherine, her blue coat thrown over her fluffy pink dress.

"Sarah!" She looks delighted to see me, then wary; she hasn't forgotten how we parted. "What are you doing here?"

"I need to talk to you."

"About what?" Catherine's manner turns cool; she's not the same girl who was once eager to discuss with me every aspect of life.

We leave the theater via the back door. As we emerge into the alley, I say, "I'll walk you home. I'll tell you on the way."

"I'm not going home yet. I've met the most divine new man, and he's taking me out for a bite to eat."

Apprehension creeps along my nerves. "Who is he?"

"There you go again." Catherine sounds impatient. When she lived with me, she chafed at what she thinks is my overprotectiveness. She once told me that she left home because her parents were too strict, and they wanted her to marry a man who owns a farm near theirs instead of going on stage. Other than that, she hasn't spoken of her family. I don't press her; I never told her about mine.

"His name is Randolph," Catherine says.

"Where did you meet him?"

"At the park today."

"You hardly know him, and you're going out alone with him?" I exclaim in dismay. "Have you heard that Polly Nichols was murdered last night?"

"Who? Oh, that whore in Whitechapel. Isn't it gruesome?" She seems mildly titillated, mostly indifferent.

I lower my voice as I say, "She was one of my models. So was Martha Tabram, who was murdered a few weeks ago. So are you. You may be in danger."

"Oh, pooh! I'm not like them. And Randolph isn't like the men they pick up in the streets. He's clean, and rich, and nice."

"It isn't only dirty, poor, obvious scoundrels who patronize streetwalkers in Whitechapel. Randolph could be the one who killed Polly and Martha. Please, come home tonight."

"But I promised Randolph I would go out with him." We arrive in the street. "Look, he's waiting for me." Catherine points to a carriage parked outside the theater.

A man inside opens the door. I envision Polly walking the streets last night and a carriage drawing up beside her. "Please. Don't go."

Catherine turns on me, suddenly angry. "You said it was time for me to grow up and be on my own. That's exactly what I did. So you've a lot of nerve showing up now and telling me how to run my life." She dashes to the carriage, climbs in. Never able to stay angry for long, she smiles at me from the window and calls, "I'll be fine. I'll come over first thing tomorrow morning and prove it. Don't be such an old worry-wart."

7

The next morning I breakfast in my studio and listen to the knocker-uppers rapping on windows along the streets while I wait for Catherine. Finally, at eleven o'clock, the doorbell jingles. I look through the window and there is Mick the street urchin. My spirits plunge. I thought I'd seen the last of him, and I'm afraid that Catherine has fallen prey to the Ripper.

Mick opens the door and offers me a newspaper from a stack he's carrying. "I got me a job selling papers, Miss Sarah. Want to buy one?"

I give him coins and take a copy. He smiles expectantly. I sigh. "Would you like something to eat?"

"Yes, please!"

He hovers in my kitchen-darkroom while I fry eggs and bacon. They're barely on the table with bread, butter, and jam before he devours the whole meal. I bought the food for myself, and my funds are scarce, but I don't begrudge Mick the food; he's hungrier than I am.

"Here's a story about the murder." Pointing at the newspaper, Mick reads aloud, " 'The inquest for Polly Nichols will be held at the Working Lads' Institute at one o'clock today.' What's an inquest?"

"It's a kind of court that's held after someone's died."

The doorbell jingles again. Catherine bustles into the studio, dressed in a rose-colored, lace-trimmed frock, smiling and scented with lavender perfume. My relief is tremendous.

"Here I am." She spreads her arms and pirouettes. "The Ripper didn't kill me."

She doesn't notice Mick. His face takes on the openmouthed, dazzled expression that virtually every male wears when seeing Catherine for the first time.

"You mustn't keep testing your luck. Someday it may fail you." My tone is sharp.

"Pooh! Look what Randolph gave me." She holds out her wrist to display a bracelet.

Its gold veneer is already wearing off the tin, and the diamonds are paste. Even if Randolph isn't a murderer, men who woo actresses with cheap trinkets expect favors in return, and Catherine is too willing to

91

oblige. My mother taught me to avoid men, but hers evidently taught her nothing about chastity. I once warned her not to sleep with her latest boyfriend because she might get with child. She told me bluntly, "No, I won't. He uses a rubber." She's like a wild creature with no notion of sin, pure despite the fact that she isn't a virgin.

"Please don't go out at night," I say now. "At least, not until the Ripper is caught."

"Oh, Sarah." Catherine spies Mick, and a frown puckers her brow. "Who's this?"

As I introduce them, Mick drops his gaze and flushes. It's painfully obvious that he's fallen in love with Catherine at first sight, but she wrinkles her nose at his raggedy clothes and stale smell. She sits at the table, scooting her chair as far away from Mick as possible.

Mortified, he rises, picks up his newspapers, and mumbles, "Got to go." I feel sorry for him as he slinks out the door.

"How did you meet him?" Catherine asks. When I tell her, she says, "You made friends with a street urchin who stole your camera?" She shakes her head; her blond ringlets quiver.

"He didn't, actually."

"And you tell me that *I* should be careful with strangers!" Puffed up with righteous indignation, Catherine clearly enjoys turning the tables on me. I wonder if she's also jealous of my attention to Mick. "That boy is mooching off you, and if you turn your back on him, he'll rob you blind."

It could be said that Catherine mooched off me while she lived with me, but I don't want to quarrel. I've been afraid of quarrels since my childhood, when I often heard my parents' angry whispers from the other side of their closed bedroom door. To cut short this exchange with Catherine, I say, "I have to get ready to go out."

"Where are you going?"

"To the inquest for Polly Nichols, the woman who was murdered yesterday." There I can learn what the police know about Polly's murder.

"I'll go with you. I've never been to an inquest before. It might be fun."

It won't hurt to remind Catherine of the danger she's putting herself in, and if I let her come, at least it will keep her away from men.

The Working Lads' Institute is a club for boys, a red brick building adjacent to Whitechapel Station. As Catherine and I approach it through the lingering fog, I see a large crowd of boys, local tradesmen, and housewives amid newspaper reporters and photographers armed with notebooks and cameras. Police officers guard the entrance. I pause, steel myself, and move forward. Heads swivel in our direction; people stare. Catherine's beauty always attracts attention. She nods and smiles like a princess making a royal visit. I, in her shadow, am free to observe without fear of being noticed.

The man who catches my eye isn't one of the crowd. Tall and slim, he strides toward me. He wears rumpled black evening clothes, and he looks to be in his late twenties. His top hat covers his fair hair, whisker stubble glints on his cheeks, and his eyes are bleary, but his face is astoundingly handsome and instantly recognizable. He is the beautiful blond man from the hotel yesterday. He must be on his way home. As our gazes meet, he halts in his tracks. His Adam's apple jerks. The expression on his face is pure horror as he recognizes me and sees the police: he's thinking I could report him for committing a crime against nature.

"Lord Hugh!" Catherine waves at him, smiles, and hurries toward him, dragging me along. "Sarah, I want you to meet a friend of mine. Lord Hugh Staunton!"

I recognize his name from the society columns in the newspapers. He's the youngest son of the Duke of Ravenswood, an eligible bachelor-about-town, and often rumored to be having affairs with actresses and married noblewomen. My dismay is nothing to his as Catherine accosts him, bats her eyes, and says, "My lord, what brings you here?"

His features freeze into a supercilious mask. "I'm sorry, Miss. I don't believe we've met." His voice is a smooth tenor, aristocratic, and coldly polite.

"But of course we've met!" Catherine says, all confusion. "At the Oxford Music Hall. You took us girls out for drinks last week." I suppose Lord Hugh consorts with women in order to hide his true nature. Catherine pouts prettily. "Don't you remember?"

His gaze is riveted on me, as if I'm some horrible, fascinating spectacle — a train wreck, perhaps. "Sorry." He ducks into Whitechapel Station.

"I could tell he knew me. Why did he pretend he didn't?" Catherine sounds perplexed; she must have met few men who would cut her like that.

"I don't know." What happened between Lord Hugh and me is too embarrassing to tell her, and I somehow feel compelled to protect him.

"And he looked at you so oddly." Catherine regards me with doubt and suspicion. "Do you know Lord Hugh?"

"No, of course not." I hasten toward the Institute before she can question me further. Caught in the crowd, we are separated.

Suddenly, Police Constable Barrett appears. Grinning and toughly handsome, he confronts me before I can hide. "If it isn't Miss Bain again." He sounds pleased, as if he's caught me in some guilty deed.

Alarm quickens my heartbeat. My guard goes up. I don my chilliest expression and nod a greeting.

"Are you here for the inquest?" Barrett says. "It's not open to the public."

So I will have no chance to learn more about Polly's murder, and I've put myself back in Barrett's sights. "I was just passing by."

He isn't fooled; amusement glints in his gray eyes. "It's funny you should be here. I thought you said you didn't have any special interest in the murder."

For once in my life, I think of a good rejoinder at the moment I need it instead of later. "It's funny you should be here when you're not part of the investigation."

Barrett reacts with gratifying chagrin. "How do you know I'm not?"

I don't admit that I spied on him yesterday. "You just told me I'm right."

"Damn it to hell!" he bursts out.

Although I flinch from his anger, I realize that it isn't directed at me, and I'm less afraid of him here, in public, than when we were alone in my studio. Curious, I say, "What happened?"

He hesitates, frowning. "Suppose I tell you?" He sounds reluctant, as though it will cost him. "Will you tell me why you've come to an inquest for a woman you didn't even know?"

Here is a bargain with the devil, but if I agree to it, I may learn something important. "Very well," I say. While Barrett is talking, I can think of what to tell him. And I again feel that current of excitement running through my fright.

He motions me down the street, out of his colleagues' earshot, and speaks in a low, furtive voice. "I was on duty the night Martha Tabram was killed. At about two in the morning, I saw a soldier loitering in George Yard. I asked him, 'What are you doing?' He said he was waiting for a friend. I went on my way. The next morning, I heard that Martha had been killed in George Yard shortly after I left. The soldier might have done it."

Barrett sounds vexed because he'd been there at the wrong time to prevent the murder or to catch the killer afterward. "I told my inspector, and he asked me if I could identify the soldier if I saw him again. I said yes; I recognized his uniform — he was a private with the Grenadier Guards. Inspector Reid took me to the Tower of London and lined up all the Grenadiers. I walked up and down the line, and I tapped the shoulder of the private who looked the most like the man from George Yard." Barrett wipes his brow. "But it turned out he had an alibi. He'd been with another private, and they'd never set foot in George Yard.

"Inspector Reid was furious. He dressed me down for wasting his time on a false lead." Shame flushes Barrett's olive-tinged skin. "He said that if not for my blunder, we might have caught the killer already. He put me out of the investigation."

If not for his blunder, Polly Nichols might not have died. But I feel sympathy for Barrett because I, too, bear responsibility for Polly's death and the fact that Catherine, Liz, Kate, Annie, and Mary Jane are still in danger. We have something in common, and I have to respect him for his willingness to lose face in the interest of catching the killer. "It was an honest mistake," I say.

"Yes, but Inspector Reid is right." Barrett hastens to defend the law he serves. "The police can't afford mistakes. But I'm obliged to do whatever I can to help the investigation even if I'm not wanted in it." I suppose another man in his position would go off in a sulk and let his colleagues struggle on by themselves. Now Barrett says, "Your turn, Miss Bain."

I'm ready. "I knew Martha Tabram. I also knew Polly Nichols." That is the truth; now I lie. "When I saw her body, I didn't recognize her. I didn't know it was her until I read her name in the newspaper this morning."

Barrett regards me with interest. "How did you know those women?"

"They came to my studio. Martha was thirsty and wanted a cup of tea. Polly asked if I needed a charwoman." It has occurred to me that someone may have seen Polly and Martha enter my studio for our photographic sessions, and I need an excuse. "I felt sorry for them. I let them in to sit and rest for a while."

"Oh." Barrett sounds disappointed because he's shown his own embarrassing hand for naught.

I wish I could tell him what I really know.

Maybe he could use it to catch the killer, make up for his mistake, and save Catherine and my other models. But if I did tell, he would sooner throw us in jail.

Barrett's eyes narrow; he thinks I know more than I'm telling. "If I can get you into the inquest, would you still like to go?"

He wants another chance to grill me, but I seize the chance to attend the inquest. "Yes. Thank you." As we walk to the Working Lads' Institute, Catherine joins us. "Can you get her in, too?"

Barrett looks surprised; he probably thought all my associates were drabs like me. When I make introductions, Catherine bends her smiling charm on him. She loves male attention, and the admiration in Barrett's eyes doesn't disappoint her. I feel a twinge of jealousy.

"Wait here," Barrett says, then speaks with the police at the Institute. They let him escort us inside to a library where royal portraits hang above the bookshelves. Rows of chairs hold an audience composed mainly of policemen and local officials. At the front of the room, a dignified man with spectacles and gray hair sits at a table.

"Mr. Wynne Baxter, the coroner," Barrett whispers as we head toward empty chairs in the third row. Barrett takes the chair on my left, Catherine on my right. She and I are among the few women present. Five officials sit at another table, near the coroner's. "The jury," Barrett whispers.

"I call Mr. Reese Llewellyn to testify," says Mr. Baxter.

Mr. Llewellyn walks up to a podium. He is the doctor from Buck's Row. Without his derby, his bald head shines. "On Friday morning at about four o'clock, I was called to Buck's Row. I found the deceased woman lying on her back. She had severe injuries to her throat."

The chairs are too close together. The slight lessening of my fear of Barrett has freed other emotions to prevail. The warmth from his body is like fire painted down my left side. Catherine's perfume is suffocating.

"This morning, I did a postmortem examination," Mr. Llewellyn says. "The body was naked when I arrived at the morgue. There was a circular incision terminating about three inches below the right jaw. It completely severed all the tissues down to the vertebrae. The large vessels of the neck on both sides were severed."

The audience murmurs in horror at the description of what I saw with my own eyes. Catherine giggles, her nervous habit when distressed. Barrett gives me a puzzled look:

101

he's wondering what my relationship with her is. I can smell his scent — a mixture of soap, the wool of his uniform, and fresh sweat. It is at once clean and earthy, animal and all male. I grasp at the memory of my mother's warnings.

"On the lower part of the abdomen, on the left side, was a very deep, jagged wound," Mr. Llewellyn says. "On the right side, there were three similar cuts. All the injuries had been done by the same instrument — a sharp, long-bladed knife, used with great violence."

"You mentioned that when you arrived at the morgue to perform the examination, the body was naked." Mr. Baxter asks the police occupying the first row, "What happened to the clothes?"

Hearing the word "naked" repeated in public causes heat to rise in my cheeks.

The police mutter among themselves. One raises his hand and identifies himself as "Detective-Sergeant Enright, J Division." His voice and shape are familiar; he's the big officer I saw upbraiding Barrett last night. "The body was stripped by the mortuary attendant."

"The clothes were examined for evidence, I presume," Mr. Baxter says.

After an uncomfortable pause, DS Enright

says, "No, sir."

"Then we shall do so now. Go fetch the clothes and the attendant."

As Enright walks past us, Barrett whispers to me, "J Division will be in trouble over this. They should have examined the clothes." He sounds pleased yet embarrassed on their behalf. His breath is warm against my ear.

Mr. Baxter calls more witnesses. Charles Cross is the carriage driver who found the body. Emma Green and others take their turns. All testify that they observed nothing out of the ordinary.

Barrett whispers, "Could there be somebody who knows something but isn't talking?"

DS Enright returns with another man and a bundle of clothes. Mr. Baxter unfolds the bundle, revealing Polly's brown coat, brown dress, petticoats, chemise, and corset, all stiff with dark bloodstains. He calls the mortuary attendant to come forward. "State your name, place of residence, and occupation."

"Robert Mann. I live at the Whitechapel Workhouse. I'm the keeper of the mortuary."

Workhouses give room and board to the poor in exchange for labor. Robert Mann, who appears to be in his fifties, wears frayed, patched cotton garments, his hair cut short to discourage lice.

"How did you remove the clothes from the victim?" Mr. Baxter asks.

"I cut them down the front, sir."

Mr. Baxter holds up the clothes, displaying the slashed fabric, and frowns. "What did you do with the clothes after you removed them?"

"I threw them in the workhouse yard."

"And they've been lying there, exposed to the elements, ever since?"

"Yes, sir."

Mr. Baxter stares over the top of his spectacles at the police. "I must state for the record that police procedure has been very slipshod, and evidence may have been lost."

The police sit with their backs straight and stiff. Barrett mutters, "Serves them right."

"Let's proceed," Mr. Baxter says. "I call Inspector John Spratling of J Division."

Inspector Spratling takes the witness seat. His large nose dwarfs his small chin.

"Would you please describe the investigation of the murder and the results thus far?" Mr. Baxter says.

"My officers and I searched the area around Buck's Row, but we found no bloody footprints nor other trace of the killer. No murder weapon, either."

"Have you searched the dustbins and sewers?"

"Er, not yet."

"I suggest you do so." Mr. Baxter's tone is icy.

"And they think *I'm* not fit to investigate murders," Barrett says. To avoid looking at his face, I glance at his hands. They are well shaped, with long fingers, strong knuckles, and clean nails.

"I call William Nichols," Mr. Baxter says.

We turn to watch Polly's husband, a man with an earnest, homely face, walk up the aisle. His coat strains across his broad shoulders; his trousers flap around his thin legs.

"When did you last see your wife alive?" Mr. Baxter asks.

"When a married woman is murdered, the husband is a logical suspect," Barrett tells me.

"We were separated." Nichols twists his hands, which are stained black. Polly told me he was a printer's machinist. She also said he was kind and he couldn't stand her drinking and fighting. "Last time I saw her was about three years ago."

"Where were you during the night of the

thirtieth of August?"

"At home with our children."

"I heard that his alibi was verified," Barrett whispers.

The last witness is Mrs. Emily Holland, once Polly's landlady. She testifies that as far as she knew, Polly had no enemies.

Barrett sits back in his chair and folds his arms. "They've no evidence, and no suspects either."

Mr. Baxter dismisses Mrs. Holland. "Gentlemen of the jury, you may now deliberate on your verdict."

The jurymen huddle together in low, serious conversation. Catherine asks, "What was the purpose of all that?"

Barrett speaks to her across me. "The purpose of an inquest is to determine the cause of the death, whether it was foul play, and who might be responsible." His tone is patronizing; he, like many other men, equates beauty with stupidity.

"But isn't the cause of death obvious? I mean, she was all cut up. If that's not foul, then what is? And it doesn't seem as if they" — Catherine points to the jury — "could figure out who the killer is based on what's been said. It sounds like the police have made a mess of things."

Barrett looks disconcerted, crestfallen. I

hide a smile. Catherine often states bluntly the facts that other people overlook, obfuscate, or would rather not face.

"In some cases, new information comes out during the inquest, or the evidence takes on new meaning when it's added up. Although in this case, it didn't. Maybe there's someone else who should have been called to testify and wasn't." *Namely, you,* says the gaze Barrett turns on me. His face is so close to mine that I can see the golden flecks in his eyes. The corner of his mouth lifts in an accusing smile. My own lips burn.

"Sarah." Catherine sounds surprised. "Did you tell him about —"

I kick her foot before she can mention the boudoir photographs. Fortunately, Barrett doesn't notice because the jury is signaling Mr. Baxter that they're ready to give a verdict. An expectant hush descends. The jury foreman whispers in Mr. Baxter's ear.

"The jury has returned a verdict of willful murder against some person or persons unknown," Mr. Baxter announces. "This inquest is hereby concluded."

Everyone rises. I hurry Catherine out of the room, leaving PC Barrett behind. I do not want him to see that I am distraught because the inquest and its verdict have dashed my hopes that police will soon catch

the killer. Nor do I want him to wonder why
I care so much.

8

During the days that follow, I dread news of another murder, and I crave another encounter with PC Barrett as much as I fear it. My keyed-up state has various effects. On the Saturday evening after the inquest, I develop the photographs of the Lipskys' daughter, but on Sunday morning, I cannot achieve prints of good quality and ruin many sheets of paper. On Sunday afternoon, Catherine drops by. I again beg her to give up men until the killer is caught, she again refuses, and we quarrel. She thinks bad things only happen to other people, and she suspects I'm hiding something related to Lord Hugh Staunton. Mick is a daily visitor who chatters, eats, and runs. My orderly world has become chaotic. On Monday, while photographing customers, I drop and break three negative plates. By Tuesday evening, I'm rattling around my studio like a pebble in a shaken cup. I'm also more concerned than ever about Kate Eddowes. Needing action, I put on my coat and go outside, never mind that I may run across PC Barrett.

The tower of St. Botolph's Church vanishes into the fog that fills the darkening sky. The church is nicknamed "Prostitutes' Church," for the streetwalkers who parade around it at night, soliciting customers. Dressed in ragged finery, they appear under the haloes of the gas lamps. A bright dyed-green feather adorns a bonnet here; a red taffeta petticoat swishes above mismatched shoes there. Men lurk and watch before taking their pick.

One of them could be the killer.

Liz, Annie, Mary Jane, and Kate are nowhere in sight. It's futile to hope they decided to heed my warning. Has one of them gone off with the Ripper?

The night echoes with disembodied voices. The rattle of wheels on cobblestones announces the jakesmen, who shovel waste from the privies and transport it to the countryside in carts. A vicious stench trails them. Loath to be mistaken for one of the prostitutes, I stand outside the church and ask each, as she passes by, if she's seen Kate Eddowes.

A toothless redhead says, "I saw her today at Cooney's Lodging House on Flower and Dean Street."

Kate is alive; I can warn her; it's not too late.

Flower and Dean is a short, narrow road crowded with people queuing for beds at the lodging houses. I squeeze past men and women who wear layers of soiled, ragged clothes and carry their few possessions in sacks. Their odor is foul from living on the streets as often as not. Coughs rattle from bad lungs. I try to avoid touching the people. The line between solvency and poverty is thin, and I don't want their bad luck to rub off on me. At Cooney's, the deputy at the door, who takes fees, assigns rooms, and keeps order, is muscled like an ox.

"Wait your turn," he orders me as he accepts eight pence from a woman with a crutch.

I'm disconcerted because he's mistaken me for one of those who need lodging. "I'm here to visit Kate Eddowes. Is she here?"

"Second floor, room three."

The house is noisy with people settling in for the night. Their odor permeates the stairwell and passages. As I knock on Kate's

111

door, I think of Lord Hugh Staunton and wince.

"Go away," a man's rough, slurred voice calls. "We're trying to sleep."

"It's Sarah Bain," I call. "I have to speak with Kate."

Inside, rustling sounds accompany muttered conversation. The door opens to reveal small, thin Kate in a woolen dressing gown. Dark auburn hair straggles around her face, whose pitted complexion and carved lines make her look older than her forty years. Her hazel eyes are puffy, she exudes the stale smell of sleep, and she's a far cry from the laughing minx who wiggled her bare bottom at my camera, but rarely have I been so glad to see anyone. If I had to pick a favorite from among my models, she would be second to Catherine. She's cheerful, clever, and resourceful. The boudoir photographs were her idea, and although they've put me in a compromising position — and possibly endangered all my models — I admire Kate's initiative. If not for bad luck, she might have become a more successful businesswoman than I.

"Where have you been?" I exclaim.

"Picking hops in Kent," she says with a drowsy smile. "We just got back today."

Many London folks go to the countryside

for the hops harvest, a sort of paid working holiday with fresh air. Kate was safe; I worried needlessly.

"What are you doing here, Miss Sarah?" Kate asks.

"I've something to tell you. May I come in?"

"Kate!" the man calls. "Get rid of whoever the hell that is! Come back to bed!"

She mouths his words, mimics his annoyance, smirks, and lets me in. John Kelly, her companion, is sitting in bed in a small chamber cluttered with strewn clothes and miscellany. He looks sleepy and disgruntled. I say hello and try not to look at his bare chest, which is matted with hair the same reddish color as the shaggy mane on his head. Kate snuggles against him and motions me to the chair.

I experience a pang of envy. John Kelly is no prize, but Kate's bed, unlike mine, is warm at night. I sit on clothes piled atop the chair. "While you were gone, there were two murders."

"You woke us up for that?" John says. "Christ!"

"It was Martha Tabram and Polly Nichols," I say.

"Oh?" Kate blinks, sits up straight, and glances at John. When she introduced us some months ago, she told him I had hired her to clean my studio. Now she flashes me a look that says he still doesn't know about the photographs and I shouldn't tell him. She wants to keep the money for herself.

"You knew them?" John is interested now.

"Just to say hello," Kate lies, then asks me, "So what happened?"

"They were stabbed to death."

Kate has a habit of holding and rolling her tongue in her open mouth like a pink marble. "So they met up with the wrong blokes. That's too bad."

"I think it was the same one," I say.

"Why's that?" John asks.

I seek a way to tell Kate without giving away our secret. "Because of the connection between them. You could be next."

"What're you talking about?" John demands, baffled by the undercurrent he senses in the conversation.

Kate rolls her tongue faster as comprehension glints in her eyes: she's gotten my hint that the killer could be a man who's seen the photographs of her, Martha, Polly, and my other models and that that is how he is choosing his victims.

"I'm talking about the fact that there's a killer on the loose," I tell John, then address Kate. "Be careful. Stay indoors at night.

114

Don't go with strange men."

"She don't need to go with 'em," John says. They've lived together in poverty for seven years, he knows Kate is a prostitute, and he can't afford to care. "We made enough picking hops to last us awhile." He puts his beefy arm around Kate. "I'll keep her in."

Kate pushes him away. "You'll do no such thing, John Kelly. You don't own me."

The left sleeve of her robe slides up, and I see, on her forearm, the tattooed letters — "T. C." They are the initials of Thomas Conway, a soldier she once lived with, by whom she had three children. He left her because she has a willful, independent streak, and when she drinks — which is often — she can be mean. Her relationship with John is rocky for the same reasons. She is estranged from her married daughter, grown sons, and two sisters, who dislike her drinking, her streetwalking, and her demands for money.

I attempt to sway Kate by detailing what could befall her. "Polly's throat was cut so deeply that her head was almost severed."

Kate chuckles. "A horse slaughterer probably mistook her for a gimpy nag." John laughs, too.

"This is serious!" I say, angered by her

flippancy. "Polly's stomach was cut open!"

Kate's eyes go still like thrown dice when they stop rolling. "Cut open?" Her voice contracts to a whisper.

"Yes." I am so glad I have finally put fear of the killer into Kate, I don't bother to ask why she finds the thought of Polly cut open more disturbing than Polly almost decapitated. "That's why you must be careful."

Her tongue circles inside the O of her mouth. "Are the police offering a reward?"

"Reward for what?"

"For information about who killed Polly and Martha."

"Not that I know of."

"What do you care if there's a reward?" John asks Kate. "The coppers won't give you nothin'. You don't know squat."

Even as she pouts at his scornful tone, I see a gleam of cunning in her eyes. "*Do* you have information?" I ask.

"Course not." But her tongue rolls faster, and her gaze skitters away from me.

"You should tell the police even if there's no reward." I'm insistent, hopeful that she can direct them to the killer and that my models will be safe.

"I just said I don't know anything." Kate hugs herself, as if holding in something she's afraid I'll snatch away.

"What is it?" I demand, clutching her wrist. "Do you know who the Ripper is?"

As we tussle, John says sharply, "Hey! Leave her alone!"

"Forget about money," I plead. "Lives could be at stake."

Kate wrenches free of me and shouts, "Go fuck yourself, stupid cow!"

"Your life especially! If you know, he'll come after you and kill you to keep you quiet!" I don't mention that he may think Kate told me who he is and he'll kill me, too. She won't care; she's never considered me a friend.

She spews a stream of loud obscenities. People in the other rooms yell at her to be quiet.

"See what you done?" John glares at me. "You set her off. Now there'll be hell to pay."

I am so desperate that I ignore his temper. "Please, Kate, tell me!"

"Get out!" John Kelly clambers out of bed like a bear disturbed while hibernating, yanks me up from my chair, and shoves me out the door. "Don't come back!"

9

I decide to let Kate ponder my warning and hope she'll change her mind about sharing her information with me. On Thursday, I finally print satisfactory photographs of the Lipskys' daughter. I put them and my miniature camera in my satchel and head for Spitalfields to deliver them and photograph the scenery along the way.

Whitechapel Road is blocked by crowds and the police pushing them back to clear the way for a black hearse, two coaches following it, and an escort of mounted policemen. Curiosity overcomes my fear of the law, and I join the crowd.

"What is this?" I ask a woman beside me.

"The funeral for Polly Nichols."

Spectators trail after the hearse and coaches. I have heard that criminals haunt the scenes of their crimes; why not their victims' funerals? Maybe Polly's killer is here. On impulse, I hail a cab, say, "Follow the hearse!" and jump in.

The cab takes me to the City of London Cemetery, where I rush through the gates. The funeral cortege has already gone in; all I can see of it is the police guard at its rear. In the vast cemetery, grave monuments line a broad avenue over which trees arch, their leaves turning red and gold. The air is cooler and cleaner here, the sky blue between patches of cloud. The fresh, earthy, tangy scent of autumn transports me back to my childhood. My father and I often traveled to the countryside and took photographs. I managed to save the few that now hang in my studio. My mother destroyed the others — and most of his work — after he died. Those trips were precious to me, an enchanted time that my father and I shared as kindred spirits. Now the autumn air, the birdsong, and the peacefulness evoke a sense of his presence. I can almost feel his gentle hands on my shoulders as we peered into the viewfinder of his big camera together.

The funeral cortege stops in an area of graves marked by simple stones or plaques. Mourners emerge from the coaches and gather around a freshly dug hole. I recognize Polly's husband William Nichols. The police eye the spectators; I suppose they, too, hope to spot the killer. The crowd seems composed of ordinary people, some I know by sight, and no one looks like a murderer, but I step behind a tree, open my satchel, and take out my miniature camera. It is a metal box covered with black leather, small enough to hold in one hand. The lens protrudes from the front. Technical problems easily solved in the studio loom large in the field, and estimating the length of the exposure is guesswork, ambient light less reliable than flash powder. When I photograph people without their knowledge, I can only hope they stand still long enough for me to capture their images.

Men lower the coffin into the grave. The mourners stand like soldiers. I peer through the viewfinder at the crowd . . . and see PC Barrett looking straight at me. My heart leaps of its own inexplicable volition, then sinks because he must be wondering why I came to Polly's funeral. I drop my camera in my satchel and run into the woods. Trees with gnarled trunks flash past me, their roots lump up through the ground, and I don't dare look backward, lest I trip. I hear footsteps crunching the dried leaves, gaining on me.

"Sarah Bain!" Barrett calls.

I'm running from the feelings he provokes

in me as well as his suspicion. I emerge into a vast tract of tall monuments arranged in rows, a city of the dead. As I run, carved angels spread their wings above me. I veer around tombs until I'm too breathless to run anymore. Crouched behind a monument topped with a praying cherub, I hear Barrett curse, his footsteps recede, and then nothing but the wind that blows petals from roses in urns. Now Barrett will wonder why I ran away. I feel a pang of contradictory regret. I can't help wishing I'd let him catch me. I've only made things worse for the next time I see him — and no doubt there will be a next time.

Abandoning my plan to photograph Polly's funeral, I trudge toward the gates and come upon a stone chapel built in Gothic style, with an octagonal tower and a rose window. A funeral party exits the chapel and moves toward the carriages and footmen waiting along the road. The people are elegantly dressed, a sharp contrast to the mourners at Polly's funeral. One gentleman, blond and handsome, calls farewells to his friends and walks briskly toward me.

Here, once more, is Lord Hugh Staunton.

We gape at each other, chastened by the realization that we are doomed to meet again and again.

We both burst out laughing.

"I hoped never to see you again this side of hell!" Lord Hugh cries as he doubles over.

"I could say the same about you!" Mirthful tears roll down my face. Maybe this isn't as funny as it seems, but I've never laughed so hard. Catharsis releases the tension that has built up in me since Polly's murder.

Our laughter stops as suddenly and simultaneously as it began. In the long, solemn silence that ensues, thoughts pass between us as clearly as if spoken. Lord Hugh intuits that I am tolerant of his habits and will not tell tales on him. I intuit that he is someone I can meet frankly as an equal despite the difference in our stations.

Lord Hugh says, "Fate must have some reason for throwing us together, Miss . . . ?"

I know his name; it's only fair that he should know mine. "Sarah Bain."

"I think we're meant to be friends, Sarah Bain. May I give you a lift back to town?"

But this is too much, too fast, and my habitual caution and distrust chills the warmth of our rapport. I shrink from Lord Hugh like a sensitive plant from a bruising touch. "Thank you, but no."

His face falls; he thinks he's misread the situation and my refusal means I'm disgusted by him after all. "I see. Well, never mind." His eyes, which are crystalline green, fill with hurt.

I stare in disbelief. How could anything I do hurt a rich, handsome aristocrat? Sudden insight dismays me: My rejection of people may be just as painful to them as if I'd physically struck them. I'm sparing them the danger of associating with me, rejecting them before they can reject me, but they don't know that. I think guiltily of Catherine, who must think I dumped her because I was tired of her. And my standoffishness has surely repelled customers from my studio.

Lord Hugh turns away. I say, "Wait, please!" All my life I've tried to avoid hurting people, and I don't want to hurt this man who I do want as a friend. "I would like a lift back to town."

He looks surprised, then relieved. His smile is brilliant. "Right this way, then."

During the ride in his carriage, he tells me about himself. "I'm the youngest son. My family is rich enough that I can indulge in drinking, fashionable clothes, clubs, balls, and gambling, but not rich enough to marry me to a girl with a good pedigree and a big fortune. They'd like an American heiress for me, but they haven't been able to find one whose family wants to take me on. It's just as well."

He's silent and pensive for a moment, and I glimpse a sadness beneath his blithe manner, the dark reality beneath the smooth surface of his privileged existence. He can never enjoy a normal marriage, never share his private self with his friends and relations, and never love openly where he wishes. In a way, he's as lonely as I.

Then he cheers up and regales me with hilarious stories about his social set. I talk about my photography business. His flattering interest renders me more articulate than usual. He shines, and in his presence, so do I. The subject of whose funerals brought us to the cemetery never comes up. Neither do the feelings a woman might experience toward such a handsome, charming man. Lord Hugh and I are meant to be friends, nothing more nor less. He is a man from whom I need never fear advances, and I am a woman who won't demand them from him. We're free to be ourselves.

When he proposes to treat me to tea at Brown's Hotel, I demur. *Don't let people put you in their debt,* my mother's voice whispers. Hugh says, "Oh, come on, Sarah!" By this time, we're on first-name terms. "It's not like I'm asking you to run away to Tahiti with me."

At Brown's Hotel, we sit at a table by the fireplace, amid the fashionable patrons. The scones with clotted Devonshire cream, the cucumber and the smoked-salmon finger sandwiches, the fruit tarts, and the India tea are delicious. After we've reduced the huge spread to crumbs, Hugh smiles and says, "You know my deep, dark secret, Sarah. Suppose you tell me yours?"

Tit for tat. I feel myself closing up again. I also experience a powerful, long-repressed yearning to spill over to someone. But I can't tell Hugh about the boudoir pictures. It isn't that he would be disgusted or report me to the police; it's that he thinks me a respectable person, and the fact that I can know him and still respect him is a comfort to him. I shan't take away that comfort. Furthermore, the secret of the photographs isn't only mine. That leaves me with but one story to tell.

I take a deep breath, like a swimmer plunging into an unknown sea. "It's about my father." Tears sting like salt water in the wound that opens wider. I tell of his photography studio in Clerkenwell, the protest marches, and his beating by the police. Hugh gives me his handkerchief; people at nearby tables glance at us; but I can stop neither the tears nor the words that have been pent up for most of my life. I tell Hugh how my father disappeared and I later learned he'd been killed in a riot.

Hugh blows out his breath, stricken because he's elicited such an awful tale and flood of emotion from me, yet compassionate. "Sarah, I am so sorry. Your father was a hero. He sacrificed himself trying to change the world."

I can't recall ever receiving comfort from anyone. My mother kept a stiff upper lip and expected me to do the same. I'm crying so hard I can barely speak. My body hurts as if I'm straining muscles I've never used before. People around us smirk; they probably think I'm in love with Hugh and he's jilting me. I don't care. It's such a relief to talk openly about how much I loved my father and miss him, and Hugh's kindness is a balm to my wound.

"I can understand why you're still upset about your father's death," Hugh says. "It was a terrible tragedy at a sensitive time in your life."

The balm of his kindness dissolves the barrier of secrecy. "But I've never been certain what happened to my father. I've always wondered if he's not dead."

"How can that be?"

Hugh's surprise is nothing compared to

my surprise at the fact that I'm about to confide my most private secret to a man who was a stranger to me just hours ago, the last person in the world I expected to confide in. I tell him about never seeing my father's body, never knowing the location of his grave.

"That would be a reason," Hugh agrees. "Have you ever tried looking for your father?"

"No."

"Why not?"

In truth, I'm afraid of what I might learn if I found him. Did he deliberately abandon my mother and me? Didn't he love me enough to return?

Hugh misinterprets my silence. "I see. You would have to go to the police, and they weren't exactly friends to your family."

My adult rationality prevails over childish wishes. "He probably did die, and I just pretended he was alive because I wanted him to come back." I've told Hugh most of the story; I may as well confess my secret guilt. "I've always felt that I'm to blame for his death, because I didn't look hard enough for him the day he disappeared."

Now Hugh looks startled and dismayed. He leans across the table, takes my hand, and says urgently, "Sarah, it wasn't your fault." His hand is warm, its clasp gentle yet tight. "Nothing you could have done would have made a difference."

My tears abruptly stop. Hugh's plain, sincere words have an unsettling impact. "Nobody has ever said —"

"Well, somebody should have," Hugh says. "A man is killed in a riot, and his ten-year-old daughter assumes it was because of her negligence? As if she could have altered the course of fate? If I may be blunt, that's hogwash."

From his objective standpoint, my long-held conviction does sound like a mere figment of a child's imagination, born of my need to believe I had control over fate. I'm not entirely persuaded by Hugh's words, but the simple fact that I finally voiced my secret thoughts, and heard them debunked by someone I instinctively trust, has shifted my outlook a few degrees off its axis. I feel cleansed, lighter, and refreshed, but the shift is frightening.

My conviction has been the anchor of my life. *What am I without it?*

My change of mood affects Hugh. We're both quiet, although no less companionable. He pays the bill, then helps me to my feet as though I were an aged, lame aunt. "I'll take you home."

Picking up my satchel, I remember the Lipskys. "First, I must deliver some photographs."

Hugh drives me to Spitalfields and waits in his carriage while I go to the Lipskys' flat.

Mr. and Mrs. Lipsky sob over the three enlarged photographs. "Yulia. So beautiful." Mrs. Lipsky holds her hand above her daughter's face, wanting to touch but afraid of leaving smears on the prints. "Thank you, Miss Bain."

"How much you want?" Mr. Lipsky asks.

"Nothing." I can't accept their money, not after I fainted on them and they were so kind. "The photographs are my gift to you."

They protest and try to pay me, but I stand firm. At last, they reluctantly concede. "You stay for dinner," Mrs. Lipsky urges.

I'm alarmed because I've made the mistake of beginning another friendship. Then comes a sudden, dizzying sense that I've been turned upside down. *Maybe my father died because of circumstances beyond my control.* If it's true — and I'm beginning to believe it is, thanks to Hugh — then maybe I don't cast a shadow; maybe I needn't fear making friends lest I bring harm to them. But my distrust lingers. *Stab you in the back.*

Worn out from emotion, I'm glad for an

129

excuse to refuse Mrs. Lipsky. "I would like to stay, but I've someone waiting for me."

The Lipskys escort me to the street, and there is Lord Hugh in his carriage, looking as out of place in this poor Jewish neighborhood as an orchid blooming on a pine tree. He smiles and tips his hat to the Lipskys.

Consternation appears on their faces. Mrs. Lipsky whispers, "It is none of my business, but . . . men like that, they no good for you."

She thinks Hugh is a rich cad who is sporting with me, a poor, gullible spinster. That's how it looks on the surface. "It's all right," I say, touched by her concern. "He's just . . . a friend." The word tastes strange but nourishing.

Mrs. Lipsky looks unconvinced, and her husband glowers at Hugh as if ready to pummel him if he harms me.

During the ride to Whitechapel, Hugh says, "I've been thinking about your pretty little friend Catherine. I feel bad about snubbing her the other day. I'd like to make it up to her."

I have much more to make up to her than Hugh does. Although it goes against the grain, I propose the only remedy I can think of. "Why don't you come to tea on Saturday? I'll invite Catherine, too."

"In the meantime, we can make up a story about how we met and why I behaved so atrociously." As the carriage draws up outside my studio, Hugh says, "Excellent idea. I'll see you here on Saturday."

10

By Saturday morning, 8 September, there hasn't been another murder. I dare to hope my idea that the Ripper is after my models and won't stop killing until they're all dead is wrong. I begin to fret about my tea party for Hugh and Catherine. I've never hosted a party before. Even if I haven't a shadow and therefore am no danger to them, I'm overwhelmed by practical concerns. What shall I feed them? I go to the bakery and overspend on fancy puff pastries cut into half-moon, star, and leaf shapes and filled with raspberry preserves. As I wait for the pastries to be boxed up, I hear two women in line behind me talking.

"Another slag's been killed in Whitechapel."

Coldness trickles through my heart. I turn to the women. "Who was it?"

Surprised by my urgent tone, they shake their heads.

"Where did it happen?" I demand.

"In Hanbury Street. Behind Mrs. Richardson's house."

I grab my bakery box and make haste for Hanbury Street. The house is a three-story building identified by a sign that reads, *Mrs. Amelia Richardson, rough packing case maker.* Many landlords in Whitechapel operate businesses on their premises, and the house also contains a cat's-meat shop. A crowd is standing outside. When I reach the door, a man says, "End of the line's back there," and points down the street.

I belatedly notice that the crowd is queued up at Mrs. Richardson's house. "The line for what?"

"To see where Dark Annie was murdered."

The event I feared has come to pass: another of my models has been killed. When I last saw Annie Chapman, she was fighting with another woman over a bar of soap. She must have taken to the streets last night because she'd again run out of money. Now the scene of her death is a public attraction. I join the queue, ashamed of my own curiosity.

"It's three pence," says an old woman ahead of me. "Mrs. Richardson's grandson John is giving tours."

Some people will seize any chance to

make a profit. An hour passes before it's my turn to enter the door that leads to a long, dim corridor. Past a staircase is a door to the backyard. There stands John Richardson, a pimple-faced boy of perhaps fourteen years. He collects pennies from me and three other women and ushers us down the stone steps to the fenced yard. A cellar door leads to the packing case workshop, from which I hear hammering. A woodshed and a privy occupy the yard's far corners. Blood is spattered thickly on the ground near the house; red clots dribble down the fence. Bile sours my mouth.

"That's where she were killed," John says, pointing to the blood on the ground, his eyes bright with glee. "She were lying on her back, like this." He sticks out his tongue, clamps it between his front teeth. "Her skirts were up. Her legs were apart. And her throat were cut." He draws his finger across his own throat.

The manner of Annie's death is similar to Martha's and Polly's. Two similar murders of women who posed for my boudoir pictures could be deemed a coincidence, but three comprise a pattern. My fear for Kate, Liz, Mary Jane, and Catherine is unfortunately justified.

"Her stomach were sliced open. There

were pieces of skin lying beside her." John is so excited, he spits saliva as he talks. "Her guts were pulled out and spread around like sausages."

This is even gorier than what happened to Martha and Polly. I still believe that Annie's killer is the same man, but this time he's mutilated his victim even more cruelly.

"But that ain't all." John speaks in a low, sly voice appropriate for confiding dirty secrets. "Her female organs was missing. The killer musta stole 'em."

Exclamations come from my fellow spectators. One of the women faints. The other two catch her and drag her out to the road. I ask John, "How did Annie get in here?"

"The door's always unlocked. There's seventeen people lives here, and they come and go all day and night. Grandma don't want to have to keep letting them in. And whores sometimes use the yard."

I envision Annie soliciting a man and leading him here; I imagine her terror when she sees the knife. I glance at the windows that overlook the yard. "Didn't anyone hear her being attacked? Why did no one try to rescue her?"

"The police doctor said she were strangled, she couldn't scream. We didn't know a thing until it were too late."

"Have the police caught the killer?" My heart flutters with eager hope.

"Not that I've heard. They looked all around, but he didn't leave a trail. Not even a single bloody footprint."

Once more, he'd dissolved like an apparition in the fog.

I've brought my miniature camera in case I should see anything I wanted to photograph, but as I pull it from my satchel, John says, "Your time's up, mum. Other people are waiting."

"Do the police have any clues or witnesses?" I ask, putting the camera away and mounting the steps.

"They found a leather apron in the yard. And I heard that Mrs. Long from over on Church Street was on her way to market early this morning and saw Dark Annie talking to a man. She didn't get a good look at him, but she thinks he were foreign."

My hopes are dashed again. The killer, still at large, has neither name nor face yet.

Catherine and my other models are in such grave danger that I can no longer wait for the police to catch the killer.

I hasten along Commercial Street, laden with my bakery box and satchel. Carriages clog the thoroughfares, people queue at shops and stalls, and a tout stands outside the waxworks, calling, "See the murder victims for a tuppence!" Giggling, shrieking women come out. Before the door swings shut, I see three wax dummies splashed with red paint. Other folk besides the Richardsons are finding ways to capitalize on the crimes.

Two police officers come suddenly upon me. One is PC Barrett, the other an older man in a fancier uniform that signifies a higher rank.

"Miss Bain," Barrett says.

"Good afternoon," I say in a voice that's intended to be cool but sounds as stricken as I feel.

"This is Inspector Reid, my superior officer." Barrett seems nervous yet elated. "He's head of CID, Metropolitan Police, Whitechapel Division." He turns to Inspector Reid. "This is Sarah Bain, the photographer."

"How convenient," Inspector Reid says. His quiet voice is more authentically refined than Barrett's. "We were about to call on you."

He holds out his hand, and I am forced to shake it or risk offending him. His hand is soft and pink. So is his face. He has soft iron-gray hair worn in a fringe across his forehead. A fluffy mustache and beard frame his smiling pink mouth, but his teeth are pointed like a fox's. His deep-set brown eyes crinkle jovially. They're like autumn leaves under ice. His long nose is as sharp as an accusation.

"Call on me, why?" I ask.

"A streetwalker named Annie Chapman was murdered last night." Reid narrows his eyes, perceiving that it isn't news to me. "PC Barrett tells me you have information regarding the Whitechapel murders."

I regard Barrett with dismay. "You told him about me?" I had somehow expected Barrett to keep our relations to himself, and I have only my foolish naïveté to blame for my sense of betrayal.

Barrett nods. "This is a murder investigation. You're a potential witness." He looks sheepish, as if he, too, thinks he's betrayed me.

"He lost some credibility recently during a little fiasco at the Tower." Reid flashes a cheerful, malicious glance at Barrett. "What better way to regain it than by bringing me a new lead?"

I suppose that Inspector Reid, too, lost credibility because of Barrett's mistake, and he needs new clues to appease his own superiors. Barrett flushes; he's ashamed of using me to buy his way back into the investigation.

"But I already told Police Constable Barrett I have no information." I'm angry at myself as well as Barrett; I should have known to expect nothing better from him than this. I hold my satchel and box in front of me like a shield.

Reid smiles his jovial, sharp-toothed smile. "Sometimes people know things they're not aware of. Let's talk and see if we can ferret anything out of your mind."

If we talk, he might ask me where I've just been, and I don't want to tell him. That I visited the scene of Annie's death would signify that I have a suspicious interest in the murders. "I must be getting home." My voice quavers.

"We'll take you." Inspector Reid hails a cab.

I tried to prevent Catherine from getting into a vehicle with a man she hardly knew, and this is a no less hazardous situation, for the police are above their own law. "No, thank you! It's not far."

Inspector Reid opens the door to the carriage. "PC Barrett and I don't mind short rides, do we?" He gestures for Barrett to enter first.

With an apologetic, worried glance at me,

Barrett obeys. My panic increases because I realize that he's afraid of what Reid will do.

"After you, Miss Bain," Reid says.

Afraid that if I refuse, Reid will arrest me, I climb into the carriage. I grip the satchel and bakery box on my lap. Reid speaks to the driver, sits beside me, and slams the door. The carriage rackets past my studio. I am wedged so tightly between Reid and Barrett that I can feel their body heat. I press my knees together and my arms against my sides.

"How well did you know Annie Chapman?" Reid asks in a casual tone.

"Not very." At the same moment I answer, I realize that by pretending he already knows I was acquainted with Annie, he's tricked me into admitting it.

"That's interesting." Reid smiles across me at Barrett. "Miss Bain knew Annie Chapman as well as Polly Nichols and Martha Tabram."

I feel Barrett squirm, see his clenched jaws. Reid has already learned something from me that Barrett didn't. Reid is more expert, and dangerous, than Barrett.

"I haven't had a chance to ask her about Annie," Barrett mutters.

Reid ignores him and asks me, "How did you meet Annie?"

I can't tell him that Kate Eddowes brought Annie to me as a model. While I seek a credible, innocuous lie, anxiety quickens my breathing. I smell the men's wool uniforms and Barrett's fresh scent. Reid smells of shaving soap scented with harsh, astringent pine.

"Did she come to your studio?" Reid asks. "Did she want a cup of tea? Or ask if you needed a charwoman?"

He's letting me know that Barrett has told him everything I said about Martha and Polly, that he has a good memory, and that if I lie, he will catch me later.

"She came to my studio," I say, because people might have seen Annie there as well as Martha and Polly. "She used to crochet antimacassars, and she tried to sell me some."

Reid notices my discomfiture and smiles; he knows I'm not telling the truth. "What did you and Annie talk about?"

"Not much. She wasn't there very long."

"Oh?" His fluffy eyebrows rise. "My sources say that she was inside your studio for more than an hour."

A mixture of confusion and fear addles me. Have my neighbors told the police they saw her, or is Reid pretending? I look at Barrett, whose expression warns me to tell

141

Reid whatever he wants to know.

Reid nudges my arm. "What did Annie say?"

I can't say she was nervous about taking off her clothes for the camera the first time. "She talked about her children. Her little boy is crippled. One of her daughters died. The other joined a circus." As long as I'm talking, Reid can't ask more questions.

Reid interrupts, "What about Polly Nichols?"

I've never been quick at following conversations that take unexpected twists. I try to think of something that's safe to say.

"Telling the truth is easier than making up a lie," Reid says with false mildness. "The truth is also easier to remember if you need to repeat it."

"Polly's husband left her for her nurse while she was with child for the fifth time."

"You seem to know Polly and Annie better than you would have me believe," Reid says. "What gems did Martha Tabram pass on to you?"

I can't think of anything innocuous. "I don't remember."

Reid frowns. I have accidentally hit on the right answer — all I need do from now on when he asks me a question is say I don't remember, and he will tire of me and let me go. A glance out the window shows me that we're going in circles around the block. I could be home in an instant.

"Did the women talk about their customers?" Reid asks.

"I don't remember."

"Or their boyfriends?"

"I don't remember."

Reid turns to me. His face is so close to mine that I can see the pores in his pink skin. "Miss Bain." His voice is still quiet but threatening. The sourness of his breath mingles unpleasantly with his pine-scented soap. "I think Annie Chapman and the other two victims had a male acquaintance in common — the person who killed them. Any information about their customers or men friends is therefore of utmost importance. Try harder to remember."

If only I could tell him, I would. My fingers clutch the handle of my satchel. "I'm trying. I can't."

"Maybe she really doesn't know anything," Barrett says. I can tell he doesn't believe it, and I'm surprised he's intervening. He must feel bad because Reid is bullying me. "Maybe we should let her go."

"Would you like me to stop the carriage and let *you* go?" Reid swiftly redirects his displeasure toward Barrett.

"No, sir —"

"Then don't interrupt my interrogation."

Barrett compresses his mouth. I can feel him thinking that to leave me alone with Reid would be worse than not sticking up for me. He must often be a party to business like this, which is too bad. I think the world lost a nice person when Barrett joined the police force.

Reid asks, "Where have you been today, Miss Bain?"

"To market. I bought cakes." I untie the string around the box. "Would you like to see?"

"That won't be necessary. What's in the satchel?"

My grip tightens convulsively on the handle. "A camera."

"I'll have a look at it, if you don't mind."

Every instinct warns me not to let Reid touch my most precious possession, but unless I cooperate, he'll take it by force, and it will break. I give him the camera. He examines its black leather case, aims the lens out the window, and peers in the viewfinder. "Quite a handy invention. You could photograph people without their noticing."

I wonder if Barrett told him about seeing me at Polly's funeral. Reid says, "One more question, and then you can go. What else do you know about those women and their murders that you aren't telling me?"

His soft pink hands hold my camera hostage. I feel like Prometheus, trapped between the rock to which he is manacled and the eagle that devours his viscera. I'm tempted to tell Reid everything, just to stop this interrogation, but if I do, my torment will have only begun.

"I don't know anything else." I force myself to look him straight in the face.

Reid stares back at me with angry frustration. Quaking with terror, I brace myself. Then Reid gives me the camera. I feel Barrett draw and expel a deep breath. As I slip the camera in my satchel, my hands are so damp and clumsy that I almost drop it. Reid smirks.

"You'll have to come to the station and give an official statement." He calls to the driver. The carriage stops; he opens the door, steps out, and bows. "Good-bye for now, Miss Bain."

11

Running toward my studio, I drop the bakery box. Raspberry-filled stars, half-moons, and leaves fly out. I'm twenty paces from my door when I see Catherine and Lord Hugh standing outside the studio. Hugh twirls a gold-handled cane, tosses it in the air, and catches it behind his back. Catherine claps her hands and laughs. Hugh must have told her something that satisfactorily explained why he snubbed her. I stagger to a halt, too upset to face them. I'll have to sneak in the back door and pretend I'm not home. Then I see Mr. and Mrs. Lipsky walking toward my studio. Mr. Lipsky carries a covered basket. They must be coming to see me; there's no other reason for them to be here. I'm about to turn and run, when two young men come out of the public house and swagger up to the Lipskys.

"Hey, Jews!" one man says.

The Lipskys stop. Mrs. Lipsky draws her shawl tighter around herself.

"What've you got there?" The man points to the basket.

"I bet it's a baby," his comrade says. "The Jews kill 'em and eat 'em."

The men grab the basket. Mr. Lipsky shouts in Russian while they try to wrest it from him. I have seen ruffians like these torment Jews, and there's no telling how far they'll go. I can't abandon the Lipskys. As I hurry to their aid, the basket tips. Out falls a bundle wrapped in greasy, bloodstained paper. I smell the savory odor of beef roasted with onions. The Lipskys must have come to reciprocate for the photographs of their daughter, and the meat is a gift from the butcher shop where Mr. Lipsky works.

"Dead baby!" the men yell, then set upon Mr. Lipsky. "Murderer! Cannibal!"

Mrs. Lipsky screams while the men punch her husband. He tries to fend them off without hitting back; a Jew who strikes a Christian is likely to be killed by a mob.

"I say, leave the poor fellow alone!" Hugh wields his cane against the two men, rapping their backs and buttocks. Catherine, amazed, covers her mouth with her hands. The men scream in pain and rage. They turn to assault Hugh, but he smacks their faces with the cane. Blood pours from their noses. "Get lost before I make you eat your teeth."

The men slink off. The Lipskys politely thank Hugh. Catherine beholds him with stars in her eyes. My help isn't needed, but my momentum carries me forward. I trip on my skirts. As the cobblestone pavement rushes up at me, I clutch my satchel against my body with my left arm to protect the camera inside. I fling out my right hand to break my fall — too late. My knees, chin, and hand simultaneously strike the pavement. I lie facedown, stunned, struggling for breath.

"Sarah!" Catherine kneels beside me. "Are you all right?"

I roll over and feel warm wetness trickle from my chin down my neck. Catherine cries, "She's bleeding!"

Overwhelmed by the pain from my fall and residual terror of Inspector Reid, I sob between gasps. Hugh says, "Let's get her inside."

Catherine rummages in my satchel for my key. Hugh slings my arm around his neck and lifts me. I've never been touched so intimately by anyone except my parents. He carries me through the door, as if we're a bride and groom. He smells of bay rum shaving lotion — lime and spice. My brief, absurd thought of romance flees while he climbs the stairs. His warm breath against my hair, his steady heartbeat under my cheek, and the rhythm of his steps remind me of my father carrying me to bed when I was a child. I close my eyes for a moment, comforted.

When Hugh sets me down at the top of the stairs, I run inside my bedroom and shut the door. Hugh calls, "Sarah, what's the matter?"

"Please just go."

Catherine says, "Not until we know you're all right. We'll wait for you in the studio."

I'm trembling so hard that when I pour water from the jug on the washstand into the bowl, the water sloshes on the floor. My knees hurt. When I look in the mirror to bathe my cut chin, a ghostly white face with hollow eyes stares back at me. I tidy my hair and force myself to go downstairs.

Catherine, Hugh, and the Lipskys are at the table, eating. The beef roast sits on a platter beside a loaf of bread, a crock of mustard, and a jug of beer. Everybody smiles at me with relief. Everybody has invaded my sanctuary at once, just when all I want is my usual solitude.

"Come have some of this delicious meat

that Abraham and Rachel brought," Hugh says.

Mrs. Lipsky smiles at Hugh; his dispatching of the two hooligans has changed her opinion of him, and their shared concern for me has made the Lipskys friends with Hugh and Catherine. I'm surprised to notice that the Lipskys are younger than I thought — in their thirties. Their foreign clothes, accents, and manners made them seem older when I first met them. Mr. Lipsky carves a slice of the roast with his large, sharp knife and puts the meat on a plate for me. I collapse into the chair. I've not been at table with so many people since boarding school. I can't eat. I realize that Inspector Reid didn't tell me when I must go to the police station. It had to be deliberate; he wants me to wonder and fret. The suspense is worse than knowing for certain when, or how, the summons will come, and when it does, I'll have to brave a whole building full of police.

"Sarah, what's wrong?" Catherine asks.

I shake my head. Her I could tell, but not in front of Hugh and the Lipskys.

"Get it off your chest," Hugh urges. "What are friends for?"

I'm moved by the novel idea that all these people are my friends. Their concern overcomes my reticence. "The police just picked me up and questioned me."

Hugh's eyebrows lift in surprise. "Why? What did you do — rob a bank?"

I hesitate, remembering my mother's warning about friends.

"Come on," Hugh says, "you can tell us. We won't rat on you."

A childhood memory intrudes. I'm skipping up the street to join a group of girls — my bosom companions — playing hopscotch. They yell taunts at me. Their mothers pull them inside their houses and slam the doors. I'm left alone on the street. *Stab you in the back.*

Catherine regards me with dismayed comprehension. "It was about the murders."

"Wait, I heard that two streetwalkers were murdered hereabouts," Hugh says. "But what has that to do with you, Sarah?"

"Three," I say. "Annie Chapman was just killed."

"Did you know her?" Hugh says, all the more puzzled. "And the others, too?"

"Yes."

"Tell him, Sarah," Catherine says. "Maybe he can help." She turns starry eyes to Hugh, her knight in shining armor.

Hugh smiles and bows. "At your service."

"No," I say firmly.

Catherine rises from her chair. Hands on her hips, she says, "Tell him, or I will."

"You mustn't!" I glance at the Lipskys and see a mixture of enlightenment and confusion on their faces: They're recalling the conversation we had after I fainted at their house. They've deduced that my trouble with the police is related to the murders, but they don't understand the nature of my connection with the victims.

"They won't tell," Catherine says, as if that were our only concern. In addition to not wanting to bother them with my problems, it's wrong to make them privy to a crime. And I don't want them to turn against me. "Where are the photographs?"

"I don't have any copies," I lie.

"You keep copies of everything. I'll tear your studio apart and find them."

The secret of the boudoir photographs weighs more heavily on me now that Annie is dead, and I want to believe Hugh can help. "The darkroom. Under a loose floorboard at the back."

Catherine goes to the darkroom and returns with enlarged prints of the photographs clutched to her bosom. Her expression is a mixture of reckless daring and childish faith in Hugh. She sets the first photograph in front of him as if dealing cards. "Martha Tabram."

Martha, corpulent and grinning, stands nude with her hip cocked and a silk fig leaf over her pubis. Hugh's eyes goggle.

"Polly Nichols." Catherine lays down the photograph of Polly licking her own breast. "Annie Chapman." There is naked Annie posed like Bernini's famous statue of St. Theresa, swooning with feigned ecstasy.

"You took these, Sarah?" Hugh is incredulous.

"Yes." My face is hot with shame.

Catherine slaps down three more prints. "Liz Stride. Mary Jane Kelly. Kate Eddowes."

Hugh purses his mouth and whistles. Mrs. Lipsky shakes her head and murmurs in Russian. Her husband frowns, glancing from me to the pictures, as if trying to reconcile them with my prim appearance. Now I regret my decision; now my foolish trust shall be punished.

"Sarah, you naughty girl," Hugh says in a fond, teasing voice.

I sag with relief; he, at least, isn't offended and condemning me. Catherine still has one print clasped to her bosom, its blank back facing outward.

Hugh examines the prints. "These are quite artistic. Much better than the usual sort I've seen. You've made the models look alluring even though they're not exactly great beauties." He regards me with new respect. "They must fetch a pretty penny."

"That's why I took them," I say, flattered and sheepish. "I needed the money. So did the women who modeled for the photographs."

The Lipskys nod. They have known poverty; they understand that one does what one must to survive. I am grateful that they're ready to excuse my moral transgression. "You think the killer has seen these photographs and is picking your models off like ducks in a shooting gallery." Hugh's expression turns somber as he regards the images in a new, darker light. "Three down, three to go, and you're the only person who's figured it out."

"Four to go," I grimly correct him.

"There are only six models, or have I counted wrong? Who . . . ?" Then Hugh sees Catherine holding the last photograph. *"You?"*

Catherine nods, blushing scarlet. She didn't care if other men saw her pictures, but now her knight knows she is no lady. The Lipskys look shocked, then sorry for her. Catherine drops into her chair, hugging the photograph, loath to display it, her eyes brilliant with tears of shame.

"It's all right," Hugh says gently. "You don't have to show me."

He doesn't think any worse of her. Catherine's blush fades, and she smiles gratefully. I'm relieved that my photographs didn't turn Hugh and the Lipskys against Catherine as well as myself.

"Well, I see the problem," Hugh says. "You can't go to the police and say, 'Here's a big fat clue — the murderer you're looking for is choosing his victims from my portfolio of smutty photographs.' They would throw you in jail." He adds, "But if you show the police the photograph of Catherine, she can be your cellmate. At least you won't be lonely."

"This is no time for joking!" I'm offended, and I see that Catherine is, too.

"You're right. I apologize," Hugh says, contrite. "I'm always making jokes at the wrong times. So what's to be done?"

The secret is out, and I feel better for it, but I am still in trouble with the police, and my models are still in danger from the Ripper.

The doorbell jangles. We all start. Mick bounds in through the door. His smile fades as he sees my guests. "Oh." He's dirtier than usual, with an oily grime on his neck and a reek like the river at low tide. "You're busy. I'll come back later."

His timing is bad, but I have the oddest notion that something has been missing that is no longer missing. A moment ago, I was overwhelmed by the bounty of all these friends, but now their number seems insufficient without Mick. "Wait," I say. "Don't go."

Mick hesitates; his nostrils quiver; he smells the food. He notices Catherine, and his eyes take on that dazzled look. She beholds him with an unfriendly expression. Distrust of Hugh and the Lipskys narrows his eyes, but he approaches the table, drawn by Catherine and the food.

Hugh sweeps the photographs into a stack and turns them over — too late.

"Holy Mother of God!" Mick exclaims.

Hugh laughs. "I don't think God's mother is in there."

"Are you makin' fun of me?" Mick turns on Hugh like a new dog in a pack snapping at a stronger, secure rival.

"No, no," Hugh says. "I had the same reaction when I saw those pictures. Sorry, didn't mean to offend you."

"Miss Sarah, did you take them?" Mick's precociousness deserts him; he looks like a frightened child betrayed by a trusted adult.

156

"What's going on?"

Aghast that he's seen the photographs, I wonder how much he knows about matters of the flesh.

"Sit down, Mick." I pull up an armchair for him. "Have something to eat, and I'll tell you."

The armchair is low, and when he sits, his chin is barely above the table. He looks younger than ever. His frightened gaze flits over us and settles on Catherine. She wrinkles her nose. He reddens and hangs his head in misery. When I introduce him to the Lipskys and Hugh, he eyes them with suspicion. Mr. Lipsky scowls. Mrs. Lipsky smiles reassuringly at Mick, fills a plate with beef and bread, and puts it in front of him, but he regards the food as if it's poisoned.

"I took those photographs to make money," I say, "for myself and the women in them. That's all."

Mick nods, relieved because I had no nefarious motive but not altogether re-assured. He jabs the photograph of Polly Nichols with his dirty finger. "This one — we saw her dead in Buck's Row. You knew her." He sounds put out because I didn't tell him I knew Polly and he knows there's more I've concealed.

"Yes. And the two other women who were

murdered also modeled for me." I explain what we've been discussing.

"Gorblimey." Awe hushes Mick's voice.

"Amen," Hugh says.

Mick frowns, uncertain whether Hugh is teasing him, then regards me with new, sympathetic respect; I have revealed myself as a fellow outlaw. "What're you going to do?"

"That's the question," Hugh says.

"I can't let the murderer kill more women," I say.

"Maybe police catch him," Mrs. Lipsky says hopefully.

Mick has begun furtively cramming food into his mouth; he's not certain it's safe to eat, but he's too hungry to resist. At Mrs. Lipsky's remark, he lets out a disdainful splutter that sprays mustard on the tablecloth.

"My sentiments exactly," Hugh says. "One, then two, then three murders, and from what I hear, the police aren't making any progress."

"The police don't know their arse from a hole in their head," Mick agrees, but his look at Hugh is still distrustful.

Catherine makes a moue of disgust at Mick's vulgarity. Mick notices and looks stricken by the fact that his liking for

Catherine is unrequited and will remain so. He resorts to blustering. "When somethin' needs to be done, you got to do it yourself, that's what I always say."

"Do you mean catch the killer?" Although I've been trying to learn as much as I can about the murders, I never equated it with actually hunting down the murderer, which seems such an absurd idea that I laugh. Hugh and Catherine laugh, too. The Lipskys look as if we've made a joke that they don't understand.

"Sure. Why not?" Our reaction puts Mick on the defensive. "Ain't that better than sittin' on your thumbs while the coppers are on your back?"

I don't want to hurt Mick's feelings, and my desperation is so great that I would entertain advice from a twelve-year-old. "I could at least try."

He gives me a grateful smile. Catherine says, "Sarah, be serious!"

"Sarah, no!" Mrs. Lipsky perceives that I am serious the moment I realize it myself. "You could get hurt."

The Ripper might find out I'm on his trail and kill me. "But if I can give the police his name and prove that he killed the women, then they'll arrest him. My photographs need never come into it, and everyone will be safe." If I were to succeed, it would show PC Barrett that I'm someone to be reckoned with, and I won't be troubled by Inspector Reid again.

"I'd love a mystery to solve," Hugh says. "Why not give it a whirl, Sarah? I'm happy to help."

"Me too," Mick says, eager not to be outdone by Hugh. He obviously cares less about saving the prostitutes than impressing Catherine.

Catherine throws up her hands. "Have you all gone mad?"

"It's not so mad an idea," Hugh says. "Sarah has information that the police don't. She knows how the killer selects his victims and who his targets are. And that may not be all." Excited, he seizes my hand. "Tell me, Sarah — how do you sell your photographs?"

"I don't. Kate Eddowes does. The whole scheme was her idea. I give her the prints, and she takes them to a bookshop in Holywell Street. I've never been there."

"Holywell Street," Hugh says triumphantly. "Another clue!"

"I could go there and ask who bought the prints." I'm carried away by his enthusiasm, giddy with revelation. By flouting my mother's advice, I've learned that not all people repay trust with a stab in the back.

"I'll go with you," Mick says.

"I have friends in the press," Hugh says. "I'll ask them whether the police have any new information we can use."

These two have risen to my aid. It's as if I've fallen and a net has appeared.

Catherine gazes at Hugh's hand clasping mine. Her brow puckers; she's wondering what my exact relationship with Hugh is. "What shall I do?" she asks, still skeptical yet not wanting to be left out.

"Avoid becoming the killer's next victim," I say sternly.

"That's right," Hugh says.

Catherine frowns, distressed because now that she's seen my portfolio turned into a gallery of murder victims, she finally realizes she's in danger. Mick looks startled as he gathers that Catherine is among my models.

"How about a trip home?" Hugh asks Catherine. He turns out his pockets and tosses coins on the table. "This should cover your train fare."

"No! I'm not going home!" Catherine seems more alarmed than the idea merits. "I'm just beginning to make my way on the stage. If I leave, I'll lose my part, and when I come back, I'll have to start all over. And I love London and my friends. I don't want

161

to go away." Her voice is breathless as she piles excuse on top of excuse. "I have to be at the theater soon," she says, putting on her coat.

Mr. and Mrs. Lipsky have been politely listening to the conversation. They must regret that they've become mixed up with this peculiar photographer and her motley friends. Mr. Lipsky gets to his feet. I think he and his wife are about to make their escape, but he says, "I go with Catherine. I protect."

"You needn't!" It's not that I don't welcome his help. These are grieving parents, and I shouldn't involve them in something that is probably against the law, possibly dangerous, and certainly not their problem.

"I protect Catherine," he says, and his wife firmly nods in approval.

Do they see their daughter in Catherine? Do they think that even though they couldn't save Yulia, they can keep Catherine safe? These questions are too personal to ask. Perhaps the Lipskys feel they still owe me a favor, but perhaps they share the idea that has lodged in my mind — that we are members of a circle that was completed when Mick arrived.

"But I don't want a chaperone," Catherine protests, obviously thinking it will curtail her social life.

"It's the perfect solution," Hugh says. "Nobody will attack you with our Russian strong man by your side."

Catherine argues until we refuse to let her out the door unless she agrees that Mr. Lipsky will be her bodyguard and bring her straight home after the shows. Outside, dusk is falling. I light the gas lamps. They illuminate the somber faces around my table. I feel as if I've stitched together a cloak from random scraps of fabric that the wind has blown in my direction. The cloak is blessedly warm.

"We're all in, then," Hugh says with a strange inflection, as if our impulsive plan has taken on a gravity he never foresaw.

Mick, Catherine, the Lipskys, and I nod. I feel a sudden foreboding as I recall that my association with Martha, Polly, and Annie began in similar fashion — because I unwisely let them into my life. I wonder if I will bring harm to my new circle of friends. I should warn them not to step into my shadow . . .

Then comes a sudden, unsteadying sensation like the one I experienced when Hugh told me I wasn't to blame for my father's death. Maybe he's right. I'm almost ready to believe it. I've already flouted my mother's advice without harm; why not risk challenging the notion that I cast an evil shadow? In for a penny, in for a pound. But there is danger for my new friends, even if not from me.

"If you get involved with this, the killer could come after you," I say. "So could the police."

"Let 'em come," Hugh says, flexing his muscles.

"Yeah!" Mick says, and Mr. Lipsky grins. Catherine and Mrs. Lipsky smile admiringly at their bravado.

I concede because I have an inkling that what Hugh said about himself and me is true for all of us: fate must have some reason for throwing us together. Perhaps the purpose of our circle is to venture into the shadow of the Ripper and hunt him down.

12

On Monday morning, a brisk, fresh wind disperses the fog. As Mick and I set out for Holywell Street, the sun seems brighter than ever before, the odors of food and garbage more intense, the noise from hawkers, carts, and carriages louder. It's as if a protective skin was stripped off me yesterday, and I'm open to a world whose full intensity I never experienced. I have high hopes for today, but I'm uneasy about conducting secret inquiries in stark daylight. I miss the fog's concealing veil and the melancholy yet familiar comfort of solitude.

I glance at Mick, skipping along beside me. Banding together to hunt the Ripper seemed so right yesterday, but my new friends are virtual strangers, and my lifelong caution toward people hasn't been entirely rooted out.

Mick suddenly lets out a loud whoop. Alarm catches my breath. He runs after a carriage, jumps on the back, and rides to the next block. He laughs as he runs back to me. My heart is still pounding as we continue on our way. Enlisting the help of a twelve-year-old daredevil now seems like a foolish idea.

When we reach Holywell Street, we find many bookshops. Mick asks, "Which is it?"

"Kate wouldn't tell me." I'm worrying about what mischief he'll make next. "She was afraid that if I knew, I would sell the photographs there myself and cut her out of the deal."

We stroll up and down the street. The shops occupy old, grimy buildings; books are displayed behind smudged windows. Other people are few, mostly male, with a furtive air.

As we stop outside a bookshop, Mick whispers, "Remember, it's not just the customers we have to beware of."

The bookseller who bought my photographs might himself be the killer. My hands grow clammy with nerves as we enter the shop. I wish I could put a leash on Mick, the better to keep him under control. A hunch-shouldered man is arranging books on shelves.

"May I help you?" he asks, peering down his beaked nose at us.

I clutch the handle of my satchel. "I should like to see . . ." I clear my throat. "Some photographs of women."

The proprietor glances suspiciously at Mick, then opens a book. "How about these?"

The pictures show ladies' fashions. "Er, no."

"You got any where they're naked?" Mick says.

A muzzle, too! He was supposed to let me do the talking.

The proprietor seems shocked that a lady of my respectable appearance would want what Mick is asking for. He's probably also wondering what our relationship is. "Ah. I understand." His manner turns sly. He must think I'm among those women who like other women. He locates a clothbound portfolio and shows me the photographs. They are similar in subject matter to mine, but they're not ones I took. I understand what Hugh meant when he said mine were better than the usual. Although the models are prettier, the pictures are poorly composed, lit, and focused.

"I'm sorry, these won't do."

Mick and I try three more shops, with no luck. When we come out of the third, I spy a strange figure on the sidewalk. It has a small head on a square, truncated body. As we draw closer, I discern that it is a man seated in a wheelchair. A plaid blanket covers his legs. He has a round face as pink as a baby's and reddish hairs fringing his bald crown. Gold-framed spectacles magnify his blue eyes.

"I've been watching you," he says with a cheery smile. "You evidently aren't satisfied with the wares offered by my colleagues. I think you'll find a better product here." He wheels himself through a shop door. The sign over it reads, *Russell's Fine Books.*

"Don't let your guard down," Mick whispers as we follow. "He might be the one."

"He's crippled," I whisper.

"Maybe not really. I knows some beggars who just pretend to be."

The shop has pretensions to elegance. A worn Turkey carpet covers the floor; plaster busts of Roman emperors serve as bookends. Mr. Russell leads us to his back room, lights a gas lamp with a stained-glass shade, and seats us on a threadbare green brocade divan. He opens a safe. It contains three albums covered in maroon velvet. He places one in my lap. Mounted on the first page is a familiar photograph of Polly Nichols undressing.

"The photographer is a genius," Mr.

Russell says. "His models aren't pretty, but observe the lighting and the composition and the mood. His work could be considered art."

Never have I experienced so little pleasure in hearing my work praised or so fervently not wanted credit for it. I turn pages. My models are all there. Mick gulps at the sight of Catherine posing nude as Venus. I shut the album in which Mr. Russell has compiled my latest collection of photographs and glance at the other two albums in the safe. I gave Kate three copies of the collection to sell. The only other prints, and the negatives, are in my studio.

"I would like to buy this album and all other work by this photographer." I must remove them from circulation, lest they come to the attention of the police and the police somehow connect them to me.

"I'm sorry, I'm sold out of his earlier work. These photographs are spoken for, and the customers are coming to fetch them today. But I can order a set made for you."

"She'll pay you more," Mick says. "How much do you want?"

"Well, I don't like to renege on a deal . . ." Mr. Russell ponders, then says, "They're yours for a hundred pounds."

I haven't that much money in the world!

Mick says, "How about ten?"

Not ten, either!

Offense wipes the smile from Mr. Russell's face. "I'm afraid not." He takes the album from me and sets it on the desk beside a black ledger. Mick and I reluctantly rise. As Mr. Russell maneuvers his wheelchair, herding us out to the front of the shop, I ask, "Who has purchased photographs like these?"

"I can't divulge that information. It's confidential."

Mick sidles around behind Mr. Russell and makes a rotating gesture with his hand. I frown; I don't know what he means. Then he tiptoes into the back room. He wants me to distract Mr. Russell while he steals the albums! Even as alarm petrifies me, I wish I could tell Mick to steal the ledger, too; it must contain the customers' names, the killer's among them. I'm so nervous that the only thing I can think to do is bluff. "The police would be interested to know what you are selling here. Tell me who bought the photographs, or I will report you."

Mr. Russell's pink face reddens with anger. "Get out of my shop!"

Mick bursts from the back room, clutching the three albums and the ledger against his chest. "Run!" he shouts.

Panicking, I speed out the door, but Mr. Russell rolls his chair between it and Mick. As Mick tries to push him out of the way, Mr. Russell grabs Mick's arm. Mick lunges for the door. His momentum yanks Mr. Russell from his wheelchair. They fall onto the sidewalk. Albums and ledger go flying. Mick scrambles to retrieve them while Mr. Russell cries, "Stop! Thief!"

People in the street turn and stare. The blanket is wadded under Mr. Russell. His legs in their flannel trousers are withered, paralyzed. "Help! Police!"

"Mick! Never mind!" I call as I back away from the shop. "We must go!"

We race down the street, around corners. Breathless, we take refuge in a marketplace, among the crowd. "Mick, you shouldn't have done that. You could have gotten us arrested!"

Chagrined, he says, "Yeah, well, I thought it was worth a try. Sorry I dropped the goods. At least we found out he really is a cripple."

"Yes. He couldn't have killed the women and run away afterward."

"What do we do now?"

"I have a new idea." I lead Mick down an alley. From the end, looking across Holywell Street at an angle, we have a clear view of Russell's Fine Books. I reach in my satchel and take out my miniature camera.

"I get it," Mick says. "When the customers come to get the pictures, you'll take theirs!"

"Yes. The killer is likely to be one of them, and maybe his picture will help us discover his identity."

At ten o'clock in the morning, the sun shines on Holywell Street. Shadows immerse the alley. Mick subsides into morose silence. I don't want to pry, but I ask, "What's wrong?"

He avoids my gaze. "Those people at your studio last night."

"Do you mean Catherine?" I wish I could make it up to him for the way she treats him.

"No." Mick turns red to the tips of his ears. He doesn't want to talk about her or his feelings for her. "I mean the Jews. You shouldn't trust them."

"Why not?"

"Jews ain't like us. You never know what they're thinking."

His prejudice reflects a common attitude. "They're not so different. And the Lipskys are good people. When you get to know them, you'll see."

Mick shakes his head. "I know him already. He works in Butcher's Row. He once threw me in a mud puddle."

I recall how frightening Mr. Lipsky's temper was, and I'm alarmed to hear of his violence against Mick, but a reason for it occurs to me. "Did you steal something?"

"It were just a measly lamb chop," Mick hurries to defend himself. "I was hungry."

"Mr. Lipsky was just protecting his merchandise. Let's hope he didn't recognize you."

"He recognized me. I could tell," Mick says darkly.

I'm distressed to learn that there's bad blood between two of my new friends and that our group is far from as unified as it seemed yesterday.

"And that Lord Hugh is worse than the Jews," Mick says.

"He wasn't trying to tease you. You mustn't take offense at what he says." I want everyone in the circle to get along with everyone else.

"It's not just that. He goes around pickin' up men. I seen him. He's a nancy boy."

I'm even more distressed because someone else knows Hugh's secret. Bringing my acquaintances together has created a whole set of new problems.

Mick grimaces in disgust. "It's a dirty, nasty sin!"

"Lord Hugh is my friend. Try to get along with him. And keep quiet about him for my sake."

Mick shrugs. Although I don't think he would report anyone to the police, I'm afraid he'll spread the word about Hugh and someone else will. I'm also afraid of how Catherine and the Lipskys would react if they found out about Hugh. The circle that felt so warm and heartening last night is riddled with cracks. I wish I weren't so inexperienced at solving problems between people.

Mick and I gaze across the street at Russell's Fine Books. Three hours elapse. Men enter and leave the bookshop empty-handed. Nature calls.

"Mick, I have to leave for a moment." Afraid that the customers will come to buy my pictures while I'm gone, I give Mick the camera. "If anyone comes out carrying an album, you take his picture."

"Really?" Awed, Mick holds the camera as reverently as if it were the crown jewels.

Only days ago, he stole it from me, but I've no choice except to trust him. I show him how to use the camera. "Keep the shutter open for ten seconds, if he stays in the frame that long. Hold the camera perfectly still."

I hurry off to find a public privy, hoping Mick won't abscond with my camera and that I'll be back before the customers arrive. When I return to the alley, laden with food purchased at the market, I find Mick still there, and I sigh in relief. He hands the camera back to me.

"Somebody bought pictures," he says, looking woebegone.

"What's wrong, then? Didn't you get a good shot?"

"I did. She came out of the shop with the red book under 'er arm. She stood there the whole ten seconds, facing straight toward me."

Now I understand the problem. "It was a *woman*?"

Mick nods. "I don't think a woman could be the Ripper."

I open the camera, remove the case that holds the exposed plate, tuck it in my satchel, and insert a fresh one. Mick and I eat our meat pies and pickled oysters and drink our ginger beer while watching the bookshop. A little after two o'clock, a tall man strides up the street. He's better dressed than the other people we've seen, in an overcoat and hat styled on expensive lines. A mere slice of his face shows between his hat brim and turned-up collar. He slips into the bookshop. I aim the camera at the door. Mick and I wait, tense. Minutes pass before the gentleman reappears. I see his miniature image in the viewfinder. He carries a tiny red album. I open the camera's shutter. He strides rapidly out of the frame. Not more than two seconds have elapsed. I close the shutter.

"I didn't get him," I lament. "He moved too fast."

"Not too fast for me. I'm gonna follow him."

Mick runs off before I can warn him to be careful because that man might be a murderer who doesn't like being watched and doesn't draw the line at killing prostitutes. I resume spying. Three o'clock comes, then four. Worries multiply in my mind. Is Mick safe? PC Barrett has a propensity for turning up suddenly at the wrong times and places. Will he discover me before I can photograph the third customer? If I can, will the picture be good enough to identify him? What if my theory is wrong and the killer is not one of the buyers? I also miss Mick. Despite his rashness, I've already come to rely on his moral support.

A carriage, drawn by two gray horses,

rackets toward the bookshop and halts, partially obscuring the entrance. I hear the door on the far side open, the passenger disembark, and a thump as the door closes. I see a man's shoulder and back, clad in dark gray, as he enters the bookshop. While he's inside, I lean out of the alley. I still can't see the whole doorway, nor the driver. I photograph the carriage, counting off seconds, jittery with impatience. While hurriedly changing the plate, I almost drop the camera.

The man exits the shop, appears in the viewfinder. Focusing his image in the tiny glass rectangle, I see half his face and a telltale flash of red. He's holding my last album to his chest. I open the shutter. He vanishes as he climbs into the carriage. I close the shutter and sigh; the exposure was too brief. The door slams, and the carriage speeds down the street.

13

Mick returns two hours later, breathless and triumphant. "I got a good look at his face! And I followed him home!"

"That's good, because I wasn't as lucky." I tell him about the customer in the carriage.

"At least we know where mine lives," Mick says, undaunted. "Maybe he's the Ripper."

A premature twilight of clouds, chill fog, and thick smoke descends as we trudge homeward. Corrosive mist saturates the yellow haloes around the gas lamps, wet grime coats my face, and every breath I inhale stings. Thousands of people mill about Commercial Street, clustering outside the public houses and market stalls; their voices rise in an excited din. People flock around a man who reads aloud from a newspaper: " 'London lies under the spell of a great terror. The ghoul-like creature who stalks the streets is simply drunk with blood.' "

His audience exclaims in gleeful horror.

"Word of Annie's murder has spread." I'm disturbed by the spectacle, the enjoyment my neighbors are deriving from violent death.

"There's my mates, by the police station." Mick points to a group of boys. They are chanting something; I can't discern the words. "I'll find out what's going on."

He runs off. I eavesdrop on conversations. A woman says, "There's been another body found behind London Hospital. The killer left a message written on the wall. It said, 'I will murder sixteen more.' "

Rumor or fact? I fear for Liz, Mary Jane, and Kate. At least Catherine is protected by Mr. Lipsky. Mick returns, hopping up and down with excitement. "The police have a suspect!"

Eager with hope, I ask, "Who is it?"

"A Jewish shoemaker. The coppers are lookin' for him. Somebody seen him with Polly the day she died. A big, thick bloke with shifty eyes an' a black mustache. They calls him 'Leather Apron,' 'cause he always wears one."

"There was one left in the yard where Annie was murdered," I recall.

The street urchins by the police station are chanting, "Leather Apron! Leather

Apron!"

A sign at the confectionary store reads, *New today! Leather Apron Toffee!* In the window are boxes printed with a sinister drawing of a man in a black apron and mask. For the first time, it strikes me that there are now two separate hunts for the Ripper going on — the one in which my friends and I maneuver like shadows behind the scenes, and the other, official one that has produced this public commotion.

"Look!" someone shouts. "It's him, over there!"

People rush down Old Montague Street. Mick and I join the stampede. Men jostle me, trod on my heels; women push me. The mob is like a rabid, shrieking monster. We come upon a gang of youths circling a man, taunting him. "Leather Apron! Leather Apron!"

It's a man in a skullcap, cringing from his harassers. He wears a black suit, not a leather apron, but he is a big Jew with a black mustache. Down the street, more youths hurl blows at two more Jews, who protest that they've done nothing wrong. I watch with growing alarm. In this volatile climate, innocent men could be massacred.

Police whistles blare. The crowd turns and rushes down Commercial Street, carrying

Mick and me along. I stumble. Fright slices through me; we could be trampled. Mick grabs my hand. I see, far ahead of us, the tall helmets of policemen who are chasing someone. Blowing their whistles, shouting, "Stop!" the police race down Flower and Dean Street. The mob joins the pursuit. The murders have unleashed the current of insanity and violence that runs beneath Whitechapel's surface. It's stunning in its raw, uncontrollable power. The forefront of the mob suddenly halts. People behind Mick and me crush us against those in front. The narrow street is lined with tenements. The mob climbs onto wagons parked in the road, the better to see.

"Here!" Mick vaults aboard a wagon and helps me up.

Squeezed between other spectators, we see police armed with truncheons gathered by a tenement, holding back the mob. Howls rise from inside the building. Out of the door bursts a tangle of blue uniforms and pale, thrashing limbs — six police constables wrestling a naked young man, whose clothes have apparently been torn off him. He yowls and fights, his pugnacious features wild with terror. His muscular chest and arms are blue with tattoos, smeared with blood.

"It's the Ripper!" the crowd roars.

"That's Squibby!" Mick says.

I turn to him in surprise. "Do you know him?"

"Yeah." Mick stares in disbelief as the police force Squibby into a carriage. "If he's the killer, then I'm Jesus Christ."

"Why do you say that?" I don't think he's one of the customers from the bookshop, but I wish him to be guilty so that my responsibility for catching the killer can end.

"He's small fish. Worst he's ever done is throw bricks at the coppers."

The carriage driver cracks his whip, the horses plow through the mob, and the carriage — engulfed in hundreds of raised arms, thumped by fists — rocks and nearly overturns. The mob surges after it. Soon Flower and Dean Street is deserted. Mick helps me down from the wagon. Plodding toward my studio, I am weak with residual panic, suspended between overexcitement and fatigue. My heart won't stop racing, but I could fall asleep on the roadside. Mick skips along, chattering about the spectacle we've just seen. Then he abruptly stops and falls silent.

Lord Hugh, elegantly attired in top hat and tailcoat, is leaning against my door. Hope of good news quickens my pace toward him, but Mick lags behind.

"There's a frightful mob hereabouts," Hugh says. "What's going on?"

I tell him about Leather Apron and Squibby. Mick sullenly watches Hugh from a distance.

"Our lads in blue have been busy," Hugh says. "I came to tell you what I learned from my friend in the press. Leather Apron's real name is John Pizer. He allegedly loiters outside public houses, waits for a woman to come out, and follows her. He corners her on a dark street, pulls a knife, and demands money. If she's uncooperative, he beats her. The police have found at least three women who've sworn statements against Pizer. And there are seven other suspects in custody. The police are getting so much pressure from the top, they're arresting people right and left. Too bad we can't tell them that their investigation is going in too many wrong directions."

"Inspector Reid would demand to know why we think so." I feel more than a little responsible for the public unrest, the innocent people attacked and incarcerated.

"How was your expedition to the bookshop?" Hugh asks.

I describe our clash with Mr. Russell. Hugh laughs, says, "I'd have paid a quid to see that," and tousles Mick's hair. "Good try."

Mick recoils. "Keep yer hands off me!"

Surprised by his hostility, Hugh frowns, then looks at me. I shrug regretfully, at a loss for words, then tell Hugh about the photographs that Mick and I took.

"What are we waiting for? Let's develop them," Hugh says.

Inside my studio, I light the gas lamps and carry the negative plates to the darkroom. Hugh tosses his hat on the rack and follows me, but Mick says, "I'll wait out here."

I can tell that he wants to watch the photographs develop, but he doesn't want to be close to Hugh in the cramped dark-room. I close the door, sorry for Mick yet bothered by his attitude.

"What's the matter with him?" Hugh asks as I fill trays with chemical solutions.

Knowing Hugh's secret doesn't make me comfortable talking about it, and for the first time since we met, I'm shy with him. "He knows about you. He's seen you picking up men."

"Oh." Hugh looks mortified, shaken. "My God, how many other people have seen me?"

"You'll have to be more careful." My cheeks warm because it was a stupid, obvious, useless thing to say.

Hugh rubs his mouth. "Do your other friends know?"

"No. I haven't told them. I won't tell anyone. Neither will Mick." At least I hope not.

Hugh still looks worried, and I glimpse the awful fear he must live with every day. Now he's afraid that Mick will spread the word about him, it will filter up to his level of society, and he'll be ruined. My heart sinks because Hugh might quit our group rather than risk his reputation. I extinguish the lights and, in total darkness, remove a tiny negative plate from its case. I feel as if Hugh has already disappeared and left behind only his pleasant odor of bay rum, so unlike Inspector Reid's harsh scent. Relying on touch like a blind woman, I lay the plate in the developing solution and set the timer. The timer ticks off the seconds. Hugh and I wait in silence until it rings. I transfer the plate to the stop bath, then the fixative. I repeat the process for the other three plates, then light the safe lamp. Hugh reappears, colored eerie red by the light. I rinse the plates in water, then lay them out.

"Hmm." Hugh sounds disappointed.

"It's hard to tell anything from negatives, especially when they're so small." I'm trying

185

to keep up our hopes. "But we have to wait for the plates to dry before I can make enlarged prints. Let's have a cup of tea."

As we leave the darkroom, I hear voices. Catherine and Mr. Lipsky are in the studio. "We're on our way to the theater," Catherine says with a bright smile for Hugh and me. She ignores Mick. Her gaze moves to the darkroom, then back to Hugh and me, and her smile fades; she's wondering what we were doing in there. "We came by to see if there's any news. Mrs. Lipsky sent this." Catherine holds up a basket.

I unpack the picnic supper while Hugh tells Catherine and Mr. Lipsky about the photographs from the bookshop. Mr. Lipsky glares at Mick, who's miserable in the presence of these two men he despises. Catherine flirts with Hugh. She needs to know that she's barking up the wrong tree, but how can I tell her without giving away Hugh's secret? Mick realizes that Catherine is interested in Hugh; he looks hurt, jealous, and more hostile toward Hugh than ever. I'm uncomfortably aware that it's up to me to settle things but have no notion as to how. Tonight the circle feels like a whirlwind, full of self-destructive energy.

After Catherine and Mr. Lipsky leave, Mick and Hugh and I consume Mrs.

Lipsky's cabbage rolls stuffed with meat and rice. Hugh and I make stilted small talk until the negative plates are dry. While Hugh waits outside the darkroom, Mick watches me insert one negative plate at a time in my enlarger, adjust the image size, and light the gas lamp to expose a sheet of photographic paper. After processing the papers in chemical solutions, I carry the damp prints out of the darkroom and spread them on the table. Hugh points to the gray figure smeared across the bookshop, in the photograph I took.

"I can't make him out."

"Neither can I. But Mick followed him and found out where he lives," I say.

"Good work," Hugh says.

Mick scowls.

I study Mick's photograph. "This is excellent."

My praise earns a hint of a smile from Mick. "Beginner's luck," he says modestly.

The woman stands outside the bookshop, the album tucked under her arm. She's perhaps thirty-five years old, wearing a voluminous dark cloak and a dark bonnet that hides her hair. Both garments are long out of fashion. Her hands, raised to her throat, appear to be retying the bonnet's ribbons. Her fingers are blurred by motion, but her face is sharply focused. Her lips are thin and prim above a double chin.

"She's not a person one would imagine stabbing and mutilating women," I say.

"She reminds me of my old governess, who only tortured children with spankings that left red handprints," Hugh says.

My attempt at capturing the last customer resulted in a blurry image of the man who'd been briefly visible before climbing into his carriage.

Hugh glances at it and does a double take. "Look at this!" He points at the carriage door.

Part of an oval design is cropped off, but I can see a griffon clutching an arrow in its talon. I didn't notice it before. Sometimes, while photographing, I lose sight of the subject and am later surprised when the picture contains details that my eyes missed.

"That coat of arms belongs to Alfred Palmer, the Duke of Exford," Hugh says.

"Could he really be the killer?" I, like the public, have a mental image of the killer as a blood-spattered monster, certainly not a nobleman.

Hugh frowns. "I would be surprised. He has an impeccable reputation. Member of the House of Lords. On every important charitable committee. Never a hint of scandal."

"How well do you know him?"

"Not very. He moves in higher circles than mine."

My spirits fall. My head aches from the chemical fumes. The memory of Inspector Reid pressed against me in the swaying cab makes me nauseated. "It seems we have the same problem as the police. Multiple suspects and no evidence."

"But we know they bought your pictures," Mick hastens to say.

"It doesn't prove one of them killed Martha, Polly, or Annie," Hugh says. "Sarah is, unfortunately, correct."

Mick bristles, taking Hugh's words as a put-down. "Oh yeah? I'll get proof."

"I'd better go." Hugh rises and retrieves his hat from the rack. I can tell that he wants to avoid a quarrel with Mick, who could, if antagonized, expose his secret. "I'm late to a ball."

Although I hate to side with Hugh against Mick, I say, "We haven't any authority to interrogate the Duke of Exford or the man Mick followed. I don't know what to do."

"Think, Sarah!" Hugh urges. "You've gotten us this far."

A plan springs into my mind.

It's so risky that I don't want to air it and be talked into it, but I can't cease my hunt for the killer that the police seem unable to catch. Annie's murder and Inspector Reid have made that impossible. I can still hear shouts, running footsteps, and police whistles outside; Whitechapel is a powder keg ready to explode across all of London at the spark of another panic.

"I have an idea," I say reluctantly.

14

At eleven o'clock on Tuesday night, we reconvene in my studio. Hugh says, "I just spoke with my friend at the press. John Pizer, also known as Leather Apron, was arrested."

"Arrested?" My heart leaps. I pause while checking the equipment needed for our venture. Mick is pointedly ignoring Hugh, pretending to study the photographs on the walls. "When?"

"Yesterday morning. He was already in custody while the mob was calling for his blood last night. But he was released." Hugh explains, "The police did an identity parade, and the women who'd sworn statements against Leather Apron couldn't pick him out. And he has an alibi for Annie Chapman's murder. He was in bed with his landlady. The police have no evidence to connect him to Polly's and Martha's murders. They had to let him go."

So much for my hope that the crime would be solved, my models safe, and myself spared the dreaded visit to the police station and the equally dreaded expedition we are about to undertake. "Well, if we're correct in thinking that one of the customers Mick and I saw at the bookshop is the killer, then it's certainly not Leather Apron."

"Yes, Leather Apron couldn't have been at the bookshop because he was in prison at the time," Hugh says.

"Can we go now?" Mick asks impatiently.

The fog is heavy tonight. As we walk together up Montague Street, I'm glad of its concealing veil, but the sensation that I've lost an insulating layer of skin persists. The fog's damp tendrils invade my pores and chill me even though the weather isn't cold. Every day I feel more vulnerable, as if my blood is running closer to the surface, its scent easier for predators to detect. Mick, beside me, carries my tripod; I lug my flash lamp and stand and a bag containing supplies. Hugh trails us with my large camera in its case.

"Why does he have to come?" Mick asks.

"Because I need a man along for this."

"I'm a man," Mick says, his voice filled with hurt because I've impugned his masculinity. He stalks ahead of me.

I slow down to walk with Hugh.

"He's never going to accept me," Hugh says ruefully.

I'm sad to think of how many people would shun Hugh if they knew his secret. "Give him time," I say without much hope that Mick will change his attitude. "By the way, what did you tell Catherine about how we know each other?"

"I told her that we met when you were taking photographs in St. Dominic's Church, and you walked in on me kissing a nun. When I ran into you and Catherine, I snubbed her because I was so disconcerted to see you again that I wanted to get away fast, but then we kept bumping into each other and decided to be friends."

"Well," I say, impressed by his twist on the truth.

"Catherine believed it. But there's a problem: she likes me."

"I noticed." Here is another unfortunate situation, which I am ill equipped to handle.

"Could you discourage her? I don't want to hurt her feelings."

The onus is mine because although Catherine was acquainted with Hugh before I met him, I brought them into closer proximity. "I'll try."

"Thank you." Hugh changes the subject.

"Are you sure this idea of yours will work?"

"I can't vouch for it based on personal experience, but I read an article in the *British Journal of Photography*. It said an American physician named Sandford has had great success with the technique."

"I wish Sandford were here now. Better him than me. I'm not looking forward to this."

"Neither am I." We pass through the murky glow of a gas lamp, and I glance nervously at Hugh's handsome, tense face. As much as I like Hugh, he's an unknown quantity, unpredictable. I peer through the fog, but I can't see Mick. Has he changed his mind about coming with us? At past midnight, no one else is about; fear of the Ripper has emptied the streets. Lights shine from few windows in the dark tenements. When we arrive at a green-painted gate, Mick is waiting there. I'm relieved, but I rather wish he'd decamped for the sake of his own safety.

"It's barred," he says.

Hugh sets down my camera, laces his fingers together, and lowers his hands. Mick hesitates, leery of any contact with Hugh, then reluctantly steps into Hugh's hands. Hugh boosts Mick over the gate. In a moment, I hear the bar clank. The gate opens, and Mick beckons. Hugh and I lug my equipment into a yard that fronts a low shed — the mortuary, attached to the dingy brick Whitechapel Workhouse. Mick quietly closes and bars the gate. Hand in his pocket, he tiptoes to the shed. I hear his picklocks jingle as Hugh and I follow with the equipment. My heart hammers because we're about to break and enter and tamper with evidence.

A figure stands up near the door. Mick skids to a halt. I gasp as I stop; Hugh bumps into me. The fog is so thick that we didn't see the man seated in a chair, guarding the mortuary. He says, "Hey! Who are you?"

Despair entwines with fright in my gut. Our plan is thwarted, I may be seeing Inspector Reid again sooner than I expected, and Hugh and Mick will be in trouble with the police, too. I whisper, "That's Robert Mann, the mortuary keeper who testified at Polly's inquest."

"Let me handle this," Hugh says. He smiles gaily and calls, "Good evening, Mr. Mann." He introduces the three of us with false names spoken so quickly that I can't discern them. Neither can Mr. Mann, whose grizzled face wrinkles in confusion.

"What are you doing here?" Mr. Mann asks.

"We've come for a look at Annie Chapman's body," Hugh says.

"Forget it." Mr. Mann blocks the door. "No one's allowed in the mortuary."

After the fiasco at the inquest, the police are being more careful with their evidence, including the corpse. I should have expected it.

"Come, my good fellow. We won't disturb anything," Hugh says. "Swear to God."

"Get out, or I'll call the police."

Mick and I start toward the gate, but Hugh motions us to stay.

"How about a little wager?" Hugh asks.

Mr. Mann's bleary eyes shine. Hugh's intuition is remarkable; he has correctly pegged Mr. Mann as a gambler. "What kind of wager?"

"I bet I can tell you where you got your shoes," Hugh says. "If I'm right, you let us see Annie. If I'm wrong, I pay you a quid."

Mr. Mann grins, thinking Hugh a sucker. "You're on."

"You got your shoes on the ground outside the mortuary," Hugh says.

Indignation erases the grin from Mr. Mann's face. "You tricked me!"

Surprised, I burst into laughter. Mick does, too, then scowls; he doesn't want to show Hugh any approval.

"I told you where you got your shoes," Hugh says. "Pay up."

"I ain't letting you in." Mr. Mann folds his arms.

"How about a consolation prize?" Hugh says. "I'll give you a crown."

"Sod off!"

"A florin. The prize is shrinking," Hugh taunts.

Mr. Mann says crossly, "Oh, all right." Hugh hands over the coin. Mr. Mann unlocks the shed.

"Well done," I murmur, impressed by Hugh's cleverness.

Hugh grins proudly. Mick sulks.

Mr. Mann flings the door wide. The smell of old, decayed meat pours out. My stomach clenches. Hugh says, "Ugh." Mr. Mann strolls into the shed and lights the gas lamps. Their flames reflect in the glass fronts of cabinets that line the walls. Mick bounds after him. Hugh and I carry in my equipment. The small, cold room contains a table that holds a figure covered with a soiled sheet. When Mr. Mann whips the sheet off Annie's body, I try not to look at anything except her face. It's gray like dirty wax, bruised on the right temple, cheeks, and left jaw. Her curly dark hair looks gray, too, as if death has leached out the brown color. Her thick tongue protrudes from her puffy, bluish lips. I remember John Richardson mimicking her expression. My gaze moves, against my will, down her body. Her throat is cut, the gash jagged and deep. Her stomach is an open red cavity from which the innards have been scooped. The smell rising from it is fetid with rotten blood and excrement.

Hugh moans, his face green. He drops my equipment on the stone floor, doubles over, and retches.

"Not in here!" Mr. Mann shoves Hugh out of the mortuary.

As I hear Hugh vomiting outside, bile engorges my own throat, but folks who live in Whitechapel are more used to the sight and smells of death. I feel bad to have brought him here. Accustomed to working alone, I didn't think to ask if he had a strong stomach.

"I coulda told you he'd lose it," Mick says with contempt. He opens cabinets and drawers, fingering beakers, knives, and saws, hunting for something to steal, but his face is as green as Hugh's. I can tell that he wants to leave as desperately as I do, and I feel even worse for exposing a child to such a sight, but this is an opportunity we mustn't waste.

"Mick, I need your help," I say.

We position the tripod by Annie and mount the camera. Mick sets up the light stand while I load the negative plate. The activity calms my stomach, distracts me from the odors, and restores the healthy color to Mick's cheeks. Peering through the viewfinder at Annie's waxen face, I needn't see her mutilated body, but I see, to my dismay, that her eyes are closed.

"Her eyes are closed," Mick says.

We look at each other; neither of us wants to touch Annie. I steel myself, reach out with my fingertip, and push her eyelids up. They feel like the skin on a dead, cold, plucked chicken. Her eyes are cloudy, gelatinous.

Mick peers at them. "Miss Sarah, you said that the last thing Annie saw was her killer's face and that there should be a picture of him in her eyes. But I don't see nothing."

"Neither do I, but the camera can record images that are invisible to us. When Dr. Sandford developed a photograph of a murder victim, the eyes showed an image of a man wearing a light-colored coat. And there was another case in France, where a killer was convicted based on similar photographic evidence."

I open the camera's shutter. The flash

powder explodes, lighting up Annie's grue-some cadaver. Sulfurous smoke overlays the reek of death.

Mr. Mann returns. "Hurry up! Anybody finds you here, I'll be in trouble."

On impulse, I change the negative plate, move the camera farther away from Annie, frame her entire body in the viewfinder, and take another photograph. Then Mick and I repack my equipment and haul it out of the mortuary, through the gate. The night air is blessedly fresh. We inhale great, relieved gulps. Hugh sits against the wall, groaning. Mick mutters, "Sissy!"

I can't rebuke him, not after he stood by me through the ordeal. I won't blame him and Hugh if they both decide they have bet-ter things to do than hunt the Ripper with me.

"I haven't been so ill since I drank a whole bottle of wine when I was twelve," Hugh says. "Did you get a photograph of the killer?"

"I hope so."

Footsteps approach. We turn to see a police constable. The lantern he carries shines through the fog. My heart lurches as he sees us and the open gate to the mortu-ary. "What's going on here?" he demands.

"Run!" Mick cries.

I lumber away with my tripod and heavy camera. Hugh moans, staggering to his feet. The constable is already upon us. Mick throws himself at the constable and shouts, "Go, Miss Sarah!" A wrestling match ensues — small boy against big, strong man. "I'll hold him off!"

Hugh grabs the constable, pulls him away from Mick, and rams him against the wall. The constable's head bangs, Hugh releases him, and he crumples to the ground.

"Let's get out of here," Hugh says, panting.

"Where did you learn to fight so well?" I ask as we run through the streets; I'm remembering how he rescued Mr. and Mrs. Lipsky.

"At Eton." Glancing at my surprised face, Hugh grins. "The old school may look civilized from the outside, but inside, it's war."

Back at my studio, after we catch our breath, I say, "Who wants to watch me develop the negatives?"

Mick and Hugh exchange the sort of glance that I imagine passes between soldiers who've gone into battle together and one has saved the other's life. All offenses are put aside if not completely forgotten or forgiven. They both follow me into the darkroom. Now that they're both apparently sticking with me, I realize how much I would miss them if they quit. I'm not the same person who once survived on a steady diet of solitude.

At three o'clock in the morning, we examine the two dripping prints that hang from clothes pegs on the string stretched above the worktop. The closeup image of Annie's face gazes back at us. Her eyes are blank.

Mick curses. Hugh says, "Dr. Sandford's technique was a bust," then tells Mick, "I'll get a cab and give you a ride home."

"No thanks," Mick says hastily. "I'll walk." He's not afraid to be with Hugh; he doesn't want us to know where he lives.

I'm studying the other photograph of Annie, frowning in surprise because the camera captured something I didn't notice at the mortuary.

"What?" Mick asks.

"Look." I point to Annie's left hand, lying on the table. Where once she had worn three lucky brass rings she bought from a black man, now three white indentations circle her finger below her thick, abraded knuckles. "Annie's rings are missing."

15

The day after our trip to the morgue, neither Mick nor Hugh makes an appearance at my studio. Restless because there seems nothing I can do to further our investigation, I go out to market. I see, posted in a shop window, a handbill that reads,

Important Notice

To the Tradesmen, Ratepayers, and Inhabitants of Whitechapel and District:

Finding that the Murderer in our midst is still at large, we the undersigned have formed ourselves into a Committee, and we intend on gathering information that will bring the Murderer to justice. The Mile End Vigilance Committee will meet every evening at nine o'clock at the Crown Tavern, 74 Mile End Road, and will be pleased to welcome and receive assistance from the residents of the District.

I'm intrigued to see that my friends and I aren't the only citizens who have banded together to apprehend the Ripper. Might collaborating with the Mile End Vigilance Committee further our mutual interest? I feel guilty about keeping the boudoir pictures and the customers a secret, and how terrible if the Ripper killed Mary Jane, Liz, Kate, or Catherine! Maybe, if I were to tell the committee, they would help me and not report me to the police.

At eight thirty that night, the omnibus conveys me east along Mile End Road. I get off at the Waste — an open area occupied by a market. Despite the heavy fog and the threat of the Ripper, the stalls that sell old clothes, hot baked potatoes, crockery, jellied eels, and other goods are doing a lively business. Under the flaring gas lamps, a crowd applauds a half-naked black man swallowing swords. The Crown Tavern is packed with customers, ripe with the smell of beer and the damp sawdust on the floor. This is a respectable crowd; the women look to be wives with their husbands. The meeting room upstairs is full, all the fifty or so chairs taken. I stand by the wall with dozens of other folks. I'm the only unaccompanied woman.

At the front of the room, four men sit at a table. One bangs a gavel and says, "Order, order!" The room quiets. "I hereby call this meeting to order. My name is George Lusk. I am the president of the Mile End Vigilance Committee." He's about fifty years old, with muttonchop whiskers. "For those of you who don't already know me, I'm a builder and contractor, a member of the Metropolitan Board of Works, and a vestryman of the Mile End Old Town Parish." He introduces the three other men — the vice president, the treasurer, and the secretary.

They have the same affluent, self-important air as George Lusk. My spirits fall because I can't tell these men about the boudoir photographs. They would have neither respect nor sympathy for the likes of me. I decide to stay anyway, in case I can learn something.

"The first item on the agenda is raising money for a reward to encourage people to report information that might lead to the arrest of the murderer," George Lusk says.

Kate Eddowes asked me about a reward. If the committee offers one, maybe she'll tell them what she's hiding from me.

"Raise money for a reward?" says a man

in the front row. "Is that all we're going to do?"

Another man says, "We should get out there and hunt for the Ripper!"

Amid the clamor of agreement, people call out scathing remarks about the police's incompetence. George Lusk bangs his gavel. "We're not here to criticize the police. The mission of the committee is to work with them."

I look around to see if any police are present, and there is PC Barrett in his uniform, standing by the door. A thrill of alarm, not entirely unpleasant, shoots through me. Barrett sees me, frowns, then smiles. He's thinking I can't run away as I did at the cemetery. The only exit is the one by which he's stationed. I'm trapped.

Amid jeers and hoots, a woman says, "Work with the police? What are they doing besides strutting around and scratching their heads?" The whole audience turns to Barrett.

Put on the spot, he rises to the police force's defense. "This morning, we arrested a new suspect."

George Lusk looks annoyed that the meeting has veered from his agenda, but I'm eager to learn whether the police's suspect is either of the male customers we photographed at the bookshop. I'm also glad of an opportunity to look at Barrett without attracting attention.

The audience quiets to listen as Barrett says, "His name is Jacob Isenschmid."

It's not the Duke of Exford.

"He's a butcher," Barrett says.

My hopes dwindle. The other customer didn't look like a butcher. The news provokes disdainful remarks from the audience.

"Leather Apron is a butcher, and you decided he's not the Ripper and let him go!"

"Are you going to haul in every butcher in London?"

Barrett raises his voice over the jeering. "Witnesses saw a foreigner with Annie Chapman shortly before she was murdered. Jacob Isenschmid is Swiss. He has a violent temper, and he roams about at night carrying knives. He had two on him when he was arrested. Since he's been in custody, he's threatened to stab his wife and children to death, throw acid on his neighbors, and blow up the queen with dynamite. He was sent to Grove Hall Lunatic Asylum."

Some folks in the audience nod, ready to believe the police have the Ripper. Others offer their own theories.

"*I* think he's killing women so he can sell

their bodies to doctors, like Burke and Hare."

"No, he's a Mason! The murders were Masonic rituals!"

George Lusk bangs the gavel again and says, "The police could very well have the wrong man again. Which brings us back to the subject of the reward." He ignores groans from the audience. "Someone, somewhere, knows who the Ripper really is. They need an incentive to turn him in. We'll start raising money for the reward now."

The vice president speaks up cautiously. "But George . . . maybe we should consider doing something more."

"No buts," George Lusk declares. "It's already decided."

There's tension within their ranks, just as in my band of comrades, but George Lusk prevails. The treasurer passes a basket. When it reaches me, its bottom is littered with small change. I throw in a halfpence. When George Lusk receives the basket, he's obviously discouraged by the small size of the take. He and the committee members formulate plans to solicit donations from local businessmen. Then he adjourns the meeting.

The audience flocks to PC Barrett and peppers him with questions, demands, and criticism. Resisting my urge to linger, I make my escape.

The fog along Mile End Road is even thicker now; the sooty, eye-stinging murk is brown in the glow of the streetlamps, dense black everywhere else. The market is closed, the omnibus nowhere in sight. I trail behind people who are heading toward Whitechapel. The road empties as they scatter into the lanes that branch off the road. My fear of the Ripper is stronger now that I'm after him. *Does he know I'm after him? Would he kill me to protect himself?* I wish I'd asked Hugh to come with me. Walking faster, I'm almost home when the fog in front of me suddenly thickens into the figure of a man. He's upon me, seizing my arm, before I can run.

"Gimme your money!" His red-rimmed eyes gleam in a whiskered face. It's not the Ripper, just a common thief, but just as dangerous at this moment. As I scream and try to pull free of him, he brandishes a knife. "Gimme it, or I'll kill you!"

"Get away from her!" a man's familiar voice shouts.

The thief's grip on my arm wrenches loose. He yells, and the fog obscures the scuffle that ensues. One figure runs off into the darkness. The other — PC Barrett —

stumbles, regains his balance, and says, "Are you all right?"

I'm so shaken that all I can think to say is, "You followed me."

The light from a streetlamp shows his irate expression. "It's a good thing I did."

Now I'm ashamed because I sounded so ungrateful. But it's better than if he knew what I'm really feeling — a thankfulness so strong that I could fall on my knees before him. "Thank you. Yes, I'm fine." There's a dark, oozing line on Barrett's cheek. "You've been cut." I tap my own face to show him where.

He touches the cut, glances at his bloodied fingertips, and shrugs. "It's just a scratch."

I've recently seen so much blood that a little more doesn't faze me, but I feel an unsettling, tender pang at the sight of Barrett's. His bleeding makes him seem suddenly human and vulnerable.

"Here." I offer him my handkerchief.

He dabs it against the cut, then looks at the red stain on the white cloth. "Sorry," he says, chagrined yet proud that he's been injured in battle.

"It'll come out." I tuck the handkerchief in my pocketbook.

"I'll walk you home," Barrett says.

After my brush with death, I shouldn't

refuse. To my surprise, I don't want to refuse. As we walk through the fog, he says, "We got off on the wrong foot." His voice has lost its usual officious, badgering tone. "How about if we start over?"

"Very well." Saving my life is compensation enough for serving me on a platter to Inspector Reid and good enough reason to reset the clock on our acquaintance back to zero. The sounds of distant factory machinery fill the air that has changed between us. My own blood is strangely warm and effervescent under my fog-chilled skin.

"Have you always lived in Whitechapel?" Barrett asks, making conversation.

"No."

"Where else?"

That subject verges too close on my private history for comfort, but refusing to answer would ruin the mood, which I'm enjoying. "I grew up in Clerkenwell."

"And your father was a photographer."

I nod, unexpectedly pleased that Barrett remembered, and the pleasure alleviates the grief I feel when I think about my father.

"You can ask me something if you like," Barrett says.

I don't know anything about him, and I would like to. "Where do you live?"

"In the police section house at the Mitre

Street station. But I spend a lot of time in Bethnal Green with my folks. They're getting on in years, and I'm the only child, so I stick around to help them out." Barrett sounds as if he takes the arrangement happily for granted, and I feel a twinge of envy as I imagine him ensconced in his cozy family nest. I can picture him as a devoted son, the apple of his parents' eyes.

Barrett adds, "My father's a retired police officer. So I suppose that means you and I have something in common: we both went into the family business."

We smile at each other. Neither of us mentions that his father the policeman probably wouldn't have liked my father the rabble-rouser, or vice versa. For the moment, hard, cold facts seem part of a distant, other world. But although I like this rare harmony with Barrett, if I play along with this game of question-and-answer, he'll eventually ask me why I was at the meeting. And I've much more to hide than last time I saw him. We're a few blocks from my studio, and I say, "I can walk by myself from here."

Barrett sticks with me. "It's no trouble."

Thinking of the photographs concealed in my studio, I walk slower until we're at a standstill. Neither of us, it seems, is ready to part. Now the air between us is charged with expectancy. We turn to each other. The nearest streetlamp is ten feet away, and it's too dark to see Barrett's expression. He moves closer to me, and my heartbeat accelerates like a deer jumping when it hears a gunshot. I've never been kissed, and I've always wondered exactly how a man and woman cross the barrier of propriety, shyness, or fear. In romantic novels, a kiss is often preceded by a request for permission, if not a lengthy courtship, declarations of love, and a marriage proposal. But Barrett simply inclines his head toward mine. A sudden, alarming heat flares between us, and the barrier evaporates like snow in fire. A force I can't resist lifts my face to his and closes my eyes.

His mouth comes down on mine, his lips soft and warm, experienced and insistent. My body is like a rosebush parched and withered by drought, and this first intimate contact with a man is the water for which its roots thirst. I feel myself unfurl like petals bursting open. I've tried to hide from myself the fact that my attraction toward Barrett was physical, but now I'm blinded, dissolving in desire that floods through me. Behind my closed eyelids, fountains of sparks scintillate like exploding flash powder. My mouth opens of its own volition.

His tongue enters. The wet, slick, outrageously sensual pleasure magnifies desire into a fierce ache. Barrett's arms tighten around me. We embrace as if we've plunged into the sea and we'll drown if we let go. I can't breathe, I'll suffocate.

We break apart, gulp air, and then lock our mouths together again. Barrett's hands caress my bosom. I moan, frustrated by the ribs of my corset and my thick layers of clothing. Barrett pushes me against a wall. The hardness at his loins presses on me. This is wrong, this is dangerous, but my excitement banishes all concern for chastity and self-preservation. That the world has spun out of my control is as thrilling as it is frightening. His knee pushes my legs apart. I eagerly open them. I don't care who sees us or what happens.

Barrett pulls my skirts up and my knickers down. He fumbles at the buttons of his trousers, then lifts my legs around his waist. I want him inside me, to fill up the emptiness, to dispel the ache of loneliness. I don't care if it hurts or what the consequences are. I feel myself rising to the pleasure that I have only experienced alone in bed by my own hand. To experience it now, with Barrett, seems the only all-important thing that matters. Now I understand why Catherine has affairs. I understand how men can rut like dogs in the street with prostitutes such as Kate, Liz, and Mary Jane.

The thought of Kate, Liz, and Mary Jane is like a splash of ice water that brings me back to my senses. Now I see how I must look — like a whore giving a three-penny stand-up! I picture Annie Chapman in that yard in Hanbury Street, coupling with a faceless man. I see him reach in his pocket and pull out a knife. Exclaiming in horror, I kick and struggle.

Barrett lets go of me. "What . . . ?" His voice sounds hoarse, breathless, surprised.

I'm running, my legs shaky and my body swollen with unsatisfied desire, as Barrett calls my name. I'm furious at him; he could have ruined me! I'm even more furious at myself because I was a willing participant. But despite my fury, I still want him, and even while I berate myself for my stupidity, I feel exhilarated. Barrett wants me! There can be no mistake about it, and his feelings toward me must be more than just physical. Things changed between us even before we kissed. He cares for me, perhaps in spite of himself, but cares nonetheless. I can't help smiling.

16

Restless nights are common for me lately, but this one passes more happily than usual. The sensual pleasure of reliving my encounter with Barrett while I lie in bed alternates with the anxiety of wondering what he's thinking. *Is he angry at me? How I should act the next time I see him? Will he want to take up from where we left off? If he does, what then?* In the cold solitude of my bed, I realize the dangers of playing with fire. And Barrett is still a police officer, while I, with my secrets, am on the wrong side of the law.

When dawn comes, on that Thursday, 13 September, I go to market. While visiting the shops, I look around for Barrett. On Commercial Road, I see him standing outside a public house. My steps halt. My heart thumps with excitement, then terror: he's with Inspector Reid. I quickly hide behind a parked wagon.

"So the locals don't think we're doing

enough to catch the Ripper, but they wouldn't chip in more than a few pennies for a reward," Reid says with disgust. "They'd rather just complain. That's typical."

Barrett must have told him what occurred at the Mile End Vigilance Committee meeting. I'm irresistibly fixated on Barrett; I feel the heat of arousal.

"We'd better keep an eye on George Lusk and his friends." Barrett's tone betrays no hint of what happened after the meeting, no unseemly emotions. I see the dark line of the cut on his cheek, and I touch my own cheek, remembering that when I got home last night I found it smeared with his blood.

"Good idea." Inspector Reid asks, "Who else was there?"

Barrett gives a few names, then says, "Sarah Bain."

Alarm leaps in me. Is he going to tell Inspector Reid what happened between us?

"How convenient." Reid sounds pleased. "Did you do as I told you?"

"I talked to her." Barrett sounds all business.

"Turned on the old charm. That's the way to soften up a lonely, deprived spinster."

Reid told Barrett to romance me! My alarm turns to horror. His conversation, his wanting to start over, was just a ploy!

"Yes, sir," Barrett says.

"Did you try a little grope and tickle?" Reid nudges Barrett with his elbow. They chuckle.

My face flushes hot as my insides roil with mortification. When Barrett kissed me, he was only following orders! That his body responded signified nothing except animal lust.

"Did Miss Bain tell you what she's been hiding?" Reid asks.

"Not yet." Barrett's tone implies that he's confident I'll soon capitulate.

Reid slaps Barrett on the back as they walk away from me. "Keep up the good work, and you'll be in line for a promotion."

I run home and scrub myself from head to toe with cold water and carbolic soap until I'm shivering, my skin is raw, and I've washed off any trace left of PC Barrett. I brush my teeth vigorously, so that my mouth tastes like the camphor, powdered cuttlefish bone, and soot in the toothpaste instead of the memory of his kiss. But I can't cleanse myself of my anger or shame.

That Barrett played such a cruel, callous, self-serving trick on me!

That I fell for it!

His laughter echoes in my ears, as does

my mother's warning: *A man will always put something else ahead of you.* For my mother, it was my father's work as a social reformer that came before her. He spent time on protest marches when he could have been earning money to support us after his death. For Barrett, it's his career that matters more than me. I should never have laid myself open to him! I curl up in bed and stay there until my pillow is tear-drenched, my head aching, and my eyes puffy. Then I force myself to drink tea, eat toast, and prepare the studio for customers because I still have a living to earn.

Catherine surprises me by arriving at nine o'clock. "I decided to keep you company today!"

I'm glad to have her safe under my eye, but I can't fathom why she wouldn't rather gallivant with men as usual.

"What's that redness around your mouth?" she asks.

My face is rubbed raw by Barrett's whisker stubble. "Just chapped skin." I turn away so she won't see my blushes or my tears.

"If I didn't know you better, I would think it was whisker burn."

I can't tell her what happened. I can never tell anyone. I feel myself closing up like a blossom when the cold night falls.

When the door opens, Catherine looks up eagerly. Mick comes in, carrying a pink rose. As he and Catherine see each other, his face lights up; hers falls. He looks from her to me to the rose. I can tell he meant to give me the rose, but he's changed his mind. Shy and mute, he thrusts it at Catherine.

The flower is fresh, fragrant, and lovely, but Catherine regards it with distaste. "Where did you steal it, you dirty little brat?"

Mick blushes crimson. He probably did steal the rose from a flower stall. His eyes brilliant with humiliation, he turns and runs out of the studio. Through the window, I see him toss the rose in the street before he disappears from my sight.

Pitying Mick and angry at Catherine, I say, "Can't you be nicer to him?"

"Why? He likes me, but so what?" she says with the callousness of a girl who has too many male admirers. "That's his problem."

I can't force her to like Mick, but I'm in no mood to indulge her. "From now on, you'll be civil to him because he's my friend," I snap.

Catherine, hurt by my tone, sighs with exasperation. "Oh, all right."

Thinking of Barrett and myself, I feel sorrier than ever for Mick, but at least Catherine is honest about her feelings toward him; he knows where he stands with her. I feel guilty because she doesn't deserve the brunt of my bad mood.

"I'm sorry, Catherine. I didn't mean to snap at you."

"That's all right."

But she's cooled toward me a little, the way she did after I brushed her off. I've chipped another crack in the circle that I've been so eager to keep intact. Nevertheless, she stays the whole day, watching me photograph customers. She's still here at dusk, when I fry up onions, cabbage, potatoes, and sausage for our supper.

"He's rather marvelous, isn't he?" she says while we're eating.

"Who is?"

"Hugh." Catherine adds, "He doesn't come round the theater anymore."

Now I understand why I've had the pleasure of her company. Hugh is avoiding her, and she's here in case he drops by.

Catherine clasps her hands under her chin. "He's the handsomest, most charming man I've ever met!"

And the least available.

"He's also a lord, and he's rich," Catherine says dreamily.

I can almost hear wedding bells ringing in

her mind. I've no stomach for the talk I promised Hugh I would have with Catherine, but now is the time to nip her infatuation in the bud as painlessly as possible.

"Hugh could never marry you," I say. "His family would forbid him."

"Pooh!" Catherine tosses her head. "If he falls in love with me, we'll elope."

"You had better not count on it."

She fixes a somber gaze on me. "Sarah . . ." She twirls her blond ringlets around her fingers. "Is there something between you and Hugh?"

"No," I hasten to say. "We're just friends."

"But it seems like you're trying to put me off Hugh. Are you secretly in love with him?"

"Of course not."

"But why else would you try to keep Hugh and me apart?"

I have no choice except to speak bluntly. "Because he's not interested in you. Because I don't want you to get hurt." I want to protect her even though she's so careless with poor Mick's feelings. I would not have her, like myself, suffer over a man she can't have.

"How do you know he's not interested?" Catherine demands.

I can't tell her the whole truth; it's his

secret. "He told me so. He asked me to talk to you and discourage you from liking him as anything but a friend."

"I don't believe it." Catherine speaks with the confidence of a beauty who can get any man she wants. "Maybe you wish Hugh would fall in love with you, and he won't as long as I'm around."

She thinks no man would choose me over her. It's so true that my pride, injured by Barrett, isn't further wounded. "Some men wouldn't be interested in you." I wonder if she's aware that men of Hugh's inclinations exist. "Unfortunately, Hugh is one of those."

Catherine makes a visible effort at patience. "Sarah, you've done so much for me. I don't want to hurt you. If you're in love with Hugh, tell me, and I'll keep my hands off him. Otherwise, don't be a dog in a manger."

The doorbell jangles as Hugh, speak of the devil, sweeps into the studio. He wears a long black evening cape and top hat; he carries a valise. In high spirits, he doesn't notice the embarrassment on Catherine's face and mine.

"Good news! We're going to investigate Alfred Palmer, Duke of Exford."

"How?" I am startled because he seems to have gained access to the only suspect whose identity we've determined. "Where?"

"Palmer's hosting a ball tonight at his house in St. John's Wood."

My immediate resistance to going isn't due only to my fear of meeting this man who may be the Ripper. I have a deep dread of social events. The only ones I ever attended were at school, the fetes given by the wealthy patrons. I stood alone in a corner, mortified by shyness.

"A ball! What fun!" Catherine jumps up and down like a child offered a treat. "Hugh, will we have time to dance together while we're investigating?"

"Uh." It's obvious that Hugh doesn't want to be with Catherine in a situation tailored for romance. "I'd planned to take Sarah."

Catherine's eyes widen as her gaze moves from Hugh to me, then narrow. "Why not me?" She's surprised and hurt, suspicious that there really is something between us.

I try to take the sting out of Hugh's rejection. "Because it's too dangerous." How I wish I could send her instead of going myself! "If the duke sees you, he'll recognize you from your photographs."

"If he's the killer, you'll be putting yourself right into his path," Hugh adds.

Catherine frowns because we've taken sides against her. I say to Hugh, "I thought you didn't know the duke. How did you obtain an invitation?"

"I didn't, actually. I happened to learn of the ball when I was in town, making discreet inquiries about Palmer."

"You intend for us to crash the ball?" Although we may lose our chance at the duke, I seize on an excuse not to go. "We won't be let in."

"Never fear." Hugh opens his cape. He's dressed like a medieval troubadour, in particolored tunic and hose. "It's a costume ball." He reaches into the valise, extracts two black velvet masks, holds one over his eyes, and grins. "No one will know we're not on the guest list."

"But I haven't a costume."

"I brought you one." Hugh pulls from the valise a bundle of pale blue silk and white fur. "Pinched it from my sister."

Catherine brightens. "The duke won't recognize me if I wear this." She unfolds the costume — the gown of a French lady from the past century, matching slippers, a tall white wig, and a fur cape. "Oh, how beautiful!"

"No," Hugh and I say together.

Tears glaze Catherine's eyes. "Never mind, then." She drops the costume. "I shan't beg to go where I'm not wanted."

She flings an angry glance at Hugh and one filled with the pain of betrayal at me; then she runs out the door, calling, "I'll find someone who does want me!"

I'm afraid I've made her angry enough to spite me by roaming the town and putting herself in the Ripper's sights.

"This happens too often," Hugh says sadly. "I flirt with women so that everybody will think I'm a normal, red-blooded Englishman. Sometimes they want more than I can give them. Lord, I hate hurting that sweet girl." He adds darkly, "I'm bound to get my comeuppance someday."

"It's not your fault," I say, trying to absolve him the way he absolved me when I blamed myself for my father's death. "Catherine will be all right." But young hearts are tender, and she'll have a harder time forgiving me — her trusted friend — than Hugh.

"I hope so," Hugh says. "In the meantime, you'd better dress. Our coach is waiting."

Upstairs, I reluctantly don the costume. The gown hangs loose on me, its neckline alarmingly low; my collarbone juts. I cover myself with the white fur cape. The elaborate white wig renders my complexion even paler than usual. I look like a courtesan wasting away in the Bastille. I imagine what PC Barrett would think if he could see me, and my eyes well as I powder the whisker burns around my mouth.

When I totter downstairs in the blue silk slippers, Hugh makes a valiant attempt to pretend nothing is wrong with my appearance. We decide not to take my miniature camera — neither of our costumes offers a good hiding place for it. As we climb into the carriage, I'm thankful for the fog; my neighbors won't see us and gossip about me. We ride north through Regent's Park. The farther we go, the deeper I lapse into misery.

"You're awfully quiet," Hugh says. "What's wrong?"

"Nothing." I can't tell him about PC Barrett.

Hugh waits a moment, then says, "All right."

Now there's a coolness between us; I've hurt his feelings as well as Catherine's. We ride in silence to St. John's Wood. The wide streets are overhung with trees whose lush foliage obscures gardens and villas. The quiet is unsettling. We turn down a narrower lane and arrive at a brightly lit, Italian-style mansion with white stucco walls. Hugh sheds his cape, tells the driver to wait by the other carriages parked on the road, and helps me from the carriage.

We don our masks. Walking up the stairs to the mansion, I stumble, unaccustomed to high heels. Hugh catches me and draws my arm through his. I hear voices, laughter, strange music, and a deep, rhythmic pulse. When Hugh opens the door, the noise blares out at us from a grand foyer. Through an arched doorway, I see a huge ballroom dimly lit by a gas chandelier. A crowd dances to a frenetic dirge played by an orchestra of black men dressed in formal evening clothes, blowing horns, sawing fiddles, and pounding drums. Guests are disguised as Chinese mandarins, Roman gladiators, ballerinas, knights, Greek gods and goddesses. They gyrate singly or in pairs. Many costumes are even less modest than mine. Bare flesh gleams. Masked faces leer. Painted mouths laugh, gulp wine, and kiss.

This is the dark side of high society. Unnerved, I shrink backward, but Hugh pulls me into the ballroom, and we're enveloped by the hot, raucous crowd. "Let's dance."

He clasps my waist. I place one hand in his, the other on his shoulder. The floor is so packed, it doesn't matter that I don't know how to dance. Troubadour and French courtesan, we can only sway in place while jostled by other revelers.

"I see why Palmer has this remote hide-away," Hugh shouts in my ear. "He can't do this at the ducal manor. Ah — there he is. The pirate."

I see, across the room, a tall man wearing a tricorn hat with a yellow feather. A black patch covers his left eye. His face is red and fleshy. He guffaws at someone's joke, then turns and moves away from us.

"Come on." Hugh pulls me toward the duke.

As we squeeze past other dancers, a knight cuts in on us. He yanks me close to his tin-armored chest. "Let go of me!" I struggle while he leads me in a waltz that plows a swath through the crowd. "Hugh! Help!"

Far away, Hugh's masked face bobs among others as he fights to reach me. I wrench myself from the knight's chain-mailed embrace and fall. Prancing feet trample my gown, knock my wig askew. A boot steps on my wrist. I scream in pain.

"Sarah!" Hugh is pulling me to my feet.

"Get me out of here!"

He drags me, shouting, "Pardon us," to the people he elbows. I've lost my slippers, like Cinderella. Someone stomps on my toes. Leaving the ballroom, we enter a dim corridor. There, couples kiss and fondle. I cringe from them as we pass, ashamed of myself for behaving in the same fashion with PC Barrett. Hugh pushes open a door. We find ourselves in a cold, silent cavern that smells of turpentine and linseed oil. A silvery glow pours from a skylight; the fog is clearing around a lop-sided moon visible through the glass.

"Are you all right?" Hugh asks.

My heart is still hammering; my wrist and toes hurt. "I think so." I straighten my wig.

"What have we here?" Hugh says, looking around.

I survey easels, plaster torsos, a table strewn with jars, brushes, and paint tubes. "An artist's studio."

Hugh flings back cloths from easels. The canvases show poorly done portraits of Annie Chapman and Kate Eddowes posing in my studio. "Did you paint these, Palmer?" he asks the absent duke. "You could use some anatomy lessons."

"He's copied my boudoir photographs," I say.

"Maybe that's all he wanted them for." Hugh's voice echoes my disappointment.

"Maybe he didn't kill the women." I fear we've come here to learn nothing except that the duke indulges in lascivious parties and bad amateur art.

"He could still be our man. Let's have a

look at the rest of the house."

We climb a narrow staircase. With dark-red wallpaper that gleams in the light from brass sconces, it resembles a giant throat. We reach the second-story landing. Sudden screams emanate from a doorway that leads to another staircase.

My blood chills.

We halt abruptly, exchanging wide-eyed glances.

"I'll go first." Hugh starts up the stairs.

As I follow, the screams grow louder; they resonate with terror. At the top is an attic. A bed stands in dim light cast by lamps on side tables. On the bed lies a naked, full-breasted woman, her arms and legs spread wide, her wrists and ankles bound to the bedposts. Her slender body is slick with sweat, her long auburn hair tangled, her pubis shaved. Her eyes are crazed like a trapped animal's as she strains at her bonds and screams.

Shock slams my heart.

Out of the shadows to the woman's left steps a tall, muscular man, naked except for a white shirt with billowing sleeves. He's not wearing the pirate hat, but I see the black patch over his eye. It's the duke. He holds a long, thin object in his right hand. The woman gasps. The duke lashes at her with the object — a black leather whip. It cracks against her thighs. I scream the instant before she does.

The duke whirls toward us. His red face is engorged with violent lust. The woman shouts words I can't discern because now Hugh and I are racing down the stairs.

"It's him! He's the Ripper!" I cry as we speed through the dark studio.

"I'm afraid not," Hugh says.

We run along the passage where the couples embrace, into the crowd and wild music in the ballroom. I insist, "He killed Martha, Polly, and Annie! We must fetch the police!"

"Shut up, Sarah, for God's sake!" Hugh drags me out of the house. The air is fresh but icy, I've lost my fur, and my bare feet tread on rough ground. Hugh bundles me into our carriage.

As we ride toward London, I grab Hugh's arm and shake him. "We have to go back! The duke is going to kill that woman!"

He clasps my hands and says, "Sarah, it's not what you think. That woman suffers his abuse willingly. She enjoys it as much as he does."

Incredulous, I stare.

"Some people are like that," Hugh says, embarrassed at having to explain to me.

"Didn't you hear what she shouted as we were leaving?"

I shake my head.

"She said, 'Hit me harder! Please!' " Hugh clarifies, "The duke isn't going to kill her. It's just a game. Not a very nice one, to be sure, but not a crime. And not evidence that the police will accept as proof that he's the Ripper."

17

"Even if the duke's not the Ripper, there's still the other chap I tailed from the book-shop," Mick says, wolfing down bread and bacon.

The day after the ball, my wrist is sore where it was trampled; the lurid sights I saw are etched in my brain. Hugh hasn't come over, and neither has Catherine, who must still be angry. Only Mick arrived, in time for lunch. Mud cakes his shoes, his knickers are wet up to his thighs, and he smells like a sewer, but his fresh, youthful face revives my spirits. After I gave him an abridged version of what happened last night, he assured me that not all is hopeless.

"How 'bout I show you the other chap's crib?"

"All right." I'm curious, and if the dreaded summons from the police comes, I will be safely absent.

Carrying my miniature camera in my

satchel, I walk with Mick along Cable Street into Stepney, which is near the London Docks. At the storefronts, Indian merchants sell strange fruits and vegetables to women in saris. It's as if we've traversed a hemisphere instead of the few blocks from Whitechapel. The foreign tongues have a different flavor, and so does the cold, gray air. The sweet smell from the sugar refineries is pleasant at first but soon overpowering.

I take the chance to say, "I want to apologize for Catherine. She's selfish and mean."

"No! She's not! She's the most perfect girl I ever saw!" Embarrassed because he's pinned his heart on his sleeve, Mick looks down at his dirty shoes and mumbles, " 'Course she doesn't want nothin' to do with me."

"She should at least appreciate your trying to find out who the Ripper is."

"It's not just for her I'm doing it." Mick blushes because we both know it mostly is. He ends the conversation by saying, "We gotta turn here."

He leads me down an alley lined with tenements. Chinamen, their hair in long pigtails, recline in opium dens, smoking pipes amid pungent smoke. We enter a square bordered by terraces of old brick-

and-stone houses, once elegant, now dilapidated. In the green, dark-skinned children play amid trees and weeds that have grown up among the ruins of a demolished church.

"That's where I followed him to." Mick points at a narrow house, its doorway framed by stone pillars and a broken pediment. Its brick walls are studded with small, irregularly shaped stones. The windows are curtained.

"Is he foreign?" I whisper, although my brief glimpse of him said not.

"He's as English as you or me. And he's a gentleman, I could tell."

I conjecture why an English gentleman would live here. "If he's the murderer, he needs a place near Whitechapel where he can quickly go to ground after he kills."

Seeing no sign of life inside the house, I ask, "What now?"

"We wait over here." Mick leads me to the opposite side of the square. Loitering behind a tree, we have a good view of the house. "If he comes, you take his picture. Then we sit tight until he leaves, and then we follow him and see what he does."

Church bells ring three o'clock. An hour elapses while we wait. The house remains still and quiet. Passersby look at us curiously.

"Try to act inconspicuous," Mick whispers.

A gray mist rolls in over the rooftops. It feels as if the river is crawling ashore. The stench of the Thames marries the sickly sweet exudation from the sugar refineries. Soon we won't be able to see across the square.

"Halloo!" calls a voice.

Mick and I look up at a man leaning out the attic window of the nearest house. He's sallow-skinned, wearing a turban. "Why are you spying on the man who lives yonder?" His English is accented but precise.

"So much for actin' inconspicuous," Mick says, chagrined.

"Do you know if he's home?" I ask.

"He is not," the Indian says.

"What time does he usually return?"

"Oh, no usual time. He keeps odd hours. Sometimes he is absent for days on end."

"What is the gentleman's name?" I ask.

"Mr. Smith, according to the landlord."

"Who else lives there?"

"He lives alone."

I thank the Indian and hurry Mick away before we can attract more attention. Fog shrouds the square. When we near the house, Mick runs to the door and knocks.

"Mick! What are you doing?"

Nobody answers his knock. "Just makin' sure he's really not home." Scampering around the block, he calls, "Come on!"

At the back of the house, a cobbled alley lined with dustbins separates the buildings on the square from those on the street behind them. The fog glows yellow from lights in windows. Foreign chatter echoes. Our quarry's house is the only one dark and silent. Mick tests the back door. It's locked. He peers at its second-story windows, barely visible in the gloom, then begins to climb the wall, using the stones that stud its surface. My heart gives a mighty thump of alarm.

"Mick!" I say in a loud, frantic whisper. "Come down!"

He pulls himself onto a window ledge, crouches there, and tugs at the window, which slides up with a scraping noise. "Hah!"

"You can't go in there! It's against the law."

"Be back in a jiff." Mick scoots through the window.

I pace and clutch my satchel, hoping the man doesn't come home or the police stroll by. I'm responsible for Mick's safety even though breaking into the house was his decision.

The back door creaks open. I choke on a scream.

"It's only me." Mick stands in the doorway, holding a lit lamp. His face somber above the flame, he beckons. "I've found something."

I want to leave before it's too late, but Eve could not have felt more tempted by the apple. Fearful yet avid to see what Mick found, I step through the door.

Mick closes it behind us. "Don't worry. The house's empty. I checked."

I follow him through a dingy kitchen that smells faintly of meals cooked long ago. The only sign of recent use is a tea-cup by the kettle on the stove. The parlor on the first floor is unfurnished, the scratched wooden floors bare, the fireplace swept clean. The air is colder and damper than outside, and peculiarly still.

"Upstairs," Mick says.

The stairwell seems darker than the lack of artificial lighting can account for. The darkness shrinks the lamp's flame, and I have the strange feeling that we're going down underground instead of up. In the second-story passage, we enter a room. A sofa covered with a blanket stands under the curtained window that overlooks the square. An open armoire contains clothes that exude a faint, masculine odor. Everything looks ordinary, but my skin prickles at the sense of something *not normal.* The darkness is a palpable presence like the velvety black mold that grows in cellars. I can almost feel its fibers take root in my lungs with every breath.

"There." Mick points to a desk.

Newspaper clippings are taped to the cracked plaster wall above it. They're stories about the murders of Martha, Polly, and Annie. Boudoir photographs, not mine, are scattered on the desk. The images of the nude strangers are blurred by movement. The sense of *not normal* is stronger now. Panic clangs in my mind, tenses my leg muscles to run, and jars loose a memory from a lesson that my father once taught me, on photographing objects in a still life. He said that the darkest area within a cast shadow is the area where the light doesn't reach because the object blocks the source of illumination. The darkest area of the shadow is called the umbra.

This room is in the umbra of the shadow of the house, the city, the world. The man who lives here is surely the Ripper. He must have used boudoir photographs as a guide when choosing his victims. Maybe he chose my models because in my photographs, the faces are clear enough for him to identify them.

"Look at that." Mick points to a large photograph in a silver frame on the desk.

The picture shows a laughing man dressed in an army uniform. He leans on a rifle. His eyes squint in bright sun that shines on some hot, southern bush country. At his feet lies a pile of something I can't immediately identify. Mick holds the lamp closer. The pile is bodies of Negro women. I can tell they are dead from their vacant eyes and slack faces. Their corpses are riddled with bullet holes and knife wounds that have bled onto the white blouses and printed skirts they wear. Their stomachs are gutted. Horror fills me as I see, superimposed on the photograph, an image of Annie laid out on the slab in the morgue. Nauseated, I close my eyes for a moment and take deep breaths before I can look again.

"It's him," Mick says. "The chap I followed from the bookshop."

The man in the photograph has a square face, light hair clipped short, and a long nose. A mustache covers the upper lip of his laughing mouth. Under a wide forehead, his brows bristle low over his narrow eyes. He looks exultant, like a hunter posing with his trophies. It's as though killing the

women wasn't enough; he needed to mutilate them and record it for posterity.

"Is this in Africa?" Mick asks.

I vaguely remember that England has
waged wars in Africa. "I suppose so."

"He killed over there. He must be doing it
here."

I take out my camera and photograph the
picture of the man. I wonder who took it,
but I don't dare remove it from the frame
and look for a signature; I'm afraid to touch
it, be poisoned by the evil portrayed in it,
and leave some trace that will alert the man
that we've been here. Next, I photograph
the newspaper clippings and boudoir photographs. Waiting out the long exposures, I
hope he doesn't return before we're gone. If
he catches us, he'll kill both of us to protect
his secrets. Finished, I say, "Let's see if he's
left any clues to his identity."

The desk drawers are empty. The clothes
cupboard yields nothing. Mick points at the
washstand and asks, "What are those?"

Beside the china water bowl and jug sit
three carved brass rings. "They're Annie
Chapman's rings!" They left indentations
on her swollen, dead fingers after her killer
pulled them off.

Mick and I look at each other. His face
wears the same goggle-eyed, open-mouthed

expression that I can feel on mine. We begin laughing uncontrollably, our hands pressed over our mouths. This man whose house we've broken into is the Ripper, and we have found the proof! We can hardly believe our good luck.

We abruptly stop laughing as we remember that the Ripper is still at large and we are trespassers in his den. We are in the umbra, and if he finds us here, we won't get out alive.

I aim the camera, open the shutter, and capture the image of Annie's rings on my last negative plate.

"Excellent job, young man!" Hugh says to Mick.

He was waiting outside my studio when Mick and I returned. Now the three of us are in the darkroom, where my wet prints of the newspaper clippings, the African photograph, and Annie's rings hang on the line.

Hugh claps Mick on the back, and Mick grins proudly. "This calls for a celebration," Hugh says. "I'll send for Catherine and the Lipskys."

When we're all gathered at the table in my studio, we toast our success with champagne that Hugh bought. We gobble sliced brisket, potato pancakes, and pickled beets furnished by the Lipskys, as Mick and I relate every detail of our expedition to Stepney. The food is delicious, my appetite keen; my stomach, once constricted by anxiety, has relaxed, as have the tensions between my friends. Mr. Lipsky claps a brawny hand on Mick's shoulder. A smile transforms his sinister face; he looks touchingly sweet. Mrs. Lipsky heaps more food on the young hero's plate. Mick basks in the Lipskys' esteem; he's forgotten his antipathy toward Jews. Catherine, giggly from the champagne, has put aside her pique at Hugh and me. Our euphoria even soothes my turbulent feelings about PC Barrett. A kind of golden haze softens the edges of everything outside our circle, including the past. We stop celebrating just long enough to discuss what to do with our evidence.

"Tomorrow, Sarah and I will go to the police station," Hugh says. "We'll show the photographs to Inspector Reid and tell him about the house in Stepney."

"He'll ask how we found the house and how we got inside," I say.

"I'll bring my solicitor," Hugh says. "He'll negotiate a deal with the police — the goods on the killer in exchange for letting us go, no questions asked."

I am so grateful to Hugh. With him and his solicitor by my side, I need not fear the law. I am grateful to Mick for his intrepid bravery and to the Lipskys for helping me when they needn't have. Tonight we seem a family. My tears of happiness blur the smiling faces shining in the gaslight. I can almost feel the warm, loving presence of my father, and I think the others are similarly comforted by our friendship. Mick and the Lipskys have also suffered losses — Mick his parents, the Lipskys their daughter. Catherine's relations are far away in the country, and Hugh must feel some estrangement from his because of the secret he keeps from them, but tonight none of us is alone. Our sense of accomplishment is more exhilarating than I have felt after anything I achieved by myself. How glad I am that I opened my heart to these friends!

"Inspector Reid will be so glad to take credit for catching the Ripper, he won't care how we got the evidence," Hugh says. "Catherine and the other models will be safe, everyone in Whitechapel will breathe a sigh of relief, and Sarah will have seen the last of the police."

That I won't see PC Barrett again is an added blessing. I have a glimpse of my life as it could be after tomorrow — a life filled with luminous scenes such as this. Perhaps someday there will even be a man whose motives I need not question when he kisses me.

A cheer goes up around the table. "Another toast!" Hugh pours the last of the champagne, then says, "Wait! We need a photograph. Quick, Sarah!"

I jump up from the table, position my tripod and large camera. I set the timer device, then hurry back to my place. The others lean toward me. Glasses raised, we freeze and smile. The flash powder explodes, dazzling our eyes, the light like fireworks.

I still have that photograph. It immortalized the joyful, innocent moment in our lives when we did not know what lay ahead of us, when we could look at one another and not think of the things we did to stop what I unwittingly started and what those things cost.

18

I am looking forward to giving Inspector Reid the surprise of his life.

Last night, Hugh said that he and his solicitor would call for me at nine o'clock this morning. It is now eight thirty. The fog dissipates, and sunlight shines through the window of my studio. I'm actually excited about visiting the police station, and I wish I could see the look on PC Barrett's face when he learns that I've tracked down the Ripper. How I will relish knowing I stole his chance to solve the crime! It will be retribution for his robbing me of my dignity and peace of mind.

The doorbell tinkles. Hugh is early. But when I open the door, there stand two police constables I've never seen before. One of them says, "Miss Sarah Bain?"

Warm, happy excitement vanishes as if a blanket were snatched off me during a winter night. "Yes?"

"Come with us."

This is the summons I thought I'd managed to avoid. Stricken by fear, I look outside for Hugh, but there's no sign of him. "I have to wait for my friend."

"Sorry, that's not possible. We have orders to place you under immediate arrest."

"Arrest?" This is even worse than I first thought. My heart is a cornered animal bounding against my ribs. "What for?"

"Obstructing police inquiries."

I frantically look around for rescue. Neighbors stand on the sidewalk, eavesdropping. They won't intercede; they don't care about me. Now I regret not making friends with them. My only coin with which to dissuade the constables is the information that Hugh and I planned to give Inspector Reid. Breathless with desperation, I say, "If you'll not take me to jail, I can tell you who the Ripper is."

"Oh, aye. So can everyone else in Whitechapel." He and his partner exchange amused glances. "We're swamped with false tips."

They apparently haven't been told that Inspector Reid thinks I have valuable information about the murders. "But I have proof! If you'll just allow me to —"

The constables seize me, clamp shackles

around my wrists, shove me into a prison van — an enclosed, horse-drawn wagon with barred windows — and lock the door. The empty van smells of urine, liquor, and vomit. I sit on the dirty plank floor. As the van rattles through the streets, I peer out the window for Hugh, but I see only strangers jeering at me. A rotten apple flies between the bars. When the van draws up outside Newgate prison, fog closes in on the massive brick fortress. In the distance, the hazy domes and spires of London swim in the mist like a mirage. Disbelief compounds my anguish. This can't be happening.

Shouts from inside Newgate fade without echoes, as if absorbed by the prison's own deadening atmosphere. The constables pull me from the van. Catcalls from gawkers outside the prison walls follow me through the gate. Wrists shackled, my head ducked, I'm as ashamed and terrified for my life as if I were a criminal. Inside the prison courtyard, my escorts leave me with the guards, one a female warder who runs her hands over my body to search for hidden weapons or other contraband. I flinch. From barred windows above, men call out lewd remarks to me. I dredge up the courage to speak.

"There's been a mistake. I'm supposed to give a statement, not go to jail!"

The warder marches me through the jail beneath galleries of cells three stories high. My ears are deafened by chatter from hundreds of women prisoners. The stink of privies turns my stomach. We progress via a dim corridor to a quiet wing of the jail. The warder removes my shackles, pushes me into a cell, and locks me in. I've lost my freedom and my chance to save my models. I'll never see Hugh, Catherine, Mick, or the Lipskys again. The new life that I envisioned last night is over before it started.

I sink onto the iron bed and calm myself by inspecting my surroundings as if to compose a photograph. I turn an imaginary lens on the small window that's cut at eye level in the door and crisscrossed with bars. At the far end of the narrow cell, foggy daylight seeps through a larger barred window. A wooden chair stands opposite the bed. As I focus in on illegible words scratched on the plaster walls, I think of my father, who spent a night in jail twenty-two years ago. Was he as terrified as I am? Will I be beaten as he was? When he came home the next morning, he and my mother had an argument while she bathed his wounds, and they sent me outside so I wouldn't hear what they said. Now I resist the urge to dissolve into helpless tears and try to think.

Inspector Reid is bound to come sooner or later. When he does, I will tell him about the man who has Annie Chapman's rings in his house and about the photographs in my satchel at my studio. Surely that will buy my release.

Hours pass. At last, I hear footsteps outside the door and a key rattle in the lock. I spring to my feet as Inspector Reid opens the door. I'm happier to see him than I ever thought possible.

"Good morning, Miss Bain," he says. "The Chief Commissioner of Police, Sir Charles Warren, will take your statement."

I am too disconcerted to speak. Reid stands aside to let in another man; then he departs, closing the door. Chief Commissioner Warren is tall; his long-legged gait is unhurried, but each step covers a wide distance, and he is instantly in front of me. At first, all I see is his uniform, decorated with badges and medals.

"Sit down, Miss Bain." His voice is a resonant baritone with a Welsh accent.

I perch, tense and wary, on the edge of the bed. Why would such a senior official take my statement? This must be a tactic designed to intimidate me into surrendering information. Revived courage straightens my spine. This time I have something to tell the police, and it will rock them on their heels. I only wish I had the photographs with me.

Chief Commissioner Warren sits in the chair. His knees jut upward because the chair is too low for him. The light from the window strikes his features.

Instant, shocking recognition stabs me.

His hair and mustache are darker; lines crease his wide forehead and radiate from the corners of the narrow eyes beneath the low, bristly eyebrows; but Chief Commissioner Warren is the man in the African photograph that Mick and I found.

For a moment, I cannot move or breathe.
He is the Ripper.

As I stare at him, petrified by incredulity, he leans forward. His eyes twinkle with the same cruel humor he displayed while standing over the corpses of the black women that he killed. For once, my fear for myself is greater than my fear for my models. I am now the one in the Ripper's sights, and the Ripper isn't some cretin from the underbelly of London; he's an important, powerful man — a more formidable adversary than I ever imagined.

He sees, and enjoys, my sudden terror.

Does he know why I'm terrified? "You've been taking an interest in the Whitechapel murders," he says. "Why is that?"

My plan for delivering the murderer to the police dissolves like coins in acid. I can't tell them about the house in Stepney, the African photograph, or Annie's rings. I can't tell them that Chief Commissioner Warren is the Ripper. They won't believe me. The idea that today would bring a welcome end to maneuvering behind the scenes, and a new, better life for me, seems pathetic now. If Chief Commissioner Warren learns that I know he's the Ripper . . .

He has already killed Martha Tabram, Polly Nichols, and Annie Chapman as well as the African women. He will never let me leave Newgate alive.

Thank Heaven that I wasn't allowed to bring my pictures of the rings and the African photograph! He would destroy them, and then seek out and destroy the negatives stored in my darkroom. I want to avert my face for fear that Commissioner Warren will read my thoughts; I want to run to the door and call Inspector Reid to come back, but I am as immobilized by Commissioner Warren as a butterfly pinned on a velvet-covered board. My heart flutters like helpless wings. Verbal evasion is my only defense.

"I'm interested in the murders because I knew the women." The trembling inside me afflicts my voice.

Warren's eyes are colorless, as if bleached by the African sun, and unnaturally bright, as if they absorbed its fierce radiance. "Is that the only reason?"

"Yes." I mustn't think of the African photograph or Annie's rings.

"You claim that the women told you sad stories about their pasts. It would seem that you and they were quite the bosom friends." Warren's smile is as false as his friendly tone. I suddenly understand why he's interested in me: he suspects that I took the photographs from which he selected his victims. I'm a photographer; I work in Whitechapel; I knew Martha, Polly, and Annie. A fool could draw the obvious conclusion, and Warren isn't a fool. "Did they also confide in you about their customers?"

I am too ashamed to recount their sordid descriptions of their relations with men. "No."

His eyes narrow further, in distrust. "Did they ever describe the men?"

Martha joked about their anatomy. Polly complained because some had the pox. "No."

"How about the places where they solicited the men? Did they mention those?"

I am so preoccupied with trying not to think about Mick and me breaking into his house that a moment passes before I answer, "No."

The distrust in Warren's gaze deepens. The skin on his face and thick, strong hands is leathery from exposure to the African sun. "Think hard," he says with the stern impatience that an army commander must use to coax dull-witted soldiers through drills. "Those men are potential suspects in the murders. Any details about them could help solve the case."

"I'm sorry; I have none." I also gather why Warren is asking me about the women's customers: he was one of them prior to the nights on which he killed Martha, Polly, and Annie. I envision Annie going with him into the yard on Hanbury Street, unafraid because she'd been with him before. When he attacked her, nobody heard anything because she, like Martha and Polly, was too surprised to scream. Warren wants to know if the women said anything to me that could incriminate him. This means that I am not the only one of us who is afraid of the other.

"If you did remember any details, would you tell me?"

Emboldened because the balance of power between us has tilted a bit in my favor, I lie, "Yes." But why would he risk confronting a witness who may suspect what he's done?

Warren rises, drops all pretense of civility, and stands over me the way he stood over those mutilated black women. "Forget about the Whitechapel murders." Savagery as hot as the African sun blazes from him. "Mind your own business."

Now I comprehend why he chose to confront me rather than keep his distance, even though a confrontation might induce me to say something that endangers him. He not only wants to intimidate me; he views this as a game that he's determined to win. With a shock of recognition, I perceive that he's like me: he's attracted to danger. The old saying has never seemed so true: *It takes one to know one.* But even if he fears I have knowledge that implicates him in the Whitechapel murders, my fear is a world greater than his.

Warren perceives my fear, nods with the satisfaction of a man who has easily won the first round of a duel. "Our conversation is finished . . . for now." He opens the door.

He could keep me locked up, but what fun would that be for him? I picture African women screaming and running while he chases them on horseback and fires his rifle. How much more fun if they were allowed to hope they could escape!

As I lunge for the door, his thick hand closes on my arm, and its heat burns through my sleeve. "Keep this in mind, Miss Bain: unless you behave yourself, you aren't the only person who will suffer."

19

Liberated from prison, I run. Carriages and people blur past me in the fog. I don't look where I'm going; I'm so distraught, I want only to flee as far and fast as I can. The fog impairs my sense of direction. I'm lost. Looking skyward, I see the hazy dome of St. Paul's Cathedral, but I can't tell which way is home. I trudge past warehouses, around corners, and down alleys for hours, only to wind up outside Newgate Prison again.

Someone calls my name. PC Barrett hurries toward me. "I heard you were arrested." He looks glad to see me. "I have to talk to you."

Barrett is the last person on earth that I want to see. A resurgence of humiliation adds to my distress. As I run away, Barrett catches up, jogs beside me, and says, "Wait."

I stumble to a halt. Facing Barrett, I can tell by his expression how bedraggled I look.

I care, even though vanity should be the least of my concerns.

"Are you all right?" He puts his arms around me and strokes my hair.

He's pretending that what happened between us has given him the right to take more liberties with me. I push him away. "Don't touch me!"

Barrett reacts with surprise. "What's the matter?"

I want to throw it in his face that I've discovered his trick, but I mustn't. How much more humiliating for him to know how upset I am because our "grope and tickle" was a ploy devised by him and Inspector Reid. Instead, I air my other grievance against Barrett.

"It's all your fault! If you hadn't told Inspector Reid about me, I wouldn't have been arrested."

His hands fly up, as if I'm a witch, he's a peasant boy who wandered up to my cottage in the woods, and I'm putting a curse on him. "I think you're withholding information. Since you won't tell me what it is, I had to go up the chain of command. It was my duty."

I am not appeased. "Couldn't you have warned me that I was going to be arrested?"

"Inspector Reid and Commissioner Warren wanted to take you by surprise. I had to go along with them." Barrett extends his hand to me. "I want to say I'm sorry."

His apology is so useless that I laugh, and my laughter has a crazed, forlorn edge. That I ever let Barrett kiss me! I despise my own lack of self-control. "I'm going home. Leave me alone."

As I limp, tired and clumsy, Barrett follows. "You're going the wrong way."

Utterly lost, I stop and burst into tears.

He looks frightened and abashed, as some men are when faced with a crying woman. "Please don't cry. I'll take you home." He hails a cab.

Although mortified to break down in front of him, I let him help me into the cab and sit beside me. Swallowing sobs, cold from wandering in the fog, I shiver so hard I can't speak. When we reach my studio, I huddle in a chair. The studio is frigid; I can't stop shivering. Barrett lights a fire in the grate, then makes tea. If he's thinking about our frantic almost-coupling, he shows no sign, but for me it's as if a huge photograph of it were plastered on the wall. Once a man and a woman have been intimate, everything is changed between them. I can act as if it never happened, but I can't completely shut myself to Barrett, for my shell is broken.

He brings two cups, hands me one, and pulls up a chair beside me. I drink. "Better?" he asks.

The tea is hot, sweet, strong, and bracing. I nod. The coals in the grate whisper and glow, while outdoors the fog is dense and gray. I have to remind myself that I'm onto Barrett and not to be fooled by his pretense of taking care of me.

"I heard that you stood up to Commissioner Warren." Barrett's irritation is tinged with respect.

The mention of Warren sends another shiver through me. I set down my cup before the tea spills. Barrett says, "Commissioner Warren is a tough one. Last year he put down that demonstration at Trafalgar Square."

Thousands of socialists, radicals, unemployed workers, and Irish Home Rulers marched on Trafalgar Square and fought a fierce battle with the police, who eventually chased them away. Why is Barrett mentioning it?

"It was called 'Bloody Sunday' because so many people were hurt or killed. Warren got tons of hate mail. He was criticized in the press. But he hasn't stopped cracking down on demonstrators. When he makes up his mind to go after someone, he doesn't let

261

anything stand in his way." Barrett's expression is serious, compassionate. "What I'm trying to tell you is that Warren will keep after you. Whatever happened today, next time will be worse."

Dread wraps me like an iron chain around my ribs, dragging me downward as if through the cold depths of a lake.

"There's only one way to get out of trouble with Warren: admit what it is you're hiding."

I notice that the cut on Barrett's cheek has hardened into a thin, brown scab. His concern is but a ploy to elicit information. Remembering what Inspector Reid said to him, I laugh bitterly. "Get me to talk — that's a surefire way to a promotion."

"I'm not out to score points with my superiors," Barrett says, loud and vehement. He sets down his empty cup so hard that the noise makes my ears ring. "I just want you to be safe."

The worry in his eyes and the sincerity of his manner are so genuine that if I didn't know better, I would think he really was interested in me. There's still a charge in the atmosphere between us, and if he were to touch me, we would take up where we left off the other night, and I'm not sure I could stop this time. The shameful self-knowledge ignites a rage that overrides my inhibitions.

"You're doing it again." I fling the accusation at Barrett.

Puzzlement draws his eyebrows together. "Doing what?"

" 'Softening up the spinster.' What's next — a little 'grope and tickle'?"

"What?" Barrett's mouth drops as he recalls his conversation with Inspector Reid and realizes that I overheard it. "But I didn't mean . . ." Alarm fills his eyes; he reaches for me. "It wasn't what it looked like."

I raise my hands to ward off his touch and his protests. "Oh, spare me the excuses!" I'm triumphant because I've let him know I'm onto him, but I already regret it. The pity in his expression says that he can see how badly hurt I am. I wish I could hit him back. Now an idea foments within the chaos of my anger, shame, and humiliation.

I could tell him about Commissioner Warren.

And I can see other reasons besides my desire to turn the tables on Barrett. What a temptation, to relinquish the burden of my secret! What a relief to stop feeling guilty because I'm hoarding information that could lead to the capture of the Ripper. That my friends and I once thought we should hunt the Ripper by ourselves now seems ludicrous; we're no match for Warren, and Barrett is our only potential ally, never mind how bitter I feel toward him. Although telling Barrett about Warren would necessitate telling him other secrets, my inclination is to gamble on him. Furthermore, I have proof to support my accusation.

"All right — I'll tell you what I'm hiding." I expel the words past the racing heartbeat in my throat.

Barrett is startled by the abrupt turn of the conversation and my equally abrupt capitulation. "You will?" His expression and voice are tense with contained excitement.

I take a deep breath, inflating my lungs, trying to loosen the sudden fear that constricts them like a steel net. "It's Commissioner Warren."

Barrett frowns. "What's Commissioner Warren?"

Here is my chance to change my mind. "The Ripper," I blurt. "Warren is the Ripper."

"If that's a joke, it's not funny."

His reaction is a letdown. Another chance beckons. I ignore it and give in to the urge to wipe the disdain off Barrett's face. "It's not a joke." Even though I know how ridiculous my claim must sound, I'm angered by Barrett's refusal to take seriously the information that Mick and I risked our lives to obtain. "You haven't even heard me out."

"I won't listen to lies!" Barrett stands, his face dark with offense. "You're accusing *my superior* of murdering those women. That's just dirty slander."

I'm only more determined to convince him. Jumping to my feet, I say, "I can prove it's true. Just wait."

My satchel is in the darkroom. I run there, fetch the three photographs I took in Warren's house, and spread them on the table. Barrett bends a suspicious gaze on me. "Is this a trick?"

"*I* don't play tricks," I snap. "You and Inspector Reid do."

"Look, I'm sorry if your feelings are hurt," Barrett says, with an effort at patience and sympathy, "but it's no excuse to lie about Commissioner —"

Then he looks at the photographs. He frowns at the ones of the newspaper clippings and blurry boudoir pictures.

"What the hell?" As he scrutinizes the picture of the soldier standing over the dead, mutilated black women, his face goes blank with shock.

"That's Commissioner Warren," I say.

Barrett shakes his head and says loudly, "No." His voice rings false; he recognized Warren. "It can't be," he says firmly, as if to convince himself. He squints at the picture of the three brass rings. "What's this?"

"Those rings belonged to Annie Chapman, the Ripper's third victim." I'm vindictively glad I've unsettled Barrett, but maybe I shouldn't have told him. Whether or not he believes my story about Warren rides entirely on the photographs, and suddenly they don't seem like such conclusive proof of Warren's guilt.

Barrett's eyes betray his perplexity, his consternation, and his struggle to resist belief. "Did you take these photographs?"

"Yes." I have the sensation of skating onto thin ice.

"Where did you take them?"

"In Commissioner Warren's house in Stepney."

"His house?" Barrett stares in amazement.

I give him the address, watch him instinctively commit it to memory. I can almost hear him thinking that what I've been up to is beyond his wildest imaginings.

"How did you get in there?"

I mustn't admit that Mick and I broke in. "It doesn't matter. What matters is that the newspaper clippings, the photograph of

Commissioner Warren, and the rings are all there. Go and look."

He gazes at the photographs, then at me, with naked horror. He understands the story that I, and they, are telling: Commissioner Warren killed and mutilated women while in Africa, and he's brought his habit to London. He has souvenirs from one of the Ripper's victims. He takes pride in the newspaper clippings, which describe the public's fear of him and the futile efforts of his own police force to catch him. The collection of items is a shrine to his sins.

A look of revulsion comes over Barrett's face. "They aren't real! You faked them. You're trying to frame Commissioner Warren."

"How?" I can't imagine where he thinks I obtained Annie's rings, let alone found a young Commissioner Warren look-alike or slaughtered Negro women.

Barrett turns his head from side to side, anxiously seeking an explanation. "I don't know." His expression combines anger at me with anger at his inability to discount the evidence that the top police officer is the Ripper. "But you must have." He's breathing hard, like a bull in a ring, his fists and teeth clenched.

The door flies open. Hugh rushes into the

studio, followed by Catherine, the Lipskys, and Mick. "Sarah!" Hugh cries. "Thank God! We've been looking all over for —"

My friends see Barrett, and the relief on their faces turns to consternation. Barrett glares at me. "Damn you to hell! I'm sorry I ever —"

He's sorry he ever met me. He can't deny to himself that my evidence against Commissioner Warren is genuine, and he hates me because I've saddled him with the heavy burden of knowing that his superior is the Ripper. If he's also sorry he tricked me, because it led to this, it would be the only good outcome of my revelation.

Barrett snatches up the photographs and stalks out the door, slamming it so hard that the bell strikes and cracks the glass.

20

"I shouldn't have told him," I say to Catherine, Mick, Hugh, and the Lipskys.

We're gathered around the table in my studio, drinking tea. Hugh told me that he and his solicitor came by for me this morning, and when I failed to appear, he knew something was wrong, and he notified Catherine and the Lipskys. When the four of them came to my studio to see if I had returned, they found only Mick waiting for me. The neighbors told them I'd been arrested. My friends went from one police station to another, trying to find me. They never imagined I'd been taken to Newgate. Now that I've described what's happened, they sit mute, shocked to learn that I discovered that the man in the African photograph is the chief police commissioner and that I told PC Barrett that Warren is the Ripper, all in a few hours.

"If only I could take it back!"

"Spilled milk," Hugh says with a nonchalant shrug, trying to console me by minimizing the disaster. "Look on the bright side: we now know who the Ripper is."

A pensive hush descends on us. Rain spatters the window. Machinery in a distant factory pounds a slow, thudding pulse. "Barrett will give the prints he took to Inspector Reid." I feel an awful sensation that I'm speeding away from my friends, downward to a dark place beyond all help.

"Maybe he won't," Catherine says with her typical naïve optimism. "At the inquest he seemed rather nice, and perhaps a little sweet on you, Sarah."

"He certainly isn't sweet on me now. He won't protect me."

Mr. Lipsky glowers and shakes his head. He knows better than to hope for mercy from the police.

"Well, we'd better figure out our next step." Hugh rolls up his sleeves and looks around the table.

"Maybe we should do what this man Warren told Sarah," Mrs. Lipsky says. "Mind our own business, keep out of trouble." Her manner is stoic, resigned; it must have been so when she and her family chose to leave Russia.

"Let police get away with murder? No!"

Mr. Lipsky clenches his fists in a sudden burst of temper.

"You're right," Mick says, afire with eagerness to rebel against the law that he's always skirted, wanting to show off for Catherine. "We have to take Warren down!"

Catherine ignores Mick, but she chimes in, "It's not fair that I have to be afraid of getting murdered."

Her safety, and that of my models, is the best reason for pursuing Warren's downfall.

"There's one course of action we can take against Warren," Hugh says. "Prevent him from killing again."

"How?" Catherine asks.

"Abraham will continue chaperoning you. Sarah, Mick, and I will guard the three other women," Hugh says. "We'll follow them and make sure they're never alone outdoors after dark. Warren won't attack them in front of witnesses."

"But he'll see us," I say. "He doesn't know you and Mick, but he'll recognize me, and he'll think it unusual that the same people are always cropping up around the women. He'll realize what we're doing."

"Not if we're in disguise." Hugh sparkles with ingenuity. "Male dress for you, Sarah. I'll find costumes for Mick and me. Warren will never get wise to us."

Mick cheers. "You're on!"

Catherine and the Lipskys nod their approval. I look out the window at the deepening darkness and think of following Liz, Kate, or Mary Jane through the fog, my frail self the only thing standing between her and death. But I haven't a better idea.

That night, dressed in a jacket and trousers that Hugh purchased at a rag shop, I trail Mary Jane Kelly as she strolls around the Prostitutes' Church. I watch her solicit customers, I wait outside courtyards while she services them, and I see her safely back to her lodgings at dawn. On the next two nights, I do the same for Kate Eddowes and Liz Stride. It's less frightening than I expected — in fact, curiously liberating. The absence of my usual corset, long skirt, and cumbersome petticoats makes my body limber and agile, and I can walk alone at night without being accosted by men. Male disguise is akin to a suit of armor.

In the mornings, I come home to find Hugh and Mick swapping stories of masquerading as laborer and beggar boy while acting as bodyguards. I drowse in bed all day, too tired to open the studio yet too anxious to sleep well. If Commissioner Warren catches us, what will he do? We are merely stalling him, no closer to bringing him to justice. There's not been another murder, and PC Barrett has apparently not shown anyone the photographs, but this calm is like the space between a lightning bolt and the thunderclap.

On Tuesday, 18 September, Mick doesn't show up at my studio. While I'm cooking breakfast, there's a knock at the door, and I think he's finally come, but when I answer, it's a dark-haired boy about ten years old, wearing a tam and ragged clothes.

"I'm a friend o' Mick's. He asked me to tell you he's in Sick Children's Hospital. He's had a n'accident."

The Hospital for Sick Children, on Great Ormond Street, is a tall brick building that resembles a Gothic castle. The ward is a sunny, high-ceilinged room, cozily warm, unlike other charity wards, which are so squalid that the patients often end up dead instead of cured. Young patients occupy cribs ranged against opposite walls decorated with pictures of scenes from nursery rhymes. A table in the center aisle holds cut flowers in vases. The smell of the flowers and disinfectant mask the sickroom smells. Nurses wearing pink uniforms and starched white caps and aprons carry in trays of food.

Visiting families cluster around many of the beds. Conversation and laughter echo. A few patients lie still and pale, but others don't seem very ill. Two little girls in nightgowns are having a dolls' tea party.

Mick is propped up in his bed, a meal tray on a table attached to the railings, a nurse seated by his side. If not for his red hair, bright as a flame against the white pillows, I wouldn't have recognized him. Scrubbed clean, he wears a blue cotton nightshirt. A gauze bandage covers his left temple, his right arm wears a white sling, and as the nurse spoons tapioca pudding into his mouth, he eats obediently. I've never seen him so passive.

"Miss Sarah!" Mick seems ashamed for me to see him treated like a baby. His face firms up into its usual precociously mature, confident expression — his armor against the world.

The nurse is a buxom woman in her forties with a handsome, stern face. "Are you his relation?" she asks me.

"No, just a friend." I'm glad he's all right, but I feel a pang of regret because he never trusted me enough to let down his armor in front of me.

"I'm the matron of this ward. How good of you to come." Her tone implies that I took my sweet time.

She couldn't make me feel any guiltier. "I came as soon as I heard." I shouldn't have let Mick roam about Whitechapel at night guarding my models. "What happened to Mick?"

"He almost drowned in the Thames this morning."

Alarm besets me. "How?"

"I saw an anchor stickin' up out 'o the river," Mick says. "It must 'ave broke loose from some ship. I thought I could sell it, so I waded out to get it. Then a ship come along, an' the wake swept me into the current."

"His little friend saw him floating unconscious in the water and called for help," the matron says. "He's lucky to be alive, with only a bump on his head and a dislocated shoulder."

I sense this isn't the real story. Uneasiness creeps into my heart. "Matron, may I have a private word with Mick?" When she's gone, I ask, "What really happened?"

"After I left Mary Jane at her house, I saw two coppers comin' toward me. I ran. They chased me and cornered me by the docks." Mick sounds disgusted at himself for not managing to evade them. "They grabbed me an' threw me in the river. I must've hit my head and passed out, 'cause the next thing I knew, I was lyin' on the dock, and a bloke was pushin' on my chest, and I was throwin' up water, and my shoulder hurt somethin' awful."

I stare in horror and bewilderment. "Why did the police chase you?"

As I wonder if they saw him stealing, Mick says, "Before they threw me in the river, one of 'em said, 'From now on, mind your own business. And tell Sarah Bain to mind hers.' "

A sharp chime of dread resonates through me as I remember Commissioner Warren's warning: *Unless you behave yourself, you aren't the only person who will suffer.* He's found out who my friends are. By trying to protect Liz, Mary Jane, and Kate, I've almost gotten Mick killed. The ward spins into a blur of light, distorted voices, and nauseating smells of flowers, food, and disinfectant. I breathe deeply to relieve my sudden faintness.

"Those police must have been sent by Commissioner Warren. He must have been stalking my models and seen you, Hugh, and me following them." Another possibility disturbs me just as much. "Or PC Barrett showed him my photographs and told him what I said."

A strange expression comes over Mick's face. "Maybe it ain't because he saw us or because Barrett ratted on you."

"What else could it be?"

Mick gazes down at the pudding, milk, and stewed apples on his tray. "I think he knows we were in his house."

"How could he? We didn't disturb anything, and we closed the window and locked the door before we left. And the neighbors couldn't have seen us sneak in. The fog was so thick."

Mick hunches his shoulders. "I took some money from the desk."

"*What?* When was this?"

"When I was lookin' around the house by myself." Mick sees the appalled expression on my face. "It were three quid ten shillings," he says, wretched with guilt. "I couldn't resist."

"Where is the money now?"

"In your darkroom. Behind some jars in the cupboard." Mick says, "I'm sorry."

Spilled milk, as Hugh would say. "It's all right. Commissioner Warren can't possibly know it was you who took the money."

Relieved, Mick settles against his pillows. But I fear Warren does suspect Mick. Maybe he thinks one of my models told me something about him that led me to his house and I enlisted the aid of my friend the street urchin who is clever at burglary. But I don't tell this to Mick because I don't want him to blame himself when I never should have involved him in this scheme. It's my nightmare come again: my actions have brought harm to someone I care about. When Hugh helped me shed my notion that my father's death was my fault, I thought I'd been wrong in believing that I cast a shadow and anyone who came near me was in danger. I decided it was safe to open myself to the friendships I craved so badly. But I was right all along: I *do* have a shadow — created by Commissioner Warren — and my friends are in jeopardy.

The matron returns, all efficiency and starched skirts. "Time for you to finish your lunch and take your nap, young man." She says to me, "I'll see you out."

"As soon as I'm better, Miss Sarah, I'll get out of here and help you with you-know-what," Mick says.

But I can see that he's not eager to leave the hospital, where he's fed, pampered, and safe. I don't blame him. Wherever he lives can't be as comfortable, and after a brush with death, he's unwilling to pit himself against Commissioner Warren — not even for Catherine's sake.

"Such a sad case," the matron says as we walk down the hall. "His mother was an unwed fifteen-year-old girl. Mick doesn't know who his father is. When he was six, she ran away with another man. His grandfather was a drunk, and his grandmother had too many other children to take care of, so they gave Mick to St. Vincent's orphanage. But I suppose you knew."

I bow my head. I trusted Mick in my studio, with my possessions, but he didn't trust me enough to confide in me. I'm not the only one of us to keep secrets about the past.

"Those Irish Catholics." Her manner is stiff with disapproval. "Shiftless. No morals. Popping out babies as if they're relieving themselves."

I'm offended on Mick's behalf, but before I can protest, she says, "Mick is a good, clever boy. He deserves a future. I spoke to the nuns at St. Vincent's, and they're willing to take him back. If you care about him, you'll persuade him to go there and stay put."

Now I feel ashamed because she, despite her prejudices, is a better friend to Mick than I. As I leave the hospital, I make up my mind that even if Mick wants to help me, I won't let him; it's too dangerous.

Commissioner Warren must indeed be afraid of me; why else would he set his dogs on Mick? Not just because he enjoys hurting my friends, but to scare us off his trail. I can't let Mr. Lipsky and Hugh help me protect my models. It's dangerous for them, too. If I have to choose between their safety versus that of Kate, Mary Jane, and Liz . . .

I selfishly decide in favor of my friends. I'll do the best I can by myself for my models. They won't look after themselves, and they've been rude to me, but I feel guilty because they've drawn the short straw. Before I go out to guard one of the women tonight, I'll tell Hugh and Mr. Lipsky that their services are no longer needed. I must find some other way to keep Catherine safe.

21

Three days later — on Friday, 21 September — I return to my studio at just before eight o'clock in the morning. Hugh and I have been shadowing Liz Stride, Kate Eddowes, and Mary Jane Kelly. The two of us can't be in three places at the same time, but Hugh pointed out that it was better than if I tried to protect all of them by myself.

"I'm not quitting," he said after I told him what happened to Mick. "Even if Commissioner Warren set his dogs on Mick, they won't dare throw *me* in the river."

Catherine and Mr. Lipsky are equally impervious to my pleas to protect themselves. Catherine still won't go home, and Mr. Lipsky refused to stop guarding her. My friends and I have a trait in common: hardheaded stubbornness. None of us wants to capitulate.

This morning, somebody is huddled in my doorway — a woman in an emerald green taffeta frock. She lies curled on her side, turned away from the street. Her long, wavy blond hair is disheveled. Her hands are covered with black velvet gloves that extend above her elbows. One of her feet wears a high-heeled, rhinestone-studded slipper; the other is bare. She's trembling, and she reeks of liquor. She's drunk. I nudge her with my foot.

"Excuse me. Please go somewhere else."

She whimpers and lifts a face that's smeared with pink powder, black mascara, and red lip rouge. Blood clots her nostrils and drools from her swollen mouth. Her wide, blank green eyes are shockingly familiar.

She is Hugh in female dress and a blond wig.

My first reaction is horror laced with confusion. Why is Hugh dressed as a woman and lying battered and bloody on my doorstep? My second reaction is a fierce urge to protect him. I look around and see men standing outside the pub, watching us.

"Come inside!" I whisper as I hurriedly unlock the door. "Quick!"

Moaning, he crawls into my studio. I lock the door, then say, "We have to get you out of those clothes and cleaned up. Can you walk?"

Hugh weeps as he struggles to his feet and trips on his skirts. I help him up the stairs, recalling how he helped me only days ago. In my bedroom, I undress him and take off his wig. Beneath the green frock, he's wearing a corset padded to simulate a bosom, petticoats, garters, and silk stockings. As I remove the clothes, we're both too distraught to care if I see him nude again. His beautiful body is covered with reddish-purple bruises. I wrap him in a blanket, sit him on the bed, and sponge the makeup off his face. He cries and trembles the whole time.

There's a loud knocking at the door. A man's voice calls, "Miss Bain!"

"Is that the police?" Hugh groans. "Oh, no."

"It's Mr. Douglas, my landlord. If I don't answer, he'll use his key to get in." I rush downstairs and open the door.

With his crooked nose and heavyset build, Mr. Douglas looks like the boxer he was twenty years ago. His face is red with anger. "You let a whore inside my building." He also owns the pub down the street. He must have been among the men watching me and Hugh.

"She's not a whore," I say. "She's my friend, and she, er, had an accident."

"Don't lie to me. You have all kinds of whores coming and going."

My heart sinks; I was right to fear that Annie, Polly, and the others were seen.

"I let you get away with it because I'm a nice guy, but I just heard that you've been bringing in Jews and street urchins, too. I don't want that kind of scum on my property. This is the last straw. If that whore's not out of here in ten minutes, I'll bring the police to get her out." Mr. Douglas huffs away down the street.

Catherine comes running up to me. "Sarah, what was that about?"

This is a fine time for her to visit! I pull her into the studio, lock the door, and say, "Hugh is here. He's been hurt."

"How? What happened?"

"I'll explain later." I have ten minutes to relocate Hugh. "Wait here."

But she follows me upstairs and sees Hugh curled on my bed. With the makeup washed off, the injuries to his face are glaringly apparent. Purple bruises circle both his eyes.

"Hugh!" Catherine cries. "What happened to you?"

"I was guarding Kate Eddowes. She went home early, so I went to a party." Hugh's swollen lips muffle his voice. "It was raided by the vice squadron."

Dismay fills me as I comprehend that the party was one of the illicit, all-male affairs that men of Hugh's persuasion attend. The vice squadron often raids these affairs. Guests caught engaging in forbidden carnal acts are put on trial and, if convicted, sentenced to two years of hard labor in prison. The dark side of Hugh's life is darker than I imagined.

"The police beat me up," Hugh says.

"What party? Why did they raid it?" Catherine notices the wig, green frock, and undergarments lying on the floor. "Hugh, are these yours? Were you dressed as a woman?"

"Yes." Hugh turns away, embarrassed. "I do sometimes."

Catherine's pretty mouth falls open. I, too, am surprised to learn this detail about Hugh. Here is another of my friends' secrets exposed. Catherine says, "Are you . . . ?"

"Do I need to spell it out?"

"Oh." Catherine's expression alters from shock to enlightenment. "You're like Frankie and Maurice." I gape at her in confusion. "The costume-makers at the theater," she explains. "They're the dearest fellows, but some people don't like them because they like men instead of women. I don't see why it matters who does what in private, when they're not hurting anybody . . ." Distracted by her own thoughts, she frowns, shakes her head, then demands, "Why didn't you tell me?"

"I was afraid of what you would think," Hugh says. "I didn't know I had the good fortune of an acquaintance with two openminded women."

Catherine turns on me. "You knew! And you let me make a fool of myself!"

"I'm sorry. It wasn't my secret to tell." I'm glad because I can see that only her pride, not her heart, has been wounded. She smiles as she comprehends why Hugh isn't romantically interested in her.

"Why didn't the police arrest you?" Catherine asks Hugh.

"Damned if I know."

"How did you get here?" I ask.

"They put me in a carriage. The driver dumped me at your door."

This is another shock, a second cruel blow after Mick's brush with death. "They knew who you are. Commissioner Warren must have ordered the raid."

Hugh closes his eyes, as if this news is too much for him to cope with. Catherine frowns. "How could Commissioner Warren have known about the party and that Hugh would be there?"

"He must have seen Hugh guarding Kate and followed him." Breathless with fright and anger, I slump against the wall. "He had Hugh brought here as another warning to me."

He could have had me beaten up, but that wouldn't have titillated him enough. He could have just shot the African women, not tortured and mutilated them. Now he's having fun with me, at my friends' expense. A terrible guilt sickens me.

"Well." Catherine looks unconvinced. "It could be just a coincidence."

She doesn't think Commissioner Warren was behind the attack on Mick or Hugh's mishap; she thinks all policemen are the friendly constable in her home village. But I have no doubt whatsoever. Now a different emotion sends tremors rising up in me. They're not the helpless, debilitating tremors of fear; they're the fierce, hot energy that makes flames crackle, twist, and roar. The emotion is anger of an intensity such as I've never experienced. The anger is directed at Commissioner Warren. It's as if he set off an eruption in a deep pit of volcanic lava I never knew I had in me.

"What shall we do about Hugh?" Catherine asks.

"My landlord gave me ten minutes to get him out before he calls the police. And it's not safe for him to be around me." Warren is not just threatening me by hurting my friends; he's also forcing me to cut myself off from them lest he hurt them again. He's isolating me, the better to weaken me, as ruthlessly as a lion separates an antelope from the herd. It's not safe for Catherine or the Lipskys, either, but there's no time to discuss that.

"Hugh, you have to go home," I say.

"No!" Hugh begins weeping again. "I can't face my family."

I didn't realize until this moment how big a risk his way of life posed for him. For his own good, I steel my heart, cuff his shoulder, and say, "Get up! Now!"

Hugh gazes at me, his blackened eyes streaming tears, shocked and hurt because I've never treated him so roughly before. He pushes himself upright.

"I'll find something for him to wear," Catherine says.

She rummages in the cupboard and finds a dark-blue wool dressing gown that belonged to my father. It's soft and thin from wear. For months after he died, I slept with it. His smell comforted me. Now I let Catherine give it to Hugh. He stands naked, his back turned to us, and groans as he forces his sore, stiff arms into the gown.

Catherine ties the sash around his waist. "How are we going to get him out of the house?"

"Mr. Douglas will be watching for a woman in a green dress to leave." In the throes of shock and anger, I can't think anymore.

"I have an idea." Catherine hastily strips down to her undergarments and puts on Hugh's green dress and blond wig. I wonder if she remembers the costume she wanted to wear to the Duke's ball. "I'll run out the front door. You take Hugh out the back. Bring my clothes. I'll go hire a cab and meet you at the end of the alley."

While she's gone, I help Hugh down the stairs. By the time we reach the alley, Catherine is waiting in the cab. Hugh and I climb aboard, and as the carriage rattles down Whitechapel Road, Catherine says, "Your pig of a landlord told me never to come back. He thought I was the woman he saw lying outside your door. We fooled him." She strips off the wig and green dress, puts on her own clothes, fluffs her hair, and asks Hugh where he lives.

He mutters an address in Belgrave Square. Slumped miserably between Catherine and me, he drools blood onto my father's robe. I try not to think beyond the task of conveying him home, but I can't ignore the troubles that gather around us like wolves in the shadows outside a campfire. In Belgrave Square, couples stroll, children roll hoops, and nannies push babies in prams along paths below trees resplendent with brown, gold, and red autumn foliage. Around the square rise tall, elegant townhouses with white marble steps and brass railings. The Staunton family home has marble urns filled with marigolds outside its glossy, black-painted door. Catherine gazes, fascinated, out the cab's window.

"It's so beautiful," she murmurs, "and so clean and quiet!"

The ubiquitous stench of cesspools is fainter here, and the sun shines. Wealth encloses Belgrave Square in an invisible dome that excludes the smoke and noise from the factories. Hugh buries his face in his hands and weeps. This is his world, but his illicit desires and my need for his friendship brought him to my dirty, dangerous one. He can't help his desires, but I had a choice. That day we met at the cemetery, I should have walked away from him and not looked back.

I don't notice the crowd of men outside

the Staunton house until Catherine, Hugh, and I climb out of the carriage. Armed with notebooks and pencils, they rush upon us, shouting.

"Lord Hugh! Is it true that you were caught in a police raid?"

"Where are your clothes? Were you dressed as a woman?"

They are reporters. They know what happened to Hugh last night. "Commissioner Warren must have tipped them off," I say in dismay.

"Oh, God." Hugh covers his head with his arms.

The reporters surround us.

"What were you doing when the police caught you?"

"Were you buggering some fellow or taking it up your windward passage?"

As Catherine and I pull Hugh toward the house, my anger at Commissioner Warren spills onto the reporters like hot lava that burns anything in its path. I yell at them, "Go away! Leave him alone!"

People in the square gather to watch. The reporters follow us, crying, "Lord Hugh, what have you to say for yourself? Aren't you ashamed?"

We drag Hugh up the steps. The glossy black door opens. There stands a handsome man, dressed in a velvet smoking jacket, who looks like Hugh will in thirty years. Behind him hovers a blond woman faded by age but beautiful; she has Hugh's eyes. The Duke and Duchess of Ravenswood gape at their cowering, disheveled son.

"My lord and lady! Did you know your son is a pervert?"

Hugh's horrified parents back away. A slight, gray-haired man with a worried face steps up to the door and pulls Hugh inside the house. The door closes. As Catherine and I run to our cab, the reporters chase us.

"Who are you ladies?"

"How do you know Lord Hugh?"

We jump inside the carriage. They pound on it, yelling questions as it rolls down the street, then fall behind. Catherine and I look at each other, shaken.

"What will Commissioner Warren do to the rest of us?" Catherine asks. She finally believes that Warren is responsible for Mick's and Hugh's troubles. "And who's next?"

22

That night, I stayed home instead of guarding any of my models, much as I hated to let them shift for themselves. If Warren were to catch me at it, he would punish my friends as well as me. But my guilty conscience, and the simmering pit of my new anger, kept me from sleeping.

On this cold, smoky Saturday morning, 22 September, I buy a newspaper and read the front-page story during breakfast.

DARK ANNIE STILL
UNAVENGED BY JUSTICE

Jacob Isenschmid, arrested on suspicion of committing the Whitechapel murders, will shortly be released. His brother has given him an alibi for the time of Dark Annie Chapman's murder. It is held in several local influential quarters that all has not been done that might have been done. Great indignation has been expressed because the Government will not offer a reward for information that could lead to the murderer's capture. The inhuman murderer still comes and goes about our streets, hiding in his guilty heart the secret known only to him, Heaven, and the dead.

So much for the suspect PC Barrett mentioned at the Mile End Vigilance Committee meeting. At least there's not been another murder; all my models have survived the night.

On the next page is this article:

RAID AT THE
THOUSAND CROWNS CLUB

The Thousand Crowns Club in Fitzrovia was raided by the vice squadron during the early-morning hours of Friday, 21 September. Police surprised 35 men, dressed in female clothing or naked, engaged in indecent acts. Some were rent boys from a nearby brothel and soldiers from the Horse Guards. They were arrested and charged with sodomy. Others were quietly let go. A source within the vice squadron said that one of those was Lord Hugh Staunton, son of the Duke of Ravenswood. This statement could not be confirmed. Lord Hugh is not in police custody.

A sickening sensation washes through me as I perceive the real story between the lines of this article. Hugh's presence at the Thousand Crowns wasn't confirmed, and he is officially accused of nothing, but people will believe the insinuation that he is guilty. His dark secret has exploded into the cruel spotlight of scandal, and the fact that he's the only person named in the article leaves me no doubt that the raid was an attack targeted at him. Commissioner Warren must believe I have compromising knowledge about him, he must think I've shared it with my friends, and he wants to silence all of us. He could probably get away with killing Mick, Catherine, the Lipskys, and me, but not Hugh, a member of the aristocracy. Even if he made Hugh's death look like an accident, pressure to investigate it would come down from on high. Instead, Warren destroyed Hugh's reputation.

Should Hugh accuse Warren of murder, no one who matters will listen.

The anger flushes such heat through me that I sweep all my floors to burn it off. Then I spend the day photographing customers in my studio. I resist the temptation to visit Mick and Hugh. As much as I long to see how they're faring, I've already brought them enough harm; I must keep my distance from them. They probably won't want to see me anyway.

At six o'clock that night, the doorbell jangles. I untie the bell from its hook; lately it heralds little except trouble. My visitor is a breathless, anxious Mr. Lipsky.

"What's wrong?" I ask as I let him in.

"When I go to take Catherine to theater, she not home. She already leave."

"Why didn't you go to the theater and wait to bring her home after the show?"

"I did. Catherine not there. They say she have night off."

Catherine has seized the chance to roam free. Alarmed by her reckless stupidity, I grab my coat. "We have to find her."

We search in vain at every tavern, music hall, and supper club that Catherine frequents. In the early morning, we go to her boardinghouse. The landlady and other tenants don't know where she is. Sunday and Monday, I shuttle between my studio and her house, hoping she'll turn up at one place or the other, but she doesn't. In the evenings, I check the theater. She's not there. I grow certain that Commissioner Warren has murdered Catherine. If only I had never photographed her! A vision of Catherine lying on blood-drenched cobblestones with her throat cut sends me into frenzies of terror and guilt.

On Tuesday morning, just after nine o'clock, Catherine glides into my studio, as fresh, pretty, and gay as usual.

"Catherine!" I exclaim. "Where have you been?"

"With my friend Derek."

The powerful anger rekindles in me. "Mr. Lipsky and I searched all over for you. You shouldn't have gone out without him. It's dangerous!"

"But now that we know Commissioner Warren is the Ripper, you needn't fear that it's one of my beaux. And look at this."

Catherine hands me a newspaper. I read the story she indicates.

Monday, 24 September 1888.
Horror at Gateshead

Yesterday morning, the dead body of Jane Beatmoor was found on a railway siding five miles south of Newcastle. Her throat was cut, and her bowels were spilled from a gash in her abdomen. There were no clues as to who perpetrated this ghastly deed, but its resemblance to the crimes in London suggests that the Whitechapel

Ripper has traveled to the north of England to pursue his fiendish vocation.

"The Ripper has moved on," Catherine says triumphantly. "Everybody says so."

I throw the newspaper on the floor. Catherine looks surprised; she's never seen me in such a temper. "I don't care what everybody says! Suppose Commissioner Warren did commit this murder in Gateshead — maybe it was a ruse to make the London police decide the Ripper isn't their problem any longer, and he'll come back for you after they stop hunting him in Whitechapel."

Obstinacy tightens Catherine's mouth. "I'm through with having a chaperone, and I'm through worrying about Commissioner Warren. I want to live again!" Flinging out her arms, opening herself to the whole dangerous world, she spins around and laughs at her own dramatic extravagance.

I should convince her to be reasonable, but my anger rages beyond the point of self-control. "Mr. Lipsky has sacrificed so much of his time to keep you safe. So has Mick, and he was almost killed. So has Hugh, and he's ruined. And all you care about is yourself! You're the most stupid, frivolous, selfish creature that ever lived!"

Catherine stares, openmouthed and gasping, as if I've turned into a monster. She bursts into tears and runs out the door. Horrified at myself, I press my hands against my head and wonder what's gotten into me. Now Catherine is out in London by herself, easy game for the Ripper.

That evening, I go to Spitalfields. The streets are abnormally quiet; people rush instead of pausing to chat; shops are closing early. A woman leaving a grocer's drops a beet from her loaded basket and doesn't stop to pick it up. It lies red on the cobblestones, like a blob of blood. Police constables rove. They must still think the Ripper is a Jew. Wondering if Barrett is among them, I pull my shawl over my head to blend with the other women. I slip through the door of the Lipskys' tenement and hurry upstairs. Dim light and a low male voice issue from the open door to their flat.

Inside, Mrs. Lipsky stands by the entrance to their bedchamber. She sees me, puts her finger to her lips, and shakes her head.

"So we're conducting our own investigation," the man's voice says. It's English with an East End accent, pompous, and familiar.

I press my back against the wall of the passage and look into the room. Mr. Lipsky sits in a chair, lit by the oil lamp on the table. Puzzlement and wariness lurk behind his customary scowl. Opposite him are three Englishmen dressed in black overcoats and bowler hats. Two of them stand behind the third — the spokesman. The chair he sits on is so close to Mr. Lipsky that their knees touch. I recognize his muttonchop whiskers. He's George Lusk, president of the Mile End Vigilance Committee.

"We've been going door to door, asking if anyone's seen or heard anything that might be a clue as to who the Ripper is," he says.

The Mile End Vigilance Committee must have decided that raising money for a reward wasn't a strong enough action to take. Now my friends and I aren't the only self-appointed detectives investigating the Whitechapel murders.

George Lusk points at Mr. Lipsky. "We've identified you as a person of interest."

And the police aren't the only danger to us. This isn't just a routine visit from the committee, and Mr. Lipsky isn't just another possible witness; he is their suspect in the murders. My heart sinks.

"What is 'person of interest'?" Confusion deepens Mr. Lipsky's scowl.

"A person of interest is someone whose name has come up during our inquiries, someone that people have reported as behaving suspiciously." George Lusk speaks slowly and patiently, but the edge of menace on his voice sharpens. "Your name came up."

"Who report me?" Mr. Lipsky demands. Horror appears on his and his wife's faces as they, too, realize that he's a suspect.

"I can't tell you. Our sources are confidential."

It must have been Commissioner Warren. He's not satisfied with attacking me through Mick and Hugh. He's after the Lipskys, and he's sent the Mile End Committee to do his dirty work. It's been three days since my clash with Warren, since I guarded my models, since I or my friends did anything to provoke him, but he's not through with us.

George Lusk leans toward Mr. Lipsky. "You've been seen leaving home in the evening and returning late at night. Where did you go? What were you doing?"

Rearing back in his seat, frightened yet defiant, Mr. Lipsky says, "Not your business."

He could tell Lusk that he was escorting a friend to and from work, but he's afraid that if he does, the whole story of my photographs, our clandestine investigation, and Commissioner Warren will come out, like knitted fabric unraveling when a single thread is pulled.

Lusk smiles thinly, both vexed and pleased by Mr. Lipsky's refusal to answer. "If you were a law-abiding citizen, you would provide an innocent explanation. But then you're not, are you?" The Lipskys' faces are pictures of guilty distress. Lusk chuckles. "You've been arrested three times — twice for drunken disorderliness, once for fighting."

I didn't know. Events are exposing other secrets besides Mick's, Hugh's, and mine.

"Here's what I think," Lusk says. "You're the Ripper."

Aghast, Mr. Lipsky stares.

"Where were you on the nights of August six, August thirty, and September seven?"

Those are the nights during which Martha Tabram, Polly Nichols, and Annie Chapman were murdered. Mrs. Lipsky cries, "He was home!"

Lusk favors her with a scornful glance. "Of course a wife would lie for her husband." He stands, grabbing Mr. Lipsky's shirt collar. "You killed those women." He's much smaller and older than Mr. Lipsky, but the presence of his two friends lends him nerve. "You're roaming about at night looking for other whores to kill." He shakes

Mr. Lipsky. "Admit it!"

Mr. Lipsky rises, seizes Lusk by the wrists, breaks his grip, and shoves him. Lusk stumbles backward, upsets his chair, and falls into his friends' arms. Mr. Lipsky roars, "Get out!"

He looks so fierce that the three men hasten to the door. George Lusk pauses. "Quite a temper you've got there, Abe. You must've given those whores a real scare before you cut their throats." Shaken yet gratified because Mr. Lipsky has added fuel to his suspicions, he jabs his finger at Mr. Lipsky. "We'll be watching you."

When Lusk and his men come out the door, I experience another fit of hot, consuming anger, and I'm tempted to push them down the stairs, but I don't because they could take their revenge, on the Lipskys as well as myself, too easily. I rush into the Lipskys' house. Mr. Lipsky is slumped in his chair like a boxer who's lost a match. Mrs. Lipsky wrings her hands. They look at me with the same expression of shock and helplessness they must have worn when their house in Russia burned down.

"This is my fault." Guilt weighs like an anvil on my heart. "I never should have let you become involved in this business. I'm sorry."

They nod a wordless acceptance of my apology. There's no reproach in their eyes, but they can't deny that if they'd not joined forces with me, Mr. Lipsky wouldn't be George Lusk's person of interest. The Lipskys, as well as Hugh and Mick, have come to grief because of me, and I must remedy the situation the only way I know how.

"It's best if I sever my ties with you." My voice wobbles. I've only known them for a few weeks, but I feel a connection to them that is stronger than the short time we've spent together would forge under ordinary circumstances.

"No, Sarah!" Mrs. Lipsky clasps my hands. "We are friends."

Her hands are warm, like the last summer day before an endless winter. Tears sting my eyes. I've come to love the Lipskys for their kindness and generosity, and I thought that after my parents died, I would never love anyone again. This is what loving means — losing. I'll miss the Lipskys, and Mick and Hugh and Catherine. I see what Warren is doing. He's not only isolated me because I can't stand against him on my own; he's inflicting pain on me by attacking my friends. I wonder if, in Africa, part of his thrill was watching the black women suffer when they saw their friends hurt and killed.

Mr. Lipsky staggers to his feet. "You find Catherine? I go, take her to theater."

"Yes, I did, but you can't guard her anymore," I say at the same time Mrs. Lipsky cries, "Abraham, those men, they will get you!"

"I not hide from them! I not let Ripper kill Catherine!"

"Catherine won't have a chaperone," I say. "That's why I came — to tell you. She thinks she's safe because there's been a murder in the north and people are saying the Ripper has left London."

Mrs. Lipsky murmurs in distress. Mr. Lipsky clenches his fists, pants, and turns around in the room, like a bear in too small a pen. "I not criminal! I not coward!"

He and his wife begin arguing in Russian. He punches the wall and roars with pain and frustration. I notice spider-shaped cracks in the plaster; this isn't the first time he's punched it. Mrs. Lipsky says, "This is like Russia. When pogroms start, Abraham and his friends fight back. They throw rocks at police who come to chase Jews out of Moscow. They beat up men who break windows and loot shops." She sighs, sad yet proud. "It is same here — he was arrested for fighting English men who attack Jews.

He will not let this committee push him down."

So the Lipskys have been helping me not just because they like me or they owe me a favor. Mr. Lipsky is a man who pits himself against injustice, and his wife stands by him. Even though I admire their courage, my battle with Commissioner Warren isn't theirs to lose.

"Russian police, they want to get rid of troublemakers. That is why they set our house on fire. Abraham and I escape with Yulia." Tears fill Mrs. Lipsky's eyes. "Other two children —" She chokes on sobs.

Yulia isn't the only child they lost, and the others were murdered. This is a tragic story I didn't know about them. Mr. Lipsky starts crying. That he blames himself for his children's deaths is heartbreakingly plain to see. His grief and guilt are magnitudes worse than I deserve to feel on account of Mick or Hugh, than I ever should have felt for my father. Mr. Lipsky grabs a wine bottle, uncorks it, and gulps the liquor.

"When he thinks about Russia, he drinks." Mrs. Lipsky's expression turns grave with fear. "You should go, Sarah."

23

Early the next morning, I ride in an omnibus through pouring rain to see Hugh. I must find out how he is, and truth be told, I need advice. The threat of Commissioner Warren's wrath doesn't excuse me from the responsibility of protecting my models. My knowledge that he's the Ripper comes with the obligation to deliver him to justice, but I don't know what my next step should be. I miss Hugh; he's the only person I can talk to, and I hope my visit won't make things worse for him in any way.

When I arrive at his family's townhouse, the reporters are gone; the house is silent, the white marble steps streaked with rain, and the flowers in the urns flattened. Hiding under my umbrella, I walk down the alley behind the houses and knock on the back door. A maid in a white apron and cap and black uniform answers. She's some fifty years old, with a hard, plain face.

"I want to see Lord Hugh."

"He don't live here anymore." She starts to shut the door.

I hold it open and say, "I'm a friend of his. Please, I have to find out if he's all right."

She scrutinizes me. "Was it you that brought him home?"

"Yes."

Her face softens. "I'm obliged to you, then. Poor Master Hugh. It's terrible what happened." Glancing over her shoulder, she whispers, "Number seventy-six Argyle Square, Bloomsbury. Tell him Margaret sends her love."

Argyle Square is not in the fashionable part of Bloomsbury that contains beautiful Georgian mansions and the British Museum. Argyle Square is hard by St. Pancras Station, outside of which I alight from the omnibus amid the rumble of trains and clouds of cinder-laden smoke. I proceed on foot, through mud puddles that soak my shoes, reluctant to waste the pennies that the crossing-sweepers charge to walk on boards they've spread across the streets. Outside hotels on Euston Road loiter prostitutes dressed in vulgar finery, but Argyle Square itself retains a vestige of respectability. Terraced brick houses rise four stories high. The white paint on the trim around their windows and arched doors and the black paint on their iron fences isn't peeling, but the central garden of leafless plane trees, empty paths, and bare flower beds is as cheerful as a graveyard, and I can imagine what a comedown Argyle Square must seem to Hugh.

As I open the gate of number seventy-six, my umbrella blows inside out. I ring the doorbell while the rain drenches me. The man who opens the door is the gray-haired, serious fellow I saw at the Staunton townhouse.

"Yes?" he says cautiously. He doesn't recognize me.

"My name is Sarah Bain. May I see Lord Hugh?"

His manner becomes hostile. "Are you from a newspaper?"

Hugh's voice calls from inside the house, "It's all right, Fitzmorris." He sounds tired, apathetic. "Let her in."

In the cramped vestibule, Fitzmorris takes my wet coat and umbrella. He escorts me to the narrow parlor, where Hugh is reclining on a chaise lounge by the fire. Hugh wears a blue wool robe over striped pajamas, and a blanket covers his legs. His blond hair is lank and uncombed; the bruises on his face are the greenish color of moldy bread.

"Sarah." A listless version of his smile quickly vanishes. "Thank you for coming. Please sit down."

Even in his sorry state, he hasn't lost his manners. My heart aches for him. I perch on a green brocade chair whose upholstery has greasy stains on the arms. The yellow silk chaise lounge where Hugh lies is threadbare; the red Turkey carpet has worn patches; and the gold silk curtains are faded. The house is furnished with castoffs.

"I've been worried about you," I say. "Are you in much pain?"

"It's getting better. The doctor says I haven't any broken bones or internal ruptures. And the bruises are fading. Pretty soon I'll look like my usual self."

But nothing else will be the same for him. "Hugh, I'm sorry. It was wrong of me to put you in danger."

Hugh shrugs off my apology. "Don't blame yourself, Sarah. I don't blame you. It was my decision to join in the investigation, just as it was my decision to live the kind of life that put me in the Thousand Crowns Club that night." He broods in glum silence.

I would feel better if he did blame me for

his troubles rather than himself and his own nature.

"I never thanked you for taking care of me," Hugh says. "So I thank you now."

He and the Lipskys are far too generous. Ashamed, I nod wordlessly.

"By the way, how did you find me?" Hugh asks.

"I went to your family's house. Margaret sends her love."

A brief, sad smile crosses Hugh's face. "I'm glad there's somebody over there whose affection I haven't lost. Did she also tell you that my parents banished me to this house and decamped to their country estate to get away from the reporters and the gossip?"

"Oh, no." My heart sinks deeper.

During the awkward silence, Fitzmorris brings in a silver tray laden with bowls and spoons, a tureen of beef tea, and ramekins of rice pudding — an invalid's meal. He sets the tray on the table by Hugh.

"Fitzmorris is my valet and my companion in exile," Hugh says to me, then addresses Fitzmorris. "There's no need for you to share my disgrace. I fired you yesterday."

"You can't get rid of me that easily, my lord."

Hugh waves away the tray. "I don't want any."

"My lord, you must restore your strength."

"I can't eat. You have some, Sarah."

"I will only if you will." I've no appetite, but I let Fitzmorris serve me.

With great effort, Hugh sits up. We sip the beef tea, a hearty broth flavored with meat, butter, salt, and onions. We nibble the sweet, rich rice pudding. When Fitzmorris leaves, Hugh stops eating and so do I.

"My parents are in the process of disowning me," Hugh says. "My father told me that I can stay here, and he'll support me while I find a way to earn my own living. He's given me a year. When it's up, he'll cut me loose. In the meantime, I'm not to show my face in society."

Indignation fills me. "That's terrible!"

"It's better than it could be. My father wanted to send me to America, but my mother wouldn't let him. I'm lucky I wasn't put on trial and convicted. I wouldn't last through two years of hard labor in prison. But enough of that. What's been happening in the world?" Hugh sounds more eager to change the subject than to hear news.

"Not much." I can't tell him about Catherine or the Lipskys and the Mile End Vigilance Committee. I mustn't burden him when he has so many problems of his own. "Hugh, is there anything I can do for you?"

His smile is genuine but brief. "Sarah, it's enough to know you're still my friend." He pulls the blanket up to his chin. "I'm tired. Do you mind if I rest?"

I sit with him as his eyes close and he twitches in an uneasy sleep. Leaving the house, I blink away tears. I've come to love Hugh, and I fear he won't recover. He is the friend I feel closest to, but I must sever my ties with him no matter what he says. I shouldn't feel sorry for myself, but my own future looks as bleak as Argyle Square in the rain.

Our circle is broken. I didn't want to admit it when first Mick, then Hugh, then the Lipskys were attacked, but I must admit it now. If I'm to save Catherine and my other models and expose Commissioner Warren as the Whitechapel Ripper, I must do it entirely on my own.

24

Disguised in a man's cheap overcoat, trousers, and hat, I loiter outside a tenement on Flower and Dean Street. The door disgorges women, their shabby skirts puffed out with petticoats and their bonnets decorated with tatty cloth flowers. Their reflections gleam in the puddles left by the rain that drips though the fog.

It's Saturday, 29 September, and this is the fourth night I've singlehandedly guarded my models. My logic is becoming less solid as fatigue wears me down. I'm no longer sure that my presence as a witness would deter the Ripper from killing again, and the idea that I could defend Kate, Liz, or Mary Jane if he attacked them seems ludicrous. Catching Commissioner Warren in the act would prove beyond doubt that he is the Ripper, but would the police accept my testimony as proof? Will my efforts only call Warren's attention to the fact that I'm defying him and provoke more attacks on my friends? But I'm carrying on, like a traveler walking in a deep rut in a road surrounded by impassable jungle toward an unknown destination.

The women glance suspiciously at me, as if they wonder whether *I* am the Ripper. Liz Stride comes out of the house. The red silk rose pinned to her black jacket is like a splash of blood. Tonight she also wears a black-and-white checked scarf. She doesn't notice me following her to St. Botolph's church, where she joins the other prostitutes on parade. Men emerge from the fog, like wolves scouting a cattle herd. I don't see Commissioner Warren; I don't expect him to show himself in public. He corners his victims on deserted streets when they're alone.

What am I doing here? What can I hope to accomplish? The answers elude me, but even aimless action seems better than none.

Someone plucks at my sleeve. Startled, I turn and see Mary Jane Kelly.

"Hello there," she says, smiling her saucy smile. Her long, wavy brown hair, crowned by her straw bonnet, is jeweled with droplets of mist. Her coat is unbuttoned to show off the ample white cleavage above her green velvet bodice. "Are ye lookin' for a little fun?"

I avert my face, for if she recognizes me, she'll blurt my name and cause a scene, and if Warren is near, he'll learn that I'm defying his orders — if he doesn't already know.

I mutter in a deep-pitched voice, "No, thanks," and walk away.

"Come on, don't be shy!" Mary Jane hurries after me. I hear the desperation beneath her wheedling tone. A customer means a warm bed rather than a long, cold night outdoors. "I'll make you feel like a man!"

I think of her sad life that she revealed to me while I photographed her. Married at sixteen, her husband killed in a mine explosion before she was twenty-one, she came to London and worked in a West End brothel. A client took her to France, but soon they parted company, and she returned to England. She's had a series of unlucky affairs, and in between them, she resorts to prostitution. I feel sorry for her; we are both alone tonight. Should I reveal who I am and warn her again that her life is in danger? I could tell her and my other models that I know who the Ripper is and what he looks like, so they can beware of him, but it wouldn't keep them off the streets and out of his reach. I could take Mary Jane home with me, even though my landlord has been watching me like a hawk. But I guarded her yesterday. It's Liz's turn tonight.

I walk faster. Mary Jane yells after me, "I bet you're a wanker! Like to look, but can't get it up with a woman when push comes to shove!"

People laugh and jeer. I watch Liz, some ten feet ahead of me. She thrusts her face at the men, grins widely to show her toothless upper gums, and yells, "I can give your plugtail a good suck!"

A man exclaims in disgust. "You look like me old granny!"

Hooting and laughter echoes. Couples drift away; there goes Mary Jane. The diminished parade winds round the church. A preacher carrying a wooden cross recites Bible verses and shouts at the women, "You'll burn in hell for your sins!"

"Shut up, you damn fool!" It's Kate Eddowes, walking toward me. In the dim light, the pits and lines on her face don't show. With her curly auburn hair and small, slim figure, she looks quite pretty. A man accosts her, and they flit off together.

Liz is also leaving the parade, alone. I follow her to the Britannia Public House and wait outside while she goes from table to table, asking men to buy her a drink, until the proprietor throws her out. The scene repeats at five other pubs. Ejected from the last, Liz looks desperate. It's almost midnight, and she hasn't earned money for lodging. I take a deep breath, and cold mist tainted with smoke, chemical fumes, and the reek of the slaughterhouses sinks into the well of exhaustion inside me.

I can't keep up this surveillance forever. I can't abandon my models, either, but as I trail after Liz, I realize anew the futility of trying to protect them by myself. I wonder where the others are.

Are Kate and Mary Jane safe?

Are they worth trying to protect?

I can't help thinking they're not worth what happened to Hugh or Mick, or the threat to Mr. Lipsky, and I'm sorely tempted to give up. But these are the sick, selfish thoughts of a disturbed mind. I have to keep on because my hope of saving the women is all I have left, because I'm like a lame horse that will die if it lies down.

Perhaps Commissioner Warren knows what I'm doing. Perhaps he's lying low, waiting me out, and when I do give up, he will strike.

Liz turns onto Berner Street. This section of Whitechapel is inhabited by Poles and Germans. The tailor, shoemaker, and cigarette shops on the ground floors of the tenements are closed, but sometimes Liz finds a customer in the taverns. As she crosses the street at an intersection, two constables stroll between us. I duck into a doorway, my heart pounding.

They pass out of view.

My exhaustion overwhelms me.

How much longer must I play hide-and-seek with the police? My despair verges on the limits of endurance. How much I miss Hugh, Mick, Catherine, and the Lipskys! That I once had friends makes the night seem darker and colder. The ache of loneliness, temporarily eased, is more painful than ever. I'm living in the umbra, the darkest realm of existence. If I had kept to myself, none of this would have happened. Resisting the urge to collapse and weep, I hurry after Liz. The mist has swallowed her up. I run, spy her standing under a gas lamp on a corner, and halt. A man walks toward her — a darker silhouette in the dark fog.

"Hey!" Liz calls. "Want a ride up Cock Alley?"

On other nights, when I watched her pick up a man, I felt an initial panic, then relief when it wasn't Commissioner Warren. Truth be told, I didn't know what I would do if it was. Mick, Hugh, and I never discussed it. I suppose we were afraid to face the fact that we had no plan beyond guarding the women. Now the fog blurs the man's dimensions, his hat brim shades his profile, and his long coat conceals the shape of his body. Panic surges.

When he joins Liz in the pool of light, I see that he's too short to be Warren. The relief is immense.

Liz takes his arm and walks him through the wooden gates of a yard. On the gates, painted in white, are the words "A. Dutfield, Van and Cart Builder." Light from within illuminates the fog. The yard also contains the International Working Men's Educational Club, from which I hear male voices singing a jolly tune in a foreign language. I wait outside the gate, knowing that the transaction between Liz and the man will take less than ten minutes. I try not to think of PC Barrett and myself as I picture them coupling against a wall. Afterward, the two will go their separate ways. If the money is enough to pay for her lodgings, Liz — and I — will be finished for the night. I will see her safely home and not worry yet about tomorrow.

I count out seconds by the clanging beat of the machinery, lean on the gate, and doze. I snap awake to realize that more than ten minutes have passed, and Liz and her customer haven't come out of the yard. They must have left by a different exit, and Liz is walking home alone. I hurry in through the gates, to a narrow courtyard. The fog luminesces glaringly in the light from the windows of the International Club. There's no sign of Liz or the man. I can't hear their footsteps; the machinery and the men's singing are too loud. I turn back to the gate. Did they slip past me while I drowsed? Should I retrace Liz's route along Berner Street? As I vacillate, I see, beside the wall of the club, a dark heap lying on the cobblestones.

It's Liz, turned on her left side to face the wall, her legs drawn up inside her skirts, the black-and-white checked scarf around her neck.

I gasp. I hurry to her, crouch, and touch her shoulder. She doesn't move. Now I see the long gash in her throat and the blood that trickles from it down a gutter. The blood is as red as the rose pinned to her lapel. Her mouth is open; blood pools between her upper gums and her jagged bottom teeth. Her lifeless eyes glisten dully. I reach out my trembling hand and feel her cheek; it's still warm. I don't see any mutilation on her body — I must have interrupted the killer; he heard me coming and ran away. A high-pitched ringing in my ears drowns out the sound of the machines and the men's song. My mind flounders in bewilderment.

Liz must have been killed by her customer. She was out of my sight too briefly for him to finish with her and for someone else to find her and cut her throat. But the man wasn't Commissioner Warren! How can this have happened?

A racket of wheels and trotting hooves interrupts my frantic thoughts. A barrow drawn by a pony rolls through the gate and stops in the yard. I mustn't be caught here. Before the driver spies me, I sneak around his barrow, crouching while I move toward the gates. He jumps off the barrow; his boots thud on the cobblestones. As I flee the yard, he screams.

He's found Liz.

While I pause in the foggy darkness of Berner Street, the singing abruptly stops. Then comes a stampede of footsteps. Men's voices exclaim in foreign languages. Someone shouts in heavily accented English, "Murder! Police!"

Dizziness spirals through me. The ground under me tilts; my knees buckle. I grasp the cold, damp, rough brick wall of a building for support as I face the truth I am desperate to deny. Commissioner Warren isn't the Ripper. The Ripper is the man I saw with Liz. He cut her throat and dissolved into the fog like a ghost.

But how could I have been wrong about Warren? He killed the black women in Africa; he has Annie Chapman's rings. And if he isn't the Ripper, then why is he so determined to crush me? Why send his flunkies to drown Mick, ruin Hugh, and threaten the Lipskys? Why else except to silence us?

I still believe to the fiber of my soul that Warren is the Ripper, but Liz's murder proves that I am wrong. My mistake cost Liz her life. I left her alone with that man because I thought he was harmless.

Whistles shrill in the distance. The police are coming.

25

I run up Berner Street, then west on Commercial Road toward my studio. The police whistles shrill louder. They echo off buildings; they sound as if they're coming straight at me. I veer in the opposite direction, chased by the whistles, their sound piercing and menacing. The men at the club must have seen me run from the murder scene and sent the police after me. They must think that I am the killer!

My heart pumps hard; the night pulsates with each beat. I hear footsteps in pursuit. Did the killer see me watching Liz? Does he think I saw him murder her? I imagine a dark-hatted, dark-coated figure chasing me, brandishing a knife whose blade is red with Liz's blood. My lungs are ready to burst. The whistles shrill from every direction. Shouts answer them as police from all over the East End converge on Whitechapel. I feel as if a giant camera is aimed down at me, my image focused in the viewfinder. I run here and there, in widening circles, for what seems like hours. Desperate for refuge, I rush toward Mitre Square, which is usually deserted at night. I race down Church Passage, a narrow alley dimly lit by a lantern at the entrance. The whistles fade into silence.

Nobody is after me. I'm alone.

The instant before I burst into the square, I realize that the Ripper has no magical powers that enable him to escape the scene of a crime. I just did it, and I wasn't even trying to be quiet. The darkness, the fog, the distortion of sounds, and the police's ineptitude gave the Ripper the same advantage.

The small cobblestoned square, surrounded by warehouses, is teeming with police and bright with the light from their lanterns. Some faulty instinct has drawn me straight into their midst. My steps falter. Panting from exertion and fear, I move toward them, again compelled by curiosity. Why are they here and not in Dutfield's Yard investigating Liz's murder?

An ambulance wagon is parked on the other side of the square. The surgeon is carrying his medical bag toward the policemen grouped in the corner, and they part to let him through. Stealing up behind him, I see red rivulets between the paving stones, then a puddle of blood from which extend two feet shod in worn black lace-up boots, attached to spread legs covered in brown ribbed stockings up to thin, white, bare thighs. The woman's skirts are pushed above her waist, her arms spread. Her jacket, bodice, and white chemise are slashed down the front. A deep cut on her naked torso zigzags up her middle from the dark tangle of pubic hair to the withered sacks of her breasts. Blood and viscera have spilled from the wound. Loops of intestine, like twisted pink and gray rope, lie against her right shoulder. One of the policemen vomits, but finding Liz Stride with her throat cut has numbed my physical reactions. I can look and not be sick.

This woman's throat is cut, too. There's a red wound where her nose should be, and deep cuts carve her cheeks and eyelids. Her face is mutilated beyond recognition, but her black, fur-trimmed jacket, her dark-green chintz skirt patterned in daisies and lilies, and the auburn curls framed by her black bonnet are familiar. She's Kate Eddowes.

The surgeon crouches to examine the body. I retreat, stricken by disbelief as much as horror. I just saw Kate at the Prostitutes' Church, alive and well!

"This looks like the work of the Ripper," the surgeon says. "When was she found?"

"At about one forty-five am," someone answers.

"It's two fifteen now. I estimate she's been dead for half an hour."

The Ripper murdered Liz only moments before then! Mitre Square is nearly a mile from Dutfield's Yard. How did he leave it, hunt down Kate, kill her, and mutilate her during that short period? Maybe he really is a ghost who can vanish from one spot without a trace and appear immediately in another. I didn't believe it, but everything I thought I knew is wrong.

A heavy hand claps my shoulder. My heart jumps as I gasp. I whirl, expecting to confront the black, faceless shape of Liz's murderer. I'm not relieved to see Inspector Reid.

"Excuse me, sir, I have to ask you to leave," Reid says, fooled by my male costume. Then he recognizes me. His cold eyes glint with surprise. "Well, look who's turned up like a bad penny." A grin bares his pointed teeth under his mustache as he looks down his long, sharp nose at me. "Sarah Bain, what are you doing here?"

Words fail me; I stammer.

Reid's gaze rakes my costume. "Why are you dressed like that?"

In my alarm and confusion, I can't think of a plausible lie. Reid says, "Never mind. Explain how you happened to turn up at the scene of the Ripper's fourth murder."

Fifth murder, I think wildly. He doesn't yet know about Liz, and if I tell him, he'll ask more questions I don't want to answer. "I — I couldn't sleep. So I went for a walk."

"At two o'clock in the morning?" Reid says, incredulous. "With a killer on the loose?" He grabs my shoulders. "What were you *really* doing?"

"Nothing! Let me go!" I glance behind Reid and see PC Barrett watching us, his expression troubled.

Reid shakes me so hard that my hat falls off and my hair tumbles loose. "Tell me what you know about these murders."

Barrett says, "Guv," and steps forward as if to restrain Reid.

Whistles blare again nearby. A young police constable runs panting into the square, the tin whistle bouncing on its chain around his neck. "There's been a murder in Berner Street. It's the Ripper again!" Then he sees Kate's body. His eyes goggle; he exclaims, "*Another* one?"

328

Reid and Barrett look astonished to hear that the Ripper has killed twice on this one night. I hope they'll be distracted and I can escape, but Reid tightens his grasp on me as he orders two constables to assist at the other crime scene. Then he turns back to me, and his face shows surprise because he sees none on mine.

"How did you know about the other murder?"

So much has happened tonight; my mind is frazzled; I can't think of anything to say. A new, even more hostile suspicion creeps into Reid's eyes. "Are you protecting the Ripper? Is that why you won't talk?"

I'm so stunned, I only gape. So does Barrett. Reid isn't entirely wrong — I am, in a fashion, protecting Commissioner Warren by keeping his secrets. I think of Kate's secrets that she refused to share with me. Did Kate know who the Ripper is? Did she recognize him before he killed her? If only she'd told me what she knew!

The night erupts with loud whoops and howls, as if from a pack of savages doing battle. George Lusk bursts into the square, shouting, "We got him! We caught the Ripper!"

Reid, Barrett, and I turn to stare at the mob of men following Lusk. It's the Mile

End Vigilance Committee. Two of them are dragging a big man by his legs; another two hold his arms. Disheveled and breathless, their faces smeared red with blood from split lips and swollen noses, like war paint, they whoop in triumphant exultation. The man kicks and struggles. Blood stains the gray apron he wears over his dark clothing. His face is so battered that I can't discern his features, but I recognize his black whiskers and the voice with which he howls.

"Mr. Lipsky!"

I pull away from Reid and run toward Mr. Lipsky, but Barrett blocks my path. Reid says, "So you know this man." He asks George Lusk, "What are you doing here? What happened?"

"We were patrolling. We met a watchman who said there'd just been a murder in Mitre Square. So we rushed over." Lusk is smug and preening, happy to be the center of attention. "We saw him running away." He points to Mr. Lipsky.

Mr. Lipsky howls, his voice hoarse. He fights his captors as they wrestle him to the ground, his eyes glazed with panic like a trapped animal's. This is another bewilderment in a night filled with bewilderments. What was Mr. Lipsky doing on the streets at this hour? For an awful moment, I wonder if he really is guilty, but I know in my heart he can't be.

"He's not the Ripper!" I cry.

"Yes, he is." Lusk's small eyes narrow at me. He's wondering who I am and how I dare contradict him. "Look at the blood on his apron."

"It's from animals. He's a butcher!"

"He fits the description of the man that the witnesses saw after the second murder," Lusk says. "A big Jew with a black beard. And we've had our eyes on him — he's a person of interest. Now we've caught him dead to rights."

"You took the law into your own hands?" Inspector Reid frowns at Lusk.

"Yes, and a good thing. We caught the Ripper while your lads had their heads up their behinds." Lusk holds up his hand to forestall Reid's angry protest and says to his own men, "Show the inspector the murder weapon."

A committee man with a bruised face holds up a long knife with a discolored wooden handle and a long, gleaming steel blade. "He was carrying it."

"There's no blood on it," I point out.

"So he wiped it off," Lusk says.

Reid seems convinced, albeit furious, that the vigilantes have caught the Ripper after the police failed. He turns on me. "So it's him you've been protecting! Your Jew friend."

"He's innocent!" I cry in desperation.

"You knew he's the Ripper." Reid seizes me by the lapels of my coat and shouts into my face, "Instead of turning him in, you let him kill two more women."

This is more horrifying than any nightmare — good, kind, brave Mr. Lipsky caught in the snare of the law, blamed for the murders. My habitual reticence won't help him. Only by breaking the habit can I save Mr. Lipsky.

"I know he's not the Ripper because I know who is." My voice wobbles with lack of conviction because everything has changed. Commissioner Warren didn't kill Liz Stride, and I don't know who did. But my evidence against him is the only ammunition I have, and I don't care that he must have obtained Annie Chapman's rings by some other means than wrenching them off her fingers after murdering her. If I have to choose someone to be wrongfully blamed for the murders, I will choose Warren over Mr. Lipsky.

"I've had enough of your lies!" Reid says.

"He is the Ripper," George Lusk insists vehemently.

Mustering my courage, reckless for the sake of friendship, I say, "The Ripper is —"

"If you don't believe me, ask him!" George Lusk points to a man who stands in the shadowy main entrance to the square.

Commissioner Warren steps forward. He's in a jacket, trousers, and a bowler hat, not his uniform. His eyes shine brilliantly, as if they've caught and reflected all the light from the constables' lanterns. His flushed face glistens with perspiration; his chest heaves as if he's been running. My lungs cave in. The vacuum in my chest strangles my voice. My mouth opens wide in a futile attempt to breathe. Shocked to see Warren, I'm also terrified because if I accuse him, I'll have to do it to his face.

"He was there with us," George Lusk says. "He was the first to see the Jew running away. He told us to go after him and helped us corner him."

Fresh shock is a thunderbolt to the heart as my understanding of the crimes changes yet again. Commissioner Warren was near Mitre Square moments after Kate was murdered. He couldn't have been in Berner Street at the same time. Although he didn't kill Liz, he could have killed Kate.

His mouth twitches under his mustache, as if with his effort to control his emotions.

If he let them loose, he would look as he did in the African photograph — exuberant, wild. I'm certain that he wasn't arriving at the scene when he met the Mile End Vigilance Committee. *He was leaving it.* Two murders at far-apart locations within minutes of each other suddenly make astounding sense.

The Ripper isn't a single individual. He's two men.

The scene goes dark for a moment, then turns surreally brighter. I feel as if I've been looking at a photograph and not realizing that it was cropped. Now I see the other half, the whole picture.

Warren is one Ripper. The man I saw with Liz is the other.

My heartbeat is a thunderous banging sensation within me. My discovery thrashes every preconceived notion from my mind. My false assumptions are blasted to shards, and a whole new dreadful world rises from the wreckage.

"Mr. Lusk is correct," Warren says. "I deputized the Mile End Vigilance Committee." His exuberance, born of bloodlust satisfied, vibrates through his authoritative tone. "They were acting on my orders."

He's speaking to Inspector Reid, but I sense his attention on me. Even as I imagine myself in the crosshairs of his rifle, I perceive that the fear isn't one-sided. Has he intuited that I was about to accuse him of being the Ripper? I don't know whether Warren or the man who killed Liz is responsible for Martha Tabram's and Polly Nichols's murders, but I know that Warren's fear only makes him more dangerous to me. When a rabid squirrel is pitted against a man with a gun, it's still just a squirrel.

If I announce that there are two Rippers and Warren is one, what are the chances that these men will believe it? Warren has already ruined Hugh, almost killed Mick, and framed Mr. Lipsky; he's not going to spare me. But I've no other way to fight him. I gather my breath and my courage.

Mr. Lipsky babbles in Russian, writhes under the committee men holding him down, and shouts, "Him! He is Ripper!" He tears his hand free and points to Warren.

I'm instinctively horrified that Mr. Lipsky has beaten me to the punch. I look at Warren. The skin of his face goes taut. I'm reminded of a dog laying its ears back when threatened. The other men don't notice, for they're all looking askance at Mr. Lipsky. George Lusk stomps on Mr. Lipsky's wrist. As Mr. Lipsky howls, the constables burst out laughing.

"Jew-boy's fingering the guv to save his own dirty neck!" someone jeers.

Commissioner Warren's face relaxes into an odd, satisfied smile. Inspector Reid and George Lusk are laughing with their men. The laughter has a shrill, jagged, insane quality. The murders have put them under so much pressure, and this is catharsis. Reid laughs so hard that he lets go of me. These men don't see Warren for himself. He's like the sun during an eclipse, and they're looking at the bright rim that blinds them to the vast darkness alongside it. The only one not laughing is Barrett.

"It's true!" I cry, furious because they think Mr. Lipsky is lying. "Commissioner Warren is the Ripper!"

The laughter fades into hostility directed at me. Reid regards me with contempt. "And you would swear you were the Queen of England to defend your Jew friend."

How I wish I'd spoken up before Mr. Lipsky did! I had little chance of having my accusation taken seriously, but a Jewish person of interest, wearing a bloodstained apron and caught near the murder scene, has no credibility at all.

There's no blood on Warren's hands or clothes. He must have been wearing gloves and a coat when he killed Kate and dumped them afterward.

Desperate, I appeal to Barrett. "You know he's the Ripper. Tell them."

As the other men's gazes swivel toward him, Barrett looks aghast that I've put him on the spot. He shrugs. "I don't know what she's talking about."

I've never hated anyone so much. I also hate myself for thinking he cared about me, for letting him take liberties with me, for hoping he would take my side. I don't care that it must be as unthinkable for Barrett to side against his brother police as it would be for me to betray my friends. My anger rears its flaming head again, this time at Barrett. For the first time, I experience the violent impulse that drives humans to commit murder. If I had a knife, I could gladly stab Barrett through the heart.

Commissioner Warren jerks his chin at Mr. Lipsky and says to the constables, "Take him to Newgate."

The constables descend on Mr. Lipsky. George Lusk says, "You're welcome."

Mr. Lipsky roars, struggles, and curses as the constables handcuff him, shackle his ankles, and carry him away. Emboldened by my fury, I run after them, shout, "No!" and try to tear their hands off him. A constable swats me hard across the chest. I reel backward.

"Go home, Miss Bain," Commissioner Warren says, his voice replete with cruel mirth, "for your own good."

He's telling me that he's letting me go so he can enjoy tormenting me further, but if I try to stop the wheels of justice from turning, he will eventually kill me.

Mr. Lipsky cries, "Run, Sarah!" His next words, as he's carried out of Mitre Square, are in Russian, but I understand their gist: *I'm done for. Save yourself!*

26

At four o'clock in the morning, Spitalfields is already wakening to life. Men are driving cattle and sheep along Aldgate High Street toward the slaughterhouses as I make my way to the Lipskys' tenement. My heart heavy, I climb the stairs to their flat. Never have I had such bad news to break.

Their open door has a huge, splintered hole in its center. Mrs. Lipsky kneels on the floor amid overturned chairs, broken dishware, and the dented copper tea urn. Tears run down her cheeks.

Horrified, I rush in. "Who did this?"

"The police." Mrs. Lipsky's small, plump body is trembling.

I stare in bewilderment. The police already have Mr. Lipsky, so why ransack his house?

Mrs. Lipsky sobs. "They take Abraham's clothes, and all the knives."

I surmise that his presence near the scene of Kate's murder isn't enough to convict

Mr. Lipsky in a court of law. The police wanted his knives and his clothes — which may have animal blood on them — for evidence at his trial.

"Abraham did not come home last night." Mrs. Lipsky asks, "Sarah, what is happening?"

I dredge up the explanation from a mire of guilt. Mrs. Lipsky reacts with violent protests in English and Russian. I say, "I'm sorry," and wait wretchedly until she subsides. "Why was he out on the streets last night?"

"The fool!" Mrs. Lipsky seems as angry with her husband as worried about him. "I told him not to go, but he would not listen!"

"Go where?"

"To Stepney. He spies on Commissioner Warren's house. Every night."

I am stunned, although it shouldn't come as a surprise that Mr. Lipsky wasn't any more willing to bow to the Mile End Vigilance Committee than to the Russian authorities during the pogroms. "He wanted to exonerate himself by proving that Warren is the Ripper. He decided to catch Warren in the act of murder."

"Yes!" Mrs. Lipsky groans in frustration.

Last night, he must have followed Warren from the Stepney house to Whitechapel.

When Warren stalked Kate to Mitre Square and killed her, Mr. Lipsky must have seen. I'm ashamed of thinking, even for a moment, that Mr. Lipsky was the killer.

"Suppose he did catch Warren. What did he mean to do then?"

"I don't know. I don't think he did, either."

The ability to think beyond the immediate next step hasn't been a strong point of our group. We hardly believed our schemes would work, so why plan for their consequences? And now our plan to expose the Ripper, and save my models, has gone hellishly wrong.

Mrs. Lipsky and I start cleaning up the mess because we don't know what else to do. When we're finished, Mrs. Lipsky makes tea in the dented urn. I find two intact cups. We sit in despair, drink, and listen to the cattle bellowing at the slaughterhouses while daylight turns the window from black to gray.

Footsteps come pounding up the stairs. Catherine rushes breathlessly into the room. She's wearing a fur stole over a pink tulle frock; her face is vivid with stage makeup. "Mrs. Lipsky! Sarah!" Mick follows close on her heels.

I'm astonished to see them. "Mick, why aren't you still in the hospital?" He's dressed in whole, clean clothes that are too big for him, probably supplied by a charity. His hair is neatly trimmed under a new tweed cap, and his new shoes shine.

"I heard Mr. Lipsky was arrested," he says, gazing adoringly at Catherine.

"So did I," Catherine says.

"I couldn't just lie in bed. I'm fit as a fiddle, anyway." Mick flexes his shoulder.

Catherine hugs Mrs. Lipsky. "I'm so sorry."

Mrs. Lipsky smiles through tears. I feel like crying myself, so grateful am I for the solace of our young friends, so glad I haven't lost them. "Catherine," I say, "I'm sorry I lashed out at you. Will you please forgive me?"

"Of course!" She hugs me. "You were right — I've been stupid and selfish. But I'll try to be better from now on."

Her generous spirit brings my tears close to the surface. So does my new understanding that not all lost friendships are lost forever. The broken circle is coming together again.

Mrs. Lipsky serves Mick and Catherine tea, and I tell them what happened.

Something occurs to me that should have earlier. "The other Ripper isn't the Duke of

Exford. The man I saw with Liz was too small."

"It ain't Mr. Lipsky, either," Mick says. "We gotta get him out of the blockhouse."

Catherine nods in vigorous agreement. For once they're united, by their loyalty to Mr. Lipsky. If it were just myself and Mary Jane Kelly in peril, I would forbid Mick and Catherine to pit themselves against Commissioner Warren, but because it's Mr. Lipsky, I must accept whatever help they can give.

After Mrs. Lipsky packs a basket of food for her husband, she, Catherine, Mick, and I walk to Whitechapel Road. Noisy crowds clog the approaches to Dutfield's Yard and Mitre Square, which are cordoned off by police. Folks who've heard about the double murders are eager to view the scenes.

"Jack the Ripper kills again, twice on the same night!" newsboys shout.

So now the murderer, who is actually two people, has a nickname.

Handbills lie scattered underfoot, and I pick one up. Catherine hails a cab. As we sit in it and the driver yells at the crowds blocking our way, I read the handbill aloud:

POLICE NOTICE

On the mornings of Friday, 31st August, Saturday 8th, and Sunday, 30th September 1888, women were murdered in or near Whitechapel. Should you know of any person to whom suspicion is attached, you are earnestly requested to communicate at once with the nearest Police Station.

Metropolitan Police Office

"Why're they askin' for information when they've got Mr. Lipsky?" Mick asks.

"It does seem strange." But the news is a partial silver lining in a very dark cloud. "At least we still have a chance to save Mr. Lipsky."

We disembark outside Newgate Prison. The sight of the vast, gloomy dungeon brings back memories of Commissioner Warren grilling me. The guards inform us that "the Ripper" isn't allowed any visitors. They won't let Mrs. Lipsky leave the food for her husband. As we walk away, Catherine says, "We need Hugh."

"Yeah!" Mick brightens, and Mrs. Lipsky looks hopeful.

I know what they're thinking: Hugh was a mainstay of our circle, and he's a wealthy nobleman with influence. But I say, "We can't expect Hugh to help. Not after what happened to him."

Catherine looks grieved by the memory. Mick says, "What happened?" I didn't want to upset Mick with the news when he was in the hospital, and I was afraid of what Mrs. Lipsky would think of Hugh, but now his secret is public knowledge.

After I explain, Mrs. Lipsky murmurs, "Poor Hugh."

Mick says, "We can't let Warren get away with this! Hugh ought to be glad to pay him back!" After everything they've been through together, his attitude toward Hugh has completely reversed, and Hugh is his comrade in arms.

"Maybe Hugh is well enough now," Catherine says. "Let's go see."

We travel to Argyle Square via the underground railway, in a crowded, noisy train filled with smoke and steam. We emerge at St. Pancras Station and blink in the morning light. Everything here seems normal, untouched by last night's events. At Hugh's house, I ring the doorbell, and when Fitzmorris lets us into the vestibule, I introduce my friends. He's clearly surprised to see us — and me in male costume. His face is haggard with distress. When I ask what's wrong, he says, "Lord Hugh tried to take his own life."

We're speechless with shock. Mick looks confused, frightened, a child faced with the incomprehensible. Mrs. Lipsky puts her arm around him. Catherine and I blurt, "How — ?" "When — ?"

"On Friday. He didn't want me to tell anyone."

Attempting suicide is a sin that would add to his disgrace and enflame the scandal if it were made public.

"He slit his wrists in the bathtub." Tears well in Fitzmorris's eyes. "It's fortunate that I found him before he lost too much blood. The doctor was able to save him."

The image of Hugh lying unconscious in a tub while his blood colors the water red is horrific. I knew he was upset, but I never imagined he'd try to kill himself. Beautiful, clever, affectionate, blithe-spirited Hugh! How could we bear the loss of him?

"We should go upstairs," Fitzmorris says. "I don't like to leave him alone."

He's afraid Hugh might try again to commit suicide. I thought I was protecting him by staying away from him, but I should have been here to stop him. As we climb the stairs, my guilt multiplies. I shouldn't have let him undertake the hunt for Jack the Ripper.

In the bedroom, Hugh lies with his eyes closed, under a quilt. His face is alarmingly white except where the bruises have faded to pale blue; his matted blond hair seems drained of color; he looks like a marble effigy on a tomb. His arms lie atop the quilt, and his wrists are bandaged. The room is thick with the chemical smell of chlorodyne and a sweet alcoholic taint of laudanum. Fitzmorris arranges chairs around the bed. We sit; he quietly withdraws. I hold Hugh's right hand, Catherine the left. She and I and Mrs. Lipsky blink back tears. Hugh's fingers are limp in mine, cold even though the room is hot from the fire in the hearth. He slowly opens his sunken eyes, roused to reluctant consciousness. His pupils are dilated huge and black from the opium in the drugs.

"Well. This is a surprise." But Hugh's voice is hollow, as if he's incapable of any emotion except despair. An untouched breakfast tray sits amid the medicine bottles on the bedside table. The fire hisses and crackles in the ensuing silence.

Catherine speaks up. "Why did you — ?" Her voice trembles.

"It seemed better than going on."

I should have realized that losing his family and social position was too much to bear.

I feel so sorry for him. He must have brightened the lives of so many people besides me, and yet he thinks his life isn't worth living.

"Something's happened," Mick says. I can tell he's aware that now is the wrong time to spring the news on Hugh, yet he's eager to believe that if he can interest Hugh in our common concerns, everything will be normal again. He tells Hugh about the two murders and Mr. Lipsky's arrest.

Hugh listens without response.

"We thought you might be able to help us save Mr. Lipsky." Mick sounds disappointed but not willing to give up on Hugh.

Hugh sighs. "Sorry, but I'm not much use right now."

"Don't you know some important people?" Catherine asks. "Can't you tell them Mr. Lipsky is innocent and ask them to get him out of jail?"

"They don't know me anymore. I'm a leper. They won't do anything I ask."

Mick's and Catherine's faces fall. Mrs. Lipsky murmurs, "He needs to rest." She, who needs help the most, doesn't want him bothered while so ill. "We should go."

Catherine, Mick, and I don't move. Hugh's lethargy is contagious, and there's a comfort in being together even now, as if we're still more than a sum of our parts. Although I'm at wit's end, I feel obligated to raise morale as Hugh once did, to fill his role as instigator.

"There must be something we can do to save Mr. Lipsky," I say.

"Like what? Break him out of jail?" Mick utters a woeful laugh.

Hugh closes his eyes. I can't tell whether he's listening or dozing.

"Maybe you can ask PC Barrett to help," Catherine suggests.

Barrett, who left me on my own at the murder scene. "He won't go against Commissioner Warren," I say bitterly. The thought of Barrett and Warren brings on a resurgence of anger, the hot, molten steel inside me that straightens my sagging posture.

"We can't give up and let that rotter Warren win." Mick's face is flushed; he's caught fire from my anger, and a desire for revenge has rallied his spirits as well as mine. "We have to prove Mr. Lipsky is innocent."

Catherine rubs her eyes; her lashes are clotted with black makeup. In her pink dress and fur stole, she looks like a child playing dress-up and weary of it. "Yes, we have to." But when she lowers her hands, her gaze gleams as if with reflected flames. "How?"

I know what she's thinking: we've always relied on Hugh for initiative as well as morale. But my anger stimulates thought, inspiration, and grandiosity. "We find out who the other Ripper is."

"What good will that do? The other Ripper killed Liz. Mr. Lipsky was arrested for killing Kate. Even if we can find out who the other Ripper is, it won't get him out of jail."

Once again, she's voiced an unpalatable fact. But I see the situation with the clarity that extreme fatigue sometimes confers, when the usual inhibitions that limit the scope of our thoughts are dulled. My mind opens like the aperture of a camera, letting the light enter.

"The police don't know there are two Rippers." They're still looking at the picture with half of it cropped out. "We'll discover who the other is, and we'll find evidence that he killed not only Liz, but Martha or Polly." There won't be evidence that he killed Annie or Kate; Commissioner Warren was responsible for those murders. "We'll give his name and the evidence to the police." Unable to picture what evidence or how we would approach the police, I skip over those blank spaces in my plan. "They'll realize Mr. Lipsky isn't the Ripper and let him go."

"Yeah!" Mick says. Catherine and Mrs. Lipsky brighten. Hugh lies immobile in a drugged stupor.

"Are we supposed to forget about Commissioner Warren?" Mick asks.

I will never forget him. Someday, somehow, I will make him pay for everything he's done. "First things first. We save Mr. Lipsky, then we tackle Commissioner Warren."

"All right. So how do we go about catchin' Ripper Number Two?"

Our new quarry now has a nickname. My instincts zero in on the most seemingly direct path to him. "We start again at the beginning."

27

Overnight, the temperature plunged. Winter is coming on although it's only the first of October. An icy wind blows away the vapor from our breath as Mick and I walk up Dorset Street at nine o'clock this Monday morning.

"It's good to be back in the game," Mick says. "I just wish Hugh was with us."

I nod sadly. "Maybe Catherine will cheer him up."

Catherine is to spend the day with Hugh and the evening at the theater, which she'll be escorted to and from by one of Mrs. Lipsky's male Jewish neighbors. That leaves Mick and me to carry out our new plans. Mick's company buoys me up. So does taking action on a new day, and a new chance to right wrongs. The anger is like a stove keeping me warm, cooking away fatigue, fear, and hopelessness. And I'm in my element — poking the wolf, courting danger.

A crowd gathers around a street musician who plays an accordion and sings,

"Has anyone seen Jack, can you tell us
    where he is,
If you meet him you must take away his
    knife,
Then give him to the women, they'll spoil
    his pretty fiz,
And I wouldn't give him twopence for his
    life."

Jack the Ripper is now the subject of popular song.

Mick and I enter Miller's Court. The old tenements — built around a paved yard with a privy, a gas lamp, and a water pump, inhabited mostly by prostitutes — are quiet; the women who pay sixpence a night for a bed are asleep. I knock on the door of a room on the ground floor of house number thirteen. The window is broken.

Mary Jane Kelly's groggy voice calls, "Who's there?"

"Sarah Bain."

She mutters, shuffles, and opens the door. She wears a thin white nightdress under which her large breasts hang, their dark nipples visible. Her long hair is disheveled, her face puffy, and her sleep-crusted eyes

353

glare at me.

"So you were right. First Martha and Polly, then Annie, and now Liz and Kate. I 'spose you came to say, 'I told you so.' "

"No. Something more important. May we come in?"

She glances indifferently at Mick, shrugs, and stands aside. The room contains an old wooden bed; her few belongings litter a table and washstand. Above the fireplace hangs a cheap print of "The Fisherman's Widow" — a painting of a weeping young woman whose husband has drowned at sea. A coat hung over the window acts as a curtain and blocks the draft from the broken pane.

Mary Jane's belligerence subsides. "Thank ye for bein' concerned about me, but it's no use telling me to stay indoors at night. I would if I could, believe me. But unless I work, I can't afford my lodgings."

"That's about to change." I reach into my satchel, take out a small purse containing the money that Mick stole from Commissioner Warren's house, and hand it to her.

Mary Jane opens it and exclaims, "Mother of God! Where'd you get this?"

"You don't need to know." I think it's ironic that Commissioner Warren's money should be spent on keeping him and his prey apart. Mick looks sorry to see the money go, but we agreed that this is the best use of his stolen goods.

"You're giving it to me?" Mary Jane's blue eyes shine with tears. "Nobody's ever done such a nice thing for me. Thank ye, Miss Bain! Now I'll be safe!"

The sun plays hide-and-seek behind clouds and drifting smoke. The bookstores on Holywell Street look bright and colorful one moment, gray and dispirited the next. We stop at Russell's Fine Books and peek inside. Mr. Russell, seated in his wheelchair, dusts bookshelves with a long-handled feather duster. Mick and I raise our eyebrows at each other, take a deep breath, and push through the door.

Mr. Russell's eyes bulge behind their spectacles. "You again!" He drops the feather duster and grips the wheels of his chair. "I shall call the police!"

"Not so fast, old man." Mick grabs the handles on the back of the wheelchair.

Mr. Russell screams. Ordinarily, I wouldn't like scaring a cripple, but Mr. Lipsky is suffering in jail, and necessity is the mother of ruthlessness.

"Shut up," Mick says, "or I'll belt you."

"What do you want?" Mr. Russell cries.

"The names and addresses of the customers who bought the photograph albums you showed us," I say.

"I already told you, they're confidential!"

"Get the ledger," Mick says to me.

I look around the bookshop, but I don't see it.

"It's locked in the safe," Mr. Russell says, frightened yet smug.

"Give us the combination," Mick orders.

"I won't!"

"We'll make a deal, Mr. Russell. You give us the names and addresses, and I'll give you something I think you'll like." I open my satchel and remove an enlarged photograph, which I drop on the plaid blanket that covers his lap.

"What is this?"

"It's Annie Chapman. She was murdered by the Ripper. It was taken at the morgue."

Mr. Russell traces Annie's waxen face, cut throat, and gaping, empty stomach cavity with his soft fingertip. His round baby face flushes pinker, and a deep breath inflates his concave chest. He recognizes that the picture is a valuable moneymaking commodity. "How did you get it?" His voice is hushed with awe.

"None of your business." Mick taps his shoulder. "The combination to the safe?"

Mr. Russell hesitates. I swipe the photograph, hold it out of his reach. His gaze filled with longing for it, he mutters three numbers. While I hold the wheelchair so he can't escape, Mick runs to the back of the shop and soon returns with the ledger. Mr. Russell turns pages and points at three entries in a column of thready handwriting. They're dated 10 September, the day Mick and I photographed the customers. Mick tears out the page, I drop Annie's photograph in Mr. Russell's lap, and we run from the shop. The sky has clouded over, and the icy wind blasts us. We shelter in a church doorway and examine our prize.

" 'A. Palmer, St. John's Wood,' " I read aloud from the list. "That's the Duke of Exford. We already ruled him out."

" 'William Smith.' " Mick reads the address of the second customer; it's Commissioner Warren's house in Stepney.

"This is the one we want," I say, pointing to the third name. "Ida Millbanks, York Street Chambers, Marylebone."

"The woman I took a picture of? How could she be Ripper Number Two?"

"Not her." I voice the idea that I wish I'd thought of earlier. "I think she bought my photographs for the man who is."

■ ■ ■ ■

York Street Chambers is one of numerous stately mansion blocks near the Marylebone Road. The sun shines on this affluent neighborhood where London's hordes of beggars, buskers, peddlers, and the poor don't intrude. The few people about are well-dressed ladies and gentlemen; the carriages coming and going look expensively smart.

"Ida Millbanks must be one rich bitch," Mick says as we gaze up at York Street Chambers — four stories of solid red brick pierced by many shining windows, crowned by a pitched roof studded with white dormers and tall chimneys.

I can't imagine who Ida Millbanks is or what relationship she could have with a man who kills and mutilates women. As Mick and I wait, hoping she'll appear, I feel as out of place as a crumpled page of newspaper that I see blowing in the wind.

A uniformed doorman comes out of the building. "Are you looking for someone?" His manner is courteous but cold.

"Yes," I say, emboldened by my need to save Mr. Lipsky. "Ida Millbanks." After four murders, I've lost my patience for covert spying. If I can meet Ida Millbanks face-to-face, I will ask her outright who she bought the photographs for and where he is. "Is she home?"

The doorman says without words that he's duty-bound to protect her from unwelcome visitors. "You'd best move along."

"It's all right," I tell Mick as we ride in an omnibus toward Whitechapel. "We'll try Ida Millbanks again tomorrow. In the meantime, let's talk to Kate Eddowes's friend John Kelly."

"What for?"

"I think she knew something. I'm hoping she told John and he'll tell us."

"Something like who Ripper Number Two is? But he didn't kill her. Commissioner Warren did."

"They both saw her pictures," I remind Mick. "They both may have been her customers. It could be just by chance that Warren got to her first."

At Cooney's Lodging House, the tenement where Kate lived with John, my knock on the door brings forth the deputy who let me in last time. "Does John Kelly still live here?"

"He's moved out."

"Do you know where he went?"

"No." The deputy shuts the door.

Mick flexes his shoulder; it must hurt. He shouldn't have left the hospital. "I'll look around for John Kelly." He looks tired, and very young in his new clothes. "But first, I'll walk you home. You shouldn't be by yourself. Don't forget, Commissioner Warren's still out there."

And Warren isn't the only threat. Now I'm afraid that Ripper Number Two knows I took the boudoir photographs, and he's afraid I know who he is. I must identify him and report him to the police before he can come after me.

"Walk me to the omnibus," I say, grateful for Mick's concern. "I'll look in on Hugh."

28

At Hugh's house, I'm about to enter the parlor when I hear raised voices. Hugh and Catherine are quarreling. I don't want to butt in for fear that my ineptness at resolving disagreements and my new tendency to lose my temper would only make things worse. I stand in the vestibule and eavesdrop.

"Do you know what a bore you are?" Catherine asks.

"I do now. Thanks for telling me." Hugh's voice drips sarcasm.

"You won't play cards, you won't even bother to make conversation with me!"

Hugh laughs nastily. "I might bother if you had anything intelligent to say."

"Well, excuse me, Your Hoity-Toity Highness." Skirts rustle as Catherine rises from her seat. "*I'm* not the one who was stupid enough to be caught in a police raid!"

I'm appalled. This is how Catherine means

to cheer Hugh up?

"With friends like you, who needs enemies?" Hugh says bitterly.

"I'm just sick of watching you do nothing!"

"I didn't ask you to stay. If you want better company, go scare up one of your stage-door Johnnies."

"Do you know what I think?" Catherine asks.

"I didn't know you could think," Hugh retorts.

I peek through the door. Hugh, in his pajamas, is lying on the yellow chaise lounge; Catherine stands over him with her hands on her hips, her blond ringlets quivering with ire. "I think you would rather feel sorry for yourself than do something. Because you're lazy."

"Go away, Catherine." Hugh's voice is suddenly tearful. "Leave me alone."

"Leave you alone to wallow in your misery?" There's a thud as Catherine plops herself into a chair. "Hah! I'm going to nag you until you get back on your feet!"

Her intentions are good, but she's only making Hugh feel worse. I muster the courage to interrupt.

"It's no use," Hugh says in a tone replete with self-pity. "My life is over."

"*Your* life?" Scorn infuses Catherine's voice. "I know what you've been through, but Mr. Lipsky is in real trouble. *His* life will be over for real unless we save him."

"No, you don't know," Hugh shouts, furious. "Your life is all flowers and songs and pretty dresses and charming beaux. How could you possibly know what I've been through? You spoiled little bitch!"

Shock freezes me. I didn't think Hugh would go so far. Catherine is silent, as if physically struck down.

Before I can go in and try to make peace, Catherine inhales and expels a deep, audible breath. "You're right — I don't know what it's like to be beaten by the police and exposed in the newspapers. But I know what it's like to be hurt." She sounds sad, wise, not her usual self. Hugh protests, but she talks over him. "My father is a tenant farmer. I'm the third of six children. My mother died having my youngest brother. There was never enough money, never enough to eat."

Now Hugh is silenced by this story that both of us can tell won't get better.

"I went into service in the squire's house. I made the fires, and cleaned, and washed the dishes and the laundry, and carried out the slops. I worked from dawn until late at night. I was tired and hungry all the time. One night, I was building up the fire in the hearth in the library, and the squire came in. He talked to me, and said I was pretty, and he gave me some mince pie and cheese and milk."

I hear in Catherine's voice the memory of how good the food had tasted to a starved girl. I listen with a growing sense of dread.

"I thought the squire was nice. He told me to come to the library every night, and so I did. He always had food for me. While I ate, he would ask me about my family, and I liked talking to him. The third time, he gave me wine."

Catherine pauses; she's breathing fast, as if filling her lungs before diving underwater. Hugh releases a mournful sigh, as do I. We both know what happens to pretty, innocent girls who work for unscrupulous rich men.

"After drinking the wine, I fell asleep. I woke up with my clothes off and him touching me. I screamed and tried to push him away. He told me to lie still and be quiet or he would evict my family from our farm." Catherine's voice slides up and wobbles. "It hurt so much, I cried. When he was finished, he wiped the blood off me and told me to come again tomorrow."

This is why she wouldn't talk about her

past. She let me think it had been all sweetness and light and never hinted at the darkness.

"I had to come, or my family would be turned out to starve. He did it to me every night. He taught me to do things he liked."

This is also certainly why she is promiscuous: she learned the habit of being with men, and it is apparently a habit difficult to break.

"He paid me money not to tell anybody. He didn't want to get himself in trouble with the missus."

She also learned that her beauty gave her power over men, the ability to take financial advantage of them.

"A few months later, I started getting sick in the mornings. I knew what it was, I'd seen my mother, and I grew up on a farm. But I didn't know what to do." Catherine sniffles. "Then the missus noticed that my stomach was getting bigger. She knew, too. She fired me and sent me home. My father was so angry. He said it was my fault, that I must have led the squire on."

Catherine sobs as she speaks. "That same day, I lost the baby. My father said I'd disgraced our whole family. He threw me out of the house and told me never to come back."

This is why she can't go home. My own face is wet with tears, my heart filled with sorrow for Catherine. Hugh says nothing, but I can imagine his stricken expression.

I'm ready to rush into the room and comfort Catherine, but she gulps air, clears her throat, and says, "I took the money the squire gave me, and I got on the train to London. And here I am." Her voice is strong now, although hoarse with tears. "So don't tell me I don't know what trouble is."

A peek into the room shows her sitting straight in her chair, pointing at Hugh. "You're the one who's spoiled! One beating, one scandal, and you're ready to give up? Pooh!"

"Catherine." Hugh's tone is gentle, contrite, and respectful. "I had no idea. Thank you for telling me." He sounds moved to tears. "I'm sorry."

I feel the same new respect for Catherine. I'd thought her silly and naïve and never imagined her strength or wisdom. By speaking from her heart, sharing her woe, she managed to snap Hugh out of his self-absorbed misery.

Hugh chuckles.

I've enjoyed his knack for finding humor in any situation, but I'm horrified this time.

"What's funny?" Catherine demands.

"If this is a contest to see who's had it worse, then you win," Hugh says.

There's a long, ominous silence. I want to smack him.

Catherine giggles. Then they're both laughing uproariously. I sigh with relief. Catherine and Hugh laugh until they're both crying. They cry long and hard for all the pain they've suffered. After they're finished, Hugh says, "I suppose it's time to get off my duff. If you'll excuse me?"

I hide behind an armoire as he comes out of the parlor and goes upstairs. I wait a few minutes, then go into the parlor, pretending I've just arrived. Catherine stands in front of a mirror, powdering her face. She's breathing hard, still distraught. Then she sees me, and her reflection smiles. Except for her swollen eyes, no one else would know she'd been crying.

"Where's Hugh?" I ask.

"He went to dress."

I feign surprise. "What happened?"

Catherine shrugs and feigns perplexity. She's hidden her inner darkness as if with bright stage makeup. I think her acting career may have a future. I am more determined than ever to see that she lives to enjoy the future.

When Hugh returns, he's shaved, elegantly

dressed, still pale, but handsome again and surrounded by the clean lime-and-spice fragrance of bay rum. His shirt cuffs cover the bandages on his wrists. I can barely contain my joy; Catherine has mended a big rift in our circle.

"Sarah." Hugh smiles at me. "Good evening. How can I be of service?"

29

I send Hugh to investigate Ida Millbanks. He looks as if he belongs in York Street, and no one will be suspicious of him. Mick pursues John Kelly. I spend the next nine days working in my studio. After all the time I've spent on things other than earning money, I'm nearly too broke to feed myself and Mick. Every evening, I visit Mrs. Lipsky and tell her the latest news: "An artist made colored chalk drawings of the murders, on the pavement of Whitechapel Road. Liz Stride's funeral was a quiet affair, but a big crowd turned out to see the hearse carrying Kate Eddowes's coffin."

The Jewish community rallies to give her moral and practical support. Her flat is always full of neighbors and the food they bring. The idea that her husband is truly Jack the Ripper and that they should shun her never seems to occur to these people, and their sympathy extends to me. They welcome me, feed me, and chat with me in their broken English.

One is her husband's employer, Leo Markov, a muscular, bearded Russian who owns the butcher shop. He tells me, "Abraham Lipsky is innocent victim of police persecution. Just like in old country."

A thick, unrelenting fog — a devil's brew of smoke, chemical fumes, and the smells of fish and decay from the river — descends on the East End. Days are barely distinguishable from nights. At four o'clock on Wednesday, 10 October, it's already pitch-dark. Frigid dampness pervades my studio, and I keep my coat on rather than light a fire; I can't afford to waste money on coal. I warm my hands on a cup of hot tea while the tramp of footsteps heralds the Mile End Vigilance Committee patrol. Carrying lanterns and stout sticks and wearing whistles on strings around their necks, the men march past my window. They, like the police, seem not entirely convinced that Mr. Lipsky's arrest has put Jack the Ripper out of action.

Mick arrives and says, "I know where John Kelly is!"

Thankful for good news, I pour tea for Mick and serve him bread and sausage that Mrs. Lipsky's neighbors gave me. He eats ravenously. His haircut is growing out, and his new clothes are dirty. I worry about him living on the streets again, but he's bright-eyed with happy excitement.

"Kelly's been stayin' in the casual wards," he says.

Casual wards shelter vagrants, itinerant laborers, and the local folks who can't afford even the cheapest lodgings. These "casuals" receive bed and board in exchange for work. No one with any other choice goes there. John Kelly must have fallen on hard times.

"I talked to a guy who knows him." Mick gulps tea. "He's on the circuit." The wards provide one night's shelter. The casuals aren't allowed to return to the same one for thirty days, and some make a continuous circuit of the wards. "He'll be at the Whitechapel Casual Ward tonight. It's no place for a lady. You still got them men's clothes?"

Whitechapel seems an alien place, its landmarks dissolved into the fog that diffuses the glow from the gas lamps. I wear a scarf wrapped around my nose and mouth, but the smoke and fumes burn my throat. As Mick and I hurry along, I hear people coughing before I see them coming. Horses pulling wagons and carriages are led by boys who kick the curb at each step to make sure they don't wander off the road. Two cabs collide, and one overturns. Whistles shrill, and I hear confrontations between the Mile End Vigilance Committee members and men they've stopped to question. Prostitutes huddle in doorways. One yells at me, "Are you the Ripper? If you cut me, I'll cut you!" and brandishes a knife.

Constables herd Gypsy men and Asian sailors into the police station. The newspapers say the police are investigating the possibility that the Ripper is one of these folk. Mick and I pause at a poster on a notice board. The poster displays facsimiles of two letters handwritten in slanted script. The first reads,

Dear Boss
I keep on hearing the police have caught me but they wont fix me just yet. I have laughed when they look so clever and talk about being on the *right* track. That joke about Leather Apron gave me real fits. I am down on whores and I shan't quit ripping them till I do get buckled. Grand work the last job was. I gave the lady no time to squeal. How can they catch me now. I love my work and want

to start again. You will soon hear of me with my funny little games. I saved some of the proper *red* stuff in a ginger beer bottle over the last job to write with but it went thick like glue and I cant use it. Red ink is fit enough I hope *ha. ha.* The next job I do I shall clip the lady's ears off and send to the police officers just for jolly wouldn't you. Keep this letter back till I do a bit more work then give it out straight. My knife's so nice and sharp I want to get to work right away if I get a chance.

Good luck.
Yours truly
Jack the Ripper

Dont mind me giving the trade name wasnt good enough to post this before I got all the red ink off my hands curse it. No luck yet. They say I'm a doctor now ha ha

The second reads,

I wasnt coddling Dear old Boss when I gave you the tip. youll hear about saucy Jackys work tomorrow double event this time number one squealed a bit couldn't finish straight off. Had not time to get ears for police thanks for keeping last letter back till I got to work again.

Jack the Ripper

Above the letters is a message requesting anyone who recognizes the handwriting to contact the police.

"Do you think them letters are real?" Mick asks as we walk away.

"They don't sound like Commissioner Warren, but maybe he faked them to seem as if they were written by an uneducated person."

"He could've sent them to rib his men," Mick suggests.

"Something in the second letter is definitely false. Liz Stride didn't squeal while she was attacked. I was there; I would have heard. If Ripper Number Two is the author of the letters, he's embroidering the facts."

"They don't sound like Mr. Lipsky, either," Mick says. "Maybe that's why the coppers are still looking for Jack the Ripper."

There's a long queue outside the Whitechapel Casual Ward. Among the people in ragged clothes, carrying their worldly possessions in bundles, I recognize women who normally sleep in courtyards or alleys; fear of the Ripper has driven them to seek shelter. Some have children clinging to their skirts. Mick and I walk alongside the line, scrutinizing the men. We reach the entrance without finding John Kelly.

"He must be inside already," Mick says.

Two guards stand at the double doors to the two-story brick building. They're registering and searching the people they let in, inspecting baggage, writing names. They're confiscating knives and liquor bottles.

"If we go through the line, they'll discover I'm a woman and send me to the women's ward," I say. "Even if you get into the men's ward and find Kelly, he probably won't talk to you because he doesn't know you. And the doors will be locked soon. We won't be able to leave until tomorrow morning."

"I've got a better idea." Mick leads me to the back of the building.

A high brick wall encloses the grounds, but Mick easily scales it. Soon he's inside, opening the gate. We run across a yard containing large stones that the men will break into smaller rocks for road construction. Mick tries the back door and lets us into the oakum-picking room, filled with mountains of old, frayed ropes. Tomorrow, the women will shred it into fibers for making new rope. I imagine my fingers sore from fibers burrowing under my skin.

A life in the casual wards has never been

far outside the realm of possibility for me.

In a steamy kitchen, cooks pour watery stew made of onions, meat scraps, and potatoes into giant tureens. We hurry up the back stairs to the men's ward. The long, unheated room, with windows too high to climb out of, is crowded with men dressed in identical wool nightshirts. The beds are narrow lengths of canvas stretched between pairs of rails along each side of the room; they are like hammocks pulled tight and flat and covered with thin blankets. The sour, fecal, sweaty stench turns my stomach. A preacher walks up and down the aisle, reading from the Bible. In the light from flaring gas jets on the walls, I see a glint of red hair. I point. We approach the big man who's stowing his knapsack on a shelf above his bed.

"Mr. Kelly!" I call.

He turns. Coppery whiskers stubble his cheeks, dark circles underscore his puffy, sad eyes, and his thick shoulders sag. "Who're you?" I tilt back my hat. His eyes pop as he recognizes me. "What the hell?"

"I'm sorry about Kate," I say.

Kelly tightens his jaw. In the bed on the left of his sits a tramp who works a toothless mouth like a cow chewing cud. On the right, two hale young men who look like railway laborers play a game that involves exchanging obscene curses and hard punches.

"I need to talk to you," I say.

"Sod off! You scared Kate out of her wits with your talk about the Ripper."

"I was just trying to warn her."

"So now the Ripper's killed her. You were right. Did you come to rub it in?" Kelly abruptly sinks onto the bed. "I loved her, you know? She was a whore and a drunk, but I loved her, and now she's dead." He wipes his hand down his face. "The last time I saw her was that Saturday afternoon. We were broke. We pawned my boots." His feet are wrapped in rags. "Then I went to look for work. Kate went to borrow money from her daughter. I remembered what you said about the Ripper, and I made her promise to meet me back at Cooney's lodging house by four o'clock. Do you know what her last words to me were? 'Don't you fear for me — I'll take care of myself, and I shan't fall into his hands.' " Kelly shakes his head remorsefully. "I shouldn't have let her go. If I hadn't, she'd still be alive."

I don't want him to feel responsible for a death he couldn't prevent. "It's not your fault."

"You mean if she'd listened to you and

me, she would be alive. So it's her own fault?" Kelly's spark of anger is quickly extinguished by sad nostalgia. "Nobody could tell her what to do. She was independent. And clever."

I nod regretfully. If not for her idea of modeling for boudoir photographs, she wouldn't have attracted the Ripper's attention. But it was I who had taken the photographs.

"She didn't come back that night, but I figured she'd slept at her daughter's. On Sunday morning, I heard the Ripper had killed two more women. I didn't know one was Kate. I went to Mitre Square for a look, and I stood on the very spot where my poor old gal had been cut to pieces, and I didn't know!" Kelly utters a broken laugh. "Then today I heard that the dead woman from Mitre Square had a pawn ticket in her pocket. It was for a pair of boots. So I went to the police station, and they took me to see the body. And there were initials tattooed on her arm — 'T. C.' " His eyes roll, and he rubs his mouth.

He's remembering Kate's mutilated face, her nose cut off. I hate to bother him with questions, but all I can give him is a chance at vengeance for Kate. "I think she knew who the Ripper is. I think that's what she didn't want to tell me."

"Whatever she knew, she didn't tell me, either," Kelly says morosely.

Mick and I exchange disappointed glances. I ask, "Had anything unusual happened recently?"

Kelly shakes his head; then he freezes, startled by a sudden thought. "It wasn't recent, but you could say it was unusual."

"Screw you, prick!" shouts one of the young men at Kelly's right. He and his friend aren't just playing now. They throw punches that sound like hammers striking meat.

"We better go," Mick says uneasily.

I have the pulse-racing sensation that I'm about to hear something important. "Wait."

"It was April last year," Kelly says. "Kate comes home one morning, says she's got a new customer. She shows me two crowns he paid her. I said, 'What'd you do to earn that?' She smiles, cunning-like, and says, 'Special things.' "

That April, she'd sold our first boudoir photographs, but two crowns is far more than her share of the sale. The customer must have bought a set, found her, and engaged her services.

"Ripper Number Two?" Mick whispers to me.

"I asked what special things and who he was," Kelly says, "but she said the deal was, she had to keep quiet. I let it go because the money was good. She would spend a night with him once a week or so. Then one morning, she comes home like this." Kelly moans, shakes violently, and clutches his stomach. "She was as pale as a sheet. She took some pills she brought, then went to bed. I wanted to fetch a doctor, but she said no." Kelly rubs his mouth, closes his eyes for a moment, and whispers, "Jesus."

Other men join in the fight, yelling, flailing, and hitting. Mick prompts, "What?"

"When I gave her the chamber pot so she could piss, I seen a big cut." Kelly's finger traces a line below his waist. "It was stitched with thread. She said she'd been in a knife fight and gone to the infirmary and the surgeon sewed her up."

I remember Kate hugging herself when I questioned her. It wasn't to hold in the information; she was remembering the pain. And the reason she was upset to hear that Polly Nichols had been cut open? So had she.

"I asked her who cut her. She wouldn't tell me." Kelly says grimly, "I think it was that special customer."

Mick and I look at each other in surprise.

If the customer was indeed one of the two Rippers, then how had Kate escaped?

"Three weeks later, she was well enough to go back on the streets," Kelly says, "but she was never the same. Her monthlies stopped. At first, we thought she was expecting, but no baby ever came. She complained about feeling hot, and she would cry or get mad for no reason."

As I puzzle over this, the riot spreads. The preacher flees, men curse and roar as they fight, and a window shatters, raining broken glass. Mick says, "Miss Sarah, we gotta go!"

"I wanted to know what really happened to Kate, so I went to the infirmary and asked the surgeon. But he said she wasn't there that night." Bitterness shows on Kelly's face. "She lied."

Abiding by their deal, Kate had protected a killer. She'd stepped into his shadow and not told anyone what he'd done to her there.

Guards rush into the room and assail the fighters. Mick and I push through the brawl, and as we run down the stairs, I hear the door of the ward slam shut. Safe in the street behind the building, we breathe foggy, smoky air that burns the ward's stench out of our lungs.

"Was it Ripper Number Two who cut Kate last year?" Mick asks.

"I don't think it was Commissioner War-ren. I can't imagine him sparing his victim, let alone taking the trouble to sew her up. Maybe it was Ripper Number Two." *They say I'm a doctor now ha ha.* "Maybe he really is a doctor, and he stitched the cut."

"What if he is?" Mick sounds discouraged. "John Kelly didn't get us any closer to him."

"We need to find Ida Millbanks. She's our last chance."

30

The next morning, I decide to visit Hugh and ask if he's made any progress investigating Ida Millbanks. But as soon as I step outside my door, I see a squadron of mounted police officers riding up the street. Commissioner Warren is in the lead. His eyes under his bushy brows squint as if in bright African sunlight; he turns his head from side to side as if hunting for black women to torture.

He's after me. There's no other possible explanation for his presence.

My shock is so breathtaking, so paralyzing, that I can't will myself to run before he spots me. I had thought that he thought he'd done enough damage by hurting Mick and Hugh and instigating Mr. Lipsky's arrest. But he must feel he hasn't yet won the game he's playing. What a fool I was to think that eleven days without another attack from him meant he'd decided to leave us alone! Despite my terror, I feel something like relief, for if my friends had to suffer at his hands, then so should I.

As he rides nearer, our gazes meet. His nostrils flare as if he scents blood, and a malevolent twinkle ignites in his eyes. Following his mounted squadron are police constables on foot and a pack of reporters. I glimpse Barrett among the constables. He spies me and frowns. Alarm sucks in my breath. He must have told Warren about my pictures of the African photograph and Annie's rings after all. That must be why Warren came. Fighting the impulse to hide, I muster the shaky bravado of a hunter facing down a charging beast that's a hundred times his size and strength. Warren has the power to destroy me, but I shan't run like a coward. I've gone far beyond the point of poking the wolf. I'm going to stand my ground, like the hunter dropping to his knee and holding his spear upright, ready to impale the beast when it pounces.

The reporters assail Warren with questions. "Sir Charles, what brings you to Whitechapel?"

They can't see what he is. They're blinded by his respectable public persona. As he and his squadron stop near my studio, neighbors come outdoors to listen. Warren says,

"There's been a new development in the Ripper case." He ignores me, but his voice seems deliberately pitched for me to hear.

I glance at Barrett. Since he kept silent while Mr. Lipsky was arrested, I'm angrier at him than ever. He sees me and shakes his head. A breath of relief mixed with disappointment gushes from me. He didn't tell. Warren isn't here because of the photographs. But I wish Barrett had done something instead of nothing.

"We've identified a person who may have a connection to the case." Warren looks straight at me; the twinkle in his eyes brightens, and his mustache moves as he smiles. "His name is Benjamin Bain."

I've dodged one blow only to be slammed by another. Hearing Warren speak my father's name is like a punch to my stomach; I'm speechless with shock that it should crop up in this unexpected context. The fragile rampart of my bravado crumbles.

A reporter asks, "Who is Benjamin Bain?"

"He's a criminal with a police record that dates back more than twenty years," Warren says.

I can't believe I'm hearing this. Of course my father must have had a record because of his rabble-rousing. But surely it contains no evidence to implicate him in the Ripper murders.

"What's his connection to the Ripper case?" the reporter asks.

"I'm not at liberty to divulge that information," Warren says.

"Has Benjamin Bain any connection to Bain and Sons Photography?" another reporter asks, pointing at my studio.

"Yes. Sarah Bain, the proprietress, is his daughter." As the reporters scribble, Warren says, "She may be in contact with him. We're here to look for witnesses who've seen him." He addresses the spectators. "I ask for your cooperation. Finding Benjamin Bain is crucial to closing the case, obtaining a conviction, and removing the Ripper from your midst once and for all."

The constables fan out along the street and begin questioning my neighbors. Barrett starts toward me, but Commissioner Warren reaches me first, peering down at me from his high seat in his horse's saddle. "Do you have anything to say, Miss Bain?"

This is another attack aimed at me, and with unerring instinct, he's hit upon a powerful weapon to use — my father. Indignant as well as horrified, I stammer, "My father has nothing to do with the Ripper case!" Warren made that up for my benefit. "He was killed in a riot in 1866."

"That's interesting," Warren says. "When you were first brought to my attention, I checked into your background, and that's when your father's name came up. But here's the funny thing." Joviality crinkles his eyes. "I checked the city death archives, and there's no record of a Benjamin Bain dying in a riot in 1866 or any other year since."

A dizzy, battering sensation — as if I've been caught in a wheel of a cart and rolled head over heels along cobblestones — washes over me. Warren must be lying. And yet . . . His words drill deep into my core, from which I've never quite expunged my wishful, childish notion that my father isn't really dead.

Commissioner Warren smiles, as if he can read my thoughts on my face. "The police file only says Benjamin Bain *disappeared* in 1866."

His disappearance is the one thing I am sure of, but I've never quite lost my doubt about whether my mother's explanation for it was true.

"He's been a fugitive from the law ever since," Warren says. "The order for his arrest is still in effect. We had a tip that said he's resurfaced in Whitechapel."

Here is another explanation: my father didn't die; he ran away because the law was after him. It's too much to absorb, too far beyond belief. My mouth is open, gasping. "What tip? Arrest — for what?"

"That's neither here nor there." Warren waves my questions aside. I want to think that he doesn't have the answers because he fabricated the whole story. But maybe the story is true and he's withholding the information to torment me. "What's important is that I warned you to forget about the Whitechapel murders and mind your own business."

I'm still reeling from shock, my wits almost lost. "But I have!"

"Come now, Miss Bain." Anger hardens his smile. "We both know better."

Exactly what does he know? That my friends and I are now looking for Ripper Number Two but haven't given up on delivering Warren to justice? My thoughts scatter among memories of my second trip to Russell's Fine Books with Mick and our visit to the casual ward. Has Warren been tracking my movements? Have his officers been secretly watching me the whole time? The silence between us hums with unspoken questions on both sides. Warren's expression is inscrutable, but I think he's wondering how much I know. Blindsided by his story about my father, I feel as if I'm playing cards with a lion who will devour me rather than tip his hand.

Barrett hovers within earshot. He looks uncertain, distraught. I sense that he's considering telling Warren about my photographs; he's torn between duty and fear of the consequences. If he does tell, Warren won't like that he initially withheld the information, and he may be fired. It would serve him right, but my own consequences will be even worse if Barrett tells: Warren will arrest me for slandering him, tear apart my studio, and destroy my prints and negatives of the boudoir pictures, African photograph, and Annie's rings. And then he'll kill me and my friends.

Barrett draws a breath, opens his mouth. My heart pounds with dread. Then he clamps his lips together, vexed by his own failure of nerve.

My insides go limp with relief, but this constant cycle of terror, relief, and terror is running my own nerves ragged. I feel like a hot-air balloon that is repeatedly inflated with blasts from its burner, deflated as it cools, and inflated again, its thin fabric weakening under the pressure. The anger takes command, and it goads me to a new, reckless impulse. Why not take the offensive rather than cringe like a ninny? Knowledge confers power, and the advantage isn't entirely Warren's. I think of the hunter kneeling with his spear upright.

"With all due respect, Commissioner Warren — you think you know everything about me, but you should think again." As I stare at Warren, his image shimmers, as if in heat waves radiating from the pavement in summer.

Warren remains impassive, but his horse skitters; the animal senses he's disconcerted. He tightens his hold on the reins. His smile lacks humor. "If you think you can hide anything from me, then *you* should think again."

"You may know who some of my friends are. Mick O'Reilly. Lord Hugh Staunton." Courage seeps into me, reinforcing the anger, as if saying their names invokes a magic spell.

Caution hoods the unnatural brightness of his eyes as he tries to deduce what I'm aiming at. I get a glimpse into his life of hunting and butchering women by night, pretending to be a virtuous upholder of the law by day. I know what a strain it is to harbor secrets; there are many more people watching him than me, and he has further to fall.

"Your friends have experienced some

trouble lately, I hear. The boy almost drowned, and Lord Hugh Staunton has been exposed as a homosexual." Warren is letting me know, without actually admitting it, that he's responsible for their troubles.

Does he ever regret the blackness in his nature? One might feel sorry for him if he does, but I don't believe that is so. My anger flares hotter on behalf of Hugh and Mick, expands my courage. "My friends aren't the only people who know what I know."

A flicker of dismay in his expression tells me that Warren understands I'm saying that whatever I know about him, I've told other people besides Mick, Hugh, Catherine, and the Lipskys. And he can tell I'm not lying because my voice rings with conviction.

It's true; another person I've told is standing not fifteen feet from us.

PC Barrett's face registers alarm. He thinks I'm going to blab the whole story of the African photograph and Annie's rings and say that he knew and kept mum. I feel a gleeful, vicious sense of turnabout. I could make Barrett pay for bringing me to the attention of his superiors and tricking me, for standing uselessly idle while Mr. Lipsky was dragged off to jail.

Warren looks around, searching the street for my confidantes. Barrett fades into the crowd, out of our sight. Warren says with quiet menace, "You are playing a dangerous game."

It would be dangerous if he were only the chief commissioner of police. It is all the more dangerous to antagonize a killer who slashes women's throats, has Mr. Lipsky in jail, and could attack Hugh, Mick, Catherine, Mrs. Lipsky, and me at any time. The light from his eyes is like the hot African sun; it burns and bleaches the familiar street scene. The crowd's chatter becomes the sound of black women screaming and running. My mind reels with the panic that they must have felt, and my anger diminishes like fire when the wind dies. I cross my arms, defiant yet suddenly cold with terror.

"Suit yourself, Miss Bain," Warren says. "So far the Ripper has only killed prostitutes, but that could change."

He eyes me as if he can see the viscera and blood in me that he'll spill. "If your father is alive, I'll find him. And woe betide both of you." Then Warren rides off.

I turn to enter my studio, but a thick, stubby hand slams against the door, holding it shut. The hand belongs to Mr. Douglas, my landlord.

"You didn't tell me that you're related to a criminal." His face is so close to mine that

I can see the red veins in his eyes, which bulge with anger.

The embers of my anger flame up again. "My father isn't a criminal!" My automatic defense of him is so vehement that Mr. Douglas steps back. "Commissioner Warren is lying." I cling to that thought like a shipwrecked sailor to a rock during a storm at sea. But I can't help hoping there's truth embedded in Warren's lies, that my father is alive. "And you're a fool to believe everything you hear!" I wish to believe that my dearest wish has been granted.

Mr. Douglas looks at me as if I'm a rabbit that's bared fangs like a dragon's and roared. Then his gaze moves to the departing Warren, and it's clear which of us he believes. "First you bring whores and street urchins and Jews onto my property. Now this." He flings his arm at the police questioning the neighbors. "I've had enough. You're evicted!"

The ground seems to liquefy and shift under my feet. "You can't do that! My lease doesn't end until November thirtieth."

He laughs. "Just try to hold me to it."

I am losing my beloved studio! But despite the anguish that brings tears to my eyes, I don't crumble. Mr. Douglas is a dwarf compared to Commissioner Warren. "Very well, evict me, but you won't get another tenant while people still think the Ripper is at large, and the police are swarming this street. You'll lose money."

He scowls; he knows I'm right. Thrusting his stubby finger at my face, he says, "You have until the end of your lease. Then you're out," and stalks off.

Alone in my studio, I make tea. My hands tremble, the pot bangs against the cup, and the spout chips. My throat constricts, and I feel too sick to swallow the hot, bitter liquid. I put the "Closed" sign on my door and mull over what Commissioner Warren said. Most likely his story is but a ploy to shake me up. Despite being a rabble-rouser, Benjamin Bain was a gentle, honest, decent man; surely he's not a fugitive, and there's no warrant for his arrest. He's probably dead, and Warren could look for him for all eternity and not find him. I should put the story out of my mind, be glad that Warren didn't do something worse to me, and concentrate on tracking down Ripper Number Two and finding a new studio.

But Warren has dealt me a severe blow indeed. Doubts leak into my mind like floodwater seeping under a dam.

This is what Warren must have intended

— that I should wonder and suffer. Mental torture would be more fun for him than killing me outright.

Loath to face neighbors who heard Commissioner Warren malign my father, I don't leave my studio until early evening, and then only because my larder is empty, and I need to buy food unless I want to starve. I forgot my plan to visit Hugh, and when I return home, I'm surprised to find a note from him slipped under my door. It reads, *Meet me in York Street 8:00 AM tomorrow.*

31

Mick and I arrive in York Street a half hour early. In the gray gloom of another foggy morning, well-dressed people stream out of the mansion blocks, and carriages roll to and fro. We loiter across the street from York Street Chambers and read newspapers, which we hold up to conceal our faces from the doorman.

"An experiment was performed at Regent's Park," I say. "Bloodhounds were sent to hunt a man who'd been given a fifteen-minute head start. They tracked him for a mile and were successful for several trials. Commissioner Warren was present, and twice he acted as the hunted man, but he didn't say whether he'll use the bloodhounds to track the Ripper."

"He won't," Mick says, "unless he wants their teeth in his own backside."

"He must be under pressure to try everything possible to catch the Ripper. I think he's enjoying a private joke, conducting the experiment when he's the one the dogs would be employed to hunt. What a nerve!"

As I think of what Warren said about my father yesterday, my anger starts to boil again. It cools when Hugh, impeccably groomed and handsome, joins us. We smile at each other, and my heart feels lighter. As I tell him what Mick and I learned from John Kelly, we watch two smartly attired young women come out the door of York Street Chambers.

"It's a residence for educated, single working women," Hugh says.

"How did you suss that out?" Mick asks.

"I followed two of them into Harrods and struck up a conversation."

I'm glad he hasn't lost his talent for sleuthing but afraid to look too closely at him for fear of seeing a crack in his normalcy, a sign of permanent damage. I steal glances at him, and he notices.

"I'm all right," he says. "Do you know, I feel rather good. The thing I was afraid of has happened. It's actually a relief. And when I tried to off myself, it didn't work, so there must be a reason I'm still kicking."

I smile, reassured. But now that I know how vulnerable he is, I'm afraid he'll be hurt again.

Mick, restless from waiting, ambles down the street. Hugh asks, "Anything interesting happen lately?"

I can hardly bear to think about my father, but I feel the same impulse to confide in Hugh that I did when we went to tea the day we became friends. After I tell Hugh, he reacts with surprise and excitement.

"Of course Commissioner Warren could have been lying, but if it's true, how wonderful! Your father may be alive, just as you thought. Are you going to look for him?"

"I don't know."

"For God's sake, you should! Why would you not?"

I shrink from Hugh's enthusiasm. "I don't know where to start."

"I could make a few suggestions —"

"Not now. There's too much else going on. Maybe later."

These are just excuses; the fact is, I'm more afraid to look for my father than I've ever been in my life. Commissioner Warren planted in my mind the malignant notion that my father isn't the man I thought he was. Questions plague me. When my parents quarreled, was it really because my mother hated my father's rabble-rousing or because of something else he did? What was the real reason for his night in jail? I'm afraid of what I might learn if I found my father. If he isn't dead, why didn't he get in touch with me to let me know he was alive?

I change the subject. "Did you learn anything about Ida Millbanks?"

Hugh looks perplexed, then nods sympathetically; he understands my inner turmoil. "Do bears defecate in the woods?" he replies, trying to lighten my mood with humor. "Ida is a nurse, and she leaves for work at eight fifteen every morning . . ." Hugh looks at his watch. "Right about now. Here she comes."

An older woman dressed in an outdated, voluminous gray cloak and black bonnet, carrying a large black handbag, emerges from York Street Chambers.

"Yeah, that's her!" Mick whispers.

I recognize Ida Millbanks from the picture he took at the bookshop. Her bonnet frames a sort of face I find difficult to photograph. With her heavy cheeks, her thin, prim lips, her small eyes too close together, and her lack of a chin, it would require magic to make her look good. A pleasant expression can redeem even ugliness, but Ida's expression is pensively sad.

She walks up the street, her gait slow and stiff. We follow her to Marylebone Road. In the busy thoroughfare of shops, businesses, and cafes, she boards an omnibus, and so do we. I sit in the only empty seat, directly behind Ida; Mick and Hugh stand beside me. I reflect that Ida and I have things in common — we're both single working women — but our circumstances are so different. What is it like to be affluent enough to live in a mansion block? I envy her security. She reaches into her handbag, takes out a book, and holds it close to her face as she reads. I lean forward to read over her shoulder. It's a romantic novel; the hero and heroine are about to kiss.

Perhaps her needs are not so different from mine.

Ida puts away her novel, and we all disembark at Harley Street. Harley Street is lined with Georgian-styled terraced houses. Classical details adorn their stone, redbrick, and painted stucco façades. Although it's even more elegant than York Street, I don't feel intimidated because I'm with Hugh. His presence legitimizes Mick and me. As we trail Ida Millbanks, I whisper, "Stay back; she'll notice us following her."

"No, she won't," Hugh says. "Didn't you see how close she was holding her book? She's nearsighted."

Ida enters a three-story white stone house with a bow front on the ground floor. The black-painted door is framed with Roman pilasters and topped by a fanlight. Twin brick chimneys on either side of the house flank three arched dormers above the parapet.

"This must be where she works." As we pause to study the house, I experience a thrill of hope that we've tracked down Ripper Number Two.

"Her employer must be a physician," Hugh says. "Harley Street is all physicians."

"The sort that cuts into people and sews 'em up," Mick suggests.

Unlike the houses on either side, which have wall plaques that announce the names and specialties of the occupants, the one Ida Millbanks entered bears no identification. Curtains inside cover the windows. Carriages stop to let people out at nearby buildings, but we spend half an hour strolling back and forth in front of the house, and nobody arrives there. I sense none of the darkness that I did in Commissioner Warren's den.

"Maybe he's not in."

"Let's have a look around back," Hugh says.

We circle the block. An alley separates the terraced houses on Harley Street from the mews. High brick walls, too smooth for even

Mick to climb, hide the rear gardens of the houses, and the gate to Ida's employer's house is locked. When we return to the front, Hugh says, "Shh!" and points at the door.

Ida Millbanks is coming out. As she walks slowly up the street, we follow at a discreet distance. She returns to Marylebone Road and enters a bakery. We watch through the window as she purchases éclairs. Burdened with her handbag and a large white bakery box, she leads us back down Harley Street.

At a corner, Hugh says, "You keep going. Wait for me near the house."

He quickly backtracks and vanishes around the block. I'm suddenly afraid to let him out of my sight.

"What's he doing?" Mick asks.

"I suppose we're going to find out." I reassure myself that Hugh has been fine on his own for days, and he'll be all right now.

We trail Ida to the next corner. Hugh comes hurrying around it and bumps smack into her. The bakery box flies out of her arms, falls, and spills éclairs onto the ground.

"Oh, I say, I'm terribly sorry!" Hugh exclaims. As Ida picks up the éclairs, Hugh crouches beside her and says, "Here, let me help."

Her face is hidden by her bonnet, but her hand clasps her throat; she's stunned by Hugh's handsomeness. Hugh says, "Oh, dear, your éclairs are all dirty. Let me buy you some new ones."

As they walk toward me, heading for the bakery, he smiles down at her. She looks up at him as if her eyes are dazzled by flash powder. Hugh leads her past Mick and me without a glance at us. We could be invisible for all Ida notices. We station ourselves across the street from the house and wait.

An hour passes before Hugh and Ida reappear. He carries the new bakery box. They're chatting together like friends. Either Hugh gave her a false name, or Ida hasn't read the scandalous story about him in the newspapers. Her cheeks are pink, her eyes glowing. I imagine her thinking about the novel she was reading. Hugh must seem a romantic hero straight out of its pages. But he's only doing to Ida what Barrett did to me — softening up the spinster. I feel ashamed, and sorry for Ida. She and Hugh stand by the steps to the house, talking. I can't hear their words, but she's visibly anxious not to say good-bye. He hands her the box and gestures toward the door. She reluctantly shakes her head. He looks into her eyes and asks some question to which she reacts with delight. Then she opens the door, and he saunters away. She stands dazed at the threshold. He turns to smile at her; she smiles, sighs, and disappears inside the house.

Hugh, Mick, and I reunite on Marylebone Road. Mick says, "Where were you?"

"I took Ida for a cup of tea."

"You're already on a first-name basis with her, and you have her eating out of your hand?" I say. "That was fast work."

"I've been faster. My best time is three minutes." Hugh looks tired despite his humor; he's not entirely recovered from his ordeal, and now it must cost him more effort than ever to seduce women, to pretend to be someone he's not.

"What'd you find out?" Mick asks.

"Ida doesn't have any family or close friends, and she's lonely. She's a nice woman, and I hated taking advantage of her. I had to think of Mr. Lipsky in jail the whole time."

"What about the important stuff? Like who she bought Sarah's pictures for?"

"I'm getting to the rest," Hugh says. "Ida works for a physician named Henry Poole. He specializes in female disorders."

"A doctor!" I'm delighted with Hugh's success. I feel as if we're centering our quarry in my camera's viewfinder, bringing his blurry image into focus. "He could have performed an operation on Kate Eddowes and sewn up the cut."

"That's not all. Dr. Poole has a private laboratory in his house."

"Blimey!" Mick says. "He's got to be Ripper Number Two!"

I hate to pour the cold water of caution on our excitement. "But we need proof. Can you get inside the house?"

"I tried. Ida says Dr. Poole gave her strict orders not to let anyone in unless he's authorized them. But I think I can get around her. Next Thursday is her day off. I invited her to tea with my sister. She was thrilled to accept."

So that's what he said that made her look as if she'd received a precious gift. "Your sister? But I thought your family is disowning you."

"They are." Hugh's expression is mischievous, but the sadness I saw in him on that first day, when he talked about his life, is closer to the surface now. "I didn't mean my actual sibling." He points at me, and the affection in his eyes warms my heart. "I meant you."

32

The news that Benjamin Bain, father of the proprietress of Bain & Sons, is wanted in connection with the Whitechapel murders spreads fast. Neighbors won't look at me when we pass on the street. No customers come to my studio on Friday or Saturday. I'm to be evicted next month, but Commissioner Warren has already destroyed my livelihood. I am a pariah — not for the first time. I think of how my mother and I lost our friends the same year my father disappeared. Was it really only because friends are fickle?

It's as though for twenty-two years, I've been looking at a photograph that was taken from one angle, and now Commissioner Warren has shown me another photograph of the same scene taken from a different angle. I tell myself that I shouldn't take his story about my father as gospel. He's an expert at deception — how else could he commit murders and the police force be none the wiser? But my doubt about my family's past has grown to the point where I'm forced to think that my mother's version of it doesn't hold water.

On Monday, 15 October, a loud banging startles me. Gray daylight filters through the window curtains. A man's voice outside shouts, "Police! Open up!"

Heart-pounding alarm launches me out of bed. Commissioner Warren must not be satisfied with ruining my reputation and business, and he's sent the police to arrest me! There's no time left to identify Ripper Number Two and save Mr. Lipsky. I hurry into my clothes, compelled by an absurd need to be presentable when catastrophe strikes. Then I pull back the curtains and look down at the street.

Two constables stand outside the door to the adjacent druggist's shop. One says, "We're going house to house, looking for the Ripper. Mind if we have a look inside?"

"You think I keep him tucked away here?" The proprietor cackles. "Be my guest."

I've no time for relief to sink in. As I run downstairs to make sure everything that needs to be hidden is hidden, I hear banging on the door. The man I see through the glass is PC Barrett. "Miss Bain!" he calls.

Distrustful, I frown and shake my head.

"Every house in Whitechapel is being searched. Let me in, and I'll tell Inspector Reid I searched, but I'll not touch anything, I promise." He sounds desperate, like a fugitive wanting sanctuary.

He thinks I'm that gullible. "Go away."

"I need to talk to you." He presses his palms against the window. Their heat forms white handprints on the glass. "Give me five minutes. Please!"

Two other constables materialize in the fog behind him.

"Having trouble, Barrett?"

"Want us to break in there?"

Better the devil I know. I open the door. Barrett steps in and locks it. He's breathing hard, anxious about something. When I move to block the darkroom, where the photographs I don't want him to see are hidden, he doesn't notice.

He blurts, "I think he's the Ripper."

"You mean Mr. Lipsky?" Remembering Mr. Lipsky hauled off to prison while Barrett silently stood by, I glare. "Is that why you came? To browbeat me into admitting he's guilty?"

"No," Barrett says. "I mean Commissioner Warren."

This is so unexpected that I sputter. "Is

this a joke?"

"Do you see me laughing?" Barrett groans. "God, I wish it were."

Puzzled, I shake my head. "You didn't believe me before. Why change your mind?"

Barrett glances around the room, as if afraid someone is eavesdropping. He removes his hat and runs his hand through his flattened hair. Something momentous has shaken him. I dare to hope that he will, after all, be my ally against Commissioner Warren.

"About that photograph of Warren," he says. "I thought you must have faked it, but it looked so real. Those dead black women."

I want to ask him where the copy he took from me is, but I don't interrupt him.

"I knew Warren served in Africa during the Kaffir Wars. When he became Commissioner, it was all the talk at the station. He commanded troops against the black natives who were murdering white traders and missionaries and trying to drive the British out of Africa. He was seriously outnumbered, and he was wounded, but he won. He has all sorts of medals. He's a hero. I wanted to prove you were wrong about him, so I did some checking. The landlord at my local pub has a friend who was a captain in the army in Africa while Warren was there. I went to see the captain. And he told me —"

Barrett pauses, looking sick. "There were rumors that Warren was sent back to England because he was too cruel to the natives. Not the men he killed in battles, but the women. There was talk that he hunted and tortured and shot them, and he kept their gold earrings as trophies."

Feeling vindicated by this new, compromising information about Warren, I resist the urge to say *I told you so.*

"But they were just rumors, and even if they're true — even if Warren killed women in Africa — that doesn't mean he's doing it here." Barrett flings out his palms. "This is England!"

Warren must consider white prostitutes as less than human — fair game, like the black women. "Then why do you think Warren is the Ripper?"

Dejection slumps Barrett's posture. "Because of what happened after the double murders."

I frown, thinking over the news stories I've read. They reported nothing that should have caused Barrett's change of tune. "What happened?"

"The City Police got in on the investigation." Barrett explains, "Kate Eddowes's murder happened in their territory. That gives them a say in how the investigation is conducted, even though the other murders happened in Metropolitan Police territory. They're not convinced that Lipsky is Jack the Ripper, because there's no evidence placing him at the scenes of the other murders. And they'd like to solve the case themselves."

That's why the investigation is still going on, why the police are rounding up Gypsies and foreign sailors, and why Mr. Lipsky hasn't been tried, convicted, and hanged. Thank heaven for competing police divisions.

"The Mile End Vigilance Committee people are also divided on the issue. That's why they're still patrolling. So there's been a lot of debate about whether the case is solved. Add that to the women in Africa . . ." Misery suffuses Barrett's expression. "I can't help but think Warren killed Kate Eddowes. I think he's afraid that somebody saw him with her before he killed her or leaving Mitre Square afterward. I think that's why he's so hot to close the case and hang Mr. Lipsky."

This surpasses all expectation: Barrett truly believes Warren is the Ripper. I eagerly lean toward him. "What will you do?"

Barrett backs away, resisting the pressure

to take action.

"You have to report Warren!"

"Warren will deny everything. Nobody will take my word over his."

"The evidence —"

"Rumors from Africa. That doesn't prove Warren is the Ripper."

"My photographs —"

"Your photographs don't show Warren killing anybody."

The anger flares up in me again. "So you'll just let him go on killing and let an innocent man hang?"

"Do you know what will happen to me if I accuse Warren of being the Ripper?" Barrett points at his chest. "I'll be sacked, and he'll go on killing anyway."

"It's your duty to the public! But you would just rather protect yourself than protect innocent people from the Ripper —"

He cuts me off. "There's another problem besides the fact that the evidence against Warren is circumstantial. Liz Stride was killed at about one o'clock in the morning. It couldn't have been earlier; people from the International Club would have seen. Kate Eddowes was killed between one thirty and one forty-five. We know that from the constable who was patrolling Mitre Square.

It was empty at one thirty, and when he came back at one forty-five, he found her body. Commissioner Warren stalks and kills Liz, then stalks and kills and mutilates Kate within less than forty-five minutes." Barrett shakes his head. "That's implausible."

Despite a cold stab of apprehension, I say the only thing I can to persuade Barrett to report Warren. "Warren killed Kate but not Liz. I know."

"How do you know?" Barrett regards me with confusion.

"Because I was there."

Barrett's confusion deepens. "You were in Mitre Square. I saw you. How could you know Warren didn't kill Liz in Dutfield's Yard?"

With a sense of crossing a line I can't uncross, I answer, "I was in Dutfield's Yard before Mitre Square."

"What were you doing there?" Barrett demands.

"I was following Liz. I saw her go into Dutfield's Yard with a man. When they didn't come out, I went in and found her dead. The man was gone. He had to have killed her. And he wasn't Warren."

Barrett sputters. "Why on earth were you following Liz?"

"To protect her. Because I knew the

Ripper was after her." I voice the revelation I had that night. "There are two Rippers. The man I saw with Liz is one. Warren is the other."

His astounded expression turns ominous. "It's time you came clean with me, Miss Bain. You can start by telling me how you knew the Ripper was after Liz."

He's like a dog who won't let go of a bone even when offered a bigger, meatier one. I've told him something that has major ramifications for the police's investigation, but all he seems to care about is that now he's got his teeth into me.

"I took photographs of . . . Liz." The facts I've been concealing for so long are like rotten teeth in my mouth, and I'm afraid to have them pulled out because it will hurt.

Barrett notices my hesitation. "Just of Liz?"

"And Kate Eddowes, Polly Nichols, Annie Chapman, and Martha Tabram." Confessing that they were partners with me in a crime can't hurt them because they're dead. I won't implicate Mary Jane or Catherine.

"So that's how you knew them. They modeled for you. What sort of photographs?" When I hesitate again, Barrett says, "Tell me, or I'll tear this place apart."

"All right. I'll show you."

I back into the darkroom, shut the door, and pry up the loose floorboard. It feels like digging my own grave. I pick out some photographs, then replace the board and return to Barrett. I slap a photograph on the table. It shows Liz grinning in her chemise and petticoat.

His eyes pop.

I lay down a photograph of Kate unfastening her garters.

His jaw drops.

Confronted with Polly bare-breasted, Annie flaunting her naked buttocks, and Martha wearing only a paper leaf over her privates, Barrett plops into a chair and mutters, "Jesus."

I don't think Jesus is in those pictures. I stifle a wild urge to laugh.

Barrett looks up at me, and I watch him realize I'm not the person he thought I was. His face shows confusion, chagrin, even fear. He must also be thinking that if I'm unchaste enough to take photographs like these, then why did I run from him that night?

Blushing furiously and afraid of what he'll do, I say, "The Ripper saw these photographs. He's choosing his victims from them. After Martha Tabram and Polly Nichols were killed, I was afraid my other models would be next. After Annie Chapman was killed, I knew I was right."

Elbows planted on the table, Barrett holds his head between his hands, as if his brain is too heavy from all the information it's absorbing. "Where did he see these photographs?"

I tell him about Russell's Fine Books and my surveillance.

Barrett lowers his hands and sits upright. "Quite the amateur detective, aren't you?" Grudging admiration colors the disapproval in his voice. Then he reverts to his officious police manner. "You know these are illegal, don't you?" His fingers tap the boudoir photographs.

"Why else do you think I didn't tell you and Inspector Reid?"

"Was it really better, keeping the information to yourself? While you were trying to protect those women, two more of them were killed."

My guilt weighs upon me even as I say, "We did our best." It's small consolation that after Annie Chapman's murder, there wasn't another for three weeks, and Catherine and Mary Jane are still alive.

" 'We'?" Barrett pounces on the word. "So your friends are in on this. The actress, the street urchin, and that swell who got caught

in the raid on the Thousand Crowns Club."
His eyes shine with enlightenment, then
narrow. "Is that what Abraham Lipsky was
doing in Mitre Square — bodyguarding
Kate Eddowes?"

"No. He was following Commissioner
Warren."

Barrett mixes a laugh with a groan. "I see
— he was trying to catch Warren in the act."

"He did! He saw Warren kill Kate. You
heard."

"And he got caught himself." Barrett rubs
his temples, as if our mishaps have given
him a headache. "He's in solitary confine-
ment. No one's allowed to talk to him
except the officers assigned by Commissioner Warren."

"Because Warren doesn't want Mr. Lipsky
spreading his accusations. He's afraid
somebody important might hear about
them and believe them." It's small consolation that Mr. Lipsky is separated from the
other, dangerous prisoners. He's alone, terrified, and helpless. "You know he's innocent! You have to help me save him!"

"I . . . don't know."

"Please!" Desperate, I grab Barrett's wrist.
The feel of his warm, solid flesh and bone
sends an electric jolt through me despite
my unwillingness to experience such sensa-

tions with him, now or ever.

Barrett rises; he looks down at my fingers clasping him. I feel him tense. When he raises his gaze, the heat in it brings the blood rushing to my cheeks. Now I know for certain that he's thinking about the other night, and his lust for me is real. But lust without respect or affection is dangerous.

I let go of his arm as if burned. I've already told him the address of Warren's house in Stepney, but I recite it in case he's forgotten. "The African photograph is there. So are Annie's rings. They're evidence you can use."

He shakes his head. "This is too much." He doesn't ask how I found out about Warren's house or how I know the evidence is there. He doesn't want to hear something that will force him to jeopardize his career. Although he believes Warren is the Ripper, he desperately wants *not* to believe.

Although I don't believe he's going to help me, I play the one card I have left. "I think I know who the other Ripper is."

A loud knocking at the door drowns out my voice.

Barrett turns; he doesn't hear me say, "Doctor Henry Poole." Through the glass, we see a constable who calls, "Barrett! Get a move on! We've hundreds more houses to search."

Barrett puts on his hat. "Coming." As he heads for the door, he adjusts the front of his uniform coat. The look he flings at me over his shoulder is the look of a man fleeing the hellhounds of his conscience. Then he's out the door, slamming it.

I hear the other constable say, "Find anything in there?"

"Nothing," Barrett says.

He's gone before I notice that my boudoir photographs are no longer on the table. He stuffed them under his coat while I wasn't looking. He now has the goods on me that could send me to prison.

33

On Tuesday morning, the newspapers contain the usual stories about the police's fruitless search for Jack the Ripper. I spend that day and the next looking for a new studio. The places I can afford are dumps with no running water and no space for a darkroom. By Thursday morning, 18 October, it's apparent that Barrett has decided to keep to himself the information I gave him and the photographs he stole. I'm disappointed in him yet relieved because the police aren't going to arrest me, and there's still time to save Mr. Lipsky.

On Thursday afternoon, Mick bursts into my studio, where Mrs. Lipsky and I are preparing our tea party for Ida Millbanks. "Something's going on in Whitechapel Road!"

I rush there with Mick. The fog is dense; I don't see the crowd of neighbors and reporters until we're upon it. At the center is

George Lusk of the Mile End Vigilance Committee.

"Two days ago, I received through the post a small package," George Lusk says. "It contained a letter and half of a kidney. I turned them both over to the police. This is what the letter said." He unfolds a paper and begins to read aloud:

Mr. Lusk, I send you half the kidney I took from one women and preserved it for you. The other piece I fried and ate it was very nice I may send you the bloody knife that took it out if you only wait a while longer. Catch me when you can, Mister Lusk.

Reporters shout, "Was the kidney human?"

"Could it really have come from one of the Ripper's victims?"

Puffed up with self-importance, George Lusk says, "The kidney was examined by Dr. Thomas Openshaw of London Hospital. He pronounced that the kidney belonged to a woman who'd been in the habit of drinking, and she died at about the same time the murder in Mitre Square was committed." He adds, with dramatic emphasis, "You will recall that the dead body of Kate Eddowes was missing a kidney."

As we troop back to my studio, Mick and I debate whether the kidney was really Kate's or a mere hoax. "Commissioner Warren might enjoy taunting George Lusk," I say.

"Mr. Lipsky couldn't have sent the kidney. He was in jail," Mick points out.

"The police apparently don't think that's enough reason to let him go," I say.

At my studio, Catherine has arrived; she's setting the table. There are Victoria buns, gingerbread, and a caraway seed cake that Hugh and I bought. Mrs. Lipsky and her friends have contributed turnovers filled with mashed potato and ground meat. I build up the fire with precious coal. Everything must be nice for Ida.

Mick tells Mrs. Lipsky and Catherine about the kidney. "If this Dr. Poole really is Ripper Number Two, how can Ida stand working for him?" he asks.

"If he is, she probably doesn't know it," I reply.

Mick pinches a currant off a Victoria bun and eats it. Catherine says sharply, "Don't do that! Mind your manners!"

His face turns as red as his hair. I feel bad for him, but I don't scold Catherine because then she would treat him even worse. I admire his steadfastness. He could justifiably turn his back on her and leave her at the mercy of the Rippers, but he won't.

Pretending to ignore Catherine, Mick says to me, "Bet you ten pence Ida and her boss are in it together."

"You're on." But even though I've heard no news of a woman possibly being involved in the murders, I'm suddenly afraid of the woman I've waited a week to meet. Glancing out the window, I see a carriage, its lights blurred by the fog, stop in front of the studio.

"They're here," Mick whispers, his eyes wide and bright.

The dank breath of the fog ushers in Hugh and Ida. "Hello, sister dear." Hugh's eye twitches in a conspiratorial wink at Mick and Catherine. He hands Mrs. Lipsky a bottle of wine, then kisses my cheek. Ida Millbanks stands with her hands clasped, wearing the same old-fashioned cloak and a hideous new bonnet trimmed with fake cherries.

"Ida, this is my sister," Hugh says, "Miss Sarah Bain."

"It's a pleasure to meet you," I say, shaking Ida's hand.

I think I'm a good judge of faces. When my customers sit for photographs, they put on expressions designed to make them look their most attractive, but rarely can they hold those expressions for long. Their faces settle into lines that reveal insipidity, avarice, cruelty, or other bad qualities. But in Ida Millbanks, I see only a decent woman who's eager to be liked. She seems unsuspicious; she apparently hasn't read the news stories about the police investigating my father and me in connection with the Ripper case. It's obvious that she doesn't recognize the surname "Bain" — which Hugh claimed as his own when he first introduced himself to her — or doubt that he and I are siblings.

"Thank you for having me." Her husky voice has an educated but not aristocratic accent. Her hand is warmly damp with nervous perspiration.

Mick, Catherine, and Mrs. Lipsky hover. We're like hungry lions sizing up an antelope. Hugh names them and introduces them as "my sister's friends." Ida smiles timidly at Mick and Mrs. Lipsky. Mick looks chagrined, and I mouth *ten pence* at him. He frowns and shakes his head; it's too soon for a final verdict on Ida Millbanks.

Ida looks awed, then worried, by Catherine's beauty. She glances at Hugh, and her thoughts are transparent: Catherine is heavy competition for Hugh's favor.

"I've known Catherine since she was a

baby," Hugh says quickly. "I used to push her in her pram."

"Downhill, at breakneck speed. I was scared half to death," Catherine says, slapping Hugh's arm with fond, sisterly playfulness. "Miss Millbanks, let me take your cloak."

Relieved, Ida hands it over. She's wearing a severe gray wool frock whose high, tight collar emphasizes her lack of a chin. "Miss Bain, your brother tells me you operate your own photography business. That is quite a marvelous accomplishment."

"Thank you." It will be an accomplishment if I manage not to flub this scheme that my friends and I concocted. "Would you like me to show you around the studio?"

"Yes, that would be lovely."

As I show Ida my camera, Mrs. Lipsky retreats to the kitchen. Hugh, Catherine, and Mick trail Ida and me. Now we're like big-footed geese with one egg — we're afraid we'll break it before it hatches.

"How did you learn photography?" Ida asks.

"My father was a photographer. He got me started." The usual lump rises in my throat. It has a bitter flavor due to Commissioner Warren's claims about my father and my own new suspicions that they could be true.

"Our father thought a woman should have a profession," Hugh interjects. "Sarah took up photography because she has the eye for it. Me, I haven't. That's why I'm a lawyer instead." That is his false identity that he created for Ida's benefit.

"My late father thought so, too," Ida says. "That's why he sent me to nursing school." She adds, in a rueful tone, "My late mother said I should prepare to support myself because it was unlikely that any man would marry me."

My mother said the same thing to me, along with other harsh pronouncements, and I thought that because so many years have passed, I'd ceased to mind, but now the memory stings. When she told me that I was too plain and dull to attract a husband, it hurt me as much as when she destroyed my father's photographs, sold his equipment, and called my dream of being a photographer silly.

"Mother was correct," Ida says. "I'm still single and shall probably remain so."

"Not necessarily," Hugh says. "Marriage is a matter of meeting the right person. I thought I would never meet the right person." He fixes a meaningful gaze on Ida.

She utters a flustered laugh. Hugh looks uncomfortable; he doesn't want to lead her on, but he wanted to salve the hurt that her mother and her spinsterhood have caused her. I feel bad about his pretending he cares for Ida, but if we're to save Mr. Lipsky, we've no choice, and the least I can do is help Hugh carry the conversation.

I call Ida's attention to the photographs hung on the wall. "This is my work."

"How nice." Ida smiles at the portraits of my customers, then says wistfully, "I've never had my photograph taken. Mother said the camera makes a sow's ear into a horse's hindquarters."

Hugh, Mick, and Catherine gape at this blatant cruelty. I feel a sudden, inexplicable hatred for Ida's mother. "Why don't I photograph you now?" I say, although I know Ida would be a difficult subject.

Ida clasps her hands under her weak chin; her eyes shine. "Would you really?"

"It would be my pleasure."

Breathless with excitement, Ida says, "What do you want me to do?"

Goose bumps prickle my skin. Polly Nichols asked the same question before I photographed her the first time. I move a chair in front of the backdrop of the Grand Canal. "Sit here while I set up my camera."

"Your hair is so pretty, Miss Millbanks," Catherine says, and she's right — it's a shiny toffee color but tightly plaited and wound; the style makes Ida look like an effeminate Roman emperor. "Why not let it down?"

Ida's hands fly to her head. "But Mother always said —"

"Your mother's not here," Hugh says with an encouraging smile.

"Well . . ." Ida unpins her hair.

Catherine combs it and pins it up in a loose roll from which stray ringlets trail, then she fetches her makeup case. Ida looks panicky as Catherine applies powder and lip rouge to her face and darkens her brows and lashes with burnt, pulverized cloves. Catherine finds a blue-and-green paisley shawl in my props cupboard and drapes it over Ida's shoulders.

"There!" She hands Ida a mirror. "What do you think?"

I think Catherine has worked a miracle. If only her mother could see Ida now!

"Oh, my," Ida murmurs.

"Criminy," Mick says.

"If I were an artist, I would paint you." Hugh's compliment is sincere.

I pose Ida with her hand at her chin to hide its weakness. In the camera's viewfinder, she looks solemnly innocent — so different from Martha, Polly, Annie, Liz, and Kate. I snap the shutter. The flash heightens the shine of her hair and the glow in her eyes. She blinks, as dazed by infatuation with Hugh as by the light. Now I'm ashamed of myself because I not only want to soothe the pain inflicted by her mother, I also want to soften Ida up, and it's working.

"Excuse me while I develop this," I say, then carry the negative plate to the darkroom. When I'm done, I leave the plate to dry and join my guests at the table.

The wine makes us merry, and soon we're all on first-name terms with Ida. Bubbly with new self-confidence, Ida praises the turnovers and asks Mrs. Lipsky for the recipe. She learns that Catherine is an actress and encourages her to tell stories about the theater. She describes animals at Regent's Park Zoo for Mick. Hugh's witty comments keep the conversation flowing. As Ida talks with me about exhibits at London's museums, I wish that we could be friends, that this gay party weren't a charade.

"Tell me, Ida," Hugh says, "how long have you worked for Dr. Poole?"

The atmosphere changes as if the cold fog has invaded the room. Mrs. Lipsky pauses while passing the cake plate to Mick; his reaching hand stops in midair. Catherine and I freeze with our cups held to our lips. Hugh's expectant smile has a hungry quality.

Ida doesn't notice. She dabs a napkin against her mouth. "Almost four years."

Catherine and I set down our cups, Mick snatches a piece of cake, and Mrs. Lipsky replaces the plate on the table. My heart beats fast as we hang on Ida's words.

"After I finished school, I nursed at St. Thomas's Hospital for twelve years, but I fell and hurt my back," Ida says. That explains her slow, stiff gait. "I had to resign because I couldn't stand on my feet for long periods of time or do heavy work. When I looked for other employment, I saw an advertisement from Dr. Poole. He hired me to be his assistant."

"Very fortunate," Hugh says. "What sort of medical services does Dr. Poole provide?"

"Oh, dear." Ida is suddenly shy and flustered again. "One doesn't like to talk about it. His work is of a delicate nature."

"Well then," I say, "what services do you perform for him?"

"Oh, I keep records and run errands, I purchase books —"

"What kind of books?" I ask, remembering the album of my photographs.

"Medical treatises." It's obvious that Ida doesn't read the books and has no idea what she fetched from Mr. Russell's shop. "Mostly, I assist Dr. Poole with his patients."

"Assist how?" Catherine asks.

Fanning her red face with her napkin, Ida laughs nervously. "One can't discuss it in polite company."

Mick opens his mouth to say, "We're not polite." I kick him under the table. He frowns.

Eager to offer us something she can tell without embarrassment, Ida says, "Dr. Poole is a brilliant physician. He was appointed as a researcher at Bedlam."

We murmur, as people do at the mention of London's notorious insane asylum.

"He performs experiments there," Ida says. "He writes monographs and publishes them in medical journals. He also performs experiments in his laboratory at home."

The word *laboratory* resonates like a low-pitched minor chord struck on a piano, which everyone except Ida can hear.

"You mentioned the laboratory the other day," Hugh says. "What work does he do there?"

"I'm afraid I don't know." Ida's gaiety is gone; she's aware that her reticence has put a damper on the conversation. "I've never been inside." Fidgeting with the fringe on the shawl, she explains, "I don't assist Dr. Poole with his experiments. He works alone."

"Haven't you ever peeked?" Catherine asks.

"I would never." Ida's blackened eyebrows rise with shock at the idea of spying on her employer. "Besides, Dr. Poole keeps the door locked."

The laboratory seems a repository of everything we need to prove that Dr. Poole is Ripper Number Two and exonerate Mr. Lipsky. "Do you know where the key is?" Mick asks.

"Well . . . I once saw him put it in a tin box on the mantle in his office," Ida confesses.

"Aren't you curious?" Catherine asks.

Ida shakes her head. I can tell she's a person who unquestioningly obeys authority. She also takes people at face value, which is why she's accepted Dr. Poole as a brilliant physician even though she's in the dark about his experiments, and why she accepted us as friends.

"Well, I'm curious," Hugh says. "Maybe your Dr. Poole is like Dr. Frankenstein in Mary Shelley's novel, trying to reanimate

corpses. Perhaps we should sneak in sometime when he's out and have a look?"

"I couldn't betray his trust." Ida's eyes
shine with tears. She's eager to please Hugh,
but not at the expense of her integrity.

"He wouldn't have to know," Mick says.

"*I* would know!" Ida bursts out.

Hugh, Catherine, and Mick are pushing
her too hard. I must rescue her before she
begins to dislike us. "The negative plate
should be dry by now," I say. "Ida, would
you like to watch me print your photograph?"

"Yes!" Breathless with relief, Ida follows
me into the darkroom.

I shut the door. There's an uncomfortable
silence while I try to think of something to
say that will restore Ida to good spirits and
salvage our hope of getting to Dr. Poole
through her. I can't think of a way to do
both. "My brother and my friends can be
such awful teases. I owe you an apology,
Ida. We had no right to ask such a thing of
you. Please forgive us."

"No, it's I who should apologize," Ida says
with touching earnestness, "for disappoint-
ing all of you after you've been so kind to
me."

"Kind" hardly describes us. I consider
making a clean breast by telling Ida that we

think Dr. Poole is a murderer and asking her to help us prove it, but I quickly dismiss that idea. Who would she believe — her employer, or people who befriended her under false pretenses?

Feeling guiltier than ever, I say, "Let us put it behind us. There will be no more talk of Dr. Poole." I feel my friends listening outside the door, and I sense their alarm.

Ida nods gratefully. I turn on the red safe light, place the negative plate in the enlarger, and expose the blank paper. As I swish the paper in the developing solution and an image gradually appears, Ida says, "It's like magic."

I hold my breath as I take the red shade off the lamp, and we behold the photograph floating in the tray. The blurred focus romanticizes Ida's face. The flash created the effect of sunlight, the paisley shawl adds an exotic touch, and Ida's hand under her chin is shapely and feminine. Enchanted by Hugh, she has a radiance heightened by Catherine's makeup. I let out my breath. Her portrait is among the best I've ever taken.

Ida bursts into sobs.

My best isn't good enough. Leaning on the worktop, I bow my head. I've not only used Ida; I've hurt an innocent woman I would like for a friend. I've failed as a photographer; I've lost a battle against Ida's late mother — and a battle that I've become dimly aware that I'm waging, for some unknown reason, against my own. Hugh, Mick, Catherine, and Mrs. Lipsky rush into the darkroom. They stare in dismay at Ida weeping and turn reproachful gazes on me. I've also lost us all hope of getting inside Dr. Poole's laboratory. Ida will never want to see us again.

"It's not me!" Ida cries. "It's more beautiful than I could ever be." Her voice twitters with emotion. "Sarah, you are an artist!"

We smile with relief, and my loss becomes a sweet victory. Hugh clasps Ida's hand and says, "It's the beautiful woman inside you. Sarah merely brought her out." He looks into her wet eyes, raises her hand to his lips, and kisses it.

Mick grimaces, embarrassed by the romantic gesture. Catherine regards Hugh with the respect of one actor for another's expertise. Mrs. Lipsky and I avert guilty gazes from Ida.

"Oh, oh, oh, my." Ida cradles her hand as if wanting to preserve Hugh's kiss. I think of Barrett and feel a sad, bitter pang in my heart.

Ida's face takes on an expression fraught

435

with uncertainty and rashness. "Dr. Poole will be away at a medical conference on the eighth of November. Will you be my guests for dinner at his house then?"

She wants to repay my favor. For a moment, we can't believe our luck has turned; we're speechless. Then I find my voice. "We would be delighted to accept."

Soon afterward, Hugh escorts Ida home. She leaves with the photograph and the shawl — a gift to ease my guilty conscience and a bribe to get us inside Dr. Poole's laboratory. Elated yet exhausted from our efforts, Catherine, Mick, Mrs. Lipsky, and I sink into chairs.

"Good work, Miss Sarah," Mick says, munching leftover gingerbread.

I nod, unable to summon the energy to reply.

"The eighth of November is three weeks away," Catherine laments. "Poor Mr. Lipsky will have to stay in jail at least that much longer."

I picture him alone in a dark cell. Despair could kill even a man as strong as he.

"There must be something else we can do in the meantime," Catherine says.

Mrs. Lipsky has stayed in the background tonight, as she has during all our ventures, but now she leans forward, her dark eyes aglow. "I have idea."

34

At one o'clock in the morning on Monday, 29 October, Mrs. Lipsky and I stand outside Bethlem Royal Hospital. The insane asylum commonly known as Bedlam rises before us like a cliff capped by the massive dome. The building's opposite ends vanish into the fog, seeming to extend into infinity in both directions. Most of the windows, shielded by bars, are dark.

I've been inside Bedlam with the crowds who pay to see the inmates as though they're animals in a zoo. I've photographed the clean, bright wards and the mostly docile patients. But I was afraid that the line between sanity and insanity is thin and that the keepers would decide I belonged on the other side and make me stay. Now, as we loiter at the back gate in the dead of night, I wonder if I am indeed a mad-woman, for who else would sneak *into* an insane asylum?

Mrs. Lipsky and I are wearing coarse brown frocks with white muslin aprons and caps — maids' uniforms stolen from the laundry at Bedlam. Coming here was her idea, and she shows no misgivings. A woman who has buried three children, whose husband is in danger of hanging for a crime he didn't commit, has little to lose.

The gate opens. Dim light from within silhouettes a tall, thin, lanky man carrying a broom and dustpan. Mrs. Lipsky introduces him as Gregor. He works at Bedlam, and he stole the uniforms for us. He is part of a network of Jews spread throughout London who are connected by blood or common acquaintances, who help one another. Gregor leans in for a close look at me. Some forty years old, he smells of sweat, onions, and tobacco. His face tapers from wide, high cheekbones to his thin, pointed beard. His brows are straight slashes above deep-set eyes. His scrutiny is intense, somber.

"I hope this won't get you in trouble," I say nervously.

He flashes a smile; his stained teeth are crooked. "The bosses don't know all the things that go on here." His English is accented but fluent. "This is just one more." He beckons.

Inside the gate, the fog obscures the

hospital grounds. The door from which the light shines leads to stairs. Climbing them, we meet no one. Electrified lamps shine with an unnatural brightness. Disinfectants inadequately mask a pervasive smell of urine. I hear clangs like cages rattling, and voices gibbering. My heart is pounding with fear and exertion by the time we reach the top floor and emerge in a dim, quiet corridor with walls painted a drab green and closed doors bearing nameplates. Gregor stops at an unmarked door.

"This is Dr. Poole's laboratory." He selects a key from the ring that hangs from his belt, unlocks the door, and reaches in.

Electric light flares. Mrs. Lipsky and I cautiously enter a small room with cupboards mounted on gray walls above slate worktops. Our footsteps are loud on the tile floor. The air is pungent with disinfectant. A strange machine sits on a wooden cart with two shelves. On the top shelf, wires protrude from a dozen large glass discs arranged side by side and attached to brass rods, a crank, levers, and gears. Black cables join this contraption to a smaller one on the bottom shelf, which consists of black cylinders, mechanical parts, and a meter with an arrow pointing at white numbers. The whole apparatus, mounted on casters, is some six feet high and four feet square. I've never seen anything like it, but I distrust machinery. In the factory where my mother and I worked, one of the girls got caught in a machine. I heard her scream, saw blood fly, and glimpsed her amputated hand on the floor.

Beside the machine is what looks to be an operating table, equipped with shackles for the patient's wrists and ankles and a contraption to immobilize his head. "What is it?" I ask.

"Watch." Gregor takes hold of the machine's crank.

"Don't touch anything! Dr. Poole mustn't know anyone's been here."

"No worry. He's not coming back."

"How do you know?"

"He resigned. That is official story. Truth is, he was sacked."

Ida Millbanks didn't tell us. I suppose Dr. Poole didn't tell her. "When was this?"

"End of July."

The glass-fronted cupboards are empty. Mrs. Lipsky opens empty drawers beneath the worktops, which are filmy with dust. An enclosure with a glass screen lowered over the front contains a sink with water taps. The sink is dry. Probably no one has been in the laboratory these past four months.

Mrs. Lipsky shows despair for the first time since the night her husband was arrested. This place seems unlikely to contain evidence that will exonerate him.

"Why was Dr. Poole sacked?" I ask.

"Because of the woman who died here," Gregor says.

My heart leaps with the same hope that brightens Mrs. Lipsky's face. Dr. Poole is associated with a death that occurred before the Ripper murders. "Who was she?"

"Her name was Emma Forbes. She was governess, and she was put in Bedlam for trying to kill herself. Dr. Poole, he did her favor. He killed her with this." Gregor turns the crank on the machine. The glass discs spin. Sparks shoot from the wires, and a smell like the air during a thunderstorm fills the room. Mrs. Lipsky and I gasp. "He gave her big electric shock."

The workings of electricity are as mysterious as magic to me, but I know that a big shock is akin to being struck by lightning — fatal. "What was Dr. Poole doing?"

"Scientific experiments." Gregor uses the same hushed, fearful tone that a superstitious man would use to say "witchcraft."

"What kind of experiments?"

Gregor shrugs. "Don't ask me. I just clean up during midnight shift." His discolored smile flashes. "I was here the night she died."

Mrs. Lipsky and I listen eagerly as he says, "Dr. Poole brought inmates up here. All women. He kept door locked. I never went in because he cleaned in here himself. One night I'm mopping floor in ward, and I hear nurses talking. 'Dr. Poole took Emma Forbes three hours ago and hasn't brought her back.' Nurse goes upstairs to see what's what. I'm curious, so I follow her. She knocks on door, but there's no answer. She tells me, open the door."

Gregor jingles his keys. "She is lying there." He points at the table. "Her stomach is cut open. Her guts are there, sorted into different piles. Bloody knife beside them." Gregor points at the worktop. "Dr. Poole is taking pictures with camera. There is blood all over him." Gregor curses in Russian.

Mrs. Lipsky and I are speechless, our shock laced with glee because here is eyewitness testimony that Dr. Poole cut and mutilated a patient and must indeed be Ripper Number Two.

"Nurse screams. Guards come running. Nurse faints. Guards carry her out and take me and Dr. Poole downstairs. They lock him in conference room and me in office next door. Bosses come talk to Dr. Poole. I listen.

They ask, 'Did you kill Emma Forbes?' He say it was accident — she must have had weak heart. They ask him why he cut her up. He say he want to see what his treatment did to her insides, and she was already dead."

A curtain opens to reveal a new dimension of the crimes: The two Rippers have different motives. Commissioner Warren kills for sport, but Dr. Poole kills for science. I don't know why Dr. Poole chose my models for his experiments or what he hopes to learn, but I deduce that Commissioner Warren mutilates his victims not only because he enjoys it; he's copying Dr. Poole so that all the crimes will be attributed to one man — Jack the Ripper. Warren must have viewed the bodies of the first two murdered women — Martha and Polly — and realized that the Ripper was choosing victims from my boudoir photographs, which both men had purchased from Russell's Fine Books. I'm certain that he didn't kill Martha and Polly; Mick and I found no souvenirs from them in his house with Annie's rings. He didn't know Dr. Poole would kill Liz Stride on the same night that he himself killed Kate Eddowes.

"Bosses tell Dr. Poole, resign. If he don't, he will go to jail." Gregor shrugs. "Same as being sacked, if you ask me. They tell me to clean up his laboratory, get rid of everything. I wrap up body and guts, take them to incinerator. Machine and table are too heavy. I can't move them by myself, so I leave them. I put other things in dustbin, I mop up the blood."

He obliterated the evidence. I ask, "Would you be willing to tell the police your story?"

"Hey. Whoa." Gregor waggles his hands. "No police."

"But your story is evidence that Dr. Poole is Jack the Ripper!"

"I don't care if he is the devil! Bosses said not to tell anybody. I don't want to lose my job."

The same rush of anger I felt when PC Barrett resisted telling on Commissioner Warren overpowers me now. "I don't care about your job! You have to tell. You should have reported Dr. Poole to the police long ago. He's a murderer. You're a selfish coward!"

Gregor glares at me. "You don't talk to me that way."

Mrs. Lipsky, alarmed by my outburst, says, "Sarah, please."

Yesterday, I berated a shopkeeper who shortchanged me a halfpence; now I've blown up at this man who's doing me a

445

favor. "I'm sorry. Please forgive me." I don't understand why my temper is worse than ever. "Who is the nurse, and where can I find her?"

Appeased, Gregor says, "She quit. I don't know where she is."

"The guards?"

"Won't talk either."

My heart sinks. The only other people who know about Dr. Poole are the "bosses." They must be aware of the Whitechapel murders and the similarities between the Ripper's mutilation of his victims and Dr. Poole's of Emma Forbes, but they're keeping quiet to protect themselves from the scandal that would result were the public to hear that they covered for Jack the Ripper.

In desperation, I say, "Did Dr. Poole leave any papers?"

"I burned them." Gregor watches my face fall and grins as if he's played a joke on me. "I kept some. Just in case bosses give me trouble someday, I have something on them."

I'm about to flay him for his ill-timed humor, when he frowns and holds his finger to his lips. I hear footsteps coming. Gregor grabs his broom and dustpan, extinguishes the lights, pushes Mrs. Lipsky and me out the door, and locks it. He reaches in his pocket and pulls out a wad of folded papers, which he shoves into my hand. "Go!"

I stuff the papers in my apron pocket as we run down the passage. Gregor whistles and sweeps the floor, clanking his dustpan to cover our noise. Mrs. Lipsky and I are racing down the stairs before I realize they're not the same ones we came up. The dim spiral of gray stone leads us to a passage where rocks protrude from the walls and bare rafters support the low ceiling. Muffled screams echo. A man is straddling a woman who lies on the floor. His trousers are pulled down to his knees. Her naked legs kick as he couples with her. Her mouth is gagged; her arms are immobilized by a garment that resembles a blanket with sleeves tied around her waist. Ferocious with lust, the man looks more animal than human, and so do the three men watching. The air stinks of sweat, liquor, and terror.

Mrs. Lipsky and I falter to a stop as we realize that the men are keepers from the wards, abusing a female patient. My anger explodes so suddenly that I don't think before I snatch up a broom that leans against the wall.

"Sarah, no!" Mrs. Lipsky grabs my arm before I can hit the men.

They look up, see us, and their expressions turn savage. I drop the broom as Mrs. Lipsky and I run. The men charge after us to stop us from reporting them. Turning corners, we gasp with exertion and fright. The cellar is a huge labyrinth. Machinery thunders and clangs. With the men close on our heels, we run up a ramp and emerge into the foggy night. They're panting behind us like the hounds of hell. We find a gate and struggle to draw back the heavy iron bar. Then we're running down a street alongside the hospital. I don't dare look backward, but I hear the men gaining on us. Mrs. Lipsky wheezes; her pace flags. I slow down to let the men catch me so she can get away.

A carriage and horse appear like a mirage in the fog. "Help!" I cry.

The carriage door opens. "Sarah?" Hugh calls.

Mrs. Lipsky reaches the carriage, where Hugh and Mick have been waiting for us because Gregor didn't want to sneak more than two people into Bedlam. Hugh and Mick pull Mrs. Lipsky inside. As I lunge for the carriage, hands seize my waist. I scream. My friends clutch my arms; the men have hold of my legs. In the fracas of pulling and shouting, I feel as if I'm being torn in two. I desperately kick. The men yelp and let go.

My friends haul me into the carriage, and Hugh yells to the driver, "Go, dammit!"

The whip cracks; the carriage speeds forward. The men run after us, cursing as they're left in the dust.

By the time we reach my studio, I have told Mick and Hugh what happened in Bedlam. My anger has cooled; I'm shaken because it almost got Mrs. Lipsky and myself killed. I vow to keep a tighter rein on my temper.

As I put on the teakettle, Hugh lounges in a chair, flexing his bandaged right wrist; it was sprained during the fracas. "What did Gregor give you?"

I pull the papers from my apron pocket, unfold them, and lay them on the table. We gather to look at three creased photographs.

"Damn!" Hugh turns his back on them.

The first shows a woman lying on the operating table in Dr. Poole's laboratory. The camera was positioned above her, aimed downward. The image encompasses her naked body from neck to thighs. Her wrists are shackled. Below her flat breasts and bony ribcage, her stomach is cut open, the skin flaps held back by metal pincers. In the opening, a small organ shaped like a lumpy, inverted pear sits amid coiled intestines.

Mick, Mrs. Lipsky, and I are dumbstruck, revolted.

The second photograph shows a white butcher tray containing a ruler placed below the pear-shaped organ. A film of blood on the tray looks gray in the black-and-white print. In the third photograph, the female body on the table resembles Annie Chapman's in the morgue — innards scooped out, body cavity empty.

Everything we've learned about Dr. Poole indicates that he is indeed Ripper Number Two, but we're discouraged in spite of our success. There's a great divide between finding this evidence and freeing Mr. Lipsky.

"What's that?" Mick points to the organ on the tray.

I shake my head; all I know about human anatomy is what's visible on the outside.

"It is her womb." Mrs. Lipsky, a butcher's wife, has seen animals taken apart.

Polly Nichols's abdomen was mutilated, perhaps in a bungled attempt to remove her womb, but this possible connection between her and Dr. Poole brings us no closer to delivering him into the hands of the law. I turn over the photographs, hoping for clues written on the backs, but they're blank. Then I notice something about the photographs.

"These are two different women."

"You're right," Mick says, then points to one. "The dugs on her are bigger."

And the woman whose stomach is held open by clips has a spot on her left arm — the initials T. C. "The other woman must be Emma Forbes, but this is Kate Eddowes!" I'm excited because another piece of the puzzle has dropped into place. "Kate wasn't in a knife fight, and she didn't go to the infirmary. It was Dr. Poole who cut her — and stitched her up."

Hugh whistles; Mick cheers; Mrs. Lipsky and I smile. We've drawn a direct connection between Dr. Poole and a Ripper victim, no matter that Kate was killed by Commissioner Warren.

"Dr. Poole must have been the customer that John Kelly said she did 'special things' for," I say. "She let him experiment on her, and he cut her open."

"Didn't Gregor say Dr. Poole was sacked for mutilating only one woman?" Hugh says.

"The 'bosses' probably don't know about Kate. She wasn't a mental patient. He must have sneaked her in and out of Bedlam."

"Why would he let her go instead of taking her guts out like the other one?" Mick asks.

"Maybe he didn't mean to kill Emma.

451

Maybe her death really was an accident, and he seized the opportunity to do a dissection. Maybe Kate had a stronger heart." Another idea comes to me. "He must have taken out Kate's womb. That would explain the symptoms John Kelly described." I know enough about anatomy to know that monthly periods originate in the womb, and the loss of it must mean no more periods.

"Dr. Poole, what secrets did you think you could find inside the cradle of life?" Hugh says.

None of us can answer for Dr. Poole.

"The timing is interesting," Hugh says. "Dr. Poole was sacked in July. The Ripper murders began in August. I think that when Dr. Poole lost his facilities at Bedlam and his access to the inmates, he still wanted to pursue his experiments. He must not have tried it at his house because his patients or neighbors might notice that something fishy was going on."

"So he started cuttin' women in Whitechapel," Mick says. "But what kind of experiments could he do out there on the streets? And why Miss Sarah's models?"

None of us can answer those questions, either. Weary and discouraged, I say, "We still can't prove Dr. Poole is Ripper Number Two. And it's more important than ever to get him arrested."

"Why's that?" Mick asks.

"Because tonight we learned that Dr. Poole is capable of switching from one type of victim to another — mental patients to streetwalkers," Hugh deduces. "Sarah's models may be his favorites for some reason, but every woman who crosses his path is in danger, too." He adds unhappily, "Since Gregor won't talk, there's nothing except Sarah and Rachel's word to say that the photographs came from Dr. Poole's laboratory in Bedlam."

This is the same problem we've had all along: We've much evidence, but it's open to interpretation, not conclusive enough to risk taking to the authorities. We're like fishermen who've caught a net full of fish and aren't strong enough to pull it into our boat.

"Don't give up hope yet," Mick says. "We're going to Dr. Poole's house soon."

35

On 8 November, Mick, Catherine, Hugh, and I ride in a cab along Marylebone Road. "Shall we tell Ida what we've learned about Dr. Poole?" I ask. We've been debating the issue for days, and now, on our way to dinner with Ida, is the time to decide.

"I think we have to," says Hugh, seated opposite me, next to Mick. "We can't let that poor, sweet woman go on working for that monster."

"He won't hurt her. He only kills Sarah's models," Catherine says. The cab is fragrant with her rose-and-lavender perfume and crowded with her petticoats; there's barely room for me on the seat beside her.

"Models that include you, dear girl," Hugh says. "You and Mary Jane Kelly are still left."

"I'm not like the others. He can't know who I am because I'm not a streetwalker, I don't live in Whitechapel, and even if he figured out where to find me, he can't kill me because I have a bodyguard."

"He can't kill Mary Jane either, while she's off the streets," I say. "He might be restless enough to kill Ida even if she's not his first choice."

Our cab inches through unusually heavy traffic. The Lord Mayor's Show is tomorrow. Every autumn, the Lord Mayor of London travels in a magnificent coach from the city to Westminster to swear loyalty to the Crown. A procession of soldiers, dignitaries, marching bands, civic organizations, and followers — miles long, thousands of people — accompanies him. The Show is the biggest pageant in England, and it draws spectators from all over the kingdom. Tonight, people are gathering at the inns and public houses, strolling the city.

"If anything happened to Ida, I would never forgive myself," Hugh says. "After fooling her into thinking I'm interested in her, the least I owe her is a warning."

"You did it for Mr. Lipsky's sake. And Catherine's." Mick steals a glance at Catherine, seated across from him, her skirts puffed up against his knees. She pulls her skirts away from him. He sighs sadly.

"If we tell Ida, we'll also have to tell her that we befriended her under false pretenses." I'm torn between doing the right thing and sparing Ida's feelings.

"We tricked Ida. Being nice to her was an act. Why should she trust us instead of Dr. Poole?" Catherine asks.

"I can't keep wooing her forever," Hugh points out. "I'll have to break it off eventually, and she'll be hurt whether we tell her about Dr. Poole or not."

"Can't you make her understand why we did it?" I ask.

Hugh responds with a glum chuckle. " 'Your employer is the Ripper. All we care about is putting him out of action. You're just our tool.' That's a tall order to stuff down her throat."

"You're so smart, you can think of a nicer way to put it," Catherine snaps.

"If you think there's any way to sugarcoat it, you're not so smart," Hugh retorts.

The responsibility that comes with our knowledge is wearing on us, and we're turning on one another. It's up to me to settle the argument. "I'll tell her. After we've seen the laboratory." Guilt forms in me like stalactites dripping acid in my stomach. PC Barrett's deception still hurts me, and before this night is over, we'll have caused Ida similar pain.

We climb out of the cab in front of Dr.

Poole's house. The foggy street is quiet. In the light from the lamp over its door, the house looks as inviting as a block of moldy white cheese in a mousetrap. I shiver, glad that Dr. Poole himself is in Cambridge.

While telling the driver to wait for us, Hugh drops the bottle of wine he's brought. Glass shatters; liquor splashes on the pavement. "Damn! It's too late to get another."

Ida opens the door. She's wearing the paisley shawl over a black dress. Her hair is pinned up in a clumsy facsimile of the style Catherine created, but she's not attempted makeup. "Come in." Her eyes are bright with excitement and apprehension. She looks like a woman who is about to give up her virginity and already regrets it.

The vestibule has shiny gold-and-cream-striped wallpaper and black-and-white floor tiles. Everything looks clean, opulent, and normal. That in itself is disturbing: women who come here to see Dr. Poole are oblivious to the danger. Ida hangs our wraps on a mahogany coat tree. Her unease, and ours, casts a pall over the evening.

"Where is Rachel Lipsky?" Ida asks, fidgeting with the fringe on the shawl.

"She couldn't come. She's ill," I say. After our trip to Bedlam, Mrs. Lipsky had a fainting spell. The Jewish doctor says her worry about her husband is weakening her health.

Catherine attempts to put our hostess at ease. "How lovely you look, Ida." Eager to explore, she wanders down the hall. The rest of us follow. On the right of the staircase is a parlor; on the left, two open doors with a closed one between. The first room is a waiting room, furnished with plush chairs for Dr. Poole's patients. The far door belongs to his office. Our gazes speed past the desk to the mantle over the fireplace. There, a round tin box glows. It's only reflecting light from the hallway, but I imagine the laboratory key inside shining like the Holy Grail.

Framed photographs decorate the hall. We study the groups of men — dressed for playing cricket; seated in rowing shells on a river; posed in academic gowns outside a columned building; white-coated in an operating theater. We stop at the portrait of a man dressed in a formal dark coat, seated at a table upon which sits a microscope, with a diagram of a human skeleton behind him. He gazes past the camera, his mind apparently occupied with grave scientific matters.

"Is this Dr. Poole?" I ask.

"Yes," Ida whispers, as if afraid he can hear us.

The man we've been seeking is neither handsome nor ugly, perhaps forty years old. His brow is wide and high; his features seem crowded into the bottom half of his smooth-complexioned face. Rimless spectacles frame pale, intelligent eyes. His hair, of indiscernible color, is short and sleek. A sparse goatee surrounds a mouth that's broad and full-lipped but compressed. I feel no sense of recognition; I didn't get a good look at him before he murdered Liz. I'm surprised because he looks so conventional, so devoid of the hot passions I perceived in Commissioner Warren. But it makes sense that Dr. Poole isn't the sinister, black-mustached foreigner described by witnesses. That he doesn't fit anyone's image of a killer has surely helped him escape notice when stalking his victims and leaving the scenes of their murders.

"There he is." Mick points to a younger Dr. Poole in the photograph of the rowing crews. His limbs bulge with muscle in his shorts and sleeveless jersey.

"He was an outstanding athlete as well as a top medical student at Oxford." Ida seems puzzled by our interest in Dr. Poole.

The front door opens. Startled, we turn. Dr. Poole himself, accompanied by a whiff of the cold fog, walks into our horrified midst.

"Miss Millbanks." His voice is upper-middle-class, educated, and quiet. He's older than in his portrait; his neat hair and goatee are iron gray; but his black overcoat covers a body still muscular and vigorous. As he hangs his hat on the rack, irritation animates the features that are so sedately composed in his photograph. "Who are these people?"

Even more horrifying than his unexpected arrival is the fact that we didn't sense him coming. We're as caught by surprise as his victims must have been when this normal-looking man attacked them with his knife.

"Dr. Poole!" Ida's hand grips her throat. "These are my friends. I — I invited them to dinner. I thought you were in Cambridge."

"I decided not to go." His skin, which appears smooth in the photograph, is stippled with large pores. Dark spots fleck the pale gray irises of his eyes. "You know you're not supposed to bring anyone here. This is grounds for dismissal."

Ida extends clasped hands to him; tears fill her eyes. "Please forgive me! I'll never do it again."

We're dumbstruck. Our scheme is ruined,

and we've gotten Ida in trouble for nothing. Dr. Poole's disapproving gaze skims over Hugh, Mick, and me, and halts on Catherine. He seems not just taken by her beauty, but startled by recognition. Catherine automatically smiles and bats her eyes, then looks aghast as she recalls who he is. I thought things couldn't get worse, but they have, and I see Hugh and Mick realize it too.

We've brought Dr. Poole and Catherine together.

"Very well," Dr. Poole says to Ida, his attention still on Catherine, his expression now bemused. "Just this once, I'll let it pass. Will you introduce me to your friends?"

"Oh! Thank you!" Ida gasps with relief. "This is Catherine Price. She's an actress at the Oxford Music Hall."

Dr. Poole extends his hand to Catherine. "My pleasure."

Now he knows her name and where to find her. Mick growls softly, like a watchdog whose mistress is threatened. Hugh and I are too alarmed to speak. Catherine shakes Dr. Poole's hand and murmurs politely. She withdraws her fingers from his grasp, her smile frozen; she holds her hand stiff at her side, as if it's contaminated by the blood on his.

"This is Sarah Bain," Ida says. "She owns her own photography studio in Whitechapel."

And now Dr. Poole knows who I am and where I'm to be found. Does he suspect that I took the boudoir pictures of Catherine and his victims? Does he fear that Kate told me about his experiments on her? I'm afraid to look into his eyes and see if he does; I can't bear to touch him. I curtsey; he bows. Ida introduces Mick and Hugh. As they and Dr. Poole shake hands, Mick's expression is frightened and hostile, Hugh's grin sickly.

"Welcome." Dr. Poole's manner has the suave, practiced courtesy that he must use on his patients. "Please stay for dinner as my guests. Would you like some sherry?"

Glances fly between Hugh, Catherine, and me. If we hope to carry out our scheme, we must accept his invitation. Hugh recovers first. "That's very generous of you."

Dr. Poole hangs up his coat. He's wearing an expensive black suit over a starched, pristine white shirt. He ushers us into the parlor and pours sherry, serving Catherine first, as Ida chatters nervously about how she and Hugh met and the tea party at my studio. "Whitechapel has lately been much in the newspapers," he says. "As a neurologist, I have an interest in aberrations of human behavior, and I've been following the murder case."

He's speaking so nonchalantly, as if he has nothing to do with his own crimes. His murderous nature is concealed inside the smooth, high dome of his head. I picture a bell jar that encases a tableau of preserved scorpions and cobras.

"Would you give us the benefit of your professional opinion?" Hugh asks. "What sort of man do you think the Ripper is?"

"In my professional opinion, he is a sexual deviant who hates women in general and women of immoral character in particular. He may be impotent. If so, stabbing is a substitute for penetration, and he obtains gratification from killing." Dr. Poole conveys in a matter-of-fact tone the sort of information that normally isn't spoken in mixed company. "He views his victims as fair game, and he enjoys the thrill of the hunt."

This might describe Commissioner Warren. Is Dr. Poole also describing himself, or is science his sole motivation? It's unfair to leave the whole conversation to Hugh, so I venture, "The newspapers have said the Ripper could be a medical man. Do you think so?"

Catherine, Hugh, and Mick start in alarm at my veiled accusation. Ida smiles because we and Dr. Poole are getting along so well.

"The wounds on his victims exhibit more brutality than surgical precision." Dr. Poole sips his sherry. "The Russian butcher who's been arrested seems the probable culprit."

He's blaming his own crimes on Mr. Lipsky. I'm too indignant to speak. Hugh compresses his lips; anger sparks in Catherine's eyes; Mick glowers. Ida looks disturbed; she senses something amiss.

"Shall we go in to dinner?" she says.

"A capital idea." Hugh offers her his arm.

Dr. Poole offers his to Catherine. Mick starts forward to put himself between them. I hold him back. We follow the others to the dining room. Seeing Dr. Poole walking arm in arm with Catherine jolts me back to the night of the double murders. The shape of his body viewed from the back, his unhurried but determined gait . . .

He is the man I saw in Berner Street with Liz.

I feel a sudden, overpowering urge to run. It's the self-preservation instinct of a sparrow that feels a hawk's shadow fall over it. My muscles quiver, my heart races, and sweat chills me. To get away from Dr. Poole, if only for a moment, I offer to help Ida with the food. As we serve the mock turtle soup, I almost drop the bowl I put before

Dr. Poole, seated at the head of a table laid with a white linen cloth, burning candles, heavy silverware and crystal, and flowered china. Catherine is on his right, Mick beside her. Ida takes the place at the foot of the table. My seat is beside Hugh, on Dr. Poole's left. When I try a spoonful of rich, sherry-laced soup, it threatens to come back up. Hugh and Catherine praise Ida's cooking, but not even Mick is hungry. Only Dr. Poole eats with relish. Ida pretends not to notice that our soup plates are still full when she removes them. She and I serve the roasted duck with sage-and-onion stuffing and mashed potatoes. The duck on my plate is red at the bone. I can't manage a single bite.

We are dining with Jack the Ripper. The blood that our host has spilled taints the atmosphere like a nauseous gas, but he looks so much the civilized, law-abiding pillar of the medical community. Our scheme to expose Dr. Poole now seems absurd. I remember the night of the double murders, running through the dark streets, thinking the Ripper was after me. That same terror reawakens, stripping away the boldness that I've developed during these past months. I'm shrinking back into my shell, although it's no safe place to hide.

But my friends are bolder by nature than I, they didn't experience the terror of that night, and even if they're afraid of Dr. Poole, they're reassured by our safety in numbers. Hugh talks while he, Catherine, and Mick push food around on their plates. "Pardon my ignorance, but what exactly does a neurologist do?"

"I treat diseases of the nervous system." Dr. Poole eats tidily, often dabbing his full lips with his napkin, alternating bites of duck, stuffing, and potatoes. Ida nibbles, watching us anxiously. "My specialty is hysteria."

"What is that?"

"Hysteria is a disturbance of the uterus — the womb. It's caused by fluids accumulated due to stress. The symptoms include faintness, bloating, shortness of breath, muscle spasms, melancholy, erratic behavior, and delusions. It's common in nuns, widows, and other single women."

So I am a prime candidate for hysteria. Indeed, I am experiencing faintness and shortness of breath, although it's from fear, not accumulated fluids. My behavior certainly has been erratic, and I must have been deluded to think our scheme was a good idea!

"How is hysteria treated?" Hugh asks.

"By inducing a phenomenon called hysterical paroxysm. It disperses the excess fluids. I'm conducting research at Bethlem Royal Hospital to determine whether the treatment can cure insanity." Dr. Poole speaks as if he still has his post at Bedlam; he lies without visible discomposure. "The results are quite promising. The women are calmer, happier, and less fractious after the treatment."

Maybe it's good that I didn't tell PC Barrett about him. He could easily lie his way through an interrogation by the police. They would never believe he's Jack the Ripper. He has that much in common with Commissioner Warren.

"But that is only one aspect of my research. The other involves determining why the treatment works. My theory is that during hysterical paroxysm, the uterus produces a substance that spreads through the body and promotes healing. My aim is to identify the substance."

"How?" Hugh asks.

"By inducing a hysterical paroxysm, then removing the uterus and extracting and analyzing its fluids."

Mick looks confused by the technical language. Catherine pushes her plate away. Hugh and I try to hide our shock. Here is the reason Dr. Poole dissected Emma Forbes, operated on Kate Eddowes, and cut open Polly Nichols.

"Isn't it a problem getting specimens?" Hugh manages to say. "Wouldn't many women be unhappy to part with their, er, uteruses?"

"Some women would benefit from the surgical removal of their uteruses," Dr. Poole says calmly. "Those who have had too many children, for example."

Ida serves the dessert — ladyfingers topped with whipped cream and red strawberry sauce. Portions sit untouched on all the plates except hers and Dr. Poole's.

"Society would benefit if some women were relieved of their ability to reproduce," Dr. Poole says. "Women who are indigent, immoral, or insane, for example."

Now he has justified killing prostitutes. I wonder when he decided that science outweighs morals. Was there ever a time when he viewed women as fellow humans he wanted to cure instead of as material for experimentation? What flaw in his nature drove him to employ his talents in such a terrible fashion? I don't suppose I'll ever learn the answers. Analyzing Dr. Poole is like photographing him from a distance. His aspect would be blurry no matter how much

I enlarged the print, because I don't want to get close enough to bring him into focus.

"There must be thousands of women of that type." Hugh valiantly hides his revulsion toward Dr. Poole. "How do you pick your subjects?"

"The ideal subjects are the ones in which multiple hysterical paroxysms are easily induced." Dr. Poole must think my models fall into that category, and that, plus the fact that they were vulnerable on the streets at night, is why he chose them to kill. "They would produce the greatest quantity of the substance."

"How are these hysterical paroxysms induced?" Hugh asks.

"With a special technique." Dr. Poole asks Catherine, "Would you like to try it?"

36

"No, she wouldn't!" Mick blurts.

I'm so alarmed by the idea of Catherine subjected to treatment by Dr. Poole that I can't find the breath to object. Hugh says, "Oh, but we wouldn't want to impose on you."

"It would be my pleasure," Dr. Poole says.

Catherine rises. She looks as she did the day I found her at Euston Station — innocent, frightened, and excited. "I would like it very much — if Sarah and Ida may keep me company."

The covert glance she flashes at Hugh and Mick says that while Dr. Poole and Ida are occupied, and I am there to protect her, Hugh and Mick should sneak into the laboratory.

"Of course they may," Dr. Poole says, although I perceive he'd rather be alone with Catherine.

Hugh and Mick reluctantly assent. I

admire Catherine's ingenuity, but I wish there were some other way. Debilitated by my fear, I'm in no shape to stand between her and the Ripper. There's no element of attraction for me in this danger. I can only hope that Ida's presence will prevent Dr. Poole from hurting Catherine.

Ida also seems reluctant; she would rather stay with Hugh. Hugh winks at her and says, "Hurry back."

Blushing and smiling, Ida accompanies Dr. Poole and Catherine across the hall. I slip my miniature camera from my pocket into Mick's hand before I follow them to the treatment room, which is furnished like a lady's chamber, with floral wallpaper, rosy carpet, and a Chinese lacquer screen. A pink plush fainting couch is elevated on a platform about two feet high.

"Please lie down," Dr. Poole says.

Catherine obeys, giggly with her own daring. Ida stands by the couch. I sidle to the door to the adjoining office and surreptitiously close it. Behind the Chinese screen is a large contraption made of discs, rods, gears, and cylinders. My heart pounds with dread, for the contraption is similar to the one I saw at Bedlam, the one that killed Emma Forbes.

"What is that?" Catherine says loudly, to

cover the sounds of Hugh and Mick sneaking into the office and stealing the key.

"An electric generator," Dr. Poole says. It's connected by wires to a smaller machine on a cart that he wheels over to the couch. "This is a pelvic massager."

The massager consists of a black, leather-covered box the size of a suitcase, connected to the generator by cables. The top is studded with dials and switches. A thicker cable attaches to an instrument with a cylindrical handle and a bulbous, riveted metal head that tapers to a short snout. It looks like an instrument of torture.

"I built the equipment myself," Dr. Poole says with pride. He approaches Catherine and flips up two metal loops attached to the sides of the couch. "Put your feet in the stirrups, please."

Lying on her back, feet in the stirrups, legs spread and knees raised, Catherine looks like she's posing for a boudoir photograph, albeit fully clothed. Dr. Poole opens a leather case that contains flesh-colored rubber caps of different sizes. He selects one, fits it onto the snout of the instrument, then moves a lever on the generator. Discs spin; belts and gears turn. A hissing sound and a mechanical pulsation begin. Dr. Poole lifts the instrument by its handle and flips a switch on the black box. The instrument vibrates. Dr. Poole adjusts dials, then stands at the foot of the couch facing Catherine's spread legs.

"I shall insert the massager under your skirts and apply it to you," Dr. Poole says.

When he does so, Catherine jerks and says, "Oh!"

Ida soothingly pats her shoulder. "The vibration can be disconcerting at first."

"Just relax," Dr. Poole says.

Catherine's eyes widen as the massager hums under her skirts. I try to imagine what she is experiencing, and I feel a twinge in my own crotch. It is the same pleasure I feel when I touch myself. Dr. Poole's procedure is but a mechanically enhanced, clinically applied version. I can't believe that the medical profession has styled it as a treatment for a disease! But the so-called hysterical paroxysm won't harm Catherine.

"No, no!" Catherine sits up. She seems to be upset rather than enjoying herself. Ida presses her shoulders down, and she struggles. "Please!"

I force my voice through the barrier of my fear. "What's wrong?"

"There's no need for concern," Dr. Poole's features are unnaturally rigid. The black flecks in his eyes enlarge and coalesce.

"Outbursts are common during the procedure."

His breathing quickens, and sweat droplets bead on his skin. It's as if the dark, foul passions within him are rising to the surface, leaking through his professional carapace. I think he knows what's going on — he's not fooled by the cloak of scientific respectability he's thrown over the proceedings. He must have fornicated with his victims immediately before he killed them, and taken his own pleasure even as he attempted to induce hysterical paroxysms in them without the aid of a pelvic massager. I suppose he thought that because he'd seen them displaying carnal excitement in my photographs, they would easily and quickly reach hysterical paroxysm. He desires Catherine, and stimulating her sensations excites him. But Ida seems unsuspicious, unaffected, and innocent. I think she's never experienced the sensations herself.

Catherine moans, writhes, and tries to push the massager away. Ida restrains her while Dr. Poole holds the massager in place. Catherine cries, "Help!"

I hold her hand. Her fingernails dig into my palm. I'm afraid to oppose Dr. Poole, afraid of what he might do if angered, but I say, "Dr. Poole, that's enough! You're hurting her."

"It's all right." Catherine's red, perspiring face contorts. Her hips buck; she breathes hard and fast. She seems torn between craving the pleasure and fearing it.

Dr. Poole adjusts knobs on the black box. The humming rises to a shriller pitch. Catherine screams. Shudders course through her body. Her head tosses from side to side as her feet kick out of the stirrups. Catherine gasps and sobs as if in terrible pain.

"What's wrong?" I say anxiously.

Babbling, incoherent, she clings to me. Dr. Poole withdraws the massager from beneath her skirts. The rubber cap is shiny, wet. His hand is shaking.

"This is quite unusual." His chest heaves; his voice is ragged. "Most women are calmer after a paroxysm." Ida stares at him, surprised because he's lost his air of professional detachment. "One was not enough. She needs another treatment."

"How can you think so? She was fine before, and now look at her!" I feel a shifting sensation within me. It's the anger elbowing aside my fear. "Catherine, we're going home."

"No! I want another treatment."

She's determined to occupy Dr. Poole

long enough for Hugh and Mick to photograph his laboratory. I want evidence that he's Ripper Number Two, but not at her expense.

"The treatment didn't agree with you." I'm still baffled by her reaction to it, and my fury at Dr. Poole is nearing the now-too-familiar point beyond my control. His readiness to compromise his patients' well-being for his own pleasure must have enabled him to murder them for the sake of science. "Another will make you worse."

"Perhaps Sarah is right," Ida murmurs, clearly having second thoughts about the beneficence of her employer's work.

"I want it," Catherine says in the same stubborn tone with which she once refused to stop picking up men.

Dr. Poole induces another paroxysm. This time she screams louder, shakes and sobs more violently. Her suffering is more than I can bear. My temper explodes like an internal black thunderstorm. I snatch the vibrating massager from Dr. Poole, and for the first time, I face him one-on-one. Gripped by the same impulse to violence as I felt at Bedlam, I raise the massager to strike Dr. Poole.

He's perspiring so heavily that his male, animal reek fills the room. His pupils are so dilated, their blackness seems to fill his eye sockets. The bell jar has cracked; the air has reached the scorpions and cobras, freed them from their suspended animation. His expression is devoid of thought, as if he's become an automaton controlled by the evil forces that possess him.

This is how he must look when he kills.

In his own way, he's more terrifying than Commissioner Warren.

Fear overcomes my anger with a shattering sensation, as if I'm a blacksmith's red-hot iron rod dunked in an ice bath.

Hugh and Mick burst into the room, yelling, "Catherine! Sarah!" They stare, appalled, at Catherine weeping on the couch, me brandishing the massager at Dr. Poole, and Ida fearfully, helplessly wringing her hands. Mick grabs me before I can strike Dr. Poole. I drop the massager on the floor, and it hums and writhes like a swatted hornet.

"What happened?" Hugh asks.

Mick glares at Dr. Poole, who doesn't seem aware of him or Hugh, Ida or me. His blank, black gaze is fixed on Catherine.

"We must take Catherine home," is all I can manage to say.

Hugh carries her out of the room. Mick runs ahead to open the front door. I can't leave Ida alone with Dr. Poole. "Come with us." I grab her by the hand and pull her along as I follow my friends. On our way out of the house, I grab our coats from the stand. While Hugh and Mick put Catherine in the carriage, I say, "Ida, you mustn't work for Dr. Poole any longer." I'm so distressed, I can't find the words to explain.

"Because of how he treated Catherine. Yes, it was awful." Ida's face is drawn with misery. "Tomorrow I shall give notice."

"Don't give notice! Never go back. Let us take you home now."

"Very well," Ida says, unhappy because she's lost her job but relieved that she needn't face Dr. Poole again.

Dr. Poole's figure darkens the lighted doorway of his house. I feel his attention following Catherine like a miasma. I could pity him in the way that I would pity a lizard born without a leg, or any other defective creature, if he didn't seem so soulless. If I had to guess which Ripper has a conscience, I would have to choose Commissioner Warren. I hurry Ida into the carriage and discover that Catherine has fainted. As we make our escape, Hugh calls her name and pats her cheeks, but she's as limp, white, and still as death.

Mick sits across from her, his hands

clasped, whispering prayers. Ida opens a vial of smelling salts under Catherine's nose. Catherine jerks and coughs. Mick says, "Thank you, God!"

Catherine opens dazed, frightened eyes. She doesn't seem to recognize us. Huddling in the corner of the seat, she shivers. I cover her with her coat. When the carriage stops outside York Street Chambers, Hugh walks Ida to the door. He's gone a long time. Mick and I are silent, watching and fearing for Catherine.

When Hugh climbs back into the carriage, his face is grim. "I told Ida. She's terribly hurt, but she said she understands and forgives us. I've never felt so ashamed."

Nor have I. "Does she believe Dr. Poole is a murderer?"

"Yes. I had to lie to her again, though. She wanted to tell the police everything, but I figured they would probably throw us in jail for fraud instead of arresting Dr. Poole, so I told her we're secret agents working for the government."

"And she believed you?"

"I could have convinced her that left is right," Hugh says bitterly. "Damn me."

I ask whether he and Mick got into Dr. Poole's laboratory. Mick nods and holds up my camera, but at the moment, we're too worried about Catherine to care what's in it. Hugh says, "Sarah, were you really going to wallop Dr. Poole with that gizmo?" His voice is filled with disbelief. He's never seen me lose my temper; he didn't see me in Bedlam.

"No, of course not." But at the time, I could have split Dr. Poole's head open.

"Well, it's good that you didn't," Hugh says. He and Mick seem not quite reassured, a little afraid of me. "God only knows what would have happened."

"I'm sorry. I don't know what got into me. It won't happen again."

But I remember the overpowering force of my temper, I'm unsure I can control it next time, and I begin to perceive what's gotten into me. The anger ignited by Commissioner Warren isn't directed only at him or anyone else who's crossed me lately. At the tea party, my irrational hatred toward Ida's mother was really displaced, unacknowledged hatred toward my own mother. *She* is the source of my reservoir of hot, molten fury. Not only was she harsh and unloving, but by refusing to let me see my father's body and visit his grave, she denied me the right to know for certain whether his death was a fact. No matter her reasons, she left me with persistent questions and a habit of distrusting other people, and she consigned me to a life of loneliness. Because she never set the record straight, I don't know if Commissioner Warren lied when he said my father was a fugitive from the law. And because my mother is gone, I'm venting my rage on other people. Now I retreat into frightened silence. *What have I become?* I don't know myself anymore. I can't predict what I'm capable of doing in the future.

At my studio, Hugh carries Catherine upstairs, then goes to the kitchen to make tea. Mick watches me tuck Catherine into my bed and light the fire. She lies still, her eyes closed.

"Is she gonna be all right?" Mick whispers. Love for her shines from his eyes.

I nod even though I'm far from certain.

"You want me to develop the pictures?"

"Do you know how?"

He manages a smile. "I've watched you enough times."

After he goes, I sit beside Catherine and say softly, "Can you tell me what's wrong?"

Her eyes move beneath their closed lids as if she's half asleep and dreaming. Her lips form words that are barely audible. "I begged him not to. But he said I wanted it."

She must be talking about the squire who violated her. It hurts me to listen. I don't know what to say.

"When he did it, it happened. I couldn't control it." Her voice is tiny, woeful. "He said it meant I liked how he made me feel. I thought he must be right. Because it did feel good."

These cryptic words, together with the story I heard her tell Hugh, add up to a tale that's even more upsetting: When the squire had carnal relations with her, her body naturally responded with what Dr. Poole terms "hysterical paroxysm." She experienced pleasure that he forced upon her, and Dr. Poole's treatment brought back the painful memories.

"I was so ashamed." Tears seep from under Catherine's long, dark lashes. "When he told me I was a bad girl, I believed him. Because if I weren't, I wouldn't have liked it."

"Oh, Catherine," I whisper, sad that she still carries the undeserved burden of guilt.

"I never let it happen with other men. I never let myself feel good while they touched me. I don't want to be reminded of him. When I came to London, I thought I could forget. But I never will." Sobs erupt from Catherine. She sounds as if something is broken inside.

My heart breaks for her. That day at Euston Station, I thought I was saving her, but I was only setting her on a road back to her old nightmare.

By the time she falls asleep, it's two thirty in the morning. I go downstairs to the studio. Hugh says, "You need to see the photographs."

In the darkroom, two damp prints hang from the line. The first shows a table like the one I saw in Bedlam; it has shackles and a head restraint. Mick points at glass-fronted cabinets behind the table and says, "Those things in there are all kinds of different knives. We didn't have time to take closeup pictures."

"This setup tells us that Dr. Poole isn't planning to stop his experiments, and now he's willing to risk doing them at home," Hugh says. "I think he's already started collecting more specimens." He taps the second photograph.

Spread on the laboratory table is a dress with a white collar, cloth-covered buttons down the left bodice, and a swath of fabric draped across the full, pleated skirt — the kind a respectable, affluent woman would wear. My vision is so bleary from fatigue that I can't see why Hugh and Mick thought the dress worth photographing or why it was in the laboratory.

"It's cut down the front," Mick says.

"We found it in a cabinet," Hugh says. "We think Dr. Poole cut it off a woman so he could remove her organs, and he forgot to dispose of it afterward."

We once thought the Ripper's interest was confined to my models, and that even if we couldn't save Mary Jane and Catherine, at least he wouldn't kill anyone else. "But who was she?" I say, horrified.

"I would suppose one of his patients," Hugh says.

"What happened to her body?" I ask.

"God only knows." Hugh says. "The devil of it is, if Dr. Poole keeps on killing, Commissioner Warren won't stop either."

"He can hide behind Dr. Poole," I agree. "As long as he's careful, he'll be safe."

"Safe to switch to murdering whatever sort of woman Dr. Poole chooses next," Hugh adds. "I hate to say this, but we can't go to the police. They wouldn't believe that these pictures mean what we think they mean. We lack a certain credibility."

"Shit!" Mick says. "Was tonight all for nothing?"

"No," I say. "We found out that Dr. Poole really is the Ripper. I recognized him. He's the man who was in Dutfield's Yard with

Liz Stride."

"Which makes our job simpler," Hugh says. "Dr. Poole can't kill Mary Jane Kelly because you paid her to stay indoors, or Catherine because we're not letting her go out by herself no matter what she says, so he'll proceed to kill other women. All we have to do is spy on him and catch him in the act."

37

It was four o'clock in the morning before I crept into bed beside Catherine.

A knock at the door awakens me from a heavy, exhausted slumber.

"Miss Sarah," Mick whispers, "can you come downstairs? Something's happened."

I forgot that I let him and Hugh sleep in my studio. Blinking in the pale daylight from the window, I glance at the clock: ten thirty. Catherine is still asleep. After hastily washing and dressing, I go downstairs to find Mick and Hugh at the table. There lies a huge bouquet of red roses, so dark they're almost black. They fill the air with a funereal scent.

"A delivery boy just brought them," Mick says. His red hair stands up in cowlicks, but his eyes are bright, wide-awake.

Hugh, rubbing the whisker stubble on his jaw, gives me the card that came with the roses. The message is written in script so precise that it could have been printed on a press, but inkblots betray the author's impatient, excited state of mind. I read the letter aloud:

Dear Miss Catherine Price,
Last night was most extraordinary. I believe that together you and I can make great scientific advances. Please tell me when and where I can see you again. Perhaps at the Oxford Theater after your next performance?

Yours sincerely,
Dr. Henry Poole

PS Dare I hope that we might also become more than friends?

I drop the card as if it soiled my fingers. I feel the burn of anger again.

Hugh yawns. "Catherine's made another conquest. She can be the bride of Dr. Frankenstein." He sees me frown and says, "Sorry."

"I'll take this to the dustbin." Mick gathers up the card and bouquet.

I wonder if he's remembering the pink rose he tried to give Catherine. "Dr. Poole must think Catherine lives with me." I voice a belated thought. "His handwriting isn't anything like that of the Jack the Ripper letters. Either they're Warren's doing or someone else's hoax."

As soon as Mick comes back, there's a loud knocking at the door, and a male voice shouts, "Sarah Bain!" The shade is pulled down over the window; we can't see outside, but I recognize the voice. My heart lurches.

"It's Inspector Reid," I whisper.

"Open up, or we'll break the door down!"

Thumps rattle the door's windowpanes. I mustn't let Reid at Hugh and Mick. "Run out the back door!"

They stand pat. "We're not leaving you alone with him," Hugh says.

Wood splinters and glass shatters. I push Hugh and Mick into the darkroom just before the front door flies open. PC Barrett steps across the threshold, looking both defiant and ashamed. Then comes Inspector Reid. Fists clenched, a bounce in his gait, he sparks with combative energy, like a boxer entering the ring. The ends of his mustache are straggly; he's been gnawing on them. His disheveled gray hair hangs into his eyes, which are red from sleeplessness and anger.

"The Ripper has struck again," he says. "Mary Jane Kelly was killed in Miller's Court, early this morning."

Shock pressures the wind from me. I lean on the table and struggle to inhale. How could Mary Jane have been murdered? Mick and I paid her to stay safe at home!

"The Ripper attacked her while she was in bed. He slit her throat, cut off her arm, and ripped her stomach open. He pulled her entrails out, cut off her nose and her breasts, and skinned her legs." Reid seems to relish these appalling details that he hurls at me. "The scene looked like a bloody slaughterhouse."

Her killer must have gained entry via the broken window. Frustrated with waiting for her to come out, or afraid of meeting the police or the vigilantes on the streets, he murdered her in her own room. Was he Dr. Poole or Commissioner Warren? Whoever killed Mary Jane, we made her a sitting duck.

Reid can't see the misery on Barrett's face because Barrett is standing behind him, but I can tell that Barrett thinks Warren killed Mary Jane. He thinks that because he didn't speak out against Warren, her murder is partly his fault.

"Don't tell me you didn't know her," Reid says. "I can see that you did."

The murder is in some ways a lucky break. "Mr. Lipsky was in jail during the murder.

He couldn't have done it. This proves he's innocent!" Sick with guilt for Mary Jane yet overjoyed for Mr. and Mrs. Lipsky, I say, "Are you going to set him free?"

"Not quite." Reid speaks with scornful condescension. "Just because he has an alibi for this murder doesn't mean he's not guilty. Our theory of the crimes has changed. We now believe that they were committed by different people. There are two Rippers."

The police have finally arrived at the same truth I did on the night of the double murders.

"Lipsky is one," Reid says. "He killed Kate Eddowes. The other is still at large. He killed Liz Stride and Mary Jane Kelly. We believe he and Lipsky have been working together, stalking the women and taking turns killing. That's how the double murders were committed within such a short time frame. They're partners."

I hear whispering in the darkroom; Hugh and Mick are as outraged as I am. I speak loudly to drown out their voices and to vent the anger that's boiling up inside me again. "That's ridiculous. Mr. Lipsky isn't partners with the killer!"

"That's not what Lipsky says." Reid grins at the shock on my face. "He says over and over, 'There are two! There are two!' "

I comprehend what's happened. Mr. Lipsky learned about Liz's murder, probably when the police interrogated him about it. He's realized, as I did, that there are two Rippers, although he doesn't know about Dr. Poole.

"But he didn't confess to the murders." I'm certain. Mr. Lipsky didn't cease battling the Russian police until after his children were burned to death during the pogroms. He wouldn't knuckle under to the London police when it's only his own life at stake.

The anger in Reid's eyes burns hotter, but he says, "We'll break him eventually. And you're going to help us."

Now I understand why he came: he thinks I'll be easier to break than Mr. Lipsky. I'm terrified because of what Reid might do to force me to incriminate Mr. Lipsky, because of what Hugh and Mick might do in an attempt to defend me. And Catherine is helpless upstairs.

Reid pulls a chair away from the table and says to Barrett, "Sit her down and handcuff her."

The terror leaps in me like a whirlwind.

Barrett blinks. "Guv?"

"You heard me."

As Barrett reluctantly unhooks the hand-

491

cuffs that dangle from his belt and moves toward me, I glance at the darkroom and see the doorknob turning. "No!" I shout, at Hugh and Mick as well as Barrett. I lunge toward the front door. If I run, Reid and Barrett will chase me, and my friends will be safe. But Reid grabs my arm, shoves me into the chair, and pulls my arms around its back. I feel the thirst for vengeance that went unsatisfied when Mrs. Lipsky prevented me from hitting the keepers at Bedlam and Mick prevented me from hitting Dr. Poole. But if I start a fight, Hugh and Mick will join in. For their sake, I restrain myself from kicking Reid. Barrett locks the cold steel cuffs around my wrists. He knows I'm not hiding evidence that Mr. Lipsky is guilty, and he believes Commissioner Warren is the Ripper, but he's not going to say so, because he's duty-bound to go along with Reid.

"Who is Lipsky's partner?" Reid demands. "Another friend of yours?"

"There's no partner! Mr. Lipsky is innocent."

Reid says to Barrett, "Hit her face."

Barrett looks from side to side, as if he hopes Reid is talking to someone else.

"Yes, you," Reid snaps. "That's an order."

Outrage fills Barrett's expression. "I won't do it."

I'm amazed and grateful that he's openly disobeying Reid. Then Reid says, "If you don't, I will, and you can be sure I'll hit her harder than you would."

Barrett bites his lip. He looks at me; he shakes his head to express his reluctance; his eyes brim with apology. I return his gaze, and, in a moment of bizarre, intimate conspiracy, I nod to give him my permission. Barrett inhales, tightens his mouth, and draws back his hand.

The ceiling creaks as Catherine stirs upstairs.

The slap explodes against my cheek. Although Barrett meant to be gentle, the impact is stunning. I thought he couldn't hurt me any worse than he already has, but this feels like a personal insult, a declaration of my utter worthlessness, no matter that it wasn't intended. The spirit of my anger changes; now it's weak and helpless, like a body whose skeleton has been crushed.

Hugh bursts from the darkroom, shouting, "Stop!"

As my ears ring and my cheek throbs, Reid and Barrett turn to Hugh in surprise. Reid demands, "Who the hell are you?"

I'm less relieved that Hugh has interrupted than horrified that he's put himself between Reid and me. I sense his fear even as his brazen smile challenges Reid. My fear for him gnaws away at my courage.

"I'm Miss Bain's solicitor," Hugh lies in his most aristocratic manner. "I've been watching your disgraceful abuse of my client, and I shall file a complaint against the police department. Undo those handcuffs at once!"

Intimidated by the threat or Hugh's social class or both, Reid blusters, "She has information about the Whitechapel murders. It's my job to get it out of her."

"By torturing her?" Hugh's voice embodies a nobleman's scorn for the ignorant peasantry. "You'll make her say whatever you want her to say, but it won't be true."

"She knows who Lipsky's partner is," Reid insists.

"Bosh! You can look for this partner from here to Timbuktu and never find him, because he doesn't exist. And if you think that hanging Abraham Lipsky will put an end to the Whitechapel murders, think again. There'll be more after he swings."

"Why should I listen to you?" Reid scoffs, but I see that Hugh has touched a nerve. Reid thinks Mr. Lipsky is one of two Rippers, but he's afraid he's wrong. He takes a closer look at Hugh. "Have we met before?"

"Sorry, I haven't had the pleasure. You should listen to me because I know who the Ripper really is," Hugh says.

"How would you know?"

"I was told by Miss Bain."

Barrett's and Reid's surprised, indignant gazes turn from Hugh to me. "So you were withholding information," Reid says. "Why didn't you just give it to us at the start?"

I've no idea what to say or what Hugh is doing. Hugh says, "Because it just came into her possession. She consulted me first, and I advised her that I should be the one to hand it over to you."

Reid scowls. He suspects a trick, but he takes the bait. "Well then, put your money where your mouth is."

"Uncuff Miss Bain first," Hugh says.

Reid hesitates, then nods to Barrett.

As Barrett unlocks the cuffs, we both hold our breath. His hands are warm, sweaty, and shaking. Released, I flex my aching arms and rise. Barrett drops the open handcuffs on the floor as if they're distasteful to him. His damp fingerprints cool on my skin as I stand beside Hugh.

Like a magician, Hugh produces a folded, thick paper from his inner coat pocket. He opens it and slaps it down on the table. As

Barrett and Reid examine it, I'm no less dumbfounded than they are. It's the photograph of Dr. Poole and his fellow physicians in the operating theater. How . . . ?

Mick stole it.

"There." Hugh points at Dr. Poole. "That's your man."

"Who is he?" Reid asks.

"Dr. Henry Poole. He's a neurologist."

Reid shakes his head. "His name's never come up in our investigation."

"But we've been thinking the Ripper is a physician, because of the way he cuts his victims." Barrett's voice is eager with hope that it's not Commissioner Warren.

Reid gives him an incredulous glance, then addresses Hugh. "The man in this picture could be any random physician. Why should I even believe his name is Henry Poole?"

"He lives and practices at number forty-one Harley Street. Go see for yourself."

"Some of the witnesses saw a man carrying a black bag near the crime scenes." Barrett can't contain his excitement. "It could have been a physician's medical bag."

"That's enough, Constable!" Reid chews his mustache. He seems as annoyed by his own doubts as by the points Barrett raised. I desperately hope he'll believe Dr. Poole is the Ripper and arrest him. "Supposing this Dr. Poole is real, why do you think he's the Ripper?"

"He was a consultant at Bedlam until they dismissed him for doing this to a patient." Hugh pulls another photograph from his pocket and lays it on the table.

It's the one of Emma Forbes's gutted corpse. Barrett curses under his breath as he and Reid stare.

"He can't stick his knife into the patients at Bedlam anymore," Hugh says, "so he's taken his show on the road to Whitechapel."

Reid's obstinacy deflates, but he says to me, "Where did you get these photographs?"

"We can't reveal her source," Hugh says. Never have I been so thankful for his talent for fast talk. "The authorities at Bedlam hushed up the matter of Dr. Poole, but if you lean on them, they'll admit he murdered and dissected a patient."

"Guv, we should go investigate Dr. Poole," Barrett says urgently.

"The hell I will!" Reid turns on me. "I think you faked these photographs."

The accusation is so absurd, I laugh. "How could I?"

"With dead animal parts you got from

your friend Lipsky the butcher? You're the photographer, you tell me."

"Your knowledge of human female anatomy is sadly lacking, Inspector." Hugh taps the woman's naked breasts in the photograph. "These ain't cow udders."

"You spliced together different pictures, then. This is all a scheme to fool me and save Lipsky."

"Guv, I think it's real," Barrett says.

"Oh, do you?" Reid turns on Barrett. "I think you're sticking up for Miss Bain because you're sweet on her."

Barrett flushes and stammers. He says, "We can't ignore a lead. What if they're right about Dr. Poole?"

Reid jabs his finger against Barrett's chest. "When you flubbed that lineup after the Martha Tabram murder, I gave you another chance. You were supposed to romance Miss Bain to make her talk, but instead, she wrapped you around her thumb. And now you're contradicting your superior officer. You're fired."

"Sir!" Alarmed indignation raises Barrett's voice.

"Get lost."

Barrett looks devastated. As he walks out of the studio, his straight back radiates wounded, angry pride. I feel sorry for him.

He stood up for me, and it has cost him dearly. He'll never forgive me; I'll never see him again. I regret it even though I should be glad. The door slams behind Barrett. More glass shatters on the floor. I've just lost my only ally in the police force as well as a man I care about more than I like to admit.

Hugh says to Inspector Reid, "You're going to wish you'd listened to him, the next time the Ripper kills while you're chasing your tail."

An odd look comes over Reid's face. "Hey. I know why you look familiar. I've seen you around town. You're Lord Hugh Staunton."

My heart vaults into my throat.

"Sorry?" Hugh feigns quizzical confusion.

"One doesn't forget a pretty mug like yours. You're no solicitor." Reid's eyes gleam with sudden awareness. "You're the pervert from the Thousand Crowns Club!"

Hugh's laugh has a reedy, alarmed sound. "I'm afraid you're mistaken."

"Don't bother denying it." Startled as if by further enlightenment, Reid says, "You're not just trying to protect Miss Bain and Abraham Lipsky — you're trying to protect yourself. And she's protecting you. You're Lipsky's partner! You're the other Ripper!"

The accusation is so unexpected, Hugh

and I are dumbstruck.

"You weren't satisfied with buggering men, so you switched to slaughtering women." Reid is desperate enough to believe in the baseless scenario that's just occurred to him. "I'm arresting you both." He points at Hugh, says, "You, for murder," then at me. "You, as an accomplice."

He doesn't have any evidence to back up his accusation, and he doesn't care. He's going to railroad us the way he did Mr. Lipsky. I'm so horrified to see Hugh sucked into the abyss of the police's misguided hunt for the Ripper, I hardly mind about myself. Hugh looks stricken, terrified. Even though he's innocent, even if he's acquitted, he'll suffer. There's no telling what the inmates in jail will do to him should they learn that he's a homosexual — which Reid will make sure they do. And if Hugh and I are incarcerated, we won't be able to save Mr. Lipsky, protect Catherine, or stop Dr. Poole or Commissioner Warren.

"You and who else are arresting us?" Hugh puts his arm around me. Trembling with fright, we stand our ground.

Reid's breathy chuckle sounds like a train accelerating. "Come along easy, or you'll be sorry." He reaches for me.

My hand reaches out, and without thinking, I shove Reid, elated by my own nerve. Reid stumbles backward. Glowering, he pulls a silver whistle on a chain out of his pocket, says, "I'll have every policeman in Whitechapel all over you in a minute," and heads for the door.

Hugh looks appalled by my foolhardy action and the consequences. Mick comes running out of the darkroom, lunges at Reid, and tackles him. Reid yells as he crashes to the floor.

"Don't let him get help!" Mick shouts.

Astonished by this turn of events, I snatch the whistle from Reid. Reid thrashes his legs free of Mick's grasp. Hugh runs to Reid, kneels on his back, grabs him by the hair, and slams his head against the floor — once, twice, three times. Reid lies still.

Mick gets up, grinning. Hugh climbs off Reid and says, "Who's sorry now?"

I hear a whimper. Catherine stands on the stairs, her hands clapped over her mouth. She stares at the unconscious Inspector Reid, then at us.

The heat of the moment fades. I say, "I shouldn't have done that."

"Neither should I," Hugh says, "but I couldn't resist giving the police a taste of their own medicine."

"Nor me. And we had to stop him," Mick says.

Catherine drops her hands. "Is he dead?" she whispers.

Hugh rolls Reid over onto his back. Reid's eyes are closed, and blood trickles from his nose. Hugh puts his ear to Reid's chest. "His heartbeat's strong."

My relief is as short-lived as my satisfaction that Reid got what he deserved. "He'll be furious." We all look at one another in alarm. There's naught to do but improvise. I point to the corner. "Move him over there."

Hugh and Mick drag Reid. I pick up the handcuffs that PC Barrett dropped, then I lock one cuff around Reid's wrist and the other around the gas pipe that runs up from the floor through the ceiling.

"Good thinking, Sarah. That'll buy us some time." Hugh searches Reid's pockets to make sure Reid hasn't a key.

"Time for what?" Catherine asks.

"To run," Mick says.

38

I pack up my photography equipment. It's more precious than anything else I own. Hugh carries my large camera and tripod, Mick the flash lamp and stand. I have my pocketbook, my satchel full of miniature camera and lenses, and a trunk containing negative plates, flash powder, and photographic paper. Catherine lugs a carpetbag of books, tools, and sundry items. I wish I could bring the enlarger, but it's too big and heavy. So are my father's framed photographs. As we slip out the back door and hurry down the alley, I can't bear to look back. I feel a pain in my chest, as if my heart is wrenching away.

I'm leaving my beloved studio sooner than I expected, and forever.

"We'll go to my house," Hugh says. "Then we'll figure out our next step."

Commercial Street is clogged with thousands of people amid carriages, wagons, and omnibuses full of passengers. "The Lord Mayor's Show." I'd forgotten about it. "That's where everyone's going." In almost seven hundred years, neither wars, fires, nor the Black Death have ever stopped the Lord Mayor's Show. It's not going to stop for Jack the Ripper.

"I'll get us a cab," Hugh says.

They're all occupied. Hugh opens the door of one whose passenger is a fat, prosperous-looking man. "Excuse me, we need this cab. It's an emergency."

He and Mick pull the fat man out of the cab, and we all climb in. Hugh shouts his address to the driver. As the cab begins moving, the fat man yells, "Bastards!" We close the windows so the police won't spot us. It's dark in the cab, and cold. While we inch through traffic, Hugh checks his watch.

"It's past noon," he says. "At this rate, we won't get there until tomorrow."

The Lord Mayor must be swearing his oath of loyalty in the Royal Courts. I hear distant music from a brass band. The cab comes to a complete stop.

"Roads into the city are closed," the driver calls to us. "Can't go no farther."

"We're better off walking." Mick flings open the door. "Come on!"

Laden with my equipment, we plunge into

the crowd of chattering, laughing people who fill Aldgate High Street. They don't seem to care that they can't get near the parade; they're enjoying a holiday. Boys wave flags and blow noisemakers. Shopgirls in feathered hats shoot passersby with squirt guns.

"This way!" Hugh heads up a side lane, wielding my tripod like a baton to blaze a trail.

None too soon, we're free of the mob, but rain starts to fall — a cold, windy downpour. We trudge west on London Wall Street. The Church of St. Bartholomew the Great looms above the rooftops. Too tired to walk any farther, we make for it like pilgrims lost on a journey. We push through the massive double doors of the ancient Norman edifice and drop ourselves and my equipment onto the hard wooden benches that face the long central aisle. The dank, cavernous space is empty but for us. Drenched to the skin, we sit shivering and miserable. I feel as if a black line has been drawn around me in a small circle that contains only the present moment and its troubles. Everything else — my past, my mother and father, Jack the Ripper — is outside. My anger is like a flame licking at the circle's perimeter. I feel distanced from my friends; they're isolated in their own black circles.

Catherine closes her eyes. She's as pale as the gray stone walls that rise in arched galleries to the vaulted ceiling. Mick rubs his shoulder; carrying my equipment must have made it hurt again. Hugh props his elbows on his knees and rests his head in his hands. He was happy to have survived the exposure he'd always feared, but he probably never thought things could get worse. Self-reproach fills me because I brought this upon us. The area around Great St. Bart's was once the site of public executions, and it's said that one can still smell the odor of burning flesh, but I smell nothing except our hopelessness.

"Churches are supposed to be sanctuaries," Hugh says, "but I wouldn't want to test the theory if the police were to find us here."

Mick speaks reluctantly. "We can go to my place."

An early winter dusk, darkened by fog, settles upon the warehouses along the riverfront in Wapping. The Thames gleams with lights reflected from boats. Exhausted by our long hike, Hugh, Mick, Catherine, and I set my equipment at the top of the stone staircase that leads down to the water.

This is where I first met Mick, the day he stole my camera, the day I saw Polly Nichols dead in Buck's Row. On our right, to the east, the Tower Bridge rises; its two Gothic towers seem to hover in the mist. The low tide laps against mud flats that reek of sewage and dead fish. Spectral flames flicker on the flats, where hunched figures prowl.

"It's just the mudlarks," Mick says.

The mudlarks are folks who scavenge in the mud for coins and items they can sell that have fallen in the river. I realize that mudlarking is among the "this-and-that" by which Mick earns a living. Now I know why he's dirtier at some times than others: those were days he'd been digging in the filth.

A loud boom rocks the night, and a gold starburst lights up the sky beyond the Tower Bridge. More booms echo across the city; red-and-white pinwheels rain sparks onto the earth. It's the fireworks display that ends the Lord Mayor's Show. We lift our burdens. Mick leads us down the stairs, then past the retaining walls upon which the warehouses rise straight up from the riverbed. Our shoes squish in the mud; I trip on shells, rocks, and debris. Fiddle music and raucous laughter drift from a tavern. After we've traveled some fifty feet, Mick stops to yank bricks from a wall. The opening he exposes is about four feet high. He ducks inside, scrambles around, and then there's a flare of light. Mick emerges with a lantern that he shines into the opening. I see a tunnel whose crumbled brick floor and ceiling are covered with green algae. It leads into blackness that exudes the odors of earth, decay, and sulfur.

"It's an old sewer drain," Mick says.

It looks like an entrance to hell. I don't want to go in there.

"Did I ever tell you I have a terrible fear of dark, enclosed spaces?" Hugh says.

"The coppers will never find us here," Mick says.

Hugh, Catherine, and I follow Mick into the tunnel. He bricks up the opening and says, "Right this way."

For some twenty feet, the tunnel slopes upward, its ceiling so low that we crouch while we walk, dragging my equipment. Then it opens into a junction with three larger tunnels, and we can stand upright. The arched brick ceilings and square pillars have a strange beauty reminiscent of a cathedral. The smell of sulfur gas is stronger here, and I hear water splashing. Mick leads us through one tunnel, to a flight of stone steps. We carry my equipment up them, into another tunnel that extends about fifteen feet to a pile of rocks and earth where the ceiling is caved in. Cold drafts whistle through this narrow room. Above a pile of ragged blankets and cushions, crevices in the walls hold picture postcards — the Taj Mahal; the Leaning Tower of Pisa.

"It's very nice," Hugh says, trying to sound enthusiastic.

"Yes." It breaks my heart to see how Mick has made a sewer tunnel a home, to think this is the only place on earth that he can call his own and he was ashamed to tell me about it. That such a bright, quicksilver creature should live underground!

"I can make tea." Mick finds a kettle, a tin of tea, and four mismatched china cups. He lights coals and twigs in a circle of stones, puts a scrap of rusty iron grate on them, then fills the kettle with water from a jug and sets it to boil.

I don't want to find fault, but I have to ask, "When the tide rises, won't we be trapped?"

"The water won't cover the opening till tomorrow afternoon," Mick says, "and it never comes up this high."

I can't bear to think about tomorrow. Sitting on the bed, we drink the murky tea. Mick produces tinned beans and sardines, and we eat them cold, straight from the tins, with bent spoons. They taste metallic and too salty. Mick, Hugh, and I are too hungry to care, but Catherine says, "I don't like it. I can't eat." She flings down her tin and spoon and gestures around the tunnel. "This is awful!"

Mick wilts.

"Catherine. Don't," Hugh says.

"I hate it!" she cries. "I can't bear to stay here."

She's voiced the thoughts that Hugh and I share but didn't speak. We don't want to hurt Mick's feelings, but we're just as miserable in this cold, dank, smelly tunnel as she is.

Mick stands. He brings to my mind a young knight in a fairy tale who has tried to win the hand of the princess by performing heroic deeds, only to learn that they weren't heroic enough, and so he musters his courage, takes up his sword, and rides off again. "You don't have to stay here long," he tells Catherine. "Just until I come back."

He's gone before Hugh and I can ask where he's going or beg him not to abandon us.

39

The tunnel is pitch-dark. River water pours into Mick's cave. Hugh, Catherine, and I scream as we frantically try to swim out, but the rising tide is too strong. We're trapped.

I awaken with a gasp. Breathing foul but dry air, I open my eyes to light from the lantern Mick holds. I'm lying on his bed with Catherine, and he's shaking us, saying, "Time to go."

Hugh is already up. Lugging my photography equipment, we clamber out of the tunnel. It's still dark, the river cloaked in fog. We walk along the mud and up the stairs to the embankment. There stands a horse attached to an enclosed wagon. The driver — a big, bearded man wearing a skullcap — grins and beckons. It's Mr. Lipsky's employer.

"You went to see Mrs. Lipsky?" I say to Mick.

"Yeah. She sent Leo to get you." Mick looks disappointed because Catherine, drowsy and apathetic, seems oblivious to the fact that he's rescued us.

"I could kiss that good woman!" Hugh says. "I could even kiss you!"

I, too, am grateful. "But we mustn't involve Mrs. Lipsky. It's dangerous for her, and she's suffered enough."

"She wants to help," Mick says. He and Hugh put my equipment in the wagon. "Get in."

After a bone-jarring ride, we disembark outside a narrow building. A sign on it reads, *Jews Temporary Shelter,* with words in Hebrew below. In the lighted doorway stands Mrs. Lipsky. She smiles and brushes off Hugh's and my thanks. When we're seated in the warm, clean, plainly furnished dining room, I feel safe from the police; we've disappeared into the secret world of the Jews.

Mrs. Lipsky brings us hot, savory chicken soup with dumplings and strong tea. As Hugh, Mick, and I devour the meal, Mrs. Lipsky sees Catherine picking at her food and urges her to eat. Catherine shrugs. Later, while I help Mrs. Lipsky wash the dishes in the kitchen, I tell her about Dr. Poole.

"That monster," Mrs. Lipsky says, her usually gentle voice sharp.

We rejoin Hugh, Mick, and Catherine at the table. Daylight brightens the windows, and the shelter's other guests — men, women, and children — troop into the dining room. They speak in foreign languages as they eat. Some leave after breakfast; other Jews come. The shelter is merely a way station. My sense of isolation from my friends persists, as though we're reverting to strangers bound for different destinations. I'm as lonely as if they're already gone.

"We have beds for you," Mrs. Lipsky says, "and a place to wash."

I crave a hot bath and sleep. Mick and Hugh yawn. Only Catherine is wide awake. She gazes morosely across the room at a mother feeding a little boy who is perhaps a year old.

Leo enters the room. "You better look at this." He lays a handbill on the table.

At the top is the word "Wanted" in big, black type above sketched portraits of a fair, handsome man, a freckled boy, and a plain woman with her hair in a braided coronet — Hugh, Mick, and me — labeled with our names. The message below reads, "The police are seeking these persons in connection with the Whitechapel murders. Anyone with knowledge of their whereabouts is urged to report it at any police station." Our likenesses are remarkable, considering that the artist must have relied upon descriptions from Inspector Reid, who was apparently rescued from my studio. The handbill is surely his doing.

"These are posted all around," Leo says, then departs.

The increased gravity of our predicament jolts us all alert. Mick exclaims, "This makes it sound like we did the murders!"

"We're in a real pickle now." Hugh's light tone doesn't disguise his fear of going to jail and the special horrors it holds for a man like him.

I think of the uproar after Annie Chapman's murder, when mobs chased innocent people through the streets. Reid has thrown us on the mercy of citizens already whipped into a panic. "The Mile End Vigilance Committee will be looking for us, too."

"Stay here," Mrs. Lipsky urges. "Do not go outside."

Mick, Hugh, and I shake our heads. We can't stay indefinitely, and someone here might see the handbill, recognize us, and report us to the police. My heart aches with lonely despair, for I know what I must do.

"We should split up," I say. "We'll be too easily recognized if we're together."

"That wouldn't solve the problem of where to go," Hugh points out.

I speak through a lump in my throat. "Your father wanted to send you to America."

"Bollocks! I'm not leaving you, Sarah."

"Maybe you can take Mick," I insist despite my anguish at the thought of never seeing them again. "It would be a fresh start for both of you."

"I wouldn't skip out on you if you paid me," Mick says, adamant.

Their loyalty moves me so much it hurts.

"Besides," Mick says, "Mr. Lipsky is still in jail. Hugh and I have to help get him out."

Mrs. Lipsky wrings her hands. She knows that the likelihood of our exonerating her husband has drastically decreased, but she says, "We must protect Catherine from Dr. Poole."

Catherine silently stares across the room at the mother and little boy.

"Catherine's not wanted by the police," Hugh says. "If she goes out in public, she won't be arrested or attacked by a mob."

"There is Jewish shelter in Birmingham," Mrs. Lipsky says. "I send her there."

I nod, already missing Catherine but glad

she'll be safe. Mick gazes at her as if memorizing her face.

"But I have to be at the theater." Catherine has ignored most of the discussion. Her manner is petulant. "I'm in the show." She's grasping at her normal routine, as though it's a lifeline that will pull her out of this nightmare. Suddenly alarmed, she says, "What day is this?"

I, too, have lost track of time. I have to think before I answer, "Saturday the tenth of November."

"The performance last night! I missed it. I'll be fired!" She begins crying.

Mrs. Lipsky tries to soothe her. Hugh says, "She's in no shape for a journey. Let her settle down first. In the meantime, we'd better talk over our next move. I've an idea."

Although I'm fervently thankful that at least we're still together for now, I can't believe there's a solution to our problems.

"Let's make a last-ditch sortie at Jack the Ripper," Hugh says.

A sad smile twists my lips. He hasn't lost his sense of adventure, but I've lost my faith in us. "How, when we're hiding from the police?"

"We can't stay hidden forever. They'll nab us eventually. Why not put our remaining freedom to good use? Besides, I'd like to accomplish one splendid thing before I say hello to Hades. Wouldn't you?"

His valiant optimism has buoyed me up during these past months, and in spite of everything, it's having the same effect now. If his spirits can bounce back after a calamity, so can mine, and I, too, would like to rid the world of at least one Ripper and justify my existence on earth while I still can. "You're right."

"Yeah, we should save Mr. Lipsky!" Mick says, then looks thoughtful. "But it's more than that, ain't it?"

Hugh and I nod. The whole tone of our endeavor has suddenly changed. It isn't just about saving a friend or serving any other personal interest. It's about doing what's necessary and right, no matter the consequences.

Mrs. Lipsky smiles with relief as she holds the weeping Catherine. She must have been afraid we would abandon her husband to save ourselves.

Disliking to be a wet blanket but not wanting to raise false hope, I say, "We could spy on Dr. Poole, but how long will it be before he attacks more women? We may be caught ourselves before we can catch him."

"She's right," Mick says glumly. "With all

the coppers around, he might lie low for a bit."

Once again, I find myself in that mental territory where fatigue loosens the constraints on my imagination and prudence falls by the wayside. "We could force him to surface."

"Hah!" Hugh grins. "That creative mind of yours has hatched a plan!"

"I wouldn't quite call it a plan."

"Give me an ounce of clay to work with, and I'll build Michelangelo's *David.*"

The famous statue of the naked young man armed with a slingshot to fight Goliath is probably a more apt allusion than he intended. "It will be dangerous."

"Hell, I'd rather go down in a blaze of glory than sit twiddling my thumbs," Hugh says.

"Me, too!" Eager with bravado, Mick slaps his hand palm down on the table. "I'm in."

Hugh puts his hand atop Mick's.

"You haven't heard my idea." In order for it to work, we require something we don't have.

"We know the water's cold," Hugh says. "Best to jump in without thinking first."

"What've we got to lose?" Mick asks.

Mrs. Lipsky lays her hand on theirs. Recklessness overcomes my misgivings; I reach out my hand. The circle around me now seems like a balloon pumped up with hope, daring, and the spirit of self-sacrifice.

"What good is another plan?" Catherine bursts out. "All our plans have just gotten us in a bigger mess!"

Once again, she's spoken a truth we don't want to acknowledge. Discouraged, we withdraw our hands even as Hugh says with overemphatic confidence, "This one will work."

"Stop being silly." Catherine's streaming eyes blaze with contempt. "Admit that it's all over!"

My anger at Catherine is like a hot needle that punctures the balloon. I stifle an urge to smack her — our predicament isn't her fault. Hugh watches her with a sad, resigned expression — he knows it's no use telling her to pull herself together the way she told him to after his beating; Dr. Poole's treatment has broken her. Mick squirms in his chair, distressed by her behavior and helpless. None of us can rally the spirits she's quashed.

Mrs. Lipsky puts her arm around Catherine. "Come upstairs. I put you to bed."

"Leave me alone!" Catherine pushes Mrs. Lipsky away. "Stop treating me like a baby."

Across the room, the little boy throws

himself on the floor, drums his fists and heels, and screams. Catherine stares at him, dismayed. "Oh my God." She touches cheeks suddenly red with shame. "You're treating me like a baby because I'm acting like one."

As we behold her in surprise, she shakes herself, squares her shoulders, and composes her face in a calm mask. This must be what she does before she goes on stage. It must be what she did before she walked away from her family's farm and boarded the train to London. There's a strength in her that Dr. Poole didn't break.

"I'm sorry," she says in a wan yet steady voice. "You've all worked so hard to protect me, and I've been nothing but a bother. Will you forgive me?"

We nod.

"Good." Catherine's manner takes on a brisk cheer. "Whatever this plan of yours is, Sarah, I'm in." She puts her hand on the table.

The element that my plan requires, that was absent a moment ago, is absent no longer. Hugh beams at Catherine and puts his hand on hers. Mick and Mrs. Lipsky add theirs. When I cap the stack of hands with my own, I recall thinking that fate had brought us together to catch a killer. I feel the boundaries that isolate us dissolving with a warmth that's greater than from the mere pressure of our joined flesh, whose alchemy changes my idea of what a family is. My father and mother are only people I was born to; these friends are my family I've chosen.

It's as if we've put our hands in fire together.

40

At ten thirty on this Sunday night, 11 November, I'm riding down Aldgate High Street in Leo's enclosed wagon, peeking between the wooden slats. The canopies outside the Butcher's Row shops are rolled up. Rain patters; the fog carries the ever-present barnyard reek. I'm shivering in the cold, afraid the police will discover me, and anxious about whether our plan will work. I hold onto my photography equipment as the wagon turns down Harrow Alley, which angles behind the butcher shops. A gate opens on creaking hinges. The wagon enters, then stops. Its door opens.

Hugh and Mick unload my equipment. Catherine hovers behind them. I step down into a muddy cattle yard. There stands another wagon with an open bed full of stinking animal debris. Along the north side is the back of the butcher shop where Mr. Lipsky worked. In the distance rises the hazy spire of St. Botolph's Church, shimmering in the rain. I imagine the ghosts of Martha Tabram, Kate Eddowes, Liz Stride, Polly Nichols, Mary Jane Kelly, and Annie Chapman parading around the church.

On the yard's eastern side is the slaughterhouse. Leo, the owner, opens the wide double doors. Light spills into the yard. Five burly Jews who work for Leo walk out to meet us. They carry my equipment into the slaughterhouse, a huge, cold room with a flagstone floor and plaster walls. Hooks for hanging carcasses dangle from rails that traverse the ceiling, above troughs and workbenches. Mops, brooms, and buckets stand in a corner. The walls and floor are brown with old blood spatters, and I smell the foulness that no amount of scrubbing can eradicate. Hugh covers his nose with his handkerchief. Mick runs into the slaughterhouse, jumps up, and grabs two hooks. I set up my large camera in a place about ten feet inside and to the right of the door. There's another distant door behind me, secured with an iron bar, which leads to an alley that opens onto Aldgate High Street. Leo's men move the workbenches and troughs to the edges of the room, clearing the center.

"Do you think Dr. Poole will show?" Mick

asks, swinging from the meat hooks.

I load negative plate cartridges into the camera. "I hope so."

Yesterday, Hugh dictated to Catherine a letter inviting Dr. Poole to meet her at the Ten Bells public house tonight, and Leo sent someone to deliver it to Harley Street.

Catherine is the bait in a trap.

She and Hugh stand outside the slaughter-house. As I pour flash powder into the tray, her anxious voice says, "What time shall I go?"

"Eleven thirty should do," Hugh says. "We told Dr. Poole midnight."

"And you'll come with me?"

"No, Leo's men will. Mick and I will wait here with Sarah."

"So I go into the Ten Bells . . . ?"

"You don't go in. You wait outside for Dr. Poole." Impatience sharpens Hugh's voice. We've gone over and over the plan with Catherine, and she still forgets the details.

"When he comes, what do I say to him?"

"Nothing. You just smile, beckon him, and start walking to the slaughterhouse. Let him follow you. Remember?"

"Oh. Yes. Of course."

She's memorized all the songs and dance steps she performs at the theater, yet she can't keep her part in our plan straight. Her fear, or Dr. Poole's treatment, or both, is impairing her concentration. As I attach the flash lamp to its stand, I glance uneasily at Catherine.

She clutches Hugh's arm. "What if he attacks me before I get here?"

Hugh pats her hand. "He won't. Leo's men will be nearby in plain sight. Dr. Poole won't lay a hand on you in front of witnesses."

"And after I bring him here?" Catherine is breathless, agitated. "What then?"

"He'll attack you. Sarah will take a photograph."

The photograph will prove that Dr. Poole is the Ripper. Leo and his men will help Hugh and Mick apprehend Dr. Poole and keep him at the slaughterhouse until I've developed and printed the photograph. Where I'll develop it is yet to be determined, a hole in our plan; I can't risk going back to my studio. Then we'll turn the photograph and Dr. Poole over to the police. They'll have to arrest him, and after they investigate his business at Bedlam, he'll surely be hanged for the murders. Even if Mick, Hugh, and I go to jail for what we did to Inspector Reid, and Commissioner Warren remains free to kill again, one out of two Rippers down will be far better than none.

Women will be safe from Dr. Poole. Mr. Lipsky will be released because there won't be evidence to connect him to Dr. Poole; the neurologist and the Jewish butcher belong to different worlds and aren't acquainted. If the police still think there are two Rippers, they can keep looking for the other.

"What if I get lost in the fog?" Catherine asks.

"You won't. It's only a hop, skip, and a jump." Hugh talks her through the route. He has her repeat the sequence of streets and turns, and it takes her three tries to get it right.

Mick drops from the hooks, comes to me, and whispers, "You think she'll mess up?" His faith in her perfection has waned; he looks anxious, scared.

"No, don't worry." But my faith in our plan is waning fast.

Hugh checks his watch. "Time to go." Catherine clings to him. He kisses her cheek. "You're the star of the show. Break a leg!"

Two of Leo's men escort her from the yard. She looks so small and fragile. My fear for her grows into alarm that whines in my ears like machinery spinning out of control. Hugh's and Mick's faces wear the same aghast expression that I feel on mine. Then we're running out of the yard, down winding Harrow Alley, past a railway depot and warehouses. We see Catherine and her two escorts walk out of the alley, onto Aldgate High Street. They turn right and disappear. As we hurry after them, two policemen carrying lanterns stride into view. We flatten ourselves against a wall. The police pause, shining their lanterns down the alley, looking for Mr. Lipsky's imaginary partner or looking for the three wanted fugitives. The light doesn't find us. The police move on in the same direction as Catherine. Mick, Hugh, and I exchange helpless, distraught glances; we can't bring her back without drawing the police's attention to ourselves.

"Spilled milk," Hugh says mournfully.

In the slaughterhouse, a gas lamp on the ceiling casts a dim, greenish pool of light on the middle of the bloodstained floor. The periphery of the room is in darkness that conceals me where I stand with my camera. The doors are open just wide enough for Catherine to enter. Hugh and Mick, stationed on either side, walk into the light to check Hugh's watch every few minutes. Fog drifting through the doors swirls. The cold numbs my hands and face.

"Eleven forty-five," Hugh says.

Waiting, we breathe the odor of rotten meat and listen to the night. Factory machines pulse; water gurgles in drains; a dog barks. Despite my fear for Catherine, there's a beautiful simplicity to this moment, like a photograph of a single object — an egg, perhaps — with a plain background and stark light and shadow. It's the simplicity of living in the present with a single goal. I feel sharp, focused, and alert. I picture Catherine walking up to the Ten Bells while Leo's men loiter across the street. I'm concentrating so hard on this vision that when Hugh says, "Twelve o'clock," I jump.

Church bells throughout the city toll, dissonant and ominous. We face the doors, entranced by a mutual vision of Dr. Poole, dressed in a black overcoat and hat, taking shape under the gas lamp near the Ten Bells. He is Whitechapel's incarnated nightmare of the Ripper. Catherine's eyes flare with panic as he walks with his unhurried, deliberate gait toward her. His face is shaded by his hat; he doesn't want anyone else to see it clearly enough to describe it later. Catherine cocks her head, smiles at Dr. Poole, and crooks her finger. She turns, sashays down the street, looking over her shoulder. Her smile sparkles with flirtatious invitation. It's the best performance of her life. It's possible that none of this is happening.

In my mind's eye, I watch Dr. Poole follow Catherine. He stays twenty paces behind her; he wants no one to see them together. As he watches Catherine's slim figure stroll through the fog, in and out of the light from the streetlamps, his breathing quickens; his mouth trembles; sweat leaks from him. His hand grips the knife in his pocket. Is he thinking about the scientific advances that will justify her death, or the release he'll experience when he cuts her throat? He must be sorely tempted to attack her now, but he sees Leo's men loitering on the streets. He never kills in front of witnesses. He'll wait until she brings him into the slaughterhouse.

"It's twelve fifty-nine," Hugh says, and a chill runs through me. "Something's wrong."

We gaze at the door, as if by sheer will we could make Catherine appear. The night has never been darker, the fog never thicker, nor the dawn further away.

A sudden burst of voices comes from outside — two men arguing. I can't make out what they're saying, but one is English, the other foreign. The foreigner is Leo. He was supposed to hide nearby until we need his help, but he must have met someone coming down Harrow Alley. I surmise that he's trying to make the Englishman leave before Catherine and Dr. Poole come.

The Englishman raises his voice. "Not until you tell me why you're lurking round here."

"That's George Lusk from the Mile End Vigilance Committee!" I whisper.

Leo mutters. George Lusk says, "The hell you were on your way home. I think you're the Ripper's partner, looking for another woman to kill. I'm taking you to the police station."

I hear the sounds of a scuffle. Mick says, "Shit!"

"Help!" George Lusk yells. Then comes a shrill blast from a whistle.

"We have to get rid of him before he brings in the whole cavalry," Hugh says.

We run to Harrow Alley. There George Lusk and Leo are punching each other. Hugh and Mick yell and wave their arms. Lusk, disconcerted, backs away from Leo. Footsteps pound down Harrow Alley. Five men roaring and brandishing lanterns and sticks charge at us. It's the Mile End Vigilance Committee. I pull Hugh and Mick into the cattle yard as Leo runs down

Harrow Alley with Lusk and the other committee men after him. He's drawing them away from the slaughterhouse, clearing the scene for Catherine and Dr. Poole.

"Pray to God they don't catch him," Hugh says as we troop back into the slaughterhouse. "Now where the hell is Catherine?"

We listen anxiously. A train rumbles. As the sound fades, I hear screams. Catherine's voice cries, "Help!"

Startled, we peer out the door. She's nowhere in sight. A banging noise rackets through the slaughterhouse. "Let me in!" Catherine screams.

"The other door!" I rush across the room toward it.

"She went down the wrong alley," Hugh says. He and Mick race ahead of me. They fumble with the bar on the door while Catherine bangs and screams, "He's going to kill me!"

Dr. Poole didn't wait for Catherine to lead him into our trap.

"Damnation!" Hugh says. It's so dark at this end of the room, he and Mick can't see.

"Hurry!" Catherine screams.

Accustomed to working in darkness, I feel the bar, twist, and pull. The door, shoved by Catherine, flies open and slams against

531

me. Thrown backward, I bump Hugh and Mick, and we scatter. Catherine falls into the slaughterhouse on her hands and knees, panting.

"He's coming!" she cries. "Where are you?"

Mick calls, "We're here, it's all right."

She crawls toward the pool of light on the floor. Rapid, heavy footsteps pound down the alley. It's Dr. Poole. Catherine's panic is contagious. I can't move. Catherine staggers to her feet, into the light. She's drenched with rain, her hair hanging limp around her stark white face. Her eyes are wild with terror. Vapor puffs from her open mouth. She's at center stage, but she's not acting now.

Hugh pushes me. "Sarah, get ready to take the photograph."

I regain my wits and my place behind my camera. Hugh and Mick hide in the darkness. Dr. Poole's rapid footsteps are coming closer. Catherine wrings her hands, moans, and staggers. I'm trying to center her in the viewfinder when Dr. Poole bursts into the slaughterhouse. His breaths sound like a bear's — punctuated with growls, thick with saliva. His reek of sweat and arousal overpowers the slaughterhouse smell. I feel air blowing, like the wind that an oncoming train pushes in front of it, as he charges toward Catherine. She screams. I see, through the viewfinder, her figure set upon by a shape like a crow — Dr. Poole in a black overcoat, arms spread. The image is all movement and confusion.

"Hurry, don't let him kill me!" Catherine shrieks.

The photograph will be blurry unless they stand still. They're not going to stand still.

"Stop!" I shout.

As he seizes Catherine, Dr. Poole turns toward the camera: he realizes they're not alone, and he's trying to see who spoke.

My pounding heart beats faster. I press the shutter control.

41

The powder in the tray ignites with a bang like an overheated boiler exploding. The white fireball illuminates Dr. Poole's and Catherine's images in the viewfinder. Time stops; all motion is suspended. Dr. Poole grips Catherine by her throat with his left hand. His hat has fallen off, his whole face is visible, and he's looking straight into the lens. His eyes, behind the glass ovals of his spectacles, brim with rage. His full lips are drawn back from his small, pointed teeth in a snarl. His raised right hand holds a knife. The edge of its long, sharp blade gleams red. Catherine's terror-stricken face is also turned toward the camera. Her up-flung hands are marked with bleeding slashes.

The photograph condenses the story of the Whitechapel murders into a single frame.

It shows the truth about Dr. Poole as clear as glass. No one who sees it could doubt that he is Jack the Ripper.

It's the best shot I'll ever take.

Darkness extinguishes the flash. Catherine shrieks. I look up from the viewfinder, but all I see is a black rectangle — its afterimage. Blinded, I hear Dr. Poole growling and panting, and violent motion. My eyes adjust, and I see Hugh holding the back of Dr. Poole's collar with one hand and his right wrist with the other. As Dr. Poole tries to stab Catherine, Hugh twists his arm behind his back. Dr. Poole yowls, releasing Catherine. She falls on the floor, holding her throat, gulping. Dr. Poole turns on Hugh, punches his ear, and yanks himself free. Hugh stumbles.

"Look out!" I call as Dr. Poole slashes at Hugh.

Hugh dodges, then kicks Dr. Poole's thigh. Dr. Poole staggers. Hugh grabs for his hand that holds the knife, but Dr. Poole slashes at him again. Hugh clutches his left upper arm and drops to his knees. The horror on his face says he's badly wounded.

"Hugh!" Aghast, I run to him.

Mick bursts out of the darkness and jumps on Dr. Poole's back, knocking him away from Hugh. Hugh's face is gray, and he's wheezing, but he says to me, "I'm all right. Help Mick."

"I can't leave you like this!" I frantically unbutton his coat, trying to get at the wound, desperate to stanch the flow of warm blood that wets my hands.

Dr. Poole hobbles backward and slams Mick against the wall in the darkness where I can't see them. I hear a yell from Mick, then a thud. Hugh topples onto his side. Dr. Poole rushes at Catherine.

"Sarah!" Catherine screams.

I look for a weapon to use against Dr. Poole. *Where were those mops and brooms I saw?* It's too dark to locate them. I run to my light stand, disconnect it from the camera, and pick it up by the metal pole. I position myself between Dr. Poole and Catherine.

Dr. Poole's spectacles are steamed over from his body heat. With his eyes invisible, he seems inhuman — a killer without a soul. Terror immobilizes me, but when Dr. Poole raises his knife at me, the anger flashes through my muscles like a reanimating current. This is a man who's killed my models and hurt my family. I swing the light stand, hit him across the chest, swing again, and smite his thighs. Dr. Poole totters. The third time I swing too hard. The momentum spins me. I hear a hissing sound and feel a line of pain across my back as Dr. Poole slashes through my clothes. He grabs the pole, wrenches it from me, and swings.

"Run, Catherine!" I cry. The powder tray clangs against my head, breaks off the pole, and clatters on the flagstones. My brain judders inside my skull.

Catherine is limping toward the door. Dr. Poole swings the pole at me and bashes my legs. I drop to the floor and see the pole rushing down upon me the instant before a black starburst of pain explodes across my face. Tasting blood, I curl up, my arms clasped around my head. How grievously we underestimated him and overestimated ourselves! I hear the pole *clink-clink* on the bricks and Catherine screaming. Only my rage at Dr. Poole tethers me to consciousness. Dizzy and nauseated, my head aching, my face a sore, swollen mask, I push myself up on one elbow. Catherine is at the edge of the circle of light, struggling with two black-clad figures. I'm seeing double. I'm too weak to get up. The despair that floods me is deeper and blacker than any I've ever known.

Two of my friends may be dead while the other fights a losing battle for her life. This is the umbra of the umbra, the darkest place of all. I succumb to the terrible, shameful temptation to give up and wait for Dr. Poole to kill me, too. If my friends are done for, I neither deserve nor want to live.

The figures reel into the full light. Dr. Poole has hold of Catherine's bodice. He's raising the knife, the blade pointed at her throat. Another man has hold of Dr. Poole's wrist, his left arm locked around Dr. Poole's neck. Dr. Poole twists in his grip, Catherine tries to pull free of Dr. Poole, and the three stagger and whirl. Dr. Poole's face is red, his mouth wide. The other man clenches his jaws with his effort to choke Dr. Poole.

He's PC Barrett.

Shocked, I blink my eyes. How did *he* get here?

Barrett is fighting to hold Dr. Poole's hand and knife away from Catherine. "Police!" he shouts. "Let go of the knife. You're under arrest!"

Joy lifts me above the pain that wracks my body. Barrett will save Catherine for us!

Dr. Poole gurgles. His grip on Catherine loosens. She falls on the floor moaning. Dr. Poole throws himself backward. He and Barrett crash to the floor. Dr. Poole lands on Barrett, untangles himself, and sits up. Barrett lies motionless — stunned or killed by the fall.

I clamber to my hands and knees. The room spins, and I vomit. As the retching and spinning abate, I see Dr. Poole crawl toward Catherine. He seizes her ankle. She screams. My groping hand finds the light stand. I rise unsteadily and walk to Dr. Poole, using the light stand as a crutch. My vision is still blurred, but my anger is an internal compass that keeps me on course. Catherine kicks Dr. Poole's face and knocks his spectacles off. I raise the light stand over Dr. Poole, swing, and hit his shoulder. He doesn't seem to notice. He stabs at Catherine's skirts. I swing again and bash the floor with a clang that echoes in my aching head. Catherine screams and kicks; her skirts ride up to her waist; there are bleeding gashes on her legs. I feel the light stand taken from my hands.

"Allow me," Hugh says. He's white-faced and perspiring, and his shirt is red with blood.

I gasp, wordlessly thankful he's alive. He hits Dr. Poole on the head, but he's so weak, his blow subdues Dr. Poole for only a moment. We take turns hitting Dr. Poole. He's on top of Catherine. When it's my turn, I'm not just hitting him, I'm hitting Commissioner Warren for attacking my friends, my mother for leaving me with doubts about my father. Each thud is an exuberant release that has little effect on Dr. Poole. Catherine claws his eyes. He hits her cheek with the knife handle. Catherine shrieks. Hugh takes the light stand from me, then collapses. I grab Dr. Poole's coat and try to pull him off Catherine. He doesn't budge.

"Get out of the way, Miss Sarah!"

Mick charges toward Dr. Poole, a broom handle held high in both hands. The anger that energized Hugh and me revived Mick, too. I fall away from Dr. Poole and land on my knees. Mick yells as he brings the broom handle down on Dr. Poole's head.

There's a thudding, cracking sound. Dr. Poole jerks, then lies still. Catherine screams, writhing under him. Mick rolls Dr. Poole's limp body off Catherine. Her legs thrash; she beats the air with her hands and sobs. Mick kneels beside her, seizes her wrists, and says, "Don't cry, you're safe now."

She blinks, sees him, and swallows a scream. He gently raises her to a sitting position.

"Dr. Poole was following me down Aldgate High Street," Catherine babbles. "I was almost here when I saw some men with lanterns and sticks coming." The Mile End Vigilance Committee. "After they passed, I looked over my shoulder, and Dr. Poole wasn't there. He must have gone to hide from them." She spies me on the floor with Hugh. "I didn't want to disappoint you, Sarah. I had to bring Dr. Poole here. So I went looking for him. When I found him, he started chasing me. I couldn't get to Harrow Alley. I had to come the other way."

It wasn't failure of wits that had almost cost Catherine her life, but loyalty.

Mick helps her to her feet and says, "Dr. Poole can't hurt you. I knocked him out." He kicks Dr. Poole's thigh. Dr. Poole doesn't flinch, doesn't make a sound. "See?"

My anger dies down with a shuddering, sighing sensation, like a locomotive engine that's run out of coal. Catherine stares at the inert Dr. Poole. She turns to Mick, and her dazed eyes fill with adoration. It's an involuntary, bred-in-the-blood reaction of a woman to a man's heroics. She presses her lips against Mick's dirty cheek, then weeps violently against his shoulder. Mick doesn't smile, but his chest swells; he looks ten feet tall. I glimpse the man he'll become.

"Oh, God." Hugh's voice echoes my horror at how badly we erred, our relief that everything turned out all right.

We all look at one another, and a collective sob of joyful amazement issues from us.

Leo rushes in with his men. Glad to see us alive and Dr. Poole laid flat, they do a double take and notice the cuts on Catherine's hands, the bruises swelling on my face, and Hugh pressing a blood-drenched hand to his wounded arm.

"Let me look at that," Leo says to Hugh.

Hugh strips off his coat and shirt. The wound is even worse than I thought — a deep, oozing gash on his left upper arm that continues down across his breast. Leo tears up his own shirt and fashions a tourniquet.

PC Barrett groans and sits up. "What the hell is going on?"

I'd forgotten about him. Barrett hauls himself to his feet and stands looking down at Dr. Poole. "Who's this?" Everything has happened too fast for me to believe it, let alone comprehend the ramifications. I say, "It's Dr. Henry Poole."

Barrett regards me with stunned recollection. He rubs the back of his head; it must ache from his fall. "The man you said is Jack the Ripper."

"What on earth brought you here?" Hugh asks.

"I was walking around Whitechapel . . ." Barrett stops himself. I notice he's wearing ordinary clothes, not his uniform; I remember that Inspector Reid fired him. He was watching for Commissioner Warren! My friends and I weren't the only ones out to catch Jack the Ripper tonight. "I heard the girl's screams." He looks around the slaughterhouse, and comprehension dawns. "You set a trap for Dr. Poole. She —" he points at Catherine "— lured him here."

I square my aching shoulders. "Yes. We set a trap. And we caught him."

My friends and I exchange triumphant, exulting glances. We're not sorry for what we did, and we don't care who else knows. We four, risking our lives in the shadows behind the scenes, have accomplished what the police could not. Mick isn't the only one who seems taller. The ground beneath my feet looks farther down than usual, and I don't think it's just because of the blow to my head.

Barrett stares at me and shakes his head; I've exceeded his estimation of my nerve or my underhandedness. "Holy hell . . ."

"You oughta thank us. We caught Jack the Ripper for you," Mick says with insolent pride. "You better take him to jail before he comes to."

Barrett crouches beside Dr. Poole, who lies face up, eyelids sagging. He feels Dr. Poole's wrist, leans an ear to his chest, looks up, and says accusingly, "He's dead."

Shocked, we stare at Dr. Poole, then at one another. This wasn't supposed to happen. We talked over our scheme, anticipating how it might play out, but a scenario in which we killed Dr. Poole never occurred to us.

The flush of victory fades from Mick's face. "I didn't hit him that hard."

"Nor did Sarah and I," Hugh says.

There's fresh, profuse, wet blood on the floor around Dr. Poole. When Barrett rolls Dr. Poole onto his stomach, I see a big, awful cleft in the back of his head. The weapon I mistook for a broom handle when Mick swung it lies beside Dr. Poole. It's an axe whose blade is gory with blood, hair, and bits of shattered skull and grayish brain tissue. I wonder if Mick knew it was an axe. Hugh gags. I experience a sick, foreboding sensation that's worse than nausea.

Catherine, leaning on Mick, says, "Serves him right." Her smile at Mick is brilliant, admiring.

"You and your friends are in serious trouble, Miss Bain," Barrett says, regaining a semblance of his policeman's authority. "This was murder."

There's danger as well as strength in friendship. Alone, none of us were capable of killing; together we are. Our triumph shrivels into fright. We knew we could get in trouble, but the reality is more disastrous than we anticipated. "We were only defending Catherine," I hurry to say. "You saw him attacking her. If we hadn't stopped Dr. Poole, *she* would be dead."

Barrett glowers at us. "I think a lot of other things happened before I got here. Just how was this trap for Dr. Poole supposed to work?"

I explain. The blow to my head and the distrust in Barrett's eyes make me less than articulate.

"Maybe you were never going to hand Dr. Poole over to the police alive," Barrett says. "Maybe you meant to kill him."

"Why would we?" Mick asks, incredulous.

"You're wanted in connection with the Whitechapel murders. You could have set Dr. Poole up to get yourselves off the hook. Maybe he didn't really attack the girl. Maybe the four of you attacked *him,* and he was defending himself."

"He did attack me!" Catherine says. "Sarah took a photograph."

"Just let me develop it, and you'll see." My shot of Dr. Poole is our perfect counter against Barrett's accusations. I hurry to my camera.

It's lying on the floor. It must have been knocked over during our fight with Dr. Poole. Exclaiming in dismay, I tilt the camera upright on its stand. It looks intact, but I hear a tinkling sound. My hands tremble and my heart thuds as I remove the exposed negative in its cartridge. Glass — countless tiny shards — rattles.

"The plate is broken." I see my disbelief on Hugh's, Mick's, and Catherine's faces.

Through all our misadventures, photography is the one thing that always worked. It gave us the pictures of the people who bought my boudoir pictures, of Annie Chapman at the morgue, and of Commissioner Warren's African photograph. But now photography has failed us when it mattered the most.

"So much for proof that Dr. Poole is the Ripper," Barrett says, sounding vindicated yet disappointed.

"But you believe he is!" I cry, threatened again by the prospect of my friends and I losing one another, our liberty, and our lives.

"It doesn't matter what I believe. Inspector Reid won't believe it, and neither will the rest of the police force. When Reid finds out about this, he'll string all of you up himself."

We thought the problem of Dr. Poole was solved, but now that he's dead, it's as if his hands are clamped around our ankles and he's dragging us down to hell with him.

"How's Inspector Reid going to find out?" Mick asks.

Hugh stands beside Mick and Catherine. "He doesn't have to."

I move close to my friends. "Unless you tell him."

Confusion on Barrett's face turns to dismay as he realizes he's outnumbered by four people who've just colluded in a man's death. I feel an exhilarating sense of power, and there's a new fierceness in Hugh's and Mick's eyes. To kill a fellow human is to cross a line, and crossing that line has changed us. Having learned that we're capable of killing, the compunction against it seems less insurmountable than before.

We killed Dr. Poole to protect one of us.

We could kill again to protect all of us.

The impulse comes upon us with a heat like fire. In this moment, I realize that at some point I fell in love with Barrett, but I feel nary a hint of chagrin, because I'm not in love with him now. *He's the enemy.* Hugh and I glance at the light stand, Mick at the axe beside Dr. Poole. As Barrett reaches for his nightstick, then remembers he's not in uniform, panic glints in his eyes. Leo and the slaughterers move to block the exits, for if Barrett reports us, he'll also report them. Catherine looks around for a weapon, ready to help Hugh, Mick, and me do what's necessary.

Then the impulse fades. The fire in us isn't hot enough. Killing once in the fever of a reckless moment isn't the same as killing in cold blood. Breath seeps from us; our muscles relax. The turbulence in the atmosphere settles. Leo and his men shrug and move away from the doors. Astonished disbelief is written all over Barrett; he's wondering if what he thinks just happened really happened.

"Our fate is in your hands," Hugh says solemnly.

Our fate has been in Barrett's hands since the day that he first came to my studio. I just didn't know it until now. Every subsequent time that he came back and then left, I was relieved because danger had temporarily passed yet saddened by unfulfilled need and impatient to feel the danger and excitement — to feel fully alive — again. Now, as I wait for Barrett to leave this time, I feel only dread; he has the power to destroy us, and we're not ruthless enough to destroy him first.

Silent and looking numb, Barrett moves toward the door. This is the last time I'll see him until my murder trial, when he testifies against me. He stops to gaze at Dr. Poole's corpse, as if weighing the value of justice for Jack the Ripper against the value of the lives of the people who would be punished for his murder. The meat-and-iron smell of Dr. Poole's blood thickens the air. I put my arm around Mick. Catherine's hand grips mine. Hugh stands with the three of us.

Barrett looks up. The numbness, confusion, and astonishment are gone from his manner; his eyes are clear and alert. "There's so much blood on this floor, nobody'll notice that some's human. We just need to get rid of the body."

We.

In this moment, Barrett becomes one of our circle. My heart soars. It's partly because he's not going to report us, partly because my falling in love with him wasn't a case of poor judgment. Despite all that Barrett has done to hurt me, he's taken my side when it mattered most, and he's revealed his worth as a man. He's given me, and my friends, our lives. We're too stunned to thank him for forsaking the law he swore to serve.

"I own a rendering factory," Leo says.

Hugh finds his voice. "I'll never complain about the smell from those places again."

Leo brings the wagon full of animal debris. Two of his men heave Dr. Poole's body into the wagon, cover it with bones, gristle, and hooves, and drive it away into the fog. Barrett mops blood into the drain while Leo sluices the floor with buckets of water.

My heart begins another descent. All the mopping in the world won't erase what we've done. Even if we're not punished for it, we'll have to reckon with it eventually. And Jack the Ripper's reign of terror isn't over. We've hauled our net of fish up from the water, only to discover that there was a big hole in the net and the shark in the bottom has swum out.

"You and your friends should go," Barrett says to me. "Where can I find you?"

That I can trust him now, and will see him again, is meager comfort. "The Jews Temporary Shelter in Spitalfields."

Dr. Poole will never kill again, but Commissioner Warren is yet at liberty, and Mr. Lipsky is yet to be exonerated.

42

In the dining room at the Jews Temporary Shelter, Mick, Hugh, Catherine, and I breakfast on smoked herring, braided egg bread, buckwheat porridge, and tea. It's Tuesday morning; we've been here for the two nights since we dispatched Dr. Poole. We wear plain dark clothes provided by a local charity. My head and Catherine's are covered with shawls, like the Jewish women's. We could pass for immigrants, but we take precautions — keeping to ourselves, eating our meals after the other residents have finished. Between meals, we hide upstairs.

Hugh has the private sickroom. A Jewish doctor stitched his wounds and gave him medicine, but he became feverish and delirious. Mick sat vigil by him the whole time. This morning, Hugh felt well enough to get up. Now Mrs. Lipsky brings the newspapers, and he thanks her with a smile.

Catherine and I have separate quarters, too. The cuts on Catherine's hands and legs are healing, and she eats with a good appetite, but at night she wakes screaming from nightmares. The bruises on my face are purple, my headache, dizziness, and nausea have abated, and the cut on my back is only skin deep, but at night I lie awake, reliving the events in the slaughterhouse, pondering what we might have done differently, as if I'm rubbing them into my mind with sandpaper. We accomplished Hugh's "one splendid thing," but no matter that we put Dr. Poole to rights, Martha, Polly, Annie, Liz, Kate, and Mary Jane are still dead, and we killed a man.

The reckoning has begun. The consequences of our actions haven't. We're suspended in a state of waiting. Leo disposed of Dr. Poole's remains, but we haven't had word from Barrett, and because we're still fugitives, we rely on the newspapers to tell us what's going on in the world.

"The inquest for Mary Jane Kelly's murder was held yesterday," Hugh says, reading while he eats. "The verdict was willful murder against some person or persons unknown."

We don't know whether it was Dr. Poole or Commissioner Warren who killed her. We probably never will.

I skim the newspaper. "There's no mention of Dr. Poole. If anyone's reported him missing, it didn't make the papers."

Hugh sits up straight. "Hell's bells! Look at this!" He holds up the front page. The headline announces, "Sir Charles Warren Resigns." He reads the story aloud.

" 'On Monday evening, the Home Secretary announced that Sir Charles Warren, the chief commissioner of police, has tendered his resignation. In a brief interview, Sir Charles declined to offer a full explanation as to the reason for his resignation, but he did state that the Home Office's interference in the Police Department has been a great grievance to him. He also stated that he did not resign on account of the Whitechapel murders or the police force's failure to catch the perpetrator.' "

After we exclaim with shock, I say, "There must be more to the story."

Carriage wheels rattling outside precede the sound of the door opening and footsteps in the hall. More immigrants must be arriving. Before we can hide, a man staggers into the room, a Jew with a long, straggly beard and mustache, dressed in black clothes too large for him. Mrs. Lipsky claps her hands over her mouth, sobs, runs to the man, and throws her arms around him. It's Mr. Lipsky!

He holds his wife and kisses her forehead while she weeps. His hollow eyes well with tears. They murmur endearments to each other in Russian. Catherine and I are crying, too, for their joy and our own. Mr. Lipsky has lost much weight, and his skin has a gray pallor, but he smiles at Hugh, Mick, Catherine, and me.

"Knock me over with another feather," Hugh says, wiping his eyes.

He shakes Mr. Lipsky's hand and slaps his back. Catherine, Mick, and I hug him. "How'd you get out of jail?" Mick asks.

Into the room walks Barrett in police uniform. A sly smile plays across his face. "The charges against Mr. Lipsky have been dropped."

We clamor with bewildered excitement. "But why — ? How — ?"

"Abraham, you're so thin! I must feed you." Mrs. Lipsky turns to Barrett and says with heartfelt sincerity, "Thank you for bringing my husband back. Have you eaten?"

"I could use a cup of tea," Barrett says.

He drinks it at the table with Catherine, Hugh, Mick, and me. The Lipskys sit at another table by themselves. Mrs. Lipsky plies her husband with food, and he eats hungrily while he tells her in Russian the story that Barrett tells us.

"Yesterday, some police officers searched a house in Stepney," Barrett says. "They found a photograph of Commissioner Warren with a pile of dead African women. There were also three brass rings that were identified as belonging to Annie Chapman."

I never expected those items to come to light. "How did they know to search the house?"

"They received an anonymous tip. It said Jack the Ripper lives there."

I realize what must have happened. *"Anonymous?"*

Barrett looks over his shoulder, pretending to think that my pointed gaze is aimed at someone else.

"You're the only person besides us who knew about that house," Hugh says, "but go on."

"They also found obscene photographs of the victims and a bloodstained knife that fits the coroner's description of the weapon that the Ripper used."

"Wait a minute." The full extent of Barrett's machinations dawns on me. "There was no bloodstained knife in that house."

"Nor Miss Sarah's dirty pictures neither!"

Mick says.

"Somebody ought to fix the broken lock on the window above the alley." Barrett calmly holds our gazes. This is his only admission that he sneaked into Warren's house and planted Dr. Poole's knife, which he brought from the slaughterhouse, and my boudoir photographs, which he took from my studio.

"The officers were convinced that Commissioner Warren is Jack the Ripper. They took the evidence straight to his superior — Henry Matthews, Home Secretary. Mr. Matthews ordered them not to breathe a word of it to anybody." Barrett asks, "Did I mention that one of the officers is a friend of mine?"

"I assume that your friend is the officer who received the anonymous tip," Hugh says.

"I think Warren and the Home Secretary agreed to a deal — Warren would resign, the Home Secretary would bury the evidence, and there wouldn't be a scandal."

"That's the gentlemanly, face-saving British bureaucracy for you," Hugh says.

"Where is Warren now?" I ask.

"Gone," Barrett says. "The army posted him to Singapore. The Home Secretary must have pulled strings to make them take him back."

Our relief is so massive that Catherine, Mick, Hugh, and I groan. London is rid of Warren, but heaven help Singapore. Half of the evil shadow that Jack the Ripper cast over the city has shifted to another, unsuspecting part of the world. But we're nonetheless proud that we provided the ammunition with which Barrett dispatched Commissioner Warren. One Ripper dead and the other banished is more than we could have expected.

My only regret is that with Warren gone, I'll never know whether there's any truth to his claim that my father is a fugitive criminal who could still be alive. But of course if I were to ask Warren, I couldn't trust anything he said.

"Is that why Mr. Lipsky was released — because the Home Secretary sent down word that he's not Jack the Ripper?" I ask.

"The official story is that a confidential source gave him an ironclad alibi," Barrett says.

"Wait," Hugh says. "If you didn't get credit for exposing Warren, then how is it that you're back on the force?"

Barrett grins. There's a rapscallion look to him that he didn't have before. He, too, has crossed the line to the far side of the law, and he doesn't dislike it.

"The same day Warren resigned, the Home Secretary told me I'd been dismissed without proper protocol and he was reinstating me. I found out the rest from Inspector Reid when I reported for duty. He's furious. He said the Home Secretary reamed him out for trying to railroad Abraham Lipsky and criticized him for bad management of the officers under him. Reid's been relieved of his command while the records on his past cases are reviewed."

I can't pity Reid. "Does he know the real reason Warren resigned?"

"No. But he knows it's not a coincidence that he took a fall the same day Mr. Lipsky was cleared and I was reinstated. He said he's going to get to the bottom of the whole business. He knows I had something to do with what happened to him, and so did the lot of you. He said he'll make us all pay."

"It was too much to expect that we could get rid of all our enemies with one swell foop," Hugh says.

"At any rate, the warrant for your arrest has been withdrawn. The Home Secretary must think that getting handcuffed to a gas pipe was Reid's just deserts. You're free to move about."

Mick whoops with delight and jumps up

from the table. "I'm going out to see what's happening!"

Catherine flings the shawl off her head and jumps up, too. "I'll go to the theater and ask for my job back!"

The young are so resilient. Although still protective toward Catherine and Mick, I let them go. Not everybody I love will abandon me; they'll come back.

Catherine pauses at the door, turns to Mick, and says, "Will you come with me?" She sounds newly aware that the world is filled with dangers even though Jack the Ripper is gone.

Mick grins, newly cocksure. "Be glad to."

As they hurry off together, I smile. Maybe I'm not the only one who glimpsed the man he'll become. Catherine will never lack for suitors, but Mick is the one who killed for her — a hard act to beat.

Hugh stands, and so does Barrett. "Time to go home," Hugh says. "Sarah, you can stay with me. Fitzmorris will look after us both."

I haven't anywhere else to go, but I hesitate, daunted by the impropriety of his suggestion.

"Oh, come on, Sarah!" Hugh says. "Compared to everything else you've done, living with a man you're not married to is small beer. Anyway, your virtue is safe with me."

Persuaded, I nod. "Thank you."

"I've an idea for what we can do next," Hugh says. "We're such good detectives, why not form a private inquiry firm?"

I groan. Barrett says, "Some people don't know to quit while they're ahead."

"It would solve our problem of how to earn a living," Hugh says. "We could both use a fresh start."

Life might be dull without a new venture. My appetite for danger seems to have grown, not shrunken as it logically should have. "I'll think about it."

Hugh extends his hand to Barrett. "Thanks for all your help." They shake hands. "We owe you."

I murmur my own thanks, suddenly shy with Barrett. A new affection for him gentles the anger, need, and humiliation he's aroused in me. I'm sad because we're about to part for the last time, just when we've found common ground. I can't picture another set of circumstances that would bring us together again.

Barrett clears his throat. "Miss Bain, will you come for a walk with me?"

As Barrett and I walk along Commercial Street, I squint at the sun, which seems so bright after I haven't seen it in so long. The sky is a rare blue, but an icy wind blows smoke from chimneys into horizontal plumes. Peddlers wave crimson-covered pamphlets at the crowds. "Get yer *Book of the Whitechapel Horrors* — only a penny!" A man in a gaudy plaid coat leads a flock of fashionably dressed ladies and gentleman. "Right this way to the scene of Jack the Ripper's latest murder!"

George Lusk is giving an interview to reporters. "The Mile End Vigilance Committee sighted the Ripper last night!" His face is bruised from his skirmish with Leo. "We shall continue patrolling the streets until he's caught."

I marvel at the wide gulf between the reality that I am aware of and the delusion under which the people around me labor. They think Jack the Ripper is still at large, and they'll fear him until enough time passes without another murder. The police will search for him until all the leads peter out or his natural life span ends. I suppose it's better than a scandal that would destroy the public's trust in the law.

Barrett and I don't look at each other or speak. Anyone who sees us might not know we're together, but we're bound tightly by our secrets, as if by invisible handcuffs link-ing our wrists. By tacit, mutual consent, we go to my studio. I'm eager to see what's happened to it, and it's where we first met the day I saw Polly Nichols's dead body, when everything started.

The gold lettering on the window, which read, "Bain & Sons Photography," is gone; the door is boarded up. As I stare in dismay, Barrett says, "Allow me."

He breaks the door down. I step into the studio. It's vacant of furniture, the walls bare. I hurry to the darkroom. Everything's gone except my enlarger. I'm thankful that Mr. Douglas thought it worthless. Then I run upstairs. The flat is emptied of my clothes and other personal belongings. A crumpled photograph lies on the bedroom floor, placed there as if to taunt me, soiled by a dirty footprint. I pick up and smooth out the photograph of daffodils blooming in a graveyard and touch my father's shadowy figure in the woods. I discovered who the Ripper was, but I still don't know what became of my father. Carrying the photograph, I go downstairs.

Barrett looks somberly at me from the empty studio. "I'm sorry."

"Don't be." I realize, with astonishment, that I'm not. The studio was built by the person I used to be. "I'm glad for a fresh start. Can you help me carry my enlarger?"

"Sure." But Barrett doesn't move.

My heart begins to drum a cadence of foreboding.

"I'm sorry I hit you," he says.

"It's all right. I understand."

"And I'm sorry about — well, you know."

Blushing, I only nod to say that the incident after the Mile End Vigilance Committee meeting is forgiven. I'm so indebted to him that if he wanted to ravish me, I should let him. The thought brings on a rush of desire and more heat to my cheeks.

"Inspector Reid told me to pretend to romance you, and I'm a cad for taking liberties with you," Barrett says. "I want you to know that I wasn't just pretending, and I wouldn't have done it if I hadn't felt . . . if I hadn't wanted . . . if I didn't hope that you and I . . ." Now it's his turn to blush, because he's confessed that he was, indeed, sweet on me.

Hiding a smile, I start toward the darkroom to let Barrett regain his composure while he follows me, but he stands still.

"One more thing," he says. "Commissioner Warren's papers were cleared out of his office. I sneaked a look at them, and I found your father's police file."

This is the last thing I expected. Coldness

seeps through me. My throat is suddenly dry, my heart thudding. I'm afraid to hear what comes next.

"I stole these from it." Barrett reaches into his pocket and brings out a wad of lined papers. Yellow with age, they crinkle as he unfolds them. He offers them to me.

I'm afraid to see what they say, but here is my wish granted — my chance to find out what, if anything, Warren knows about my father. I discover in myself a reckless courage born of facing death and surviving. I take the papers . . . but my courage isn't strong enough to overcome my reluctance to open a tin of worms from Jack the Ripper.

I thank Barrett and put the papers in my handbag. Barrett says, "I haven't read them, but I saw that Commissioner Warren added his own notes. By the way, his writing is similar to that of the Jack the Ripper letters. Warren wrote them. He tried to disguise his writing, but it's obvious if you know what you're looking for."

I don't dare think about what the notes in the police file could mean.

"Warren's investigation of your father has been cancelled. But you could carry on with it if you wanted."

I picture Hugh and me perusing the file together, beginning our first inquiry. "I don't know . . ."

Barrett nods, understanding my reluctance. He goes outside and hails a cab. We carry out my enlarger, put it in the cab, and ride in silence, occupied by our own thoughts, mine a tangle of confusion. *Look for the truth,* my father said. I know that someday soon, despite my fear of what I might find, I must look for the truth about him, for better or worse.

When we stop at the Jews Temporary Shelter, Barrett says, "You and Hugh can take the cab to his place. I'll walk back to the station."

The door of the shelter opens, and Hugh comes out, accompanied by Mr. and Mrs. Lipsky carrying my photography equipment.

"Miss Bain . . ." Barrett hesitates. "May I call on you sometime?"

I feel an impulse to ask, "What for?" Maybe he's still sweet on me. Maybe he only wants to make sure I'm not doing anything illegal. I stifle the impulse. I've experienced enough revelations for today. Looking for the truth behind Barrett's request can wait.

"Yes." After facing death, I'm no longer afraid that if I let Barrett too near me, he'll break my heart; I could get over it. I give him Hugh's address. My manner is prim, his polite, our farewell handshake brief yet warm. As I slip my fingers from his clasp, I fancy I feel the invisible handcuffs joining our wrists.

Barrett jumps out of the cab and helps Mr. Lipsky load my equipment. Hugh climbs in beside me. Mrs. Lipsky says, "Come to our house for Sabbath dinner on Friday. Bring Catherine and Mick." She smiles at Barrett. "You come, too."

"I would be honored," Barrett says.

The cab bears Hugh and me along Aldgate High Street. Butcher's Row is now jammed with wagons, barrows, and carriages, and noisy with commerce. The carcasses hanging under the canopies outside the butcher shops are bright pink in the sunlight.

Hugh smiles at me and says, "We're off."